Next Exit, Pay Toll

CW Browning

CW Browning
Visit my website at www.cwbrowning.com

Second Edition: 2018

ISBN-13: 9781493780662

This book is dedicated to my beautiful daughter.

I love you more than words can say.

Next Exit, Pay Toll

"It is mine to avenge; I will repay. In due time their foot will slip; Their day of disaster is near and their doom rushes upon them."

~ Deuteronomy 32: 35

Prologue

The explosion rocked the quiet valley out of its slumber, sending deep rumbles ricocheting through the earth and up into the hills. Flames leapt high into the night sky, lighting the darkness, while high above the valley a solitary figure watched as the fire rapidly spread through the compound below. The explosives had been placed strategically throughout the estate, ensuring maximum devastation. What sounded like one explosion from this distance was, in reality, several explosions occurring together. As each individual inferno met the next, the flames engulfed the compound within seconds.

Hawk lowered his head to his night-vision scope and slowly scanned the flames, looking for movement. He was lying flat between two boulders high in the hills and both he and his rifle were covered with branches, making him invisible in the night. When he reached the end of the compound without detecting any movement, he slowly scanned back again. There were over thirty men in that compound, three of whom were the heads of the largest Mexican drug Cartels. Those three men were the reason for Hawk's visit.

Movement in the midst of the raging flames made him pause and his finger slipped over the trigger of his rifle gently. When the shadow lurched out from one of the burning buildings, Hawk waited for it to stumble into his cross-hairs before he squeezed the trigger. It fell to the ground and Hawk watched for more movement. The flames were reaching a fever pitch now, engulfing the buildings and spreading across the gardens to the SUVs and sports cars that were parked in the expansive driveway.

Another shadow appeared near the cars and Hawk squeezed his trigger. The shadow fell as the first SUV in the path of the flames ignited and the full tank of gas exploded. More flames leapt high into the air as pieces of the vehicle shot out in all directions. Hawk loaded another round into the chamber and continued to watch for movement. The hillside where he was concealed was silent in the night; the breeze was gentle and the sky clear. The smoke from the flames below hadn't reached him yet, and he took a deep breath of fresh, clean air. The fire had only been burning for about three minutes. There was still plenty of time. Hawk lowered his head to the scope again. Ten minutes later, the space between the rocks was empty. Far below, in the Mexican valley, a fire raged out of control as it licked past the fences of the estate and across the landscape. Six bodies were on the ground, the flames consuming them with everything else. If anyone bothered to examine the charred remains closely, they would find a single .50 caliber round embedded in each of their skulls.

But the shooter had already disappeared into the night, leaving no trace of a man or a rifle, his mission accomplished.

Chapter One

The Puritans in Salem had the right idea; witches were meant to be burned, burned to a crisp, until even the buzzards hovering overhead wouldn't peck at the charred remains. That was the right and just punishment for witchcraft. It was the only way to eradicate the evil within them.

The archer released her grip on the steel-tipped arrow and the bow sung briefly as the arrow whizzed along its course to the target. Tilting the bow back, she pondered the merits of fire versus arrows as her shaft buried itself in the target.

The problem with fire was that nowadays you had to actually get the witch into a place where she *could* be burned alive. While one would think that would be relatively easy, the archer knew that it would not be that simple for this particular witch. This witch would find a way out before the fire even started. She was just that annoying.

The archer reached behind her and pulled another arrow from the slender bag on her back. She notched it into the string with a practiced movement and brought the bow up to her shoulder.

No. Fire was out of the question.

There was another hiss as she released the second arrow and watched it impale itself next to the first one. She considered the target that was seventy feet away, pursed her lips, and then turned to walk back a few feet. Stopping at around seventy-five feet, she turned to face the target again.

Sadly, death by arrow was almost impossible as well. The odds of her being able to somehow maneuver the witch into an archery setting were non-existent.

The archer notched another arrow into her bow and took careful aim, her hands steady as she pulled it back.

No. It was best to stick to the original plan. As much as she would love to listen to the witch screaming as flames licked around her flesh, consuming her, it was always best to stick to the original course of action, especially when one had already embarked upon it.

The arrow soared through the air and buried itself between the other two, piercing through the picture taped to the target. The archer lowered her bow in satisfaction.

The last arrow stayed, trembling, where it had struck between two black eyes on the rearing head of a Viper.

Stephanie Walker stepped into the silent house, leaving the sliding door open behind her. The feeling of emptiness was oppressive. The electricity had been off for three months and the air was stale and hushed. No sound came from the refrigerator in the large kitchen and Stephanie found the silence disturbing. She glanced around, taking in the emptiness in the fading afternoon light. The carpeted living room was to her left and the couch and recliner were covered with furniture covers. Looking to her right, she saw that the dining room furniture was also covered. The bar separating the kitchen from the dining room had been left bare, and the once-shining black granite top was dull with a layer of dust.

Walking forward, Stephanie set her keys down on the granite, absently swiping a finger through the dust and rubbing her fingers together as her eyes traveled into the still kitchen. The kitchen island was bare and the pot rack above it hung empty. Top-of-the-line appliances stood silent, waiting for the day when they would be called into use again.

Stephanie sighed, depressed by the emptiness. She looked around again and wandered into the living room. Three months ago, her old friend, Alina, had come back to Jersey from God only knew where, doing God only knew what, and saved her life. When Stephanie came to thank her, the house was empty and locked up tight. The furniture was covered with protective covers and the entire residence had been swept clean of any trace of occupants.

A few phone calls had elicited the information that the house had been sold a few days previously to a Ms. Raven Woods. The entire sale had been completed through lawyers. A call to the lawyer representing Ms. Woods led to a dead end.

Alina had simply disappeared.

The growl of a motorcycle engine dragged Stephanie's attention from her thoughts and she went out the sliding doors again to stand on the deck that ran the length of the house. The property was buried, out of sight from the road, in the middle of South Jersey's pine barrens on about sixteen acres of land. The late afternoon sun filtered through the trees and left speckled patches of light on the manicured lawn. The house was empty, but a local lawn service had standing orders to come once a week. They had been paid up front, in cash, for the whole summer until October.

That, too, had led to a dead end upon investigation.

Stephanie watched as the motorcycle roared around the side of the house and stopped behind her car. Her partner got off and removed his helmet, turning to come across the lawn. John Smithe was tall, with blond hair and broad shoulders. He was dressed in jeans and a green shirt, with his FBI badge clipped to his waist and his 9mm holstered next to it. He didn't look happy.

"I guessed you would be at the Bird House," he said, joining her on the deck.

Stephanie grinned despite herself. When they found out the owner's name was Raven Woods, a snort from John was his only acknowledgement of the hawk that had terrorized him there. He looked past her now to the open sliding door.

"Breaking and entering?" he asked, stepping past her to the sliding doors.

"I didn't break anything." Stephanie followed him and John glanced at her, his pale blue eyes glinting in amusement.

"Of course not," he murmured. They stepped into the living room and John looked around. He was silent for a moment, his eyes taking in the furniture covers and bare walls. He walked into the dining room, glancing into the kitchen. "What are you looking for?"

"Oh, I don't know." Stephanie sighed and looked around. "Maybe just closure."

John leaned on the bar and looked across the room at her. His pale blue eyes considered her thoughtfully.

"You don't think she's coming back?" he asked softly. Stephanie shrugged.

"I don't know," she answered truthfully. "She bought the house, which would indicate that she will eventually."

"Well, according to the deed, her damn bird bought the house," John said disgustedly.

Stephanie chuckled. She had been amused by the name on the deed of sale, but John had not. In fact, John had been pretty UN-John since Alina had disappeared again. Normally very talkative and light-hearted, John had been quiet and morose for the past three months.

"That really bothers you, doesn't it?" Stephanie asked, crossing her arms and leaning against the back of the couch. John shrugged.

"You're supposed to be starting your well-deserved vacation," he said, changing the subject. "Why are you here, poking around in a house that can't tell you anything?"

"I don't know." Stephanie shrugged.

"We went over this place twice and didn't find anything. Not even DNA," John pointed out. "The place is clean."

Stephanie nodded, her dark hair falling into her eyes. She reached up to brush it out of the way.

"I know," she agreed with a sigh. "I just keep hoping that maybe we missed something."

"Honey, they're long gone," John said, straightening up and walking over to her. "The latest report this morning had her sighted in Peru."

Stephanie lifted her eyes to his and laughed shortly.

"Yesterday she was in Hong Kong," she exclaimed. John grinned.

"I thought yesterday was Moscow," he murmured. Stephanie shook her head and John put his arm around her shoulders, turning her toward the sliding doors. "Come on. You need to relax and forget about it. Enjoy your vacation and clear your mind. She'll turn up eventually. Even Alina can't hide from the US government indefinitely."

"I wouldn't be too sure of that," Stephanie retorted as she allowed herself to be led out of the empty house.

The heavy, solid wood door to the bar swung wide, allowing a gust of humid August heat to sweep in from the street. Late afternoon sun sliced through the gloom inside, glinting off the dust particles floating in the air, and caused a patron sitting at the bar to turn his head and blink owlishly at the bright light. There were only a handful of customers, but they all fell silent and turned to look at the open door.

The newcomer glanced around the bar, highlighted for a brief moment in silhouette by the ray of hot sunshine. Broad shoulders and a solid frame blocked the light before the door swung closed behind him and the sunlight was swallowed up. The gust of hot air dissipated and the patrons went back to their drinks and low-voiced conversations, their momentary interest exhausted. Setting down the pint glass he was drying, the bartender leaned on the bar and waited for the newcomer to approach.

"Hey, Danny." The newcomer nodded, stopping at the bar. "How's it going?"

"Just living the dream," the bartender replied. "The usual?"

"You got it." The newcomer looked around. Even though the summer heat outside was oppressive, few people had taken refuge in the cool, dark bar. "Slow day?"

"It's early yet," Danny replied, pouring a draft of craft brew into a pint glass. "It'll pick up later."

"I hope so, for your sake." The newcomer pulled out his wallet as the beer was placed in front of him. "Who's that at the end there?" he asked, lowering his voice as he handed Danny a bill.

Danny leaned forward and turned his head slightly to look where the newcomer had motioned. At the far end of the bar, hunched over a double scotch, was a woman. Her mousy brown hair was streaked with threads of silver and pulled back into a twist at the back of her head. She was dressed neatly, but drably, in a beige, summer-weight suit. Glasses perched on her nose and she peered owlishly into her scotch, ignoring everything around her.

"She's one of the new regulars," Danny answered readily. "She's alright. She comes in every day after work and nurses a double scotch. She works over at J.A. Associates as some sort of administrative assistant."

The newcomer grunted.

"I would need a double scotch every day too if I worked there," he muttered. "Does she always sit there?"

"Yeah, but don't worry." Danny turned away with the money to ring up the drink. A minute later, he returned with the change. "She has a hearing aid. You have to practically shout before she hears you. She got some kind of an infection in her ear a few months back and it never healed. She's learning to sign."

"Chatty with her, are you?"

The newcomer took his change and dropped a few bills on the bar. Danny picked them up with a nod of thanks and dropped them into the tip jar behind the bar.

"I'm a bartender," he retorted.

The newcomer grinned and picked up his beer. He moved away down the bar, toward the hearing-impaired woman. She glanced up as he drew closer and he encountered a blank look from dark, glittering eyes. As quickly as she caught his glance, she looked down again, and spun her glass around absently on the bar. He walked by, noting the flesh-colored piece of plastic stuck in her ear, and seated himself in the booth behind her. He watched her for a minute before losing interest. She had returned to staring into her scotch morosely. Danny was right.

She was no kind of threat.

Settling against the worn back of the booth, Michael sipped his

15

beer and watched the door. Marty was late, but there was nothing strange in that. He had never known Marty to be on time. He usually rolled in when Michael was halfway through his beer. He had learned to expect it and took the opportunity now to relax a bit. His eyes wandered over the handful of bar patrons as he sipped his beer. Aside from the woman at the bar, they were the same demographic: tired, disheartened, out of work professionals. They were all over the city now. The woman drowning her sorrows at the bar may work for a notoriously horrible company, but at least she was working. A few of her fellow patrons would probably kill for her job.

Michael brought his eyes back to the woman curiously. She had shifted on her bar stool and crossed her legs. He tilted his head slightly, looking at the length of thigh that was exposed by the short skirt of the suit. The legs were a surprise to him. Given her overall mousy appearance, he wasn't prepared for legs that were that long and perfect. He lifted his beer again, and then his eyes, meeting an amused look from Danny. He grinned sheepishly as Danny shook his head and Michael returned his attention to the front door, dismissing the mouse with the great legs from his mind.

Alina Maschik sipped her scotch and watched the man behind her in the mirror behind the bar. He was sitting with his back to the wall and staring at the door. She had had ample time to study him while he talked to Danny, the friendly neighborhood bartender. Tall, with red hair cut close to his head in a military cut, he exuded confidence. He had green-hazel eyes and was built like a tank. Broad shoulders tapered into solidly muscled arms and black suit pants did nothing to hide the thickly muscled thighs. He had loosened his tie and now, as he leaned back against the back of the booth, his suit jacket hung open and she could just glimpse the edge of the holster holding his sidearm.

Setting the glass down, she glanced at Danny under her lashes. He was shaking his head over something as he wiped down the bar with a rag, his lips curved in a grin. Alina dropped her gaze back to the glass.

She had been coming here every weekday now for two and a half weeks. She came at the same time and always ordered a double scotch. By her third visit, Danny had started talking to her. By the fifth, he had the scotch ready when she walked through the door. She sat and nursed it for an hour and then left, tipping generously. She had been patiently waiting.

Waiting for Michael O'Reilly.

Next Exit, Pay Toll

He looked older than the last time she had seen him. That was almost eleven years ago now. It was a lifetime away, and enough time for them both to change. He was a young gunnery sergeant then, serving in the Marine Corps. They shared a bottle of Jameson and parted company as near strangers, but it was a day that would be forever tucked away in her heart. It was the last time she had spoken to any member of her brother's unit.

It was also the last time she touched Jameson.

The door to the bar suddenly swung open again, pulling her attention from the man behind her. Riding the hot sunshine, and letting in another blast of humid air, was a short, stocky man dressed in khakis and brown loafers. Alina watched as the door swung closed behind him and he sauntered down the bar toward the booth in the back, nodding to Danny as he passed.

"How's it going, Danny?"

"Just living the dream, Marty," Danny responded.

"It's all we can do, right?" Marty answered. He passed Alina without a glance and joined Michael in the booth behind her. "Sorry I'm late, Mikey. Business held me up."

"Business always holds you up," Michael retorted good-naturedly, setting his half empty beer on the table and looking at the small Italian man who slid into the booth across from him.

"Yeah, I know." Marty grabbed a napkin from the chrome holder on the table and mopped his forehead. "Man, it's hot out there. Feels like a sauna."

"It's August in DC." Michael reached into his inside pocket and pulled out his notebook. "What've you got for me?"

"What haven't I got, you mean?" Marty retorted. "I got nothing. I even went up to Jersey and checked with them personally." Michael pinned him with a steady stare. "Swear to God."

"I don't need you to swear to God," Michael told him. "I need you to find out who she is."

"But that's just it!" Marty leaned forward and lowered his voice. "No one knows! Look, I know I told you that Frankie knew, and in a roundabout way, he does. But he don't know her name. He only met her once."

"When?"

"Three or four months ago. She showed up looking for information," Marty answered, sitting back in the booth. "Frankie says she did the Family a favor."

"If what I hear is true, she did a lot of people a favor," Michael muttered. "But then she disappeared."

"Why are you so interested in her, anyway?" Marty asked. "She's

17

not in your usual line, is she?"

"Do I have a usual line?" Michael put his notebook away and drained his glass. "Did you hear anything else up there? Anything at all?"

"Just that the last anyone heard of her, she was fishing in Anchorage with the polar bears," Marty retorted. "But they're keeping their ears open and…"

"Yeah, yeah, I know." Michael stood up. "When you know, I'll know."

"Don't make it sound so lame." Marty remained seated and reached for a bar menu that was tucked behind the napkins. "You know I'm your best source of information."

Michael grinned down at the little Italian man.

"Sadly, that's true," he retorted. "You know how to reach me if you hear anything."

"You got it." Marty turned his attention to the bar menu. "You won't join me in a bite? I never see you eat anything."

"I eat on my own time," Michael answered. "Enjoy your food."

He turned and walked away, past the woman at the bar and toward the door, nodding to Danny as he went.

"Night, Danny. Hope it picks up," he called.

"Take it easy," Danny answered with a wave.

The front door opened and Michael disappeared into the sunlight. Alina glanced at the clock again. Her hour was up. She finished her scotch, laid a few bills on the bar and collected her bag. She smiled vaguely in the direction of Danny.

"Have a good night," he called. She blinked at him owlishly.

"WHAT?" she yelled.

Danny grinned and signed to her. She nodded and signed "You too" back to him. A moment later, the door opened again and she, too, was swallowed by the sweltering heat outside.

Damon Miles watched the black hawk circle high above the tree tops through a pair of binoculars. To the casual observer, it was just another bird riding the wind current high above the trees. But Damon knew all too well that black hawks were rare this far north, and this particular one was even more so, having come all the way from South America.

He laid the binoculars on the passenger's seat and put the Jeep in gear, turning off the main road and onto a narrow little dirt track that was partially hidden in the trees. The wind ruffled his hair as he bounced along the rough trail through the woods. It felt good to be back in the States. Summer was in full swing and the air was warm and heavy with the scent of the forest. The hawk was lost from sight now, but Damon didn't need to see the bird to know where it had gone. It was going home and, in a way, so was he.

The dirt track narrowed until branches were screeching against both sides of the Jeep. Damon ignored the sound and continued to push through the trees. He hadn't seen Alina in over three months, not since they left New Jersey together after killing one of the world's most notorious assassins at a little, run-down farmhouse in Pennsylvania.

Damon shifted gears as the track angled down sharply and disappeared into a wide, shallow river. He coasted into the water and drove through, splashing water up the sides of the doors.

A few days after leaving New Jersey, he was called away on an assignment which landed him in Mexico. The last time he saw Alina, she was disappearing into the crowds at the airport. He had boarded his flight wondering if he would ever see her again, an all-too-familiar thought that he had every time he said goodbye to her.

Reaching the bank on the other side of the river, he pressed the gas and the Jeep lurched out of the water. He bounced back onto the barely recognizable track once more and shifted gears again. They lived far from a secure existence, he and Alina. The simple fact that he was back in the States and heading through this wilderness to join his old friend was a blessing in itself. While he was thankful for that blessing, the reasons for it were far from heavenly. The time had finally come to wrap up what they started three months before. Damon's lips thinned grimly.

The time had come to catch a traitor.

Damon punched the Jeep through some underbrush. Three months had been spent waiting patiently while Alina had lulled them into a state of confusion. Now, it was time for her to take back her life and her freedom. It was time for them to find the person responsible for bringing a terrorist onto American soil.

Despite the grimness of the situation, he was looking forward to seeing her again. The circumstances may be less than ideal, but they had faced worse together: boot camp, for one and New Jersey, for another.

Compared with those, how bad could it be?

Chapter Two

The black hawk dove down from heights unknown, circling lazily as he descended through the evening sky. The sunlight was fading and, as the bird reached tree level, he blended perfectly with the shadows before dropping gracefully out of the sky and landing gently on the outstretched arm of a slender redhead. She murmured to him softly and the hawk bobbed his head, his shiny black eyes locked onto her green ones.

Alina smiled at him fondly. Raven adopted her as his own two years ago, the day she took him in to nurse him back to health. Rather than be parted from her, he followed her out of the mountains of South America, all the way to New Jersey. When she departed from Jersey a few months before, he followed her again. He was a guardian and a companion, and Alina couldn't imagine a better pet.

Still holding her arm out like a perch, she turned and slowly walked back to the small cabin in the center of the clearing. People used to call her a witch behind her back in the military. Her uncanny knack with animals of all types had earned her the nickname, and her "sixth sense" had held it. They didn't know that she was aware of the whispers, but she had been amused by them. She certainly didn't think there was anything magical about her abilities with animals. They responded to her and seemed to understand her. It was a phenomenon that had come in extremely handy on several occasions and Alina had learned not to question it. It was just part of who she was.

She reached the back porch of the cabin and Raven stepped off her arm onto the wooden banister that surrounded the porch. Stepping up onto the worn wood, Alina turned to look out into the trees. She had been in the cabin now for three months and was getting restless. Aside from her daily afternoon romp into the Irish bar in the city, she didn't leave the safety of the woods. Those three months had been spent carefully ensuring that she had completely vanished off the grid. Her pursuers were fed a steady diet of misdirection until they weren't sure if she was in Egypt, South America,

Russia, Canada or the Alps. She could have been in Timbuktu for all they knew. They didn't have any idea where she was and they were getting nervous.

And that was part of the plan.

Alina smiled grimly as she gazed out into the gathering dusk. Soon she would be able to start moving again. While these months of near inactivity had served her well, Alina was ready to get on with it. She glanced at the black hawk, who was settled on the railing, staring out into the trees with his sharp eyes. Even Raven had been restless recently, sensing change in the air.

Alina was turning to go into the house when she caught the unmistakable sound of an engine through the trees. She paused, her hand instinctively unsnapping the holster holding the .45 semi-automatic pistol at her back. Raven was still staring into the trees to the right, his shiny eyes unwavering. Alina stepped off the porch, listening to the faint sound of the engine in the distance. Only two people knew where she could be found, and both of them were out of the country.

Alina was still, listening to the faint hum echoing through the trees. It sounded as if it was heading towards her, but it was hard to tell at this distance. She glanced at Raven. He turned his head to look at her before launching off the balustrade and disappearing into the trees to the right.

That was the only thing she needed to see.

Pulling the .45 out of her back holster, Alina ran swiftly toward the trees to the right of the house. It was entirely possible that it was a stranger, off-roading in the woods, but she wasn't about to stay put and wait to see. In a few seconds, she was in the trees, skillfully moving through them with the speed of someone very familiar with the territory. Her heart settled down into a steady rhythm, and every sense she had was focused on her surroundings. The trees moved past her in a blur, and Alina sensed the forest animals scurrying around her as she moved swiftly and silently through the woods.

The engine was louder now. It was definitely on the old trail that led from the access road a few miles away. Alina paused, judging the distance by sound, before crossing to her right to cut through the trees. She emerged onto the old trail about a quarter mile ahead of the vehicle and, leaning up against the fat trunk of an old tree, she caught her breath and waited.

A topless, black Jeep Wrangler came into view a moment later, bouncing along the trail. Alina lifted her right arm, the .45 firmly in her grasp, and brought up her left hand to steady it. Without flinching, she fired off a round at the Jeep.

The sound was deafening in the forest. Her bullet tore into the front right tire and the Jeep came to an abrupt stop. The forest fell silent around them as the driver stood up swiftly, aiming his own weapon at her. Alina's heart surged into her throat as her eyes met bright blue ones. She stared at the tall man holding a gun pointed straight at her pounding heart.

"I thought you were in Mexico," she finally called a little breathlessly, breaking the silence. The man studied her lazily.

"I thought you were a brunette," he answered.

Alina gave a short laugh and lowered her weapon as she moved forward. As soon as she did, he lowered his and tucked it away in the back of his cargo shorts. Switching off the engine, he jumped out of the Jeep and strode forward to meet her. He was six foot, two inches of solid strength, with shoulders as broad as he was tall. Dressed in khaki cargo shorts and a black t-shirt that stretched tight across his hard chest, he moved with a jungle-cat grace that was deadly. Dark hair fell over his forehead in a careless wave and Alina thought he might very well have been the best thing she had ever seen.

"Welcome back, Hawk," she murmured, tucking her gun back into its holster as she met him in the middle of the trail.

His arms wrapped around her warmly and held her tightly for a moment. Alina got a whiff of musk and woodsy scent, the smell that was unmistakably *him,* and a rush of warmth surged through her. Damon pulled away slightly and looked down at her, his cobalt eyes dancing warmly.

"Not quite the welcome I was expecting," he retorted.

Alina grinned and they both turned to look at the Jeep. The hissing that came from the front passenger tire was unmistakable.

"Sorry about that," she said sheepishly and Damon glanced down at her again.

"Nice shot."

"I've been known to make a few," she answered with a wink.

He chuckled and looked around.

"How far are we from your lair?"

"About half mile along this track."

"Get in." Damon headed back to the driver's door. "The tire just might make it there."

Alina glanced at the deflating tire dubiously as she passed it and climbed into the Jeep.

"What are you doing back already?" she asked as he started the engine and put the Jeep in gear.

"I finished sooner than I expected," Damon answered shortly, pressing the gas. The Jeep moved forward. "Harry told me how to get here. You couldn't have found a better spot. This place is the land of nowhere."

"Have you heard any chatter?" Alina asked and Damon glanced at her.

"I heard that you were sighted in China last week, and last night I heard that you were in Brazil," he told her. "Apparently, you're everywhere."

Alina's lips curved into a smile.

"Except here," she said softly and Damon nodded, turning his attention back to the trail.

"Except here," he agreed. "You've done a great job of keeping them spinning their wheels," he admitted. "I was half-tempted to start some rumors about Mexico, but then I thought better of it."

"Thank you!" Alina said with heartfelt sincerity, grabbing the roll bar as the Jeep bounced over a deep rut. "I don't want to have to worry about the Cartels on top of everything else."

"I have no idea what you're talking about," Damon murmured and Alina glanced at him, her eyes alight with laughter.

"Oh, don't you?" she demanded.

"Not the faintest," he retorted. Alina grinned.

"Ok, Hawk," she murmured. "Have it your way."

Damon glanced at her swiftly.

"If I could have it my way, we wouldn't be here," he said. The smile faded from Alina's face and she ducked instinctively as a tree branch smacked the roll bar. "This is insanity. You know that."

Alina was silent as they bounced the last few yards towards the edge of the trees that surrounded the cabin clearing.

"You know I couldn't just run away," she said finally as they broke through the trees and into the clearing behind the house. Two square buildings were set apart from the cabin at the back. One acted as a garage and the other was a makeshift workshop. Alina pointed to the building on the right.

"You can pull up there," she said.

Damon guided the limping Jeep to the right and stopped outside the garage, cutting the engine. They were both silent for a minute.

"I've been thinking a lot about this whole mess," Damon said slowly, breaking the silence. "This might be the one time when you *should* have run."

"I could never have stopped. You know that," Alina replied softly. She looked at him and her eyes met his. "I can't live any kind of life hiding from my own government. This has to end now."

Damon stared at her in silence for a long moment before nodding.

"Then we'll end it," he finally said.

Alina wasn't aware that she was holding her breath. With his words, however, she exhaled a long, silent sigh of relief. She couldn't do this without Hawk. Even with the two of them working together, the odds were heavily against them.

And heavily in favor of someone hidden deep within Washington, DC.

⊕

Michael O'Reilly poured himself a drink and carried it over to his dining room table, staring down at the papers spread out before him. Time tables jostled with the latest intelligence reports on the missing government agent known only as Viper. The mysterious agent had disappeared three months ago and just about every agency in Washington was looking for her. The problem was that no one knew anything about her, or even what she looked like. She was a phantom, and a very well-trained phantom at that.

He sipped his drink as his eyes fell on an 8x10 glossy photo of an attractive brunette. Stephanie Walker, FBI and Agent-in-Charge of the case that had blown up and made headlines three months ago. She and her partner had single-handedly prevented what was potentially the largest terrorist attack on US soil since 9/11. The terrorists had been apprehended at the last moment and not a single American life was lost. That was the print story.

The actual events, as they happened, were cloaked in so much disinformation that Michael had no idea what *really* took place three months ago on Three Mile Island. According to Ms. Walkers account, the terrorists were led by Johann Topamari, the notorious leader of the terrorist cell, Mossavid. He was killed when Ms. Walker and her partner apprehended the terrorists. Though her name had not appeared in any of the official reports, and there was no witness to prove it, the widespread theory was that Viper had been present as well on the nuclear reactor site that night.

Michael turned to look at the huge map of the world that took up most of the far wall of the dining room. He set down his glass, picked up the latest intelligence report, and carried it over to the map. He scanned the report and picked up a red thumb tack, sticking it through Panama. Stepping back, Michael shook his head as a reluctant grin spread across his handsome face.

Red thumb tacks covered the map before him. There was at least one tacked in every country, often more. If this so-called Viper had been present at even half the locations, then she had enough frequent flyer miles to fly for free the rest of her life, and she clearly had a superpower that allowed her to be in more than one place at a time. Several, in fact.

Michael went back to the table to pick up his drink again, looking down at Ms. Walker. The theory was that she was the last one to see Viper. She had been interviewed repeatedly. She had been badgered, summoned and politely threatened until her agency finally said enough. Ms. Walker had cooperated every step of the way and she was now off limits. She had no knowledge of this mysterious government agent. She and her partner had worked closely with Homeland Security to apprehend a terrorist and prevent an attack on Three Mile Island. They had acted with unsurpassed bravery and were heroes. That was the FBI's final word on the matter and the case was officially closed.

Except Michael knew that it wasn't. Ms. Walker's agency was actively trying to find Viper. The FBI had alerts out all over the country, looking for information on not only *her* whereabouts, but that of her last known companion, Damon Peterson. The FBI wanted both of them for questioning in relation to that incident that happened on Three Mile Island in the Spring. Damon, allegedly a clandestine agent with the Department of Homeland Security, was also wanted for questioning in the unrelated investigation into the death of a Homeland Security agent in DC. The FBI was getting nowhere in their search for either of them.

Michael sipped his drink and let his eyes wander back to the massive map on his wall. He had been given the task of finding this phantom named Viper. Someone higher up on the food chain believed that she was a very real threat to White House security. It wasn't his job to ask questions, but Michael found himself questioning more and more why this particular agent was considered a threat. If she was present on the Island with Ms. Walker, then chances were pretty good that it had been *her* that killed Johann Topamari. Michael frowned. If that was the case, she was a hero, not a villain. If she was a security risk, wouldn't she have been working *with* the terrorist?

And why was everyone so desperate to find her? The FBI wanted her for questioning, but for what? Their case on the terrorists was closed, crisis averted. Homeland Security was also looking for Viper. They wanted her for questioning by an oversight committee investigating God alone knew what, because they claimed she could have information that could be relative to that investigation.

Michael sipped his drink again thoughtfully. Johann was dead and his associates were in custody. What additional information could Viper possibly have for DHS?

And then, of course, there was the CIA. Michael ran a hand over his short red hair and drained his glass. The CIA had alerts out to their agents worldwide. Michael had seen the alert. They were looking for any and all information on the location of one particular agent, commonly known as Viper. Their alert had gone to every station head throughout the world and brought back zero hits. Michael wasn't surprised. The people who sent the alert had taught Viper to be a ghost. It was clear that the alert had been sent as a courtesy only. They weren't about to let one of their agents anywhere near a Congressional oversight committee.

Michael sighed and set down his empty glass. Someone wanted this agent, and they wanted her yesterday. It had nothing to do with terrorists on Three Mile Island or oversight committees.

He stared at the map on the wall.

What did she know?

Alina handed Damon a beer over his shoulder and walked around to sit next to him on the overstuffed couch. He had a laptop balanced on his legs, his feet crossed on the worn coffee table in front of him, and he was studying a map on the screen. The sun had disappeared and the lights were on in the small living room at the front of the cabin. The large fireplace that took up most of the exterior wall was cold and dark. A thick woven rug consisting of reds and whites covered most of the hardwood floor in this room, and matching red curtains were pulled across the windows, shutting out the night. The front door opened directly into the living room, and a wooden staircase led upstairs opposite the front door. The cabin was small, but homey.

And Alina was getting heartily sick of it.

"This is in perfect position," Damon murmured, sipping the beer and glancing at her. "You couldn't have found a more perfect location."

Alina smiled slightly.

"Raven needed room to hunt," she replied with a twinkle. Damon laughed.

"Of course," he agreed, sitting back and looking at her.

Alina was curled into her corner of the couch with her knees up next to her, facing him. Damon took in the red hair and the sparkling green eyes. He wasn't sure he could get used to the hair, and the green contacts were disconcerting.

"You look completely different," he told her.

Alina raised her eyebrow slightly in that gesture that was uniquely hers.

"That was the idea," she murmured. "Don't you like redheads?"

she asked with a flash of a grin. Damon smiled slowly.

"Not as much as I like brunettes," he answered.

Alina's lips curved and her heart rate quickened.

"I like the red," she said, ignoring the leap in her pulse.

"I've known too many redheads," Damon informed her and Alina laughed.

"You spoke to Harry?" she asked, changing the subject and sipping her bottled water.

"Yesterday." Damon closed the laptop with a snap and leaned forward to set it on the coffee table. "He says he'll be back in Washington tomorrow." Damon shifted slightly to face her and rested his elbow on the back of the couch. His t-shirt stretched taut across his chest and he seemed to take up the whole couch. "He asks respectfully that we don't blow anything up until he gets back."

Alina met his bright blue eyes and they shared a quick grin.

"I think I can go along with that," Alina said. "I have a few more things to set in motion. Does he think he can keep Homeland Security spinning for a few more days?"

"He didn't say," Damon sipped his beer, "but he seemed very confident that everything would go smoothly on his end."

Alina nodded and stared thoughtfully at the empty fireplace. Damon watched her for a moment.

"The Organization reinstated you with a clear record," he said. "Congratulations."

Alina nodded absently.

"Mmm," she murmured. When Damon was silent, she lifted her eyes to him again. He was staring broodingly into his beer. "They are cautiously endorsing this mission," she said.

"Meaning if we succeed, they'll protect us," he stated. Alina nodded.

"And if we fail, we're on our own," she added. "Same deal as always."

Damon looked up and they stared at each other for a moment.

"They want to know who the traitor is," Damon finally said, "and they don't want to go through normal channels."

"Something like that," Alina agreed. "They're looking the other way while we operate on US soil. Again."

Damon nodded. He was strangely comfortable with working on US soil, in the FBI's backyard. He tried not to consider the possibility that it was because he was getting tired of globe-trotting.

"Are you worried?" he finally asked. Alina's lips curved slightly.

"I don't have time to be worried," she replied. "Someone's trying to kill me to keep me quiet."

Damon nodded and got up restlessly with his beer. He prowled around the small living room once before coming to a stop in front of the fireplace.

"What about the Fearless Feds?" he asked over his shoulder.

He was referring to the two FBI agents Alina had left behind in New Jersey. The two friends from her past had become irrevocably entangled in her mission there three months ago. That mission had been her atonement mission, the one that reinstated her with The Organization after an unusual mission failure two years before.

"Running in circles with the rest," she said. Damon caught the note of regret in her voice and shot her a sharp look under his lashes. She was watching him with an unreadable look on her face. "But they're safe. For now."

"What a God-awful mess." Hawk shook his head and turned his attention to the empty fireplace. Alina was silent as she sipped her water. After a long thoughtful silence, he straightened up and turned to look at her, leaning his broad shoulders against the stone mantle. "So, what kind of odds are we looking at?"

"FBI, NSA, DHS, NCIS...pretty much the entire alphabet, except ours, is looking for me," Alina told him, capping her water and setting it on the coffee table. She shifted on the couch and stretched her legs out, crossing them at the ankles. "And now the Secret Service has thrown their hat into the ring as well."

"Secret Service was inevitable," Hawk said. "He knows we'll come after him."

Alina lifted that strange, sparkling green gaze to him.

"Yes," she agreed. Her lips curved mischievously. "But what *wasn't* expected was who would lead the charge for them."

Damon raised an eyebrow questioningly.

"Don't even tell me it's someone we know!" he exclaimed. Alina's smile grew to a grin.

"It's someone *I* know," she replied. "The last time I saw him, we killed an entire bottle of Jameson in honor of my brother."

Damon let out a low whistle.

"A Marine?" he asked. Alina nodded.

"He came to see me when he got stateside after my brother died," she told him. "He wanted to give his condolences personally and tell me that he promised my brother he would look out for me." Damon watched her through hooded eyes. "We drank an entire bottle and then he left. I joined up not long after that and I never saw him again, until today." She made a face. "I never drank Jameson again, either," she added.

Damon chuckled and went over to the couch again. He lifted her outstretched feet and sat down in their place, setting them down in his lap.

"Can we turn him?" he asked, rubbing her ankles absently. Alina was quiet for a moment, thinking.

"I don't think we'll have to," she finally said slowly. "I didn't get the impression that he was hostile. He's asking questions and poking around in Frankie Solitto's backyard."

Damon looked surprised.

"Really?" he drawled. "Now how on earth did he get wind of that old mobster?"

"One of Solitto's extended cousins is a regular informant for him," Alina said with a yawn. Damon was massaging her ankles and the warmth of his strong fingers was sending goosebumps up her legs. It felt so natural to sit like this, to allow the soothing motion of his hands relax her legs. She stretched and sat up, pulling her feet off Damon's lap and reaching for her water again, abruptly ending the contact. "They meet in the back booth of an Irish bar downtown."

Damon stared at her, his lips twitching.

"You never cease to amaze me," he murmured. "How on earth did you ferret out that piece of information? Wait. Never mind. I don't want to know."

Alina laughed and stood up.

"The important thing is that Michael O'Reilly will be on our side," she said. Damon looked up at her.

"And just how do you plan on getting the Secret Service on our side?" he demanded. The smile that curved across her lips sent a shiver of foreboding down his spine.

"Let's just say that a Marine is always a Marine," Alina told him, picking up her water bottle and turning to go into the kitchen.

"Viper!" Hawk called. She turned her head, pausing at the sudden use of her codename. "Be careful. He can just as easily say that an assassin is always an assassin."

Alina met his gaze and smiled slightly.

"Oh, I'm counting on that."

Hawk watched her disappear into the kitchen and the feeling of foreboding grew. Viper was one of the best in the Organization. Her planning and attention to detail were legendary. She had an almost perfect record and always got her mark, but she had never taken on her own government.

Hawk lifted his beer to his lips. He really hoped Viper's plan was flawless.

Anything less and they would both be finished.

29

Chapter Three

Stephanie tossed her bags into the trunk and slammed it shut. John leaned on her driver's side door with his arms crossed over his chest, watching her from behind his sunglasses. The sunlight glinted on his blond hair and Stephanie smiled as she walked up to him.

"And the vacation officially begins," she said. John nodded.

"We've earned it," he agreed. "I'm going to soak up every ray of sun I can on the beach." He straightened up and unfolded his arms. "I still don't see why you're disappearing into the mountains. What's there to do up there?"

"Nothing." Stephanie grinned. "That's the point." She reached around him to open her door. "But keep your phone on," she added as an after-thought. "I might get bored."

"That I don't doubt," he retorted, holding the top of the car door as she got behind the wheel. "To each his own, though. Whatever it takes to recharge." He leaned forward and looked down at her. "Take the time to relax."

"Oh, I plan to," Stephanie answered, starting the engine. She glanced up when John made no move to step back. "What?"

"I know you're bothered about Lina," he said seriously. "You have to let her go." Stephanie stared up at him.

"I'll let her go *after* I thank her for saving my life," she retorted.

John opened his mouth as if to say something, but apparently thought better of it. He nodded instead, pushed her door shut, and watched as she backed out of her spot. He waited until she pulled out of the parking lot before turning and slowly walking back to his own car. The motorcycle was locked up at his apartment and he was sporting his old Firebird today. John slid behind the wheel and sat for a minute thoughtfully.

Alina always loved this old Firebird. John ran a hand over the top of the dash and glanced over to the passenger seat. The leather seats were worn and cracked, but she used to say it was a classic. His eyes fell on a gray, burnt patch on the passenger's floor. He stared at it, remembering the smell of burning carpet and cigarette smoke, and her laughter as she realized that the carpet was smoldering. They had been parked outside his friend's house when they started fighting. John frowned slightly. He couldn't remember the cause, but he remembered the make-up vividly. It had led to the burn mark on the floor. Her cigarette had fallen unnoticed and burnt all the way down to the filter, leaving a two-inch burn in the floor before it ignited and started smoldering. Even then, it had been quite a while before either of them had noticed anything.

John lifted his eyes from the damaged floor and turned the key in the ignition. The engine growled to life and he pressed the gas gently, revving it. Alina had been more upset over the burnt carpet than him. It had led to yet another attempt to quit smoking, an attempt that failed when they got word that her brother had been killed in Iraq.

John pulled himself back from the past and put the car in reverse. He had no intention of going to the shore.

He was going to find Lina.

A soft ocean breeze blew into the study, carrying the unmistakable scent of saltwater and sand, while the soothing sound of waves crashing onto the beach flowed into the study as if it were part of the decor. The sun had disappeared and the beach out back was bereft of moonlight, leaving it dark and mysterious. The beach was private property, belonging to the house and rigorously guarded. This house was a fortress, yet still a summer home away from home.

Frankie Solitto had a few residences. Running the Jersey Family had made him a very rich man, and this particular house on the Jersey shore was the pride and joy of his wife of twenty-odd years. She was in residence from before Memorial Day until well after Labor Day, spending her days on the beach and her nights either on the stone patio outside or at the casinos in Atlantic City. Tonight, she was in Atlantic City. Alina had watched her leave over an hour ago.

Frankie was in the dining room, finishing his dinner. His guards were on patrol on the beach and surrounding the house within the terracotta-colored privacy wall. No one could get in or out without their knowledge, and absolutely no one was allowed in Frankie's private study without him. Ever.

Viper sat comfortably in a leather chair in a dark corner of the study, waiting.

She had left Damon at the cabin two hours away with misgivings. It wasn't that she didn't trust Hawk. At least, that was what she told herself. It was just that she was uneasy leaving him unattended with her equipment. When she left, he was fixing his tire and tinkering around with the engine on his Jeep, but she knew Hawk. He would get curious and start poking around. She knew this because she would do the exact same thing in his position.

The handle on the door of the study turned suddenly, pulling Alina from her thoughts. The door opened unceremoniously and Frankie Solitto came into the room, carrying a glass with two fingers of scotch in one hand. The head of the Jersey Family let the door close behind him and Alina had ample time to study him as he walked over to his desk in front of the open French windows. He hadn't changed in three months, except to develop a much deeper tan. He was still every bit as imposing as the last time she saw him. Tall, with broad shoulders, Frankie exuded power, both physical and charismatic. A woman could easily be intimidated or overwhelmed by Frankie Solitto, and Alina was sure that more than his fair share of women *had* been overwhelmed by his Italian good-looks and aura of sheer authority. However, she was not one of them.

"Hello, Frankie," she said softly.

She had waited until he set his drink on the desk before making her presence known. Frankie started, his dark eyes flying to the shadows where she sat.

"For the love of..." he started to bluster angrily, then abruptly stopped. He frowned and stepped forward from his desk. "Is that...."

"I apologize for the unexpected intrusion, but I really don't want anyone to know I've been here." Alina reached up to switch on the standing lamp next to the chair. "Although, you may not recognize me," she added apologetically.

Frankie stared at her sternly, his dark eyes taking in her appearance. Her red hair was pulled back into a loose braid and she was dressed in light-weight black cargo pants and a black tank top. Frankie stared at her for a long moment, struggling between anger and a reluctant grin.

"I don't care for the red," he finally informed her, moving back to his desk to pick up his drink. Alina's lips twitched as she watched him sip his scotch.

"You're the second one to tell me that," she said. "I really thought I made a good redhead."

"I've known too many redheads," Frankie retorted, perching on the corner of his desk. "To what do I owe this invasion of my privacy? I was

32

under the impression that we concluded our business together three months ago."

"And so we did," Alina agreed congenially, crossing her legs. "But now I have a problem."

"And you're calling in the favor," Frankie stated rather than asked. Alina raised an eyebrow.

"Do you owe me one?" she asked.

Frankie frowned and swirled the amber liquid in his glass, studying her.

"The whole east coast owes you one," he finally said. "I guess they'll never know that, though. Don't think I don't know what you did. You killed two birds with one stone that night and I, for one, will always remember that."

"Two?" Alina raised an eyebrow. "I recall the papers only reporting one."

"Funny thing about that..." Frankie swirled his scotch some more. "There was an awful lot of blood in a barn a few miles down on the other side of the river, but no body. My boys looked good and hard."

Alina smiled slowly and her eyes met Frankie's in a brief look of understanding.

"Is that why you didn't reach for your gun just now?" she asked softly.

"Is it still there?" he asked in surprise. "You people have a habit of removing it when you break into my home."

Alina allowed herself a low chuckle.

"It's still there," she assured him. "I'm confident that I can get to mine before you can get to yours," she added with a slow smile that didn't reach her eyes. Frankie smiled reluctantly.

"I've said it before, and I'll say it again. You find yourself at loose ends, you come see me," he told her, sipping his drink. "I like your style, you *and* your boyfriend."

"I'll be sure to pass the compliment on," Alina replied, biting back a laugh at the thought of Hawk's face when she relayed the message.

"So, if you're not here to collect the favor, why are you here?" Frankie demanded, setting his glass on his desk and crossing his arms over his chest with the air of a man getting down to business.

"You have an associate down in DC who's been asking questions about me," Alina told him. "Why?"

"Marty?" Frankie snorted. "He's nothing to worry about."

"It's not him I'm worried about," Alina retorted. "How did someone find out I had ever been to see you?"

"What says someone did?"

"Someone knew to ask Marty about me."

Frankie stared at her for a moment and then sighed, rubbing his forehead.

"I don't know how they found out," he admitted after a minute. "I suspect that it was Bruno, the guard you stepped into the ground last time I saw you."

"Ah." Alina examined her nails. "Where would Bruno be now?" she asked gently.

"At the bottom of the river," Frankie answered bluntly. She shot a look at him under her lashes and he shrugged. "Bruno and I had some.... irreconcilable differences."

Alina watched him silently for a long moment and Frankie matched her stare for stare. After a few long minutes, she sighed.

"Here's my problem, Frankie," she said slowly. "I know who's asking questions about me, and I know what you're telling them."

"Nothing!" Frankie interjected quickly.

"What I really need to know is how they found out about our...connection," Alina continued as if she hadn't heard him and Frankie found himself gazing into cold green eyes. "I really wish you hadn't put Bruno in the river."

Frankie felt a shiver go down his spine at the look on her face.

"He went in the river before Marty came up here asking questions," he told her. "By then, it was too late."

"I need you to find out who put two and two together and came up with four. I doubt it was Bruno. He didn't strike me as the intelligent type." Alina stood up fluidly. "Someone in your Family passed on information about me. That not only puts your entire Family at risk, but it puts *that* person at the top of my To-Do list. Trust me, I keep my To-Do list short."

"I won't ask how," Frankie murmured and Alina's lips curved coldly.

"Don't," she advised. "Find your leak," she allowed a note of steel to lace her tone, "or I'll find it for you."

"I'll need to know how to reach you," Frankie said as she moved toward the French windows. Viper glanced back.

"When you have something for me, tell Marty to order the Guinness Burger with extra Guinness. I'll get the message," she said over her shoulder before disappearing into the night.

Frankie watched her go before finishing his drink in one swallow. He had thought once before that he wouldn't want to be on the wrong side of her. Now, he was dangerously close to ending up there.

Frankie slammed his glass down. He had almost been expecting her ever since that idiot Marty had come to him last week asking questions about a woman who was exceptionally skilled with a gun. Frankie had sent Marty on his way with no information, but he had known she'd be back to visit him. He had known she would ask questions, and he knew that it was past time to do what he had been putting off for far too long. Somewhere in his Family was a leak, a leak to the Feds. He had suspected it for six months.

It was time to clean house.

Hidden deep in the forest, a fire burned cheerfully within the confines of a pit dug into the earth and surrounded with large, heavy rocks. Smoke spiraled up into the night, warning the forest animals to stay away. Alina stood in the shadows at the edge of the clearing and watched as Hawk stared into the flames. He was seated next to the fire with his back to her and his broad shoulders were relaxed, his arms draped loosely around his knees. A cooler next to him beckoned faint memories of a cold beer next to another bonfire, one lit on a beach ten years ago.

Alina stared at it, her mind going back to a night that seemed another lifetime away. They had survived basic training and were leaving the next day to begin their military careers. Alina sat next to Damon on that night long ago, staring into the flames and listening to the raucous laughter of her fellow sailors. Drinking her beer, she had listened with only half an ear as they joked and laughed, still wondering what the Navy had in store for her. It wouldn't be what was undoubtedly in Damon's future. He would head into SEAL's training eventually, everyone knew that. While she would have loved to have joined him there, she couldn't at the time. No women were allowed then. Alina had been irritated by that fact all through basic training, even as she broke record after record made by men that had come before her. She had the man sitting next to her to thank for that. He was the reason she had worked so hard. Ever since they met the first week of training, they were in friendly competition with each other. It was because of him that she never gave up. She didn't begrudge him his inevitable entrance into the Special Forces. She wanted him to succeed. Alina had just wished that she had that option available to her. She hadn't known, at the time, that she would end up following a similar path after being guided into military intelligence.

Ever since that first week of training camp, their lives had been intertwined, following a parallel course and crossing every so often. Hawk had always been there, in her thoughts and even, she admitted to herself now, in her career. He was always in the distance, driving her to push herself. Hawk had become a permanent part of her life without her even realizing it.

"Are you going to come over to the fire, or just stand there lurking all night?"

Damon pulled her back to the present, calling the question without turning around. Alina smiled and moved into the clearing silently. She walked up behind him as he opened the cooler to pull out a beer. He handed it up to her, tilting his head back with a slight smile.

"Are you done for the night?"

"Yes."

Alina took the bottle and sat on the ground next to him, pulling her utility knife from her pocket and using the bottle opener to pop off the top. She tossed the lid into the fire and stared at the flames as she took a sip of the beer. It was cold and filled with Dejá Vù.

"Good trip?" Damon asked, glancing at her.

She hadn't told him where she was going and he hadn't asked. Her eyes were unreadable as she shrugged.

"I think so," she answered. "We'll see."

They fell into a companionable silence, mesmerized by the dancing white and gold flames. Alina began to relax for perhaps the first time in months, lulled by the crackling wood and crickets singing around them.

"I spoke to Harry while you were gone." Hawk broke the silence after a few moments. Alina glanced at him sharply and he grinned.

"Don't worry. Any trace will send them to Kyrgyzstan," he assured her. "At least on my end. God alone knows where Harry will send them."

Alina chuckled.

"And what did Harry have to say?" she asked, turning her gaze back into the fire.

Damon shifted and stretched his legs out toward the fire pit. His thigh rested against hers as he leaned back on his elbows and his eyes were dark pools in the dancing firelight. When she glanced back at him, Alina's heart thudded uncomfortably as it skipped a beat and she lifted the bottle to her lips again, hastily turning her gaze back to the fire. He looked entirely too sexy, leaning back with his biceps gleaming in the dancing light. His thigh suddenly seemed very warm and her pulse quickened in reaction.

"He sends his love." Damon watched her turn her attention back to the fire. "Things are even better than I expected. The Organization issued a non-official statement to DHS, and all the other alphabets, saying that until they provided substantial proof of you being a national security risk, they wouldn't provide any information about you, your missions, or your possible location. They cited international security as their shield."

He grinned as her head snapped back to stare at him.

"You're kidding!" she exclaimed.

The fire behind her cast her face in shadows, but Damon could see the grin on her face.

"Nope. Honest truth," he told her. "Harry says Charlie flat out told DHS that they would be better off trying to find Houdini, end quote."

"Well, that's true," Alina agreed with a short laugh. She wasn't being cocky. The past three months had proven it to be fact. Damon watched as she tilted the bottle back again and her full lips closed over the top. He shifted his gaze quickly back to the fire, but not before his gut tightened in reaction. "Was Harry there? He heard it?"

"As far as I could understand." Damon drained his beer. "It won't stop them all from looking, and if they catch you stateside, you're done. But this is better than I'd hoped for. It sends the message that we have the Organization's protection, at least for now."

"Absolutely."

Alina turned back to the fire and stared into the flames thoughtfully. The Organization was a very small section of the CIA that most people didn't even know existed, led by a man they called Charlie. It was comprised of highly-trained, specialized assassins, taught to be elite, invisible, and deadly. They were tasked with the job of doing what the government could not, or would not, do overtly. The Organization was, by its very nature, autonomous from the government and answerable only to the Director of the CIA himself. It was virtually untouchable. Those in Washington who knew of its existence were content to keep it that way. They wanted nothing to do with the necessary, but politically devastating, role that the Organization played in the international arena. If the Organization said they didn't need to know, they didn't *want* to know. Having the Organization's open protection was much more than Alina had hoped for.

Damon watched as Alina fell into a pensive silence; her gaze on the fire. It crackled cheerfully and sparks occasionally shot into the darkness to burn out harmlessly. The flames cast dancing shadows along her arms and bare shoulders, throwing her profile into sharp relief against the night. The red hair hung in a thick braid across the back of her shoulders and Damon had the sudden urge to undo it and pull it loose, feeling the soft strands in his fingers. His mind shot back to a night three months ago, in another clearing, in a different forest. There had been a moment, a very brief moment, when he glimpsed her true feelings, a moment when he felt them. That moment passed all too quickly, however, and their relationship had fallen back into the friendly teasing one that they had always known. The professional had returned, and the woman he discovered in New Jersey had disappeared. Damon watched the fire play now against her skin, wondering if that Jersey girl was still there somewhere, dormant while the professional was focused, deep in thought.

Viper was going over her plans in her head, looking for weaknesses, looking for flaws.

He knew her well and knew that her mind was far away. Hawk dragged his eyes away from her and back to the dancing flames. He would leave what happened between them three months ago in the past and go along with her plans, working next to her once more. He would give her more time to decide just how she felt and, more importantly, what she was going to do about it. But once this was over, once they were free, they were going to have a long talk. There was only so much he was willing to endure, and working next to her without touching her was just about going to hit his limit.

"What's wrong?" her voice pulled his gaze back to her. Alina was watching him, her eyes dark in the shadows.

"What makes you think something's wrong?" Damon asked, looking up at her.

"You looked very resolute just now," she told him. Damon met her gaze steadily.

"Did I?" he asked quietly. Alina's eyes narrowed.

"What were you thinking about?" she demanded.

Hawk smiled slowly, his eyes glittering in the darkness.

"Hunting," he said softly.

Alina shivered unconsciously at the tone in his voice. It washed over her like hot velvet and goosebumps pricked along her neck. The air between them was suddenly charged with tension and she caught her breath, her heart thudding again. She stared at him, watching as the shadows on his face flickered with the flames. His eyes were dark and unreadable, watching her steadily.

"How's that working out for you?" she finally got out, her voice just as soft.

The firelight danced in his dark eyes and Damon's slow grin was downright sinful.

"I've never lost yet," he purred.

Alina swallowed, her mouth suddenly dry. Her lips curved despite herself and she shook her head slightly before finishing her beer. She could feel him watching her and was thankful for the combination of darkness and firelight which concealed the heat flooding her cheeks. Her heart thudding in her chest, Alina set her empty bottle down carefully. She was silent for a long moment, avoiding his steady gaze, while her mind clamored over the pounding emotion for some kind of articulate response.

"Everyone loses eventually," she finally whispered.

Damon sat up swiftly and silently. When he spoke, his mouth was right behind her ear.

"Not everyone," he murmured.

Alina turned her head, ready with a retort, and found his eyes inches from hers. Her reply flew out of her mind as she locked onto his eyes. They were dark blue and glittering and when they dropped to her lips, her stomach rolled over and her heart started pounding again. Hawk saw the pulse beating at the base of her throat and smiled slowly, raising his eyes back to hers.

Alina was having trouble catching her breath. There didn't seem to be enough air for both of them. Firelight danced across Damon's face and his eyes were dark, filled with lazy passion that he couldn't conceal. Her eyes dropped to his lips and he leaned forward, closing the few inches between them. His lips were warm and firm and they sent a shock of desire straight through her. Alina couldn't think anymore. She could only feel. Her lips parted on their own and passion took over. Heat shot through her, clear to her toes, and she lifted her hand to lightly grasp the side of his shoulder.

That was all the encouragement Damon needed. He slid his hand behind her head, his fingers sliding into the warmth of her hair at the base of the braid, and tilted his head slightly. The kiss became demanding and she sighed into him as passion exploded between them. Desire rocked through her in waves and Alina lost herself in the explosion. Her arm found its way around Damon's shoulders and she clung to him for support. In the back of her mind, the intensity of her reaction to him alarmed her, but desire was taking full control over her thoughts. Her heart pounding in her ears, Alina leaned into his solid warmth, allowing the emotion to sweep her along with the tide. It was a few moments before she realized that she was responding without any consideration for anything other than the man in her arms. She couldn't think at all and, with a sudden start, she came to her senses.

Pulling away, Alina got shakily to her feet, abruptly breaking the spell. Her breathing was ragged and she took a deep breath, trying to calm the blood pounding through her veins. Damon stifled a groan and flopped onto his back. He watched her step over him, bending down to collect their empty bottles, his own breathing ragged and his heart pounding.

"You're killing me, Viper," he muttered.

Her low laugh lingered as she headed back toward the cabin.

"You'll live," she shot back over her shoulder.

Damon twisted his head to watch her walk across the grass toward the house. Her long legs moved her fluidly into the darkness and she disappeared into the night. He sighed, returning his gaze to the sky. The sudden burst of desire had shaken them both, that much was clear. Well, at least he had one question answered.

The Jersey girl was most definitely still there.

"Soon," he promised the night sky quietly. "She can't run forever."

Chapter Four

Alex Ludmere, Vice President of the United States, was on the golf course. He was on the fifth hole and already so far above par that he had hit double digits. He was getting worried. When Alex got worried, he got anxious. And when he got anxious, everything suffered.

"You're over-compensating," his companion pointed out after his ball soared past the green.

"I can see that," he retorted, slamming his club into the bag that the caddie was holding. "I don't understand why it is so hard to find one woman." He waved the caddie away and began walking toward the area where his ball had disappeared, his companion falling into step beside him. "She's one woman."

"We knew it wouldn't be easy, but she can't hide forever," the woman said soothingly. "We'll find her soon."

"I mean, we found Bin Laden, for Christ's Sake," Alex muttered.

"Calm down," his companion smiled at him. "Every agency is looking for her. She can't contact anyone without us finding out. We just have to be patient."

"For how long?" Alex stopped and looked down at her. "It's already been three months. It shouldn't have taken this long. It shouldn't have even come to this. You assured me that this was going to be taken care of three months ago!"

"It would have been if you hadn't tried to interfere," she shot back. Alex scowled at her and she sighed. She reached out and put a hand on his arm. "Look, the past is done. So she was lucky. Her luck can't possibly hold out for much longer. Something will force her out into the open."

"You'll excuse me if I'm not comfortable with that something being me," he muttered, turning and continuing to stride along the fairway. "A bullet could already be in my brain before you find out where she is!"

"You know I'm not going to let that happen." The woman calmly fell back into step with him, matching him stride for stride. "She isn't as good as everyone says. I found her in South America. The Engineer found her in New Jersey. We'll find her again."

"And that's another thing!" Alex stopped again and swung around to face her. "Where is *he*? He disappeared too! I can't have all these loose ends out there!"

"I told you, The Engineer is dead," his companion reminded him. "You have no body."

"I don't need a body," she retorted. "There was blood all over that barn."

"What if he walked away?" Alex demanded.

"No way anyone was walking anywhere after that amount of blood loss." She turned to start walking again and he reluctantly followed suit. "No. It's very safe to say that The Engineer is dead."

"Well, you still need to find *her*," Alex muttered.

"I will." His companion glanced at him and took note of the high color in his cheeks. "I always take care of you," she said soothingly. "Just leave it all to me. You're worrying needlessly."

"Ha!" Alex exclaimed. "Easy for you to say. She *saw* me in Cairo. She can testify that I was there! If that ever got out...."

He shook his head and took a deep breath.

"It won't." The woman stopped and faced him, taking hold of his arm and forcing him to look at her. "You need to calm down, Alex. You have the banquet tonight and there'll be a lot of press there. You need to get a hold of yourself. Do you have any more of those pills the doctor gave you?"

"They make me dizzy," he said. She smiled.

"They help you calm down," she retorted. "You're working yourself up into one of your spells. You just do what you do best, and leave the woman to me."

"Make sure you take care of it this time," Alex replied, stopping next to a large sand bunker. His ball was in the center. "Shit."

"I will," his companion assured him. "I'll have better luck with her than you will getting that ball out of there," she added.

The parking garage was well-lit, but even the most well-lit garages had their shadows. If they didn't, it was a simple enough task to create them. Viper's bullet had done just that, creating deeper shadows in the corner of the fourth floor of the parking garage than originally present. She blended now with the darkness, a shadow herself, dressed in loose black pants and a lightweight black hoodie. The hood was pulled up securely, covering her head and casting her face into shadows. She wore tight black leather gloves that fit her hands like a second skin and flexible black boots on her feet. The sweltering heat hadn't lifted much when the sun went down, and the air was heavy and humid. Sweat trickled down her back and between her breasts but she ignored it, her eyes locked patiently on the elevator alcove.

"Where are you?" Hawk's voice spoke in her ear. "None of the cameras are picking you up."

"Surprised?" Viper spoke quietly.

"Curious," he retorted. After a few moments of silence, he added, "'I have control of the cameras now."

Alina was silent, her eyes never wavering from the alcove. Both the elevator and the stairwell exited from the same place. Regardless of which one her boy took, she would see him. The minutes ticked by slowly and she crossed her arms, leaning back against the cement wall behind her patiently. A slight, humid breeze wafted over the top of the wall, carrying a hint of fresh air into the parking area and providing a welcome break from the heavy smell of tarmac, oil, and stale urine.

The elevator dinged and Alina tensed. She relaxed back into the shadows when two women in suits emerged, laughing as they stepped off the elevator.

Parking buddies, Alina thought, watching as they walked through the quiet parking garage quickly, their heels echoing loudly on the worn cement. Their cars were parked a few spaces apart and they called goodnight to each other as they reached them. Viper returned her gaze to the alcove as the cars drove down the exit ramp. Once upon a time, she had been uncomfortable walking through a parking garage at night as well. That was before the military. Before the shadows became her friend. Before her entire body became a weapon.

Before she learned how to kill.

The sound of the stairwell door swinging open a few minutes later made Viper straighten up in the shadows again. The door swung shut and the sound echoed out of the alcove, followed by a tall man dressed in a black suit. Alina exhaled slowly as Michael O'Reilly stepped out of the alcove and into the almost empty parking garage.

"Bingo," she breathed.

"Roger that," Hawk answered calmly.

Viper watched silently from the darkness as Michael turned toward where she lurked, heading for the black F150 parked halfway down the aisle. He unbuttoned his jacket, loosening his tie as he went, and Viper caught the glint of his sidearm as he passed the shadows where she was concealed. His laptop bag was slung over his shoulder, and he still moved with the confident, steady stride of a military man, his shoulders squared and his head up.

Once a Marine, always a Marine, Alina thought, watching him.

"You're clear," Hawk told her.

Viper moved out of the shadows swiftly and silently, coming up behind Michael as he reached his truck. He never heard a thing.

In one fluid motion, she swept the back of his knees with her leg and wrapped her arm around his neck as his legs buckled. The laptop fell to the ground and she pressed her .45 against the back of his neck, turning him away from the mirror shine of his truck before he could catch a glimpse of her face.

Michael never stopped moving and Viper expected no less. When his elbow slammed backwards, she was ready. She absorbed the hit to her abdomen with a grunt, thrown back against the side of his truck with the force of the blow. Before he could follow it up with another one, Viper wrapped one leg around him and squeezed, using the truck to support her balance. She tightened her arm around his neck sharply at the same time, forcing him to change tactics. With one arm pinned by her leg, Michael tried to get his free hand under her arm to leverage it off so that he could breathe.

"I hear you've been looking for me," she purred in his ear.

At her words, he instantly stilled. Viper loosened her hold slightly and he gasped for air.

"Viper?" he choked out.

Alina gently caressed one ear with the barrel of her gun while she sighed into his other ear.

"I don't believe we've been properly introduced," she said softly.

"Let go of my neck and I'll be happy to oblige," Michael shot back breathlessly. Viper chuckled softly.

"I can't help but feel that would be detrimental to my tactical position," she replied calmly. "You Marines are so unpredictable."

"Honey, you haven't seen anything yet," Michael snarled, eliciting a genuine laugh from her.

"Promises, promises," she murmured. She tightened her arm again sharply and moved the barrel of her gun to his temple. "I'll keep this short," she hissed, "before you run out of air. You're being fed a bunch of fairy tales about bad girls that go bump in the night. Because you're a Marine, and I'm partial to gunnies, I'll give you a word of advice. Pay less attention to me and more to a dead ghost called The Engineer."

She loosened her hold slightly so that he could gulp down some air. "The Engineer?" he repeated.

"Yes. Specifically, what he was doing in Jersey three months ago and how he got there," Viper instructed. She moved her lips against his ear. "Sweet dreams," she whispered just before hitting him swiftly with the handle of her gun.

Michael sagged, a dead weight against her. Alina lowered him to the ground gently and lifted his keys out of his pocket. She unlocked the truck and tossed the laptop and his side arm inside. After locking the truck again, she dropped the keys back into his suit pocket.

A moment later, she had disappeared.

Stephanie pulled into the car park before the small building at the entrance of the cemetery. As she was getting out of the car, an older, wiry man came out of the building. He was dressed in khaki pants and a plaid button-down shirt with the sleeves rolled up. When he saw her, he paused at the door.

"Can I help you, miss?" he called.

"Yes." Stephanie slammed her door and walked up to him. "I was hoping you could point me in the right direction of a grave."

He nodded, his weathered face breaking into a friendly smile as she joined him at the door. Stephanie smiled back and brushed her hair out of her eyes. He looked like a gargoyle.

"You just caught me," he told her, holding the door open for her to step into the small building. She stepped into a room with a single desk and two chairs. "I was just closing up."

He walked around her and went behind the desk, seating himself.

"I'm glad I caught you." Stephanie sat in one of the chairs.

The gargoyle nodded and turned the computer on.

"I close up a little early on Tuesdays," he told her while he waited for the computer to boot up. "Bingo night at the firehall," he added. "I like to get there early so's I get a spot right up front. I don't hear so well as I used to."

Stephanie grinned. She could believe it. He didn't look a day under ninety.

"Well, thank you for coming back in for me," she said, settling her purse in her lap. "I appreciate it."

"Oh, it's no bother for a pretty lady like you," he replied. "Where you from? Not around here, I reckon."

"I'm from New Jersey," Stephanie answered readily. He nodded sagely.

"I thought you had to be a Yankee," he said and Stephanie blinked.

"You still call us Yankees?" she blurted out. He laughed.

"We surely do," he answered. "I'm originally from South Carolina," he told her, leaning on the desk as if he had all the time in the world. "My daughter made me move up here a few years back. She said she was worried about me, all alone after my Millie passed on. I told her I was perfectly capable of doin' for myself, but she wouldn't hear of it. I told her I would go as far as Virginia, but no further."

"You don't like us Yankees, huh?" Stephanie asked with a twinkle.

He chuckled and waved his hand.

"I like you guys just fine," he assured her. "It's all your hustle and bustle I don't like. So my girl, she compromised and moved down to Virginia."

"That was nice of her," Stephanie said.

"She's a good girl, my Sarah," he told her, peering at the computer screen. "Well, I think she's just about up," he said, leaning over the keyboard and pecking at the keys with his forefinger.

Stephanie watched as he hunt and pecked in his password, peering at the screen after each peck. She bit back a grin and waited patiently in silence, not wanting to distract him. After a few moments, he nodded.

"There now." He looked at her. "What's the name we're huntin' for?"

"Shannon Gleason," Stephanie told him. He nodded and turned his attention back to the keyboard.

"I remember her," he said as he started to hunt and peck again. "Lots of visitors to that plot. She must have been a nice lady."

Stephanie's ears perked up.

"She was," she told him. "She's had a lot of visitors recently?"

"She surely has," he agreed, peering at the screen briefly before turning his attention back to the keyboard. "You would think as many times as I've typed in her name, I would remember where she's resting, but my memory isn't what it used to be, it's surely not."

Stephanie leaned forward slightly, looking at the screen.

"I wonder...do you keep track of people who come to visit?" she asked.

He continued to hunt and peck, not looking up.

"We don't keep track of the visitors as a rule," he answered, "but all visitors are encouraged to sign the log over yonder." He waved his hand toward the back wall and Stephanie turned to look at where he was motioning. "Most folks do."

"Really?"

Stephanie got up and went over to a table with a thick log book resting on it. It was open and there were a few entries on the page, listing names of visitors and who they were there to visit. She flipped back a page, scanning the names quickly until her eyes fell on Shannon's halfway down the page. Three visitors were in the party, and they were signed in by a woman. Stephanie took out her phone and snapped a quick picture of the log entry, glancing behind her to make sure that her new friend was still typing. He was still pecking away, so she flipped back another page. Finding another entry for Shannon, she snapped a picture of that one as well.

"Here we go." Stephanie swung around as the caretaker spoke. She dropped her phone back into her purse and smiled. "I'll write it down for you."

He tore off a piece of paper from a note pad on the desk and jotted down the numbers and letters of Shannon's final address.

"Thank you so much." Stephanie walked back to the desk. "I really do appreciate it."

"Don't you mind it." He handed her the scrap of paper with a hand shaking slightly from age and then reached over to turn off the computer. "Now, it's easy enough to get to," he told her, standing up and walking back around the desk. He walked with her to the door and opened it for her.

"Now, what you want to do is go down that main road there." He pointed to the road as they stepped outside into the late afternoon sun. "Take that down past the second hill and when it splits, you want to stay to the left. When you pass the mausoleum on the right, you want to stop the car. Her plot is a few rows down."

Stephanie replaced her sunglasses on her nose and turned to him, holding out her hand.

"Thank you again," she said with a smile. "You've been so helpful."

"Well, it's always nice to pass the time with a beautiful, young woman," he told her with a grin and a wink, making Stephanie laugh.

"Why, thank you!" She shook his hand and turned to go back to her car. "Good luck at Bingo!"

She got into her car and backed out, turning the car around. With a last smile and wave, she pulled out of the little parking lot and turned onto the main road that wound its way through the cemetery. Located in Northern Virginia, it was a huge, sprawling cemetery that had been there for over two hundred years, according to the sign at the entrance. It was beautifully maintained, speaking volumes for the wealth of the patrons who graced its grounds. Shannon had mentioned in college that her family was an old one from Virginia, but Stephanie had never realized just what that meant until she read the obituary. Shannon had come from a very old and wealthy southern family.

Stephanie drove slowly, taking in the rolling hills and aged trees. She went over one hill, then drove on for a few moments before rolling over another hill. In the distance, she saw the road split in two, one going left and one going right. She stayed to the left and continued on until she saw a large, square mausoleum nestled in the center of some trees. Stephanie pulled her car to the side of the road and got out, beeping the car locked. She glanced at the address on the slip of paper and started walking. True to what her friend in the office had said, Shannon's final resting place was only a short walk down. Stephanie stepped off the pavement and started walking up the row, the thick grass soft beneath her feet. A gentle, humid breeze carried the scent of honeysuckle and she inhaled deeply, walking slowly and checking each stone as she passed.

She never had any intention of going to the Poconos when she left New Jersey. John would have tried to stop her if he had known she was coming down to Virginia to poke around some more into Shannon's death. He wanted to let sleeping dogs lie when it came to all the events three months ago, but Stephanie couldn't do that. She wanted to find out what really happened to Shannon and if that meant using her vacation to do some digging around, so be it.

Shannon's grave was near the end of the row. Stephanie stopped before it and looked down. A wreath of flowers was propped up on one side of the tombstone and Stephanie stared at the name carved in the marble, feeling hollow. She hadn't been able to make it down for the funeral, which took place the day after the incident on Three Mile Island. She supposed that was why it, somehow, wasn't real. But now, faced with the cold, hard marble with Shannon's name engraved in large block letters, Stephanie felt as if her heart had stopped. The engraving was simple, with just Shannon's name, birthday and end date. There were no cute quotes on the stone, but there *was* an engraving of a DHS badge in the marble.

Stephanie crouched before the stone with a smile. Shannon had been so proud to be part of the Department of Homeland Security. Her family had chosen well when they included the badge on the stone. She would have liked that.

"I'm sorry it took so long to get here," Stephanie whispered, blinking back a sudden rush of tears. "I'm sorry that I caused this. It's my fault you aren't with us anymore."

Her voice caught and she took a deep breath, clearing her throat and staring at the block letters in the marble.

Next Exit, Pay Toll

"I *will* find who did this, and I'll make sure that they pay for it," she promised softly.

SHANNON GLEASON.

Three months ago, she had been killed in a convenient car accident after she started a private inquiry into the mysterious DHS agent named Damon Peterson. The last time Stephanie heard from her, she had been convinced that she was being watched. The next day, she was dead.

The mysterious Mr. Peterson was conveniently absent for two days at the time of the accident. Alina had claimed at the time that Damon was in Cairo, Egypt, and nowhere near DC, but before he returned, the incident at Three Mile Island happened and the next day, Alina was gone.

And so was Stephanie's link to Damon.

Stephanie stood up slowly. She didn't know if Damon was involved or not, but she knew she had to find him and question him. She had to find the person who had put Shannon in the ground.

And when she found that person, she had all intentions of returning the favor.

"What the hell do you mean, no one's there?" Michael exclaimed, following Frank, the Head of Security, into the small room lined with monitors.

"Just that, no one's there," Frank replied. "Look and see for yourself. We saw you walking to your truck, and then we saw you on the ground. Look!"

He pointed to the monitors defiantly. Michael watched the monitors in confusion as the tech seated before them played back the camera images. Frank pointed to four monitors which corresponded with the four cameras on the fourth floor of the parking garage, and Michael watched himself walk out of the alcove from the elevators and cross the parking lot, loosening his tie. He walked up to his truck and stopped briefly, then all four cameras showed him lying on the ground next to the truck, unconscious. The transition between frames was so seamless that it appeared as if he simply dropped to the ground.

"As soon as Bill saw you on the ground, he called me and I rushed out," Frank told him, shaking his head. "We've gone back through the video stream for the whole day and can't find anything."

"But that's impossible." Michael stared at the screens.

"Not according to the cameras," Frank replied apologetically.

Michael glanced at him before returning his frown to the screens. He stared at them, his mind trying to grasp what was on them. The cameras were a live feed from the parking garage to the security room. How had someone removed a portion of a live feed?

"Bill, were you watching the monitors when I went down?" Michael asked the tech in front of the monitors suddenly after a moment. Bill looked at him apologetically.

"I was, but there are 51 other cameras to watch as well," he answered. "I saw you walk out of the alcove. I remember because that was the only movement on any of the monitors at that moment. But then the eighth level had some movement, and the sixth had a car alarm. When I went back to the fourth level, you were on the ground. I called Frank right away."

"And when you played back the stream, this is what you got." Michael shook his head again angrily.

"How did they hack into our feed? That's what I want to know," Frank said, scratching his head.

Michael glanced at him sharply. He hadn't told Frank who attacked him, just that he was taken by surprise on his way to the truck. Frank automatically assumed it was a botched robbery attempt, and Michael let him believe it. He was still fuzzy-headed and a dull headache was making his eyes hurt, but he knew that Frank wasn't going to believe that this was a robbery attempt now.

"Where's the video feed stored?" Michael asked him.

"On a server," Frank answered. "The feed comes in and then gets saved in real time."

Michael nodded slowly.

"Ok," he said, running his hand through his short hair. His fingers slid over a welt where Viper had hit him and a fresh wave of anger washed over him. "I'll take care of this. This doesn't leave this room. Understood?"

"But, our system's been compromised!" Frank protested. Michael shook his head.

"It doesn't leave this room," he repeated firmly. "I don't want this getting out."

"What about our feed?" Frank demanded.

"Make two copies of the files," Michael told him. "Give me one, you keep the other, and then delete it from the server. And I mean delete. I want it gone, like it never happened."

"And my copy?" Frank asked, looking at him.

Michael met his eyes squarely.

"You keep it safe until I tell you what to do with it."

Frank gave him a hard look before nodding.

"Ok, Mike," he agreed. "I've known you long enough to know you have something up your sleeve. I'll do it, but for God's Sake, don't make me regret it."

Michael grinned and clapped him on the shoulder.

"Trust me," he promised. "*You* won't be the one to regret it."

Chapter Five

By the time Michael got home, it was after eleven o'clock. Frank had insisted that he go to the ER to get checked for concussion. Michael refused the ER, but relented and went to an urgent care clinic instead to shut Frank up. The nurse practitioner checked him out, declared that he was fine, and sent him home with pain killers for the headache. Michael tossed the script into the glove box of his truck. He wasn't taking a prescription pain killer for a damn headache.

But he *was* going to find Viper and make sure she got a headache of her own. He was furious. He was furious with himself for being taken off guard. He was furious with her for toying with him. And he was furious with his employers for making him try to find her in the first place.

He slammed the door to his truck closed and beeped it locked. Walking down the driveway to the sidewalk, he swiped up the newspaper that had been tossed there in the morning. It wasn't until he turned around to cut back up across his front lawn that he spotted the package.

Frowning, Michael crossed to his front porch. Nestled comfortably against his front door was a brown paper bag with a white envelope propped up against it. Michael glanced around the dark and quiet neighborhood. He lived in a small, comfortable development where the neighbors were friendly and quiet. Most of the houses on his street were already dark. They worked hard here and went to bed early. The odds of anyone having seen who left the package were slim to none. He bent to pick up the envelope, careful not to touch or bump the bag. Ripping it open, he pulled out a card.

> *Sorry I missed you. I heard you were working in DC now. Just wanted to stop and say hello. It's been a long time and I feel like Dave would have liked it if we kept in touch. I understand if you feel it's been too long. I'm only in town for the*

Next Exit, Pay Toll

weekend, but my number is below if you want to
catch up. Otherwise, enjoy the bottle!

Alina Maschik

Michael stared at the name in surprise. Lina? His mind searched back and brought forth the memory of an attractive brunette with large dark eyes that looked disconcertingly like her brother's. He went to see her when he came stateside years ago after her brother Dave, his best friend, had fallen in Iraq. Dave made him promise to keep an eye on his sister and Michael had wanted to keep in touch back then. Unfortunately, Alina made it impossible to keep that promise by disappearing a few months later. He heard at one point that she joined the Navy, which hadn't surprised him, and then he lost track of her.

Michael bent down to swipe up the bag and grinned when he saw the bottle of Jameson inside. Poor Lina. By the time they finished the bottle of Jameson that night, she looked green. But she had held her own, going shot for shot with him.

Mike unlocked his front door and carried the bottle in, switching on the light as he stepped inside. He kicked the door closed behind him and dropped his keys on the hall stand. The front door opened into a hallway, which stretched back to the kitchen at the back of the house. Stairs went up the right side of the hall to the second floor. On the right was the living room and on the left was the dining room, where he had hung the world map, transforming it into his temporary command center. Carrying the bottle into the dining room, Michael dropped his laptop onto one of the chairs and set the bottle on the table. He dropped the card next to it before turning to switch on the light and take off his suit jacket tiredly.

Dave Maschik had been his best friend in boot camp, and they became brothers when they ended up in the same unit together. When Dave took a bullet to the head, half of Michael had died as well. He turned back to the table with a sigh and draped his suit jacket over the back of one of the chairs. Lifting the bottle of whiskey out of the bag, he carried it over to the side table where glasses were set on a tray and poured himself a drink. Carrying it back to the table, Michael re-read the message from Lina. She had left a cell number at the bottom of the card. He smiled slightly and dropped it back onto the table, glancing at his watch. He supposed it was too late to call now. He would call her tomorrow and arrange to meet her for dinner.

Maybe now he could fulfill that promise he made so long ago.

"I don't like it," Damon said, shaking his head. He was sitting on the edge of the kitchen counter, watching as Alina unloaded the dishwasher and put the dishes away. "You're giving him too much of an opportunity to connect the dots and realize who you are."

"No, I'm not." Alina opened a drawer and started putting away cutlery. "He's not going to see Viper. He's going to see Lina, his buddy's kid sister. There is absolutely no reason for him to connect one with the other."

"It's too risky," he argued. "What happens if he gets hold of your file somehow? Or if someone leaks your real name? Enough people know it. What if your old flame from Jersey says something that trickles back to Washington and Michael puts two and two together?"

"If that happens, it won't matter whether I've been in contact with him or not," Alina retorted. "He's going to recognize the name if someone tells him, regardless."

"So why increase the odds?" Damon demanded. "Are you *trying* to make this more difficult than it already is?"

Alina laughed and turned to face him. Her eyes were sparkling and she was tense with barely contained energy.

"I'm not increasing the odds. Ok, maybe just a little," she admitted before grinning a grin of pure mischief. "Look. There is absolutely no reason for Michael to connect his encounter with Viper to an old friend who's looking him up while she's in town. None. If I can get close to him, I can keep track of him. The only reason you don't like it is because you think my real name is going to get out. *If* that happens, it'll be better if I'm already close to Michael. It will reinforce the impression that I'm not the enemy here."

"You really think that will matter if he finds out you're the one who clocked him on the head in the parking garage?" Damon grinned. "You give Marines too much credit."

Alina shrugged and turned back to the dishwasher.

"Possibly," she admitted. "I may be relying too heavily on past loyalties. But do you have a better idea for getting inside his head?"

Damon was silent and she glanced back at him. He was staring straight ahead, thinking. Alina let him think as she finished unloading the dishwasher. She wiped down the counters and turned to face him. He shook his head reluctantly.

"No," he admitted. "This is probably the only way to get an in on the Secret Service."

"Good. Now we can move on," she said cheerfully. Damon shook his head.

"I still don't like it," he muttered, getting off the counter and following her to the kitchen table where they had set up four laptops. "I don't like any of this."

"I know."

"You're too exposed," Damon added.

"I know," she agreed. "But this is how it has to be."

"Doesn't mean I..." Damon began.

"...have to like it," Alina finished for him.

He looked at her and grinned sheepishly, his blue eyes sparkling.

"Ok. I'll stop now," he said, dropping into a chair and opening one of the laptops. Alina laughed and sat opposite him.

"Don't worry," she said. "I'll hear it from Harry as well. Charlie is the only one who agrees with me on this."

"Well, he's the only one who counts right now," Damon murmured. He glanced up at the two plasmas hanging on the kitchen wall and opened one of the laptops, directing a map onto one of the screens. "And right now, he's covering both our hides with the other agencies. He bought us a little time by backing you, but it won't do any good if we can't get proof that our guy brought a terrorist into the country."

"I'm working on it," Alina said, opening her email. "I'm still waiting to hear from one of my contacts in Egypt. She's doing some digging for me."

"You still have people in Egypt?" Damon asked, glancing at her.

"Of course." Alina didn't even look up and Damon blinked.

"Ok then," he said after a moment. "Whoever it is, they have balls of steel, I'll give them that much," he added. Alina laughed.

"I'll be sure to let her know," she retorted. "She should be able to get something for us. There's always information to be had, and she is unusually gifted in finding it."

"How long before you think Michael will bite and start running searches on The Engineer?" Damon asked, clicking open some files on his laptop.

Alina glanced up to the dark second plasma screen.

"I'm a little surprised he hasn't started already," she admitted. "I hope I didn't hit him too hard."

Damon grinned.

"Now *that* would be funny," he said. "If our main source for information from Capitol Hill gets memory loss from you hitting him over the head, I'll bounce and you're on your own."

Alina glared at him.

"I didn't hit him that hard," she retorted. "If you like, I can demonstrate for you," she added sweetly.

"I'll pass," he said with a laugh. Alina grinned and went back to her emails. "Did you get the spyware on his home network without any issues?"

"Mm-hmm," Alina murmured. "If he copies anything onto a flash drive, the tag will follow it. I'm hoping to get into his work network that way."

"Nice." Damon sat back in his chair and leaned his head back to stare at the ceiling thoughtfully. "Let's say this hair-brained scheme of yours works," he said, ignoring her snort of indignation. "Let's say Michael leads us to the person who hired Johann and brought him into the country to commit an act of terror on US soil."

"The same person who also hired an assassin to come into the country," Alina interjected and Damon glanced at her sharply, his eyes narrowing slightly.

"Let's say we find out who arranged it, and it isn't who we think it is? What then?" Damon asked.

Alina finally looked up from her screen, staring at him.

"You don't think it's him?" she asked after a moment.

Damon's blue eyes rested on her face speculatively.

"I'm not saying that," he answered slowly. "But we should consider the possibility."

Alina sat back and stared at him in silence. As much as she hated to admit it, he was absolutely right.

"Talk."

Damon shrugged and sat forward, leaning his arms on the table.

"Let's look back at everything," he suggested. "Let's start at the very beginning."

"Ok." Alina crossed her arms and nodded.

"Two years ago, you're sent to Cairo to assassinate a terrorist named Johann Topamari. You get there, he walks out of a meeting, and he has the future Vice President of the United States with him. Right?"

"Right," Alina said slowly. "They walked out of the conference room and they were discussing hiring The Engineer."

"Did you hear *who* they wanted the Engineer to go after?" Damon asked.

Alina shook her head.

"No. They saw me at that point," she answered.

"So, you hear them discuss hiring The Engineer, and then all hell breaks loose," Damon continued. "Fast forward two years. Ludmere is now the Vice President. Johann comes out of hiding and shows up, alone and without his security, in Pennsylvania. Everything has been carefully arranged so that he can enter the country and execute the largest terrorist attack since 9/11 on US soil. You're sent to take care of him and make up for your failure in Cairo."

"And The Engineer was sent to take care of the clean up," Alina said flatly. "This is a pointless exercise. Only one person knew I was in Cairo that day, aside from Johann."

"How do we know that he was the only person who knew you were there that day?" Damon asked. Alina frowned.

"No one else was there," she replied. Damon shrugged.

"You don't have to physically be there to know something," he retorted.

Alina sighed and there was silence in the kitchen for a long moment.

"All I'm saying is that, while we know the order for both the assassin and the terrorist came from DC, we need to be careful about jumping to conclusions on *who* gave the order," Damon finally said, breaking the silence.

Alina clamped her jaw shut and was silent. Damon was absolutely right. She had been convinced that the person responsible for everything was the person she saw in Cairo, the person who then moved on to become the Vice President of the United States. She had been so focused on him that she failed to consider any other possibilities. She had lost her objectiveness.

And that made her furious with herself.

Alina got up impatiently and went to the fridge. She yanked it open to pull out a beer and Damon watched her pop the lid off almost violently. He sat back thoughtfully. Alina was angry with herself, and that could only mean that she had never once considered the possibility that their mark could be someone else. That was uncharacteristic of Viper. She had a reputation for always playing devil's advocate. Viper always considered all the angles and all the possibilities. This time she hadn't.

"You're right." Alina finally spoke after taking a long pull from the beer.

"I know," Damon retorted.

Alina stuck her tongue out at him, drawing a laugh from him.

"We need Michael to start digging around," she said, returning to the table, her temper back under control. "We need to find out exactly how the Engineer got into the country."

"I want to know who they wanted him to go after two years ago," Damon said, moving on. Alina looked at him.

"You think that will tell us something?" she asked. Damon nodded slowly.

"Ludmere was meeting with Johann for a reason," he said. "If we can track down why, I think it leads us to the proof we need." He looked up. "And we *do* need proof. Charlie won't endorse you for long without it."

"Yes, I know," Alina retorted. "Ok. You take that angle and run with it. I'll take Michael and see what we can find out from that direction."

The fourth laptop on the table beeped suddenly and they both looked at it, and then each other. Alina smiled slowly.

"Speak of the devil, look who just logged in," she said with satisfaction. "Here we go. Let's see where the Secret Service takes us."

She reached over, flipped the laptop open and started typing. A minute later the dark plasma on the wall came alive with a remote access view of Michael's computer screen. Damon watched her, his lips twitching.

"So much for memory loss," he remarked and Alina glanced up with a grin.

"I told you I didn't hit him too hard," she retorted.

A phone rang shrilly, shattering the silence in the dark room, and the occupant of the bed groaned and rolled over. The second ring made her open her eyes with a start. She glanced at the illuminated numbers on her alarm clock. 3:27am. Another groan was followed by another ring. Reaching out blindly, she picked up the receiver.

"This better be important," she snapped.

"You wanted to be alerted if there was any movement on the Gleason woman," a male voice answered. She sat up on her elbow, suddenly awake and alert.

"Yes?"

"The FBI agent from Philadelphia was at her grave this afternoon," the man told her. "Just paying respects, but I thought I'd better keep an eye on her."

"Good." The woman stifled a yawn and sat up fully. "What happened?"

"She went to the site of the accident and took some pictures. Afterwards, she went and talked to the mechanic," the man reported and she pursed her lips, rubbing her forehead. "She's back at her hotel now, but it looks like she's poking around, looking for answers."

"Well, make sure she doesn't find any," the woman snapped. "Keep watching her and report in tomorrow. Don't call me at the office.

Call my private cell."

"Will do."

The man disconnected and she dropped the phone back into its cradle. Rubbing her eyes, she swung her legs out of bed. She had suspected that the agent would become an issue, but when three months went by without a murmur, she started to think that Ms. Walker had decided to leave it alone. After all, an accident was an accident.

The woman got out of bed and padded into the bathroom. Stephanie Walker was becoming a nuisance. She had been the one to ask the Gleason woman to poke around three months ago. Then, when she found out that she had been killed, she kicked up a huge fuss and demanded a full-blown investigation into the woman's death. That particular demand had necessitated a ton of extra paperwork and bribes. Even now, they still weren't sure that they had covered it all up. You never *could* be sure with something like that. In retrospect, the accident hadn't been the wisest of moves, but there was no point in crying over it now. What was done was done.

The woman opened up the medicine cabinet above the sink and pulled out a bottle of antacids. Now Ms. Walker was poking around herself. What if she found another witness they missed three months ago?

The woman popped two antacids into her mouth.

No. They had covered it up. They hadn't let anything get by them. She had personally cleaned it all up, and it was clean. She didn't make mistakes with things like that. She couldn't afford to, not in her position.

She switched off the light to the bathroom and went back to bed thoughtfully.

Maybe it was time to put an end to Ms. Walker.

She got into bed slowly. It would take care of the last person who could possibly have any suspicion over the Gleason woman, and it would have the added bonus of pulling Viper out of hiding. She had no doubt that Viper would show up if her FBI friend turned up dead. The woman settled back under the covers and stared at the dark ceiling.

It would take care of two lingering issues at once.

The woman closed her eyes and slipped back into sleep.

Chapter Six

Michael glanced at his watch as he waited outside the busy restaurant in Georgetown. His encounter with Viper had made him paranoid. He had been looking over his shoulder all day, watching everyone who passed him. Even now, he scanned the busy street again while he waited. Michael knew she wouldn't risk another meeting so soon, if ever, but he couldn't stop himself from looking. Especially now. After spending most of last night digging up information on this so-called Engineer, he had some questions for her.

A cab pulled up to the curb and the back door opened. A very high black heel emerged, attached to a long leg. Michael glanced at the leg appreciatively and watched as the rest of the woman emerged. He wasn't disappointed. The long and slender leg was part of an equally sleek woman, dressed in a short and slinky black dress that was as stunning as it was simple. The high heels added inches to an otherwise average-height frame, drawing attention to those non-stop legs.

The woman stepped onto the pavement and slammed the cab door shut, glancing around. Red waves swirled around her shoulders as she looked around the crowds on the pavement. Someone let out a low whistle and she smiled slightly, her dark eyes glittering. She caught sight of Michael, standing to the side of the restaurant entrance, and smiled at him. Michael was already smiling back when he realized with a shock that made his gut lurch that this had to be Alina.

"Michael?"

She moved across the flagged pavement towards him, still smiling, but somewhat hesitantly now.

Michael swallowed and nodded, speechless. *This* was Dave's sister? He recalled her being attractive, but this was much more than what he remembered. She stopped in front of him, her dark eyes locking with his bemused ones. She held her smile, but was quiet, waiting. Michael realized suddenly that he was staring at her in total silence. He blinked, shook his head slightly, and smiled ruefully.

"Lina!" he exclaimed, clearing his throat and holding out his hand. "I'm sorry. It's just that...well, you've changed."

Alina laughed and grasped his hand in a friendly handshake.

"So have you!" she replied lightly. "It's been a few years."

"That it has," Michael agreed, smiling at her warmly. He realized that he was still grasping her hand and let it go quickly. "Let's go in and get seated. I hope you're hungry. This place has the best prime rib in the city."

He motioned for her precede him through the doors, rebuking himself mentally as he followed her through the door and into the crowded restaurant.

Good God, man. Get it together! So she's hot. A lot of women are.

But *they* weren't his dead friend's kid sister and, as they approached the hostess stand, Michael was acutely aware of the fact that he was lusting after Dave's sister.

"Reservation for two. Michael O'Reilly," Michael told the hostess.

She checked her monitor and nodded, motioning for a waiter to come forward.

"Of course, Mr. O'Reilly," she said. "Patrick will show you to your table. Enjoy your dinner."

Michael nodded and Alina smiled at him before following the waiter through the restaurant to a table tucked away in the corner. Her eyes scanned the restaurant as she walked, taking in every face at every table and noting all the entrances and exits to the large dining area with a single glance. She felt uncomfortable being out in public like this, and in Georgetown of all places. Half this room probably worked for an agency that was hunting for her. Her lips twitched despite herself. When she left the cabin, Hawk told her that she was insane. Alina wondered briefly if he was right. She was certainly experiencing a reckless thrill at walking past people who probably had their minions searching the world over for her.

"Here we are."

The waiter stopped at the table in the corner and stepped aside. Alina smiled at him slightly and moved to the chair with its back to the wall. Michael seated himself across from her and the waiter handed them menus.

"Can I get you a drink while you're looking at the menus?" he asked.

Michael ordered a scotch and Alina ordered a glass of wine. The waiter nodded and disappeared toward the bar.

"Best prime rib in the city, huh?" Alina asked, glancing at the menu. Michael nodded.

"Trust me," he said, looking at his own menu. "You won't be disappointed."

Alina glanced at him from under her lashes. He was dressed in black slacks and a light sports jacket that she knew was concealing his side arm. His skin was tanned and he had more freckles on his face then she remembered. His red-blond hair was more blond than she remembered as well, probably from the summer sun. He glanced up and his hazel-green eyes met hers. He smiled and she smiled back, dropping her eyes back to her menu. Michael O'Reilly had turned into a very handsome man.

"Well, I don't know why I'm even looking at the menu." Alina closed it with a snap and set it down. "You had me at prime rib. I'll trust you on this one."

Michael chuckled and set his own menu aside.

"I've been thinking about steak all afternoon," he admitted before focusing his attention on her. "How long are you in Washington?"

"Just for the weekend," Alina answered readily, sitting back in her chair. "I came in for a meeting."

"I'm glad you looked me up," Michael told her. "I wanted to keep in touch after the last time we met, but I lost track of you when you joined up."

"Well, I heard that you had ended up with the Secret Service, so I took a chance and hunted you down," Alina said with a smile, looking up as the waiter returned with their drinks.

She scanned the restaurant quickly again while Michael gave their orders to the waiter. More diners had arrived and the restaurant was getting busy. They had arrived just before the rush.

"I'm glad you found me," Michael told her after the waiter had departed. "So tell me about yourself. What did you do in the Navy? It *was* the Navy, wasn't it?"

He settled his arms on the table, focusing his full attention on her, and Alina was conscious of a twinge of discomfort. She felt like she was being examined.

"Yes, it was the Navy," she told him. "I ended up in military intelligence."

Michael's sandy eyebrows soared into his forehead.

"Now *there's* a surprise!" he exclaimed and Alina smiled slightly.

"For me, as well," she agreed as Michael stared at her. "But there you have it. It also turns out that the whole marksmanship thing runs in the family. I turned out to be a pretty good shot myself," she added with a quick grin and Michael chuckled.

"Now, that *doesn't* surprise me," he said, continuing to stare at her. Alina stared back and he shook his head slightly. "I'm sorry. I just can't imagine you...I mean...well, it's just a surprise," he ended lamely.

Alina's eyes had narrowed slightly during his stumbling and Michael didn't miss the sudden flash in her glance. It disappeared almost immediately and she was smiling again faintly, leaving him to wonder if it had ever really been there.

"Because I'm a woman?" Alina asked softly, her fingers slowly spinning her wine glass. He looked up, clearly surprised.

"What? No!" he replied. "Because you're Dave's kid sister!"

Alina blinked and the simmering anger inside her receded as quickly as it had appeared.

"What?" she asked, staring at him.

Michael flushed slightly, but leaned forward.

"I'm sorry," he apologized earnestly. "You have to bear with me here. Understand that all I heard about you from Dave was the big brother talk. When I came stateside and saw you after he died, you looked like a lost soul. You *looked* like a kid sister, and *that's* what I remember. So, seeing you like this," he moved his hand to encompass the two of them at the table, "is disconcerting, to say the least. Then, to hear that you were military intelligence, well...it's like you're all grown up. It's just not what I was expecting."

"Maybe we should have ordered pizza and beer and watched baseball," Alina teased, her lips curving. He grinned.

"No." He shook his head and his eyes met hers. "I wouldn't change a thing."

"Neither would I."

Alina was glad that they had met like two adults for dinner. She was glad that she had worn this ridiculously sexy dress with the highest heels she had ever put on her feet. She had enjoyed the look of male appreciation in Michael's face when he watched her get out of the cab, and she was enjoying the obvious appreciation in his eyes now. Alina reached for her glass of wine. Regardless of the circumstances now, this man had been Dave's best friend. He became a part of her life before the military, before the Organization, and before she had forgotten what it was like to feel like an attractive, normal woman.

"Good." Michael sat back. "Besides, you're probably a Phillies fan, aren't you?"

Alina laughed.

"Absolutely," she replied. "Wait. You're from New York, aren't you?"

Michael winked.

"Brooklyn, born and bred," he answered. Alina rolled her eyes and groaned.

"Definitely no football games," she muttered. "I don't know if I can sit and eat steak with a Giants fan."

Michael burst out laughing.

"You haven't tried the steak yet," he retorted.

Alina smiled at him and sipped her wine.

"How did you end up in the Secret Service?" she asked after a moment.

Michael shrugged.

"It just fell into my lap, really," he answered readily. "When I discharged from the Corps, everything just kind of fell into place. It's a good job. It has the structure and discipline I'm used to. You know, we have a lot of ex-military work with us," he added. "What are you doing now that you're a civilian?"

"I'm a consultant. Security," Alina answered briefly as the waiter appeared with their dinners.

Michael accepted her brief explanation without comment, turning his attention to the steaming plates of prime rib, garlic mashed potatoes, and steamed vegetables. Alina watched the waiter as he arranged her meal before her, thanking him when he was finished. He nodded and disappeared again and she looked across the table at Michael.

"This looks delicious," she said and he looked up with a grin.

"I told you to trust me."

Alina turned her attention to dinner as the thought crossed her mind that, while she would love to trust him, *he* couldn't trust *her*. And with that thought, she sighed silently, the smile fading from her lips.

Damon checked his watch, glancing around the dark and deserted park. He was leaning against a tree, waiting, and a slight breeze ruffled his hair. He breathed deeply. It felt good to be out and about. Two days in the cabin in the woods had just about killed him, and he now had new respect for Alina. He was pretty sure he would go insane after three months of it.

Two women came jogging up the paved path towards where he was lurking in the shadows, the sound of their sneakers hitting the pavement breaking the silence. They ran by him without a glance and Damon realized that he was completely hidden in the shadows. Still listening to the fading sound of the runners, he straightened up as another figure came along the path. He recognized Harry's silhouette in the light cast by the intermittent park lights and Damon waited in the shadows patiently. He glanced around again in the night, his senses tuned, listening for the least sound out of place. It was dangerous to meet in such a public place.

Harry was a tall man, standing six feet in bare feet. He had been bald as long as Damon had known him, and the baldness suited him. He had broad shoulders and a thick neck and, even in his advanced years, he was still imposing. It wasn't just his position as an old spy that made him imposing. The man himself was a barely controlled force that never seemed to rest.

Damon stepped forward as Harry approached. He walked upright, yet carried a cane that he leaned on from time to time. He claimed it was an old injury that ailed him, but Damon was secretly of the opinion that Harry just liked to have an extra weapon at his disposal. The old rascal was still as fit as ever. Damon knew for a fact that he had been seen running the indoor track at one of the hotels in Brussels just last year.

"Hawk." Harry reached out and shook Damon's hand firmly. "I'm glad you could make it."

"You didn't leave me much choice, sir," Damon answered with a grin, grasping Harry's hand. "It's good to see you."

"Good to see you." Harry nodded and let go of Damon's hand. He motioned with his cane and Damon followed him along the path. "Let's walk for a bit. I heard you were in Mexico for a spell. How was the weather?"

"Hot," Damon retorted dryly. Harry chuckled.

"I heard three of the Cartel heads were killed in a fire in the foothills out there." He glanced at Damon. "Of course, you wouldn't know anything about that."

"Only what I heard on the plane coming back," Damon replied blandly. "Unpredictable, those cartels. Always arguing over something."

"That's the truth," Harry agreed with a grin. "How does it feel to be back in the states?"

"With all due respect, Harry, I doubt you brought me out here for small talk," Damon answered. Harry shook his head.

"No," he agreed on a sigh. He stopped walking and looked around. "Let's sit," he said, spotting a bench a little further up. Damon nodded and they headed for the bench. Once seated, Harry stretched out his long legs with a sigh and propped his cane against the bench next to him. "Don't get old, Hawk. It's no fun."

"I'll keep it in mind, sir," Damon answered with a grin.

Harry looked at him.

"How's our girl holding up?" he asked bluntly.

Damon sat back. He had suspected that Harry wanted to talk about

Alina. Harry had trained them both when they were in the training facility for the Organization. Even though he had moved on now to the Dept. of Homeland Security, he kept in close contact with both Damon and Alina. He had always been more interested in their emotional well-being than their physical health. When he contacted Damon earlier and suggested a meeting, Damon knew it would be to discuss Viper.

"She's good," Hawk said. "She's having dinner with Michael O'Reilly right now."

"Mike O'Reilly of the Secret Service?" Harry asked. Damon nodded and Harry stared ahead thoughtfully. "He was an old family friend, wasn't he?" he asked suddenly.

Harry had a memory like an elephant. Hawk knew this, but was surprised all the same.

"Yes. He was her brother's friend, a fellow gunnery sergeant in the Corps," Damon answered quietly. Harry nodded.

"Yes, of course," he mused. They were silent for a moment. "She's going to use him for information?"

"That's the plan."

"That might not be such a good plan," Harry murmured. "He's too close to her. Tell me, how was she in New Jersey?"

Damon glanced at him.

"She was fine," he answered. "There was some confusion, I think. She was face to face with her past, but she handled it well. She stayed focused."

"Did she open up at all?" Harry asked.

Damon thought back to the few glimpses he had seen of a woman he didn't know, the woman he privately dubbed the Jersey girl.

"I think so," he said slowly. "She softened a little. Once or twice I think I saw the real her, but who can say? I saw glimpses of a woman who was a stranger to me."

"Good." Harry nodded. "I had hoped that being faced with her past would remind her of who she really is. She was beginning to forget, I think. How is she now? Still soft?"

"No."

Damon shifted on the bench to face Harry and Harry looked at him sharply.

"You're worried," he stated. "What's wrong?"

"She..." Damon paused, trying to find the right words. "There's a lot of anger there. It's very well hidden, but she's not being as objective as I've always known her to be."

"You think she's letting her anger rule her judgment?"

"Let's just say, I think her anger is interfering with some of her judgment," Hawk said slowly. "She's fixated on the target and not seeing much else right now."

"Ah." Harry nodded suddenly in understanding. "She's angry that they came after her."

Damon nodded and Harry was silent.

"You'll need to keep a close eye on her," Harry said quietly after a long silence. "She's too well-trained to let anything jeopardize the mission, so don't worry about that. What we need to be careful of now is that the softness in her doesn't disappear completely. Perhaps the gunny isn't such a bad thing after all."

"How so?" Damon demanded. "I think he is a huge risk."

"Viper has always been partial to huge risks. They're her life's blood. She needs them to breathe," Harry retorted with a slight chuckle. "I meant that Michael O'Reilly may be just what she needs to remind her of that past life of hers."

"I'm not sure why you think that's such a good thing," Hawk said. "Harry, I love you, and you know I respect your psychology, but I need Viper."

"And you shall have Viper," Harry assured him. "That's all she knows how to be now. But when this is all over, Viper needs to remember who she really is. There is so much anger buried inside her, and it will be very easy to allow it to consume her. If that happens, Viper will only ever be what she is right now."

"What you helped make her," Damon felt compelled to point out. "What we all are."

"Yes, but with her it was always different." Harry waved his hand in the air. "With the rest of you, it was work. It was impersonal. With her, there was always more. I knew all that anger had the potential to consume her one day." He glanced at Damon. "I'm glad you're with her now. If anyone can help her not lose herself, it's you. You always had a special bond, the two of you."

"I don't know why I'm surprised you know that, but I am," Damon said ruefully. Harry grinned.

"You hid it from everyone else, but not from me. I saw how you two looked at each other when no one was looking," he said. "Keep her close, Hawk. I would hate to see her disappear into the Organization and become a drone like so many others. When I saw her last month, I saw that she was on the brink. She was reminded of herself in New Jersey, and she's fighting that now. It's not a fight she can win. Our humanity is something we should never lose. I'm afraid for her."

"I'll do what I can," Damon said doubtfully.

Harry nodded, then grasped his cane and used it to pull himself up.

"That's all I have ever asked of you," he said, turning to face Hawk as he stood next to him. "And you have always exceeded all my expectations." He held out his hand and Damon grasped it firmly. "Go. Help her take this traitor down. Then, do me a favor? Take her away. Take her somewhere sunny and warm. Get her drunk on the beach. Help her let go of some of that anger."

"I can promise you the first one, but not the second," Hawk answered with a grin. "Traitor, no problem. Viper? That's a whole other war."

"And you're the only one to fight it, my friend," Harry retorted, turning to leave. "Just don't forget her right hook," he added over his shoulder. "She still has the deadliest right hook I've ever seen."

Hawk laughed and watched Harry disappear into the night before turning to walk away thoughtfully.

"What hotel are you staying at?" Michael asked Alina as they stepped out onto the sidewalk outside the restaurant. "I'll give you a ride back."

"I'm not. I'm staying with a friend, actually. She lives in Arlington." Alina lied smoothly, turning to face him.

"Well, I'll save the you the cab fare," Michael said with a smile. "I'm parked a block over."

"No, really, it's okay," Alina told him. "I'll just grab a cab. Thank you so much for dinner. You were right. The prime rib was amazing."

"I'll never steer you wrong when it comes to steak," he answered. "No pun intended." He reached out and took her elbow, guiding her away from the door as another couple emerged. "I probably shouldn't ask, but are you going to the cemetery tomorrow?"

Alina looked up at him in surprise. It was the anniversary of Dave's death the following day, but she didn't think anyone except her family would remember. Michael's lips twisted at her surprise.

"He was my brother too, Lina," he said softly.

Alina's lips and throat went suddenly dry and she inhaled sharply as her eyes became unexpectedly moist.

"I'm sorry." She cleared her throat in confusion and brushed her hair off her forehead. "Of course he was."

Michael's eyes narrowed at her obvious fluster. She had been nothing but calm and confident all evening. Now, suddenly, her cheeks were flushed and he noted that her hand was shaking when she brushed her hair away. He frowned and reached out to take her hands. They were trembling.

"Hey." He pulled her closer and tried to look in her eyes. "Hey!" Alina looked at him reluctantly and he saw the shimmer of tears then. "Aw, hell. I didn't mean to upset you," he muttered awkwardly. A choked laugh escaped her and Alina shook her head.

"You didn't," she told him with a watery smile. She took a deep breath and forced the sudden onslaught of emotion back. "I...I don't know where that came from, actually. I'm fine now."

"You're sure?" Michael peered down at her suspiciously and Alina smiled at him.

"I'm sure," she assured him. "And to answer your question, yes. I was planning on going to the grave tomorrow. Why don't you meet me there and we can get some lunch?"

"I don't want to intrude," Michael said hesitantly, but Alina shook her head.

"It's not intruding," she told him. "I would like the company, if you can make it."

"Of course," he agreed with a smile. "I have something in the morning, but I can be finished by noon. Why don't we say noon and then we'll get lunch?"

"Sounds good," Alina agreed.

She looked toward the street for a cab and Michael let go of her hands to go to the curb and flag one down. When it pulled to a stop, he opened the door for her. Alina paused before getting into the cab.

"Thank you again," she said softly. "I really enjoyed myself."

"Well, you don't have to sound so surprised," Michael said with a grin. "I've been known as a good dinner date on occasion."

Alina laughed and leaned forward to kiss his cheek.

"And you are," she assured him with a wink before getting into the back of the cab.

Michael pushed the door closed and stepped back to watch the cab pull away from the curb. When he turned to walk away, a smile was playing on his handsome face.

Chapter Seven

John lifted his binoculars to his eyes and let out a disgusted sigh before dropping them again. He was at Arlington Cemetery on a self-imposed stake-out, seated on a bench with a bottle of water and a paper. He had arrived as soon as the cemetery opened at eight o'clock and settled himself down under a tree on a rise. The position afforded an excellent, and distant, view of the plot where David Maschik rested, but the overcast sky was becoming increasingly darker as the morning wore on. John glanced at it with a frown. The weather this morning had called for rain and his umbrella was next to him, but he was really hoping that he wouldn't need it. He was irritated enough already.

He had come all the way down to Virginia to start his hunt for Alina. If she was still in the States, which John doubted, he had every confidence that she would visit her brother's grave on the anniversary of his death. In fact, he had been sure of it.

After sitting on the bench for almost four hours, John was forced to admit that he wasn't sure of anything anymore.

He had been watching nothing less than a parade for the past few hours. It had started at quarter past eight, and was showing all indications of continuing throughout the day. Women of all heights, shapes and sizes were coming, one by one, to visit Dave's grave. They all wore light-weight, beige raincoats and they all had the same red Phillies baseball cap on their head. Some had a ponytail going through the back, while others had short hair. They all carried the same umbrella and they all laid a single rose on the tomb. The only thing that seemed to vary was the color of the rose. White, red, yellow and pink all mixed together as the morning wore on.

Some of the women had a man with them, some were alone, and some came in pairs. There was never more than one party at a time and they stayed just long enough to place the rose and have a moment of silence. Their faces were shadowed by the baseball caps and they managed to constantly have their profiles in silhouette. It was a parade of women, any and all of which could have been Alina. And yet, John was sure that none of them were.

A drop of water splashed on his paper and John looked at the sky again with a scowl. This was getting him nowhere, but it was the only lead he had on Alina. John watched as the raindrops continued to fall here and there. He was protected under the thick branches of a huge old tree, but he knew if it turned into a downpour, he would have to seek shelter so as not become conspicuous. Sighing, he watched as the distant figure in front of the grave opened her beige umbrella and moved away with her head bent, just another visitor paying her respects. John's lips twitched in spite of himself. He wondered if this parade was played out every year on this date. Somehow, he wouldn't be surprised if it was.

"Two points, Lina," he murmured. "It's brilliant, I'll give you that."

The retreating figure disappeared from view and two more appeared from the opposite direction. This time it was a man and a woman. John raised his binoculars again. The man was tall and dressed in jeans and a Yankees cap, while the woman was about Alina's height and dressed in the uniform of beige raincoat, Phillies cap and umbrella. He couldn't see any features as the man blocked her partially from view.

John dropped the binoculars again. This was how it had been all morning. No clear views, all the women wearing the same thing, and now they would all start putting their umbrellas up to further conceal their features.

John sipped his water. He would continue to wait it out.

He had no other choice.

Alina glanced at her watch as Michael pulled his truck into Arlington Cemetery's parking garage. They were right on time. They almost hadn't been. His meeting was canceled, but when he called to arrange to meet earlier, Alina told him she had a last minute meeting with a client. Possible timetable crisis averted, he picked her up outside a hotel in the city at twelve. She got into the truck wearing a beige raincoat and a Phillies cap. When he saw the cap, he grinned but didn't say a word about it.

"This is the closest parking to his plot." Michael pulled into a spot on the second level and cut the truck's engine. "Even so, if it starts to pour, we're gonna get soaked."

Alina smiled and held up her beige umbrella.

"I came prepared," she said cheerfully. "Anyway, a little rain never hurt anyone."

Michael looked at her, his eyes twinkling.

"Spoken like a true sailor," he replied, leaning over to open the glove box.

She expected him to pull out an umbrella. Instead, he pulled out a navy baseball cap. Closing the glove box, he sat back and settled the cap on his head. She burst out laughing when he took his hands away, revealing the Yankees logo.

"Dave's going to spin in his grave when you walk up to it wearing that," Alina told him.

Michael winked at her.

"Not at all," he retorted before getting out of the truck. "He bought it for me."

Alina was left speechless. Somewhere deep inside her, in a place that she had forgotten long ago, something fluttered. It was surreal to her to be talking to someone who was as close, if not closer, to Dave as she had been herself. It was even more disconcerting to see a hat that Dave bought long ago, before an insurgent put a bullet in his head. The mere fact that Michael carried it with him in his truck spoke volumes about his relationship with her brother. It also spoke volumes for the kind of man he was.

And she was trying to manipulate him for information.

Michael opened the door for her, pulling her out of her reverie. Alina climbed out of the truck and he slammed the door shut, beeping the truck alarm on. She adjusted her cap and they walked through the parking garage silently, heading into the cemetery. Alina glanced up at the sky and watched the dark clouds rolling in with satisfaction. The weather was cooperating nicely. Between the caps and the umbrellas, anyone watching would have absolutely no idea if she had been to the grave or not.

And she knew they were watching.

"Looks like we just might need that umbrella," Michael commented, glancing at the sky. Alina nodded.

"Do you visit here often?" she asked as they walked along the path through the cemetery. Michael shrugged and stared straight-ahead.

"I stop in from time to time," he answered quietly. "More so now that I'm so close."

"How long have you been in DC?" Alina asked. Michael glanced at her.

"About a year now. I was out in Texas. When I got injured, I came back in from the field and landed here."

"You were injured? What happened?" she asked, glancing at him.

"It wasn't anything major," he said, flushing slightly. "Just an accident. A bullet went astray and shattered my collarbone."

Alina blinked, her mind flashing back to a pale woman in a hospital bed, moaning in pain. A bullet had torn through her shoulder and out her chest, shattering *her* scapula. A bullet that had been meant for someone else.

"Ouch. I hear that's very painful," she murmured.

Michael nodded.

"It was," he said. "It's all healed now. I'm cleared for field duty again, but I enjoy it where I am right now."

"So if you don't guard the President, what do you do?"

Alina flicked her eyes to the distance where her brother's plot was located. She could just make out the silhouette of a woman standing before it.

"Investigative work, mostly," Michael answered. "They put me on the desk when I was going through physical therapy and it turns out I like it. I'm good at it, too."

"So, you investigate what, exactly? Threats to the President?" Alina asked, looking at him and hoping he wouldn't notice the woman in the distance.

"Among other things," Michael answered vaguely. "I'm sort of a Jack of All Trades. I do a little bit of everything. It keeps life interesting."

"It sounds it," Alina murmured dryly, then instantly regretted her sarcasm. However, he didn't seem to have noticed it.

"And you? You said you were a security consultant. How's that going for you?" Michael asked, flipping the tables.

Alina shrugged, fighting a grin. He *had* noticed it.

"Some days I like it more than others," she replied. "It's certainly not boring," she added, watching as the woman moved away from Dave's grave.

"You were engaged, weren't you?" Michael remembered suddenly, glancing at her. "What happened with that?"

"Not much," Alina said. "It ended before I joined up."

"So, no jealous husband for me to be worried about?" Michael asked.

Alina shot a look at him under her lashes, her lips curving slightly.

"Do you plan on giving him cause to be jealous?" she demanded lightly. He grinned.

"You never know," he answered. "I'm leaving my options open."

Alina was surprised into a short laugh.

"And you? Any jealous girlfriends or wives for me to be worried about?"

Michael stopped walking and faced her.

"Oh no. I asked first," he told her, "and you haven't answered."

"No jealous husband or boyfriend," Alina assured him. "I haven't had time."

"That's good to hear," he said before walking on. Alina's lips twitched and she fell into step beside him again. "I've had time, but you're catching me single at the moment," he added as they walked.

"Well, that's good to hear," Alina replied, her eyes dancing and Michael laughed.

"Do you plan on giving them cause to be jealous?" he demanded as they came up to Dave's row. Alina had been carefully keeping her head angled slightly down, but at that she glanced up with a laugh.

"I'm leaving my options open," she retorted.

Michael grinned appreciatively and then glanced around.

"This is it," he said. "Do you want to be alone? I can wait here."

"Don't be silly," Alina said briskly. "We'll go together." She stepped onto the grass just as a fat raindrop plopped onto the beak of her cap. "But if you start bawling, I'm leaving you to sob alone. I don't do well with tears," she added over her shoulder.

Michael grinned and joined her, putting a light hand on her back.

"I'll keep that in mind," he murmured. He removed his cap, tucking it under his arm as they approached Dave's stone, and blinked at the pile of roses that had accumulated on the grave. There were all colors: red ones, white ones, pink ones, yellow and orange ones and even a black one. "Well, we certainly aren't the first visitors today."

Alina's heart filled with satisfaction at the colorful blanket laying over the grave. She stopped silently before the stone and they stood together, staring at the white marker. Bowing her head, Alina closed her eyes and saw her brother before her, as he was the last time she saw him. He was in his uniform, his brown eyes laughing, and he was alive. She could almost hear his voice as he said he loved her. He was the last man, besides her father, to have said those words to her and meant them.

Rain started to fall on her hands, pulling Alina back from the memories. Taking a deep breath, she opened her eyes and reached into her over-sized shoulder bag to pull out a crimson rose. Michael watched as she bent to lay the rose with the rest. She kissed her fingers and touched the top of the stone briefly before straightening up again, her emotions firmly under control. Michael stepped out of the way so that she could move away from the grave and she stepped past him, opening the umbrella as the rain started falling more steadily. Glancing back, she was just in time to see Michael salute smartly before touching the stone with his Yankees cap. He turned and followed Alina away from the grave, settling his cap back on his head. He joined her on the path again a few moments later and was just opening his mouth to speak when his cell phone started ringing suddenly.

"I'm sorry. Excuse me." Michael pulled the phone out of his pocket impatiently. "I thought I muted it in the truck," he muttered. "Hello?" he snapped into the phone.

Alina glanced at her watch and waited patiently under her umbrella. They had about five minutes to clear the area before the next wave of women started coming through. She supposed it wouldn't be tragic if they happened to pass one of them, but she wasn't sure if Michael would notice that they were dressed alike. It was a chance Viper didn't want to take. She glanced around thoughtfully. She supposed she could take him out a different way and say she wanted to walk in the rain.

Alina glanced up from under her umbrella, looking for a possible exit point. It was when she was scanning the opposite rise that she spotted him. He was sitting on a bench under a tree quite a distance away. He appeared to just be sitting there, but her eyes narrowed and she studied the figure for a long moment.

There could be any number of plausible explanations for a man to be sitting on a bench in the rain, but Alina wouldn't believe any of them. There was something very familiar about him. Too familiar. She was still watching him thoughtfully when Michael uttered a name that made her turn her head sharply.

"Stephanie Walker? Are you sure? I didn't even know she was in town." Michael was silent, listening. "Is she okay? Where is she now?" he demanded. He listened again before sighing. "Alright. I'll be there as soon as I can."

Michael disconnected the call and turned back to Alina, tucking the phone back into his pocket.

"Everything alright?" she asked, her white-knuckled grip on the umbrella the only sign of her interest.

"I don't know," Michael said, putting a hand on her elbow and leading her back down the path. "Something happened and someone, a Fed, was involved in an accident this morning in Georgetown."

He took the umbrella out of her hand, holding it over both of them as the rain started falling in earnest. Sliding an arm around her waist, he pulled her closer so that they were both protected by the umbrella.

"What kind of accident?" Alina's voice was sharper than she intended but Michael didn't seem to notice.

"An attempted hit and run," he said. "Unfortunately, I'm going to have to skip our lunch date. I have to go check this out."

"Wouldn't that be for the police to handle?" Alina asked, her brain working quickly.

"Yes," Michael answered. "But I want to question her regarding something I'm working on. I didn't even know she was in town."

"Ah," Alina murmured.

They fell silent as they headed back to the parking garage quickly through the rain. His arm was warm and secure around her, and Alina had the absurd thought that it felt nice to have someone else holding the umbrella for once. As quickly as the thought came, she pushed it away. Aside from everything else, he was wearing a Yankees cap.

They entered the parking garage almost at a run and Michael swung the umbrella down, shaking it out before closing it. He was laughing when he handed it back to her.

"So much for not minding the rain," he said and Alina grinned.

"Getting wet is over-rated," she retorted.

He pulled his keys out of his pocket as they started back toward the truck.

"I'm sorry about lunch," he said.

"It's not a problem," Alina assured him. "I understand."

They reached the truck and he beeped the door unlocked, opening it for her. She got in and he slammed it shut, circling to the driver's side.

"Do you have plans for dinner?" Michael asked, getting behind the wheel.

Alina glanced at him.

"Are you offering plans?" she asked with a twinkle. He grinned and started the engine.

"Possibly."

"Then, I possibly have plans for dinner," Alina replied. He laughed.

"Where should I pick you up?" he asked.

"I can meet you," Alina said. "Where do you want to go?"

He was quiet for a moment before answering.

"Why don't you come to my house and I'll cook?" he suggested after a moment. He held his hand up when she looked at him sharply. "No questionable intentions!"

"I wouldn't dream there were," Alina retorted with a slight smile.

Michael looked at her in mock disappointment.

"Not at all?"

Alina grinned and shook her head.

"Nope."

"Then what were you thinking?" he asked, stopping at a red light and looking at her.

"I was wondering if you knew how to cook," she informed him calmly.

"I am a fantastic chef!" Michael retorted.

"Then your house it is," Alina agreed easily and he smiled.

"Trust me," he said with a wink. "You won't be disappointed."

John yawned and raised his binoculars again. Yet another woman around Alina's height and wearing the uniform was approaching the grave. As with all the others, her face was cast in shadows. He dropped the binoculars again and wondered for the millionth time what he was doing here. Clearly, he wasn't going to get any leads from this pointless exercise. Yet, here he remained, watching the parade. He glanced at the overcast sky. At least the rain had stopped for the time being.

"You look bored out of your mind."

An all-too-familiar voice spoke directly behind him and John started, spinning around on the bench in disbelief.

"Here. I brought you a hoagie."

She was dressed in jeans and a light-weight, black hooded jacket. The hood was up over the baseball cap on her head and green eyes sparkled dangerously from the shadows it created. Alina's lips curved slightly and John blinked, speechless. He hadn't really thought that he would ever see her again, and he was disconcerted at the wave of utter relief that crashed over him at the sight of her. She was alive and well.

He reached out wordlessly and took the wrapped hoagie she was holding out to him. Once he took it, she vaulted lightly over the back of the bench and settled down next to him. Pulling a bottle of water from her pocket, she handed it to him before sitting back comfortably, her hands buried in her jacket's pockets and her legs crossed. She kept her head down slightly to keep her face in shadows.

"So what's the verdict?" Alina asked cheerfully, watching the woman in the distance walking away from Dave's grave. "Have I showed up yet?"

"What the hell are you doing?!" John finally found his voice, and it was loud. He glanced around hastily and lowered it. "Do you have any idea how many people are looking for you?"

Alina glanced at him, her lips twitching.

"And yet here you are, waiting for me to show up," she pointed out. She nodded toward the grave in the distance. "Enjoying the show?"

"It's brilliant," John snapped, his pale blue eyes flashing. "Now tell me what the hell is going on."

"Actually, that's what I came to ask you," Alina retorted, glancing at her old flame. "Eat your sandwich in case we're being watched," she added, almost as an after-thought. John unwrapped his hoagie impatiently. "I don't have a ton of time. What's Stephanie doing in DC?"

"Stephanie?" John paused in the act of biting into his hoagie, shooting her a look of surprise. "She's not. She's in the Poconos."

"I hate to disagree, but the Secret Service is under the very distinct impression that she's in Georgetown," Alina told him quietly. "Someone tried to kill her this morning with a botched hit and run."

"Impossible," John muttered through a mouth full of Italian meat and cheese. "I left her on her way to the mountains."

"And where did you tell her *you* were going?" Alina asked pointedly.

John lifted his eyes to hers ruefully.

"The shore," he admitted after he swallowed. He put the hoagie down on the paper and nodded. "Ok. So we both lied. Tell me what happened," he said seriously.

"That's all I know," she answered, "but here's my educated guess. Tell me if I stray at all. I think she's still bothered by her friend, the DHS agent, who got herself killed down here three months ago. I think the Bureau probably told her to leave it to the local talent and let it go, and she was pissed when the investigation was closed as an accident. My guess is that it's been eating at her and she came down here to poke around herself as soon as she could get time off. Am I ringing any bells here?"

"Yeah," John agreed, taking another bite of the hoagie. Alina waited patiently while he chewed. "I'm not surprised. That's probably exactly what she's doing down here. She wouldn't have told me. She knows I wouldn't have let her come alone. Someone tried to kill her this morning?"

"That's the story I heard." Alina scanned the dripping cemetery while she spoke, looking for the eyes that she knew were out there. "Whoever killed her friend can't be thrilled to have her down here looking into it."

"Where's your old friend, Mr. Peterson?" John demanded.

Alina glanced at him in amusement.

"Are you two still convinced he was involved?" she asked, her lips curving slightly. "I really did think the FBI required more intelligence than that."

"We were never given the chance to disprove that particular theory," John shot back. "If you'll recall, you both disappeared into thin air without a word."

Alina's eyes narrowed slightly at the thread of anger in John's voice.

"Were we supposed to leave a forwarding address?" she couldn't resist asking.

"Something would have been nice," John retorted. He looked at her and his eyes were suddenly hooded. "We didn't know if you were dead or alive."

Alina studied him for a quiet moment before returning her gaze to their soggy surroundings.

"I can see that you think I owe you an explanation. Perhaps I do," she said reflectively. "I'll have to give it some thought." She paused and then shrugged, almost to herself. "I don't have time for that right now, though. We need to get Stephanie to a safe house. Whether either of us likes it or not, I have to stash you two somewhere safe until I'm finished here."

John glanced at her searchingly.

"That's really necessary?" he asked after a moment. The look he received from Alina was more convincing than anything she could have said, and he nodded slightly. He learned three months ago not to doubt her. "Ok. Where do I meet you?"

"Stay here about another hour," Alina told him. "Then give up and go back to wherever you're staying. I assume you're at a hotel?" John nodded. "Good. Call me from the lobby phone when you get there. There's a number to a burn phone on the hoagie paper."

She looked at him and the look on her face was no longer friendly.

"If I even get a whiff of the notion that you contacted anyone, you're on your own and Stephanie will be dead within twenty-four hours," Alina told him. "These people don't play around. They missed once. They won't miss again."

"And you?" John asked.

"I'm going to arrange for a safe house," she answered. "We have to move quickly before they have any idea what's happening. She's safe right now. She's being grilled by Secret Service. I'll tell you where to find her when you call. Do me a favor and don't get yourself followed. I can guarantee you're being watched."

"This isn't my first rodeo, sweetheart," John retorted without heat. "Do I want to know who we're up against this time?"

"Probably not." Alina stood up and looked down at him. "I need you to watch Stephanie's back until this is over. I can't be there this time."

John considered her thoughtfully.

"I got her," he assured her quietly. "But who's got you?"

Alina's lips curved into a chilling smile that sent a shiver down John's spine and reminded him that *this* woman was a complete stranger to him.

"Don't worry about me," she replied. "This isn't my first rodeo,

79

either."

John nodded, but as Alina was turning away, he stopped her.

"Hey," he said. Alina turned her head questioningly. "Not a fan of the red-hair. Was that really necessary?"

Alina rolled her eyes.

"I like the red," she retorted. She started to walk away, then paused and looked back again. "What's wrong with it?"

"I've known too many redheads," John retorted.

Chapter Eight

"Ms. Walker." Michael smiled charmingly as he walked into his office and held out his hand to the attractive brunette from his photo. Stephanie stood up at his entrance, taking in the tall, handsome man at a glance. "Thank you so much for coming. I know you had to wait. I'm sorry."

"That's quite alright." Stephanie shook his hand and sat down again in the chair where she had been whiling away the time on her smartphone. "It's the weekend. Even Federal agents get a Saturday," she added with a smile.

Michael nodded and moved behind his desk. He unlocked a drawer and started sorting through the neat piles of folders inside, clearly looking for one.

"I understand *your* Saturday was a little disrupted this morning," he said, glancing at her.

Stephanie didn't miss the sharp searching glance. When they told her at the hospital that someone in the Secret Service wanted to see her, she knew that yet another agency was looking for information on Viper. She agreed to come along only when she heard the agent's name.

"It was nothing," Stephanie said calmly.

Michael looked at her.

"Someone tried to run you over."

"Just an accident," she replied with a shrug.

Michael studied her for a beat before dropping into his seat.

"Well, I hope you're right," he said, flipping open the folder that he had fished from the drawer. "Are you just in DC for the weekend?" he asked conversationally and Stephanie hid a grin.

"I don't know how long I'll be staying. I'm on vacation," she said, crossing her legs. She couldn't quite contain the grimace of pain that flashed across her face and Michael caught it.

"You're in pain," he stated, concern in his voice.

81

"Just some bruising on my back," she said, waving her hand dismissively. "I had to dive over the hood of a Corolla. I didn't land on my feet."

Michael grimaced sympathetically.

"Hospital check you out?" he asked. She nodded.

"Just scrapes and bruises."

"That's good to hear." He glanced down at his folder again. "I won't keep you long. I just had a few questions about what happened on Three Mile Island."

"Of course."

Stephanie sat back and watched him. He was relaxed and calm as he scanned through the papers in the folder. When he looked up, his hazel-green eyes were nothing but friendly.

"Look, I know you've been questioned up, down, and around the block about that night," Michael told her. "I'm not going to make you repeat it all."

"I appreciate that," Stephanie said with a smile.

"Who shot Johann Topamari?" Michael asked bluntly.

Stephanie didn't blink, but she was startled. She hadn't been expecting a frontal attack. She studied him, somewhat impressed.

"It was joint effort between the FBI and Homeland Security."

She gave him the department-approved answer while her mind worked furiously. This wasn't just another agent looking for confirmation that Alina had been there that night. He *knew* she was there. Now, why would the Secret Service have an interest in her?

"Of course it was," Michael agreed, smiling slightly and sitting back in his chair. His eyes met hers and they studied each other for a moment in silence. "That was a pretty good shot." Michael finally broke the silence, leaning forward and checking the papers in the folder again. "Ballistics put it at over 300 meters with a very strong cross wind. Not many people can make a shot like that so accurately."

"Luckily for me, they could," Stephanie answered dryly.

She met his stare calmly, showing only polite interest. After another long silence, Michael's lips twitched. He reached forward and flipped the folder closed.

"Ok," he said with a sigh. "Have it your way." He looked at her. "But I can't help her if I don't know what the story is," he added softly.

Stephanie studied him in silence, torn between her loyalty and her gut. Absurdly, she really believed that he *wanted* to help Viper. Michael held her gaze and his breath. He could feel the federal agent wavering. She wanted to tell him something. He could *feel* it.

"How long have you been out of the Marines?" Stephanie asked him suddenly, surprising him. He raised his eyebrows.

"What makes you think I'm a Marine?" he asked.

"First, there was nothing in any of the reports about a cross wind. Only a shooter would know that there had to be one at that angle. I'm guessing you made quite a few of those shots yourself," she told him. "Second, you have a picture of your unit on the top shelf of the bookshelf behind me."

Michael chuckled.

"Guilty as charged," he admitted. "I've been out five years."

"A good friend of mine had a brother in the Marines," Stephanie told him after a moment. "He always said that when he became a Marine, they became his family. There was no higher loyalty than to the Corps, save to God Himself, and to Country."

"That's right," Michael agreed, his eyes narrowing slightly.

"It's admirable, that kind of loyalty," Stephanie mused. "'Greater love has no man than this, that he lay down his life for his friends,'" she quoted softly.

Michael watched her quietly for a moment.

"Semper Fi," he murmured. He sat forward and pulled a card out of his desk, scrawling a number across the back. "Well, if you think of anything you want to tell me, this is my personal cell phone."

He stood up and handed her the business card. Stephanie took it and tucked it into her purse.

"Thank you." She held out her hand. "I'm sorry I couldn't be more help," she added.

Michael grasped her hand and smiled slowly, his hazel eyes warm.

"You've told me exactly what I needed to know."

Stephanie met his eyes and smiled back before turning to leave. At the door, she paused.

"You drink Jameson?" she asked, glancing over her shoulder. Michael raised an eyebrow.

"I'm Irish," he answered with a laugh.

Stephanie pointed to a dusty empty bottle on the bookshelf, under the picture of his unit.

"I think it's time for a new bottle," she said with a grin.

Michael laughed and she disappeared out the door. After the door closed behind her, he sank into his chair slowly.

Viper had saved Stephanie Walker's life, and she had done it by putting her own life in danger. She knew that by pulling the trigger that night, she would be inviting the storm that was chasing her now. He picked up an old baseball and absently began to toss it from hand to hand as he spun his chair around, staring up at the wall. That was not the action of a psychotic assassin gone rogue. That was the action of a person fighting for something.

Michael didn't think Stephanie even knew what Viper was fighting for, but it was clear that she was not about to say what she did know. How did Stephanie even know Viper? Were they old friends? New friends? Strangers? The word friend covered a whole gamut of relationships. He couldn't make the mistake of taking the word at face value.

Stephanie hadn't told him much, but she had told him enough to be sure of one thing: Viper was not the enemy.

She was the victim.

Damon frowned slightly and watched as Alina disappeared into the apartment high rise. He didn't like the idea of being responsible for two federal agents in a safe house. He shook his head slightly and scratched his jaw where a five o'clock shadow was growing. He finished scratching and raised his binoculars, scanning the harbor once more. Everything was quiet and appeared normal. The safe house was a luxury apartment on the Baltimore Harbor. It over-looked the water and Hawk had to admit that it was perfect. No one would ever dream that two feds would be hiding in a swanky apartment so close to everything. He lowered the binoculars and yawned. The Jeep was parked in a side alley between two buildings, diagonal from the apartment. Hot afternoon sun glinted off the windshield and Damon thought briefly of turning on the engine for a few minutes to run the air conditioner. The top was up and he was sweltering. Deciding against it, he chugged some lukewarm water from the bottle next to him and scratched his jaw again.

He knew Alina had no choice in squirreling her old friends away somewhere safe. Once Stephanie had shown up in DC asking questions, she became a clear target, and it was only natural that her partner, and Alina's ex, would stay with her. But Damon didn't have to like it, and he didn't. Too many people were involved in this mess now and there were too many chances for collateral damage. He wasn't comfortable with any of it.

Hawk watched as a black 1978 Firebird eased around the corner and rolled by the front of the apartment building. He glanced at his watch as John pulled into the entrance of the underground parking garage beneath the building. He was right on time. At least he didn't appear to have had any trouble getting Stephanie to cooperate. Alina had been worried about that, which was why he was sitting out here, melting in the afternoon heat, while she was inside waiting for them. She wanted to impress the severity of the situation upon Stephanie personally and, Hawk suspected, give both her old friends an opportunity to see that she was alive and well.

Damon continued to watch the crowds and traffic, looking for any sign of surveillance. There was none. After another ten minutes without any suspicious activity, he decided that John and Stephanie had gotten away clean. He leaned his head back on the seat, his eyes ever watchful, and waited for Viper to finish.

Stephanie looked around the thickly carpeted hallway with cream-colored walls as John unlocked the apartment door. The hall was totally silent. She couldn't even hear muted sounds coming from any of the other apartments. She wondered if they were empty or if the insulation in the walls was just that good. This was clearly an expensive building filled with luxury apartments and Stephanie wondered who was paying for it.

By the time she left Michael O'Reilly's office, she had been hungry. She went to pick up a sandwich and when she came out of the sub shop, John had been waiting for her. He hadn't minced words. She and her sandwich were hustled into his car and he drove north. He hadn't explained anything on the hour and a half ride from DC to Baltimore except that he was taking her to a safe house. The ensuing argument that erupted lasted half the drive. John wasted no time in letting her know exactly what his opinions were on partners who took off on their own to start investigations that they had been told to leave alone. Stephanie felt just guilty enough about lying to him that she had shut her mouth and simmered in silence the rest of the way to Baltimore.

John took a painfully circuitous route out of DC, but once they hit the interstate, he had dropped the pedal and they had flown north. He drove as if demons were chasing them, and part of Stephanie's silence had been an effort not to distract him. She didn't entirely trust John's driving or his old car.

"Welcome to our temporary home," John said, opening the door to the apartment.

Stephanie shot him a fuming glare and stepped past him into the apartment. The floors were hardwood and gleamed with polish, not a speck of dust visible. The cream walls were decorated with standard prints in frames and the apartment was furnished in deep chocolate brown, comfortable furniture.

"Well, at least it's better than our safe houses," Stephanie said grudgingly.

She set her purse on an end table and looked around. She was standing in a large living room with a couch and two matching recliners. A 52-inch flat-screen TV was on the wall and below it was an entertainment module with a dvd player, a cable box, and even a game system. The windows were shuttered with mini blinds, and thick cream curtains hung from the ceiling to the floor. They were tied back with chocolate tie-backs and the shades were closed. She glanced down a short hall to the left and saw three doors, presumably bedrooms and bath. On the right was a dining room attached to a large kitchen with an arched opening in the wall.

Stephanie wandered into the kitchen while John closed the door behind them and glanced around. The appliances were stainless steel and the counters were granite marble. Everything was top of the line. She opened the refrigerator and was surprised to see it stocked with cold cuts, bottled water, a six pack of beer, and condiments. A peak into the freezer revealed frozen meat and vegetables.

"Hey, there's food in the freezer!" she called out. "Where did you find this place?"

Stephanie closed the freezer and frowned when John didn't answer. She turned to go back into the living room.

"I said, where..."

Her voice trailed off as she stepped out of the kitchen. Leaning against the back of the couch with her arms crossed was Alina. Her hair was red now and pulled back into a loose ponytail. She seemed thinner than she had been three months ago and her skin was darker. Her eyes were a glittering green and she smiled slightly when Stephanie stopped dead. She looked just as dangerous now as she had the last time Stephanie saw her.

"Hi Steph."

Stephanie glanced at John, who was quietly setting his keys on the end table next to her purse. He met her glance and she suddenly understood why he hadn't given her any information in the car.

"Alina!" Stephanie turned her attention back to her old friend. "Where the hell have you been? What's going on?" she demanded.

Alina straightened up and uncrossed her arms.

"You've gone and got yourself neck-deep in trouble again, that's what's going on," Alina retorted dryly.

She turned to move into the dining room and Stephanie's eyes fell to the gun tucked into the holster at the back of her jeans. Stephanie glanced at John and found him staring at the same thing, his gaze hooded. Alina grabbed a case from the dining room and came back, motioning

Stephanie into the living room. Frowning, Stephanie sat on the couch while John perched on the arm next to her and they watched as Alina set the case on the coffee table. She glanced at Stephanie, those strange green eyes glittering.

"Do you still have the back-up Glock I gave you?" she asked.

Stephanie nodded and pulled it from her holster, holding it out to Alina. Alina shook her head.

"You keep it," she told her. "I'll take it back when you're safe."

"I'm safe now," Stephanie argued.

"Oh really?" Alina raised an eyebrow. "What happened this morning?"

"A car came around the corner too fast in the parking garage. They didn't see me," Stephanie said stubbornly. Alina's eyes bore into hers steadily and, after a moment, Stephanie's gaze wavered. "Ok. They may have sped up just a little," she relented. "How did you even know?"

"I was with Mike O'Reilly when he got the call," Alina told her, sitting on the edge of the coffee table next to the case. Stephanie grinned.

"I *knew* it!" she cried triumphantly. "I knew it was the same Michael O'Reilly even before I saw Dave in the picture of his unit at his office. I guessed you were in DC as soon as he started asking questions about you."

Alina's eyes narrowed slightly.

"You didn't tell him you recognized him, did you?" she asked sharply. Stephanie frowned.

"Of course not," she answered. "He has no idea who I am."

Alina released a sigh of relief.

"Good," she murmured.

John looked at her, his blue eyes hooded.

"I take it he has no idea that every government agency is looking for you?" he asked.

Alina's lips curved slightly, but the smile didn't reach her eyes.

"Oh, he knows," she answered. "He just doesn't know it's *me* that they're looking for. It's complicated."

"Everything with you is complicated," John muttered, scowling.

Stephanie tucked the modified Glock that Alina had loaned her three months ago back into her side holster.

"So, what do you know that I don't?" she asked Alina. Alina grinned.

"I was going to ask you the same thing," she replied. The two women shared a reluctant smile.

"I don't know much," Stephanie admitted, sitting back on the couch. "I went to Shannon's grave and then tried to question what witnesses there were. I can tell you that they've all been threatened and/or paid off, and they all have the same story. Her car mysteriously lost brakes, she lost control and went over the edge of a ravine. They won't say if there was another vehicle. I think they're scared."

"Did you check with her mechanic?" Alina asked. Stephanie nodded.

"He was the only one who didn't seem nervous," she said. "I got the impression that he was tired of being bothered with the whole thing. He seemed more irritated than anything. He says that her car was in the shop two weeks before the accident for an oil change." Stephanie smiled slightly. "After some flirting, he softened up and told me what, I think, is the truth. He did a quick check on everything at her request and he swears that the brakes were fine. There was nothing wrong with them."

"Not surprising," Alina said with a nod.

"Where's your old friend, Mr. Peterson?" Stephanie asked.

"Actually, in a Jeep down the street, covering me while I'm in here," Alina answered shortly. "He had nothing to do with Shannon's death."

"I'd like to make that decision," Stephanie retorted.

Alina raised her eyebrow. She and Stephanie stared at each other for a moment before Alina sighed in resignation.

"Trust me," she said quietly. "The person responsible for Shannon's death is the same person who smuggled Johann and the Engineer into the country. It's the same person who has the entire alphabet trying to take me down, dead or alive, and it's the same person who tried to run you over this morning. That person is *not* Damon."

Stephanie and John stared at her speechlessly and Alina stared back, somewhat amused.

"Please don't tell me that you never once considered the possibility that all the events between then and now were manipulated by someone other than a dead terrorist," she said, looking from one to the other. They were silent and Alina's eyebrow soared into her forehead in disbelief.

"Well, that certainly explains alot about all the meetings and interrogations I was dragged into," Stephanie said to John. He nodded.

"You should never have come down here alone," he muttered.

Stephanie glanced at him.

"I couldn't have told you," she retorted. "You wouldn't have let me out of your sight."

"Damn straight," John shot back.

"How do they know about you?" Stephanie asked, turning her attention back to Alina.

Alina looked at her for a beat, her lips tightening.

"It was never intended for me to walk away from Three Mile Island," she finally said.

Stephanie's mouth dropped open and John let out a low whistle.

"Oh my God." Stephanie's mind was spinning as everything fell into place. All the unanswered questions from the past three months suddenly had answers. "That's why you just disappeared!"

"The blood in the barn?" John demanded grimly.

The look he got from Alina was the only answer he needed, and he nodded slightly in approval.

"Who do you work for?" Stephanie demanded. "You told me it was *our* government."

"It is."

Alina's eyes were cold and emotionless as she made the statement. Stephanie's heart plummeted to her toes and John groaned.

"I was afraid of that," he muttered and Alina chuckled humorlessly.

"So, now you understand why you both have to stay here until I...sort things out," she said, turning to the case beside her. She unlocked it and flipped it open. "Here's a secure laptop and iPad." She took them out and set them on the table. "I'll have to ask you both for your phones, ipods, and any other electrical devices you have with you," Alina added, glancing at them. "I have secure phones here too. You know the drill. No calls to anyone except me. No contact whatsoever with anyone except me."

John sighed and pulled his smartphone out of his pocket, handing it to Alina. Stephanie was frowning.

"Wait," she said, reaching over and grabbing her purse. She fished her phone out. "There are pictures on the SD card."

Alina took the phone and looked at Stephanie, eyebrow raised. "Of?"

"When I went to Shannon's grave, there was a book. People who visit the dead are encouraged to sign it," Stephanie said slowly.

"That's creepy." John remarked. Alina was inclined to agree.

"Shannon's had a lot of visitors." Stephanie ignored him. "I got a picture of two of the most recent entries. You have a starting point," she told Alina.

Alina raised her eyes slowly to Stephanie's face. Her green eyes met Stephanie's brown ones and Alina felt a surge of excitement run through her.

"Thank you," she said softly.

Stephanie nodded and looked around.

"At least this is a comfortable safe house," she said, forcing cheerfulness she didn't feel.

Alina grinned and stood up.

"My safe houses are a lot more comfortable than the rat-infested, hygiene-deficient, federally-approved huts that you're used to," she informed them. "But you can't step foot outside that door."

"I won't," Stephanie agreed. Alina looked at John.

"That goes for you too," she told him. "When they can't find her, they'll come after you."

He nodded.

"I got it," he assured her. He stood and his pale blue eyes met hers. "I'm more worried about you," he said quietly. "This is *not* a healthy situation that you've gotten yourself into, Lina. When I came looking for you, I didn't really expect to find you. You should be on the other side of the world."

"If I start running now, I'll never be able to stop," Alina said quietly, her eyes meeting his. "That's not acceptable to me."

She turned toward the door, pulling her jacket on as she went.

"Don't worry about food," she said over shoulder. "On the iPad is a grocery app. It links into a private provider. Just enter what you want and it'll be delivered same day. It will always be the same delivery person and they're trustworthy."

Stephanie stood up.

"What about you? Will we hear from you at all?" she asked.

"Either me or Damon will check in."

"He's not really DHS, is he?" John asked.

Alina's lips twitched and she shook her head slightly. John nodded.

"What about my car?" Stephanie asked suddenly.

"I'll take care of it," Alina answered, smiling slightly. "Don't worry. I'll take care of everything. You even have clothes in the bedroom."

"How long are we looking at being here?" John demanded.

Alina glanced at them both, her hand on the door handle.

"Not long," she replied shortly.

Her voice had a chilling edge to it that made Stephanie shiver involuntarily. The dangerous stranger was back and Stephanie almost felt sorry for the person or people responsible for all this. Alina opened the door and then paused, turning to look at them.

"Just relax and let Damon and I do our jobs," she said softly. "We're very good at this."

John nodded and Alina disappeared out the door. He went to lock the door after her before turning to look at Stephanie. She was frowning.

"It won't be too bad," John said, misinterpreting the frown. "We have cable and a game system. We can make this work."

Stephanie rolled her eyes.

"John, sometimes I wonder if you have any brain at all," she muttered, turning around and picking up her purse. "I'm not worried about camping out here with you for a couple of days."

"What then?" John followed her down the short hall and watched as she looked into one bedroom and then the other. Deciding on the master bedroom, she disappeared into it. "Are you worried about Lina?"

He leaned on the door jam and watched as she dropped her purse on the bed.

"Yes!" Stephanie swung around in exasperation and John blinked at the shimmer of tears in her eyes. "She already saved my life once, and now she's probably saved it again. Do you realize what all this means?" Stephanie demanded, her voice rising. "This means someone in the government, *our government*, is trying to kill her. Then, here I come, bumbling around and put myself right in the middle of it. Again! You realize that I was probably impromptu bait, right? Kill me and they know damn well Viper will surface. And she did! For all we know, they could be out there right now, waiting to put a bullet in her head the way she did to Johann."

John moved into the bedroom and grasped Stephanie's hands tightly. He shook them gently.

"Calm down, Steph," he murmured soothingly. "Damon was outside, making sure that didn't happen, and we made it out of DC without a tail. They don't know where we are and therefore, they don't know where she is."

"You were right. She should be on the other side of the world," Stephanie moaned. "Not here. Not right in their backyard."

"Ssshhh." John put his arms around her and rested his chin on her head. His expression, however, was grim. "She knows what she's doing," he said soothingly. "We need to let her do it and worry about keeping you safe."

Even as he tried to calm his partner down, John was frowning at the opposite wall. With a sinking heart, he realized that the odds of Alina succeeding were slim to non-existent.

And there wasn't a damn thing he could do to help her.

Chapter Nine

Alina glanced at her watch as Damon pulled into the parking garage of Stephanie's hotel. Damon caught the motion and glanced at her.

"What time is dinner?" he asked.

"Seven," Alina answered, scanning the first level for Stephanie's car.

Damon did a loop around the first level and she shook her head. He turned onto the ramp for the next level.

"At his house?"

Alina glanced at him, her lips twitching.

"Yes."

Damon looped around the second level and she shook her head again.

"You could have asked her what level she was on," he muttered, heading up to the next level.

Alina looked at him under her lashes. Hawk was decidedly cranky.

"I'm sorry. Is this boring you?" she asked politely. Damon glanced at her and was silent. Alina's lips twitched again and she turned her gaze back to the cars in the parking lot. She caught sight of a silver Maxima on the other side of the garage. "That's it," she said, pointing.

Damon nodded and continued on to the ramp going up to the next level. Once he topped the ramp, he slowed down and Alina opened the door, rolling out of the Jeep. She closed the door quietly and he continued on to loop around the parking level.

Pulling the hood to her jacket over her baseball cap, Alina turned to move in the opposite direction. She pulled out her gun and reached into her cargo pocket, pulling out a suppressor and attaching it to the barrel as she moved. While Hawk swept the parking level, making sure it was safe from hidden assassins, she moved swiftly. Raising her arm, she fired at the camera that was angled toward the ramp before moving around a cement pillar to shoot out a second camera angled along the aisle. Once she had cleared the side of the parking level of video, she moved to the wall and looked over to the parking level below. Viper aimed and took out the camera angled along the aisle where Stephanie's car was parked and then she turned and took out the camera on the other end. She unscrewed the suppressor and dropped it back into her cargo pocket, tucking her gun back into its holster and glancing back as Hawk rolled around the corner. He gave her a slight nod.

Alina jogged down the ramp quickly, slipping around the barrier and onto Stephanie's parking level. Glancing at her watch, she sighed. She was going to be late for dinner. They had caught traffic on the way back into the city and it was already five-thirty. There was no way she was going to be able to stash Stephanie's car away and still make it to Michael's for seven.

Alina glanced behind her and slid between two cars when she heard the sound of a car pulling onto the ramp, coming up from the lower level. She ducked in front of one of the cars, concealed between the front grate of a Cadillac and the cement wall of the parking garage. Peering around the Cadillac, she watched as a black Toyota parked near the elevators and a couple got out. They went to the elevators and disappeared into the glass alcove. Silence fell again and Alina slid out from her hiding place and started moving through the garage towards Stephanie's car. She frowned as she walked and scanned the few cars that were dotted around the garage.

Something was wrong. She couldn't see anything amiss, but the closer she got to Stephanie's car, the more convinced she was that something was very wrong. All the hair on the back of her neck and across her shoulders was standing on end and her spine was tingling. She shot a look up to the level above her and scanned the top of the cement wall. It was clear. She couldn't see anyone.

Damon rolled down the ramp on the other side of the level as Alina moved across the parking garage. He stopped at the bottom of the ramp and watched as she reached behind her to pull her gun out of its holster. He frowned, scanning the parking level quickly. He didn't see anything out of place, but Viper was definitely bothered by something. Having learned in the past not to discount her instincts, Hawk turned the Jeep onto the parking level and stepped on the gas, looping around to come up behind her. His eyes never stopped moving, looking for the threat that Viper sensed was there.

Alina glanced behind her and saw Hawk pull around the curve behind her. Stephanie's car was ahead of her at the end of the aisle and she scanned the area again. All her instincts were screaming now and Viper knew better than to ignore them. She didn't know why, but Alina knew she had to get out of there. Fast. Pulling Stephanie's keys out of her pocket, she clicked the remote-start button on the key fob.

The explosion was deafening, rocking the building to its very foundations. Alina threw herself to the ground as glass and metal shot out around her in every direction and alarms on the cars nearby started going off, triggered by the vibration from the explosion. She grunted as she hit the cement hard. Rolling over, she half sat up, her heart pounding so hard she could barely breathe as she stared at the inferno raging a few yards away.

The Maxima was toasted. Flames consumed the frame, reaching up to the cement ceiling of the garage. The heat from the fire made Alina inch back on the ground, her face scorching. A smoldering tire streaked toward her and she kicked it away quickly, watching as it rolled a few feet before flopping onto its side and coming to a stop.

Damon screeched to a stop next to her and Alina scrambled to her feet. She dove into the Jeep and he threw it into reverse.

"Stay down!" he barked as he hit the gas and the Jeep flew backwards.

Alina folded herself into the minuscule space under the glove box and ripped off her baseball cap.

"Here!"

She shoved the cap at him and Damon grabbed it, setting it on his head. He grabbed his sunglasses and put them on, then flipped the sun visor down as he flew down the ramps to the exit of the parking garage. Slowing down as he approached the street entrance, he carefully kept his head turned slightly away from the entrance cameras as he rolled up to the stop sign. Alarms were going off around the building and LED lights were flashing at the entrances warningly as Damon pulled out into traffic. A few seconds later, he turned the corner and headed away from the hotel. Weaving through the traffic, he quickly put distance between them and the hotel.

"Well, I guess I don't need to worry about stashing her car somewhere safe."

Alina finally broke the silence after about five minutes. Her pulse was returning to normal and her mind was starting to grasp what had just happened.

"Nope," Damon agreed grimly.

He shifted gears and turned down a street heading out of the city. They drove in silence until he got onto the beltway. Glancing at Alina, settled on the passenger seat floor, he shook his head slightly. Alina met his glance and their eyes locked as she rubbed her forehead, breathing deeply.

"Thank God for remote starters," she muttered.

Damon realized he had a white-knuckled grip on the steering wheel and forced himself to relax his hands. His heart was still pounding and at Alina's words, he scowled.

"Thank God you thought to use it," he muttered.

He rolled over a pothole and Alina smacked her head on the glove box.

"Oof," she grunted. "Can I get up yet?" she demanded. Damon nodded.

"We're out of the city now."

Alina pulled herself into the seat next to him, rubbing the top of her head.

"I hope Stephanie wasn't emotionally attached to the car," she commented, pulling out her ponytail and running her fingers through her hair. It smelled like burnt rubber.

"I don't give a crap about Stephanie's feelings for her car right now," Damon informed her bluntly, glancing at her. "I'm more concerned about the fact that it would've been *you* toasted in that car!"

"I'm feeling a little concerned about that myself," Alina murmured. She glanced at Hawk's profile. "But all's well that ends well. Well, not so much for the car..."

"Not funny," Damon snapped.

Alina leaned her head against the seat and studied him thoughtfully. His jaw was clenched and his eyes were concealed behind the sunglasses. He had lost his white-knuckled grip on the steering wheel and, if it weren't for the clenched jaw, she wouldn't have known anything was wrong. But she could feel the tension coming off him. Hawk was far from happy.

"You've been off all day," she said softly. "What's going on?"

Damon was silent and Alina waited patiently. It was a few moments before he answered.

"The more we get into this, the less I like it," Hawk finally said. "Why don't you leave the country?" He held up a hand as she opened her mouth. "Just listen," he said, the faint hint of a smile tugging at his lips as he glanced at her. Alina closed her mouth and nodded. "Why don't you go somewhere safe? Go to Tahiti. Or the Greek Isles. Let Harry and I take care of this. They're expecting you, not me. Let *me* do this."

"Leave you to clean up my mess?" Alina demanded. "Like hell I will."

"It's not just *your* mess," Hawk retorted calmly. "It's mine now. And the Fearless Feds. And Harry's. We're *all* involved now." He looked at her. "And you're too valuable to be flapping around exposed like this," he added, his voice softening.

"I can't just walk away," Alina said slowly. "What if you can't finish this? You would be dead, and I would be running forever. You're asking me to sign off on something that's *my* fight. You know I can't do that."

"I get that that's how you feel, but I don't see how this can possibly end well." Damon shook his head. "You're practically daring the Secret Service to figure out who you are. You've made yourself responsible for two federal agents and, God forbid this psycho finds them, *you* will be the one held accountable for them. The Organization is waiting for you to prove that you're not a psychotic national security risk and you have nothing so far to convince them otherwise. Now, you almost got yourself blown up." Damon ticked it all off on his fingers. "Do you see where my unease is coming from?"

"I wouldn't say I have nothing so far." Alina latched onto the only thing she could argue with. "We know that whoever killed Shannon Gleason is the same person who just blew up Stephanie's car. That's one count against them right there, attacking a Federal agent, and that's something concrete that I can hand Charlie. I know that someone in Frankie Solitto's camp is providing information which is making its way to the Secret Service, indicating that they're most likely also on our traitor's payroll. Trust me, when Frankie finds them, our target will know and get spooked. All I need is for them to make one mistake. Just one. You know that. One mistake and everything will start falling into place."

Damon glanced at her and sighed.

"They may have already made it. Two years ago," he told her. He dug into his cargo pocket and pulled out his phone. "I got an email from a source of mine in London. Two years ago, he was hired as extra security for a diplomatic visit," he said, handing her the phone. Alina raised an eyebrow and swiped the screen. Damon told her the code to unlock it and she pulled up the email. "He's going to dig out the file and send it along later tonight."

Alina scanned the information, her pulse increasing.

"He says it was a man and a woman, and the man left for twenty-four hours," she read. "He confirmed the flight details for the US security detail. The man went to Cairo." She scanned the rest of the email. "Dates match. Bingo," she breathed, her lips curving as she looked up.

Damon smiled back.

"We have a trail," he told her.

There was a new sparkle in her eyes and Damon turned his attention back to the road. Viper wasn't going to walk away. She was going to stay and finish this. Damon suppressed a sigh. He hadn't really thought he could talk her into going to safety, and he accepted her decision without another thought. There was no point in dwelling on what *could* happen. He just had to make sure it *didn't* happen.

Michael glanced at his watch with a frown and shook his head. He had to call Alina. There was no way dinner would be ready by seven. He turned his back to the tow truck hauling the burnt wreckage of a car frame onto its bed and pulled out his cell phone. Walking away from the bustle, he hit speed dial and listened to the phone ring.

"Hey Mike!" someone called down from the parking level above. "You want to come look at this."

Michael waved his hand to indicate that he had heard and started to walk toward the ramp. The acrid smell of smoke, burnt rubber, and oil surrounded him and he coughed just as Alina picked up.

"Hey," he said, covering his other ear to block out the noise behind him. "About dinner..."

"Are you canceling on me again?" Alina asked cheerfully.

Michael couldn't resist the smile that tugged at his lips.

"No," he answered. "I *am* pushing it back, though. Something came up and I'm still tied up with work. Can we say eight instead of seven?"

"Of course," Alina said. "If you're in the middle of something, we can cancel," she added. "I promise I won't get a complex over being canceled on twice in one day."

"No. We're not canceling," Michael retorted. "I'll see you at eight."

"Ok. If you're sure..." Alina gave him one last chance to back out and for some reason her willingness to cancel dinner irritated Michael.

"I am," he said shortly. "Come hungry," he added. Alina chuckled over the phone.

"Oh, I will," she murmured.

Michael hung up with a grin, then glanced up to the parking level above him. The grin faded as quickly as it had come as he started up the ramp to the next level. Of all the rotten luck, today had turned out to be non-stop. What was supposed to be a relaxing day getting to know Alina had turned into a bizarre rush of events, all revolving around Stephanie Walker, FBI. What was left of her car was getting towed to the FBI forensics lab, and the woman herself was not answering her cell phone.

When the Feds showed up, Michael was relieved to see their lead man in charge was Blake Hanover, one of his poker buddies. They agreed to a joint investigation after Michael explained his involvement, and now he had a sinking feeling that Stephanie Walker had just become cause for heartburn for the next few days.

"So check this out." Jerry, one of the technicians, met him at the top of the ramp. "When we couldn't get any camera footage from the cameras down there, we tried to see if we had any incidental footage from the cameras up here," he told him, motioning for Michael to walk with him. "There are two cameras on this side of the level. One faces the ramp and the other is angled to take in this entire aisle."

Michael nodded, glancing around. Jerry stopped walking and pointed up to the camera facing the ramp. Michael looked up and raised his eyebrows, whistling softly. Jerry was grinning.

"All the cameras were shot out," he stated the obvious. Michael glanced at him.

"Same gun?" he asked. Jerry shrugged.

"I won't know until we get the bullets, but my guess would be yes," he answered.

Michael looked around with a frown.

"Well, isn't this shaping up to be a big barrel of fun," he muttered. "So, we have no video and no witnesses." He glanced along the aisle and walked over to the wall over-looking the level below. "The car just detonated all by itself."

"The Fed's bomb guys found part of the explosive. They say it was pretty basic," Jerry said, joining him at the wall. They both watched as the tow truck below rumbled to life and started to ease toward the ramp with its dripping, blackened cargo. Firefighters moved out of the way as it passed, pausing in the act of cleaning up.

"How basic?" Michael asked. Jerry shrugged.

"Just a basic charge linked into the ignition," he answered. "Nothing fancy. No timers, just turn the key and boom."

"But no one turned the key," Michael pointed out. "There was no body. It exploded without the ignition."

"Maybe they wired it incorrectly," Jerry said. "The whole thing seems a little off to me."

Michael turned to look at the cameras with a frown.

"It doesn't add up," he agreed. "We're missing something."

"Unless there was a remote starter..." Jerry was still watching the tow truck absently. Michael glanced at him. "A remote starter might have triggered the explosive."

Michael turned his eyes thoughtfully back to the cameras.

"Get all the cameras down," he said after a few minutes. "Get everything cleaned up here and see if there are any videos of the entrance to be had anywhere. Something had to have picked them up somewhere. A ghost didn't come in here and do this."

Jerry nodded and turned from the wall.

"You have to get out of here," he said, his eyes twinkling. "Didn't I hear you have a date tonight?"

Michael rolled his eyes.

"You guys are worse than old ladies at bingo for gossip," he said, turning to walk back toward the ramp. "It's not a date. It's dinner."

"That sure sounds like a date to me," Jerry retorted with a grin. "Your place or hers?"

"Mine."

"Uh-huh." Jerry watched him stride away with a laugh. "You're cooking? That's a date."

"It's not a date," Michael threw over his shoulder with a frown. "She's an old friend's kid sister."

"Is she legal???" Jerry called.

He burst out laughing as Michael held up the finger before disappearing down the ramp.

Alina pressed end on the phone and glanced into the living room where Damon was cleaning his Beretta. He appeared to be paying her no attention whatsoever, but Alina knew that he'd heard every word she said to Michael. She watched him slide a thin brush into the chamber and dropped the cell phone onto the kitchen table. She had given Michael every opportunity to back out of the dinner date, partially because he just had a huge headache dumped in his lap with the toasting of Stephanie's car and partially because Damon was right. She *was* practically daring the Secret Service to figure out her identity and come after her. It was turning into something of a mess, but it wasn't entirely her fault. She had gone into the mess hoping to get some information out of Michael and maybe get an ally on her side. She hadn't expected Stephanie to pull him into an inter-agency investigation that would increase his odds of putting two and two together.

"How long do you think it'll be before your boy sends out the search party for those Fearless Feds of yours?" Damon asked, glancing down the short hallway to where she was standing next to the kitchen table, lost in thought.

"He's not my boy," Alina retorted absently, picking up a bottle of water and walking into the living room. "Once they don't get any hits on either GPS, they'll start the rounds with their boss. Probably tomorrow they'll start searching in earnest."

She sat on the couch next to him.

"You took all their electronics?" Damon asked. Alina nodded.

"I replaced them with clean ones. I told them either you or myself will be checking in with them," she told him and Damon's blue eyes lit with laughter.

"I bet Stephanie practically started foaming at the mouth," he murmured. "She still thinks I ran her girlfriend off the road, doesn't she?"

"Not so much anymore," Alina answered.

Damon sat back and looked at her, the laughter fading from his eyes.

"You told them what we're doing," he stated rather than asked. Alina shrugged.

"There didn't seem to be much point in hiding it from them," she retorted. "They were sensible enough to realize that they had to stay squirreled away. Now, they know just how important it is that they *do* stay hidden. It's not like they're a threat where they are."

Damon shook his head.

"You trust them with too much," he muttered.

Alina shrugged, her eyes narrowing slightly.

"Perhaps," she murmured.

Damon looked at her, his blue eyes hooded. After a moment, he ran his hands through his hair.

"What a God-awful mess," he sighed.

Before Alina could answer, a ding came from his laptop, sitting open next to the parts of his gun. He leaned forward to pull up his email and Alina watched the muscles ripple across his broad shoulders as he reached over to the laptop. She swallowed, grabbing her bottle of water and shifting her gaze quickly from his shoulders to the parts of the Beretta laid out on the table.

"It's the file from London," Damon said, glancing over his shoulder.

Alina raised her eyes to his and smiled.

"Fantastic!" she exclaimed. Damon lifted the laptop onto his lap and sat back, scanning through the email. Alina waited while he read, her eyes drifting impatiently to the screen. She couldn't see anything from her angle. "Well?" she finally demanded after he had been silent for a few minutes.

"It's him." Hawk looked up. "It's Alex Ludmere. There are pictures and documents. Hell, he even sent a copy of the flight manifest to Cairo." Alina leaned into him impatiently, trying to see the screen and Damon grinned, shifting the laptop so she could see. "You could have just asked," he murmured.

Alina chuckled and reached over to start clicking through the photos.

"Why did he save all this?" she asked, scanning through the mass of information.

Damon shrugged.

"Because that's how he works," he answered. "Paul was always paranoid. He says that you never know what job can come back and bite you. He probably has a couple servers filled with information. If he ever went rogue, we would be in big trouble," he added thoughtfully.

"Well, right now, I love his paranoia," Alina said. "That must be the woman."

She stopped on a grainy photo of Alex and a tall woman. They were getting off a plane and the woman had her head turned away from the camera. Alina tilted her head, studying the picture. The only thing she could really tell was that the woman was tall and had dark hair. Other than that, she was just a faceless woman.

"Is this the only picture of her?" Alina asked, glancing up at Damon.

She found his blue eyes entirely too close to hers. She swallowed, her eyes automatically dropping to his full lips.

"I think so," Damon answered, those full lips curving into a slow smile when she looked away hastily. "But I just scanned through the file briefly. You think she's important?"

"Maybe." Alina shifted away from him breathlessly and glanced at her watch. "Everything is important right now, until we figure out what isn't," she added, getting up. "I have to get ready to go."

She grabbed her water bottle and headed toward the stairs.

"Chicken," Damon murmured and Alina paused at the foot of the stairs.

"Excuse me?" she asked.

Damon didn't even turn around.

"You heard me," he retorted, his head still bent over the laptop.

Alina's eyes narrowed as she started up the stairs.

"It was a strategic retreat," she muttered.

His laughter followed her up the stairs.

Chapter Ten

Alina perched on a bar stool, sipping a glass of red wine, and watching as Michael chopped up vegetables for a salad. The kitchen was large, sporting a wood-topped island with bar stools in the center, and a counter running along the back wall with a window above the sink. A glass-topped oven was to their left, throwing out warmth, and the smell of baking lasagna filled the kitchen.

"Sorry it's not quite ready," Michael said, dropping a handful of chopped green pepper into a large bowl filled with a mix of spring greens and romaine lettuce. Alina smiled.

"Don't be sorry," she replied. "You've had a busy day."

Michael glanced at her. She was dressed in loose black linen pants and a sleeveless, dark purple shirt that fell in a drape across her shoulders. Her hair was loose around her shoulders and she looked completely at ease, perched on the bar stool, watching him chop vegetables. He smiled slightly.

"It wasn't supposed to be," he said, starting on some cucumbers. "What did you do with your afternoon?"

"I went shopping," Alina lied easily with a smile.

Before Michael could answer, his phone chirped from the counter. He glanced at it with a frown, reaching behind him to grab it. Alina watched as he read the text message quickly. The slight frown turned into a flash of irritation before he cleared the screen and dropped the phone back onto the counter without replying.

"Sorry about that," he apologized, glancing at her. "You went shopping?"

Alina nodded. Her eyes strayed to his phone briefly when he turned his attention back to the cucumbers.

"Yes." She had her eyes back on him when he glanced up. "New shoes," she added with a grin.

"Of course!" Michael chuckled. "Women and their shoes."

Alina shrugged and sipped her wine.

"It's a girl thing," she retorted. Michael nodded.

"Yes, I know," he agreed. "It's a girl thing that men will never fully comprehend." He scooped up the cucumbers and tossed them on the salad. Lifting the salad bowl, he shook it, tossing the vegetables together. "I like my salads loaded," he told her. "How about you? Do you like vegetables?"

"Pile them in!" Alina answered cheerfully.

Michael smiled and set the bowl down.

"Good." He turned toward the refrigerator and while he had his back to her, Alina glanced at his phone again. "I'm always disappointed by what some people consider a salad," Michael said, his head buried in the fridge. "Throw some iceberg lettuce, a cucumber slice, one grape tomato and some grated carrot on a plate, and people call that a salad."

He emerged from the fridge with grape tomatoes, baby carrots, red onion and broccoli.

"Then cover it with two cups of ranch dressing," Alina added.

Michael dropped his armload of veggies on the island and laughed.

"Exactly!" he agreed. "Pathetic. When I was deployed, I used to dream of salad. Your brother just didn't get it. He dreamed of cheesesteaks."

"Dave did love his cheesesteak," Alina remembered fondly with a slight smile.

Michael glanced at her.

"What food did you miss most when you were deployed?" he asked, starting to chop the carrots. Alina set her glass aside and reached for the bag of broccoli.

"I'm not sure," she said thoughtfully, opening the bag and pulling out a broccoli crown. "Honestly, I think it was an even tie between hot wings and good chili," she finally decided.

Michael's eyes met hers and he smiled.

"So you like it spicy," he murmured. Alina winked.

"The hotter, the better," she replied. "You want to pass me a knife? I can't just sit here and watch you work anymore."

Michael grinned and pulled another knife out of the butcher block on the counter. He handed it to her and watched as she skillfully flipped it in her hand and went to work on the broccoli. He went back to the carrots thoughtfully.

"Do you miss New York?" Alina asked him, changing the subject.

She hadn't missed his piercing glance when she flipped the knife. It was a habit, her way of testing the knife's balance before using it. She got the impression that Michael sensed the action was not entirely culinary.

"I get up there pretty regularly now, so I don't miss it as much as I used to," Michael answered. "My folks are still up there, so that's another

103

reason I'm happy in DC. It's close enough to go up and check on them."

Alina nodded and finished with the broccoli crown. She tossed the florets in the salad bowl as Michael's phone chirped again. He sighed and Alina glanced at him from under her lashes as he turned to grab his phone again impatiently. This time he didn't even read the text. He just cleared the screen and set the phone back down. When he turned back to the island, he encountered laughing dark eyes.

"Maybe if you answer, whoever it is will leave you alone," Alina suggested.

He shook his head slightly.

"Sorry," he apologized again. "I would normally put it on mute, but I have some people working on something through the night and they need to be able to reach me."

"Oh, I'm not bothered by the phone," she said cheerfully. "But *you* seem to be bothered by whatever is coming through."

Michael had the grace to look sheepish.

"It's annoying," he admitted, scooping the carrots into the salad bowl while Alina opened the grape tomatoes and dumped half the container into the salad.

"That sounds suspiciously like old flame troubles," she informed him, snapping the container closed. He surprised her by agreeing as he started on the red onion.

"She's persistent."

Alina raised her eyebrow, studying him.

"How long did you date?" she asked curiously and Michael rolled his eyes.

"We didn't," he replied. "We went on a business dinner once. At least, that's what *I* thought it was. She apparently thought otherwise."

"Ouch," Alina murmured, her lips twitching.

Michael looked at her in time to catch the lip twitch.

"Laugh and you won't get any lasagna," he threatened her, pointing his knife at her. "And I make a banging lasagna."

"It smells like it," she agreed, forcing the smile from her face.

Michael scooped up his onions and dropped them into the bowl before starting to clean up. Alina sipped her wine and watched him put the remaining vegetables back in the fridge and wipe up the island. She waited until he had rinsed, dried, and put the knives back in the butcher block before speaking.

"So, what's it like being stalked by a co-worker?"

Michael swung around with a short bark of laughter.

"I knew you wouldn't leave it alone! You're just like your brother!" he exclaimed. Alina grinned and sipped her wine. "She's not a co-worker.

She works in the White House."

"Don't *you* work in the White House?" Alina asked, setting her glass down.

Michael shook his head and poured himself a glass of wine.

"No. I work outside of the White House."

"But you work to protect the person who lives in the White House," she pointed out. "Therefore, it could be argued that everyone in the White House is, theoretically, a co-worker."

Michael set the wine bottle down and looked at her.

"That's like saying the sailors on a destroyer were your co-workers," he retorted and Alina chuckled.

"Point taken," she conceded and Michael sipped his wine. "So, what's it like being stalked by someone from the White House?" Alina asked, her eyes dancing.

Michael started laughing.

"You're really not hungry, are you?" he asked. Alina laughed.

"Ok. I'll stop."

She picked up her glass and slid off the stool to come around the island to refill it. Michael took it from her hand when she reached him and picked up the wine bottle to refill it for her.

"It's frustrating," he told her, handing the glass back to her, "and a little awkward."

Alina thanked him and leaned against the counter, looking at him thoughtfully.

"I can imagine it might be," she said slowly.

"Don't tell me you never ran into this problem." Michael looked at her, his hazel-green eyes very close. "You must have had sailors chasing you all over the globe. I'm sure you know how awkward it can be to try to keep a professional relationship professional."

Alina thought of a pair of cobalt blue eyes and was pricked by a sudden feeling of melancholy.

"It's not easy," she agreed.

"No, it's not."

Michael sipped his wine, his eyes studying her over the rim. The timer went off before he could continue and he set his glass down, turning toward the oven.

"Where's your bathroom?" Alina asked, setting her wine glass down.

He glanced over his shoulder.

"Down the hall on the left," he answered.

Alina nodded and turned to walk out of the kitchen as he was opening the oven. A blast of hot tomato and cheese-spiced deliciousness wafted through the kitchen, bringing with it a comforting warmth that teased long forgotten memories of laughter and family from her past. Alina frowned and pushed the unfamiliar feeling away. Finding the bathroom, she switched on the light and closed the door. Sighing, she looked at herself in the mirror.

"Stop the emotions, Viper," she hissed, looking at her reflection critically.

Her cheeks were flushed slightly and her eyes were bright. Alina stared at herself for a long moment. The sudden rush of melancholy and fleeting memories of days long gone were a direct result of the wine and congenial teasing of an old family friend. The warmth of Michael's kitchen and the smell of the hot lasagna coming from the oven had combined to make her feel comfortable and relaxed. It was pure and simple.

She was feeling the emotions of memories, and they had no place here. Not now, not ever.

Alina took a deep breath. She turned on the faucet and splashed cold water on her face. *They're going to kill you. Michael is under orders to find you so that they can kill you. And you're in his house, having dinner.*

"I must be out of my mind," Alina muttered, grabbing the hand towel and patting her face dry.

She replaced the towel and shook her head. Hawk was right. If she had an ounce of sense left in her, she would run as far away from here as possible and disappear.

Alina was stepping out of the bathroom when she heard her phone beep from her purse. She frowned as she went back into the kitchen. Michael was on the phone in front of the bay window on the other side of the kitchen. He glanced at her and smiled, motioning that he would only be a minute. Alina nodded and pulled her phone out of her purse. She swiped the screen and glanced at the text message. It was from Hawk, and it was brief.

You have company.

Awareness streaked down her spine. Hawk was out there somewhere, watching, covering her back. Alina lifted her eyes from her phone as Michael hung up. She was just opening her mouth to suggest that he move away from the window when something flashed behind him outside and there was a loud crash. Glass shattered at both ends of the kitchen as oblong objects smashed through both the bay window where Michael was standing and the window above the sink simultaneously.

Viper reacted purely on instinct. She had her gun out and cocked before the objects hit the floor. Diving behind the island, she took cover as one of the missiles landed on the other side. There was another shatter of glass and the smell of fire and gasoline filled the air. Scrambling to her knees, Viper moved quickly around the island to be confronted with the quick-burning flames from the remains of a Molotov cocktail. Without a second thought, she grabbed the lasagna from the top of the stove and dumped the pan, upside down, directly on the budding fire. Reaching over the edge of the sink, she flipped on the water and grabbed the spray nozzle. She yanked it forward and directed it onto the smoldering blaze at the base of the island. Flames were trying to escape the smothering lasagna pan and lick up the side of the island. At the first shot of water, however, they gave up. Staying below the edge of the counter, out of sight from the window, Alina held the water on the mess, ensuring the flames couldn't get hold of anything to give them life again.

Glancing over to the other side of the kitchen, she saw that Michael had contained the fire on his side by ripping down one of the heavy curtains from the window and using it to smother the budding flames. Catching the flames before they had time to gain momentum and oxygen, Alina and Michael had both fires out within a few seconds. As soon as her fire was out, Alina released the spray nozzle. As it retracted back into the sink, she reached up and turned off the water.

The acrid smell of smoke and gasoline filled the air and there was a second of complete silence. She looked across the kitchen at Michael breathlessly, her heart pounding. He had finished putting out his fire and their eyes met across the smoky kitchen. He motioned to the back door between them and she nodded, taking a slow, deep breath. Michael's eyes dropped to her gun and he raised an eyebrow slightly.

Viper didn't notice. Her ears had picked up a noise from the front of the house. She pointed to the front of the house and he nodded to indicate that he heard it, motioning that he would take the new threat from the front. She nodded and turned her head to the back door just as the lights went out, pitching the house into total darkness.

Alina immediately squeezed her eyes shut as tightly as she could and held them closed for a few seconds. She opened them briefly and then squeezed them shut again, trying to acclimate her eyes to the sudden darkness as quickly as possible. She didn't have time to be temporarily blinded. When she opened them the second time, she was able to make out shapes in the darkness and, in the split second before all hell broke loose, Viper sensed rather than saw Michael move swiftly to the wall at the side of the hallway. Standing, she moved forward along the counter in the darkness. Her breathing steadied and her heartbeat fell to the regular, rapid tempo Viper knew so well. She was ready.

When the back door crashed open, the first person through never knew what hit him. Expecting to still have surprise on his side, he never even saw the right hook that knocked him out cold. As he hit the ground,

Viper raised her pistol and met the second intruder face to face, the barrel of her gun planted firmly on his forehead.

In the darkness, she judged his height to be just under six foot and his frame solid. He froze as soon as her metal touched his skin and she watched his eyes widen in shock before he held his hands up in surrender, slowly starting to back out the door again. Before he had gone two steps, Viper heard the distinctive crack of a fist on a nose behind her, followed by a howl of pain. The howl was suddenly cut short and she turned her head in time to see Michael drop another intruder at the entrance of the hallway with a sharp hit on the temple.

That split second was all her opponent needed. He stepped forward quickly and knocked her firing arm aside. Alina's gun flew out of her hand and landed on the floor a few feet away. Viper snapped her head back to the man and swiftly blocked his fist, aimed for the side of her head. A quick jab from her right fist made his head snap back. He stumbled awkwardly backward with the force of the blow and she took full advantage of his disorientation by delivering a hard kick to his sternum that sent him flying backwards out the door. Viper followed him out as he sailed over the few wooden steps leading up to the door, landing on his back in the grass a few feet away. Before he could catch his breath and sit up, a military knife was being pressed against his throat.

"Who sent you?" Viper demanded, placing her knee on his chest and holding him flat against the ground.

He was silent, staring up at her. Viper leaned forward until her face was inches from his.

"I asked you a question," she hissed, pressing the blade more firmly against his throat.

The intruder gasped as the sharp blade broke skin.

"I don't know!" he choked out. "We were hired by some kind of go-between. We were told it was an easy mark."

"Really?" Viper drawled. "What kind of mark?"

"A man, ex-military, and we were paid to rough him up and get his laptop." He was speaking freely now as blood trickled down his neck. "They told us he was a Marine. They didn't say nothing about a chick being here."

"Always be prepared for surprises," Viper said. "When were you hired?"

"Yesterday," he muttered.

"How many of you?"

"Four."

"Paid cash up front?" Viper asked.

"Yes."

He stared up at her and Viper considered him for a moment coldly.

"Next time, I wouldn't take a job on an ex-Marine," she finally told him. "They're very unpredictable." She lifted her blade off his neck and he sucked in a deep breath. "I'm giving you one minute to get the hell out of here," she told him calmly. "Tell anyone you saw a chick here and I'll find you and make sure that cut goes all the way through. Do you understand?"

He nodded, his eyes locked on her cold ones. Viper nodded.

"Good." She slid her knife back into its holster on her ankle and lifted her knee off his chest. "Now run," she whispered.

He rolled away from her and jumped up, taking off into the night without looking back. Alina stood up and turned back toward the house. When she reentered through the back door, she heard a fight ensuing in the front of the house. The intruder Michael had dropped in the hallway was nowhere to be seen. Neither was the one she had knocked out. Alina glanced to the right and cursed softly.

Her gun was also missing.

She moved through the kitchen swiftly and into the dark hallway. The commotion was coming from the dining room and Viper stopped with her back to the wall next to the dining room door, scanning the stairs in the darkness. Seeing nothing there, she peeked around the corner into the dining room.

Moonlight filtered through the front window, lending just enough light for her to watch Michael slam his opponent's head into the dining room table. A second figure was already inert on the floor a few feet away. The intruder that Viper had left unconscious on the kitchen floor was moving up behind Michael, her gun in his hand.

Alina advanced silently in the darkness. Kicking the back of one of his knees, she grabbed the arm holding her gun as he stumbled and his legs buckled.

"This is mine, thanks," she informed him, wrenching his arm backwards at an awkward angle.

His fingers released the gun as he cried out in surprise and pain. Removing the gun from his hand, Viper used it to hit him in the temple as she released his arm. He sank to the floor, once again out cold. Michael turned his head from where he was holding his intruder pinned to the table with a strong hand on the back of his neck.

"You ok?" he asked. He didn't see Alina's cold smile in the darkness.

"Yep," she answered, tucking her gun back into the holster at her back. "Never better. You?"

"Fine," Michael answered shortly. "There's a circuit breaker box in the garage. There should be a flashlight inside the door. Think you can try to get the lights back on?"

"Sure." Alina glanced at the two men on the floor. "They won't stay out for long. You got them?"

Michael nodded.

"Yep," he answered. Alina nodded and turned to leave the dining room. "Garage door is in the kitchen," Michael added over his shoulder.

Alina headed back down the dark hallway into the kitchen. The smell of burnt fabric, smoke, and chemicals combined with the lingering smell of now-ruined lasagna and she shook her head slightly as her stomach rumbled, reminding her that she was still hungry. So much for dinner.

She found the door to the garage and opened it, feeling around inside. Her fingers touched a metal shelf and she felt around until her hand found a flashlight. Alina switched it on, playing the strong beam around the garage curiously. The fresh smell of wood and sawdust was overwhelming. Michael had turned it into a workshop, which had a wood-working bench and an electric table saw along one wall. Lawn mower, leaf blower, and snow blower were all lined up along the other wall and garden tools hung on the walls above them. In the center of the garage, there were two saw horses with what looked like a tabletop in progress laying across them. Alina raised an eyebrow in some surprise. Michael just kept getting more and more interesting.

She stepped into the garage and located the circuit breaker box on the wall a few feet away. It was already open, and all the breakers were flipped off. Alina frowned and turned, guiding the flashlight beam around the garage again more slowly. The garage door was closed and a quick glance showed an electric door-opener hanging from the ceiling. Another trip around the walls revealed a window, on the side of the lawn tools. The light paused there for a moment and Alina tilted her head thoughtfully. Someone had entered the garage and flipped all the breakers off, and she was willing to bet heavily that it was *not* any of their intruders.

She turned back to the breaker box with a slight smile, flipping them back on. Light poured out from the open door to the kitchen and she heard the sound of the refrigerator starting back up. Alina closed the box and switched off the flashlight, turning to go back into the house.

As she stepped into the kitchen, one of the intruders came barreling out of the hallway. It was the one she had knocked out twice and when he spotted her, he looked wild-eyed and held up his hands, stumbling through the kitchen. Alina raised an eyebrow and watched as he stuttered unintelligibly and lurched toward the back door. He disappeared through it a moment later. She moved to the shattered window above the sink to watch him continue to stumble as he ran out into the night.

Alina turned from the window, a faint smile hovering around her lips, and her eyes fell on the sopping, burned mess at the base of the island. Her momentary amusement vanished as her stomach rumbled again. She moved away from the window and around the island, bending to pick up her phone from where it had fallen to the floor. She dropped it back into her purse and headed down the hallway. When she entered the dining room, Michael had the intruder he had been holding against the table handcuffed in a chair. They were the only two in the dining room.

"Where's the other one?" she asked Michael.

He glanced at her and she saw that he had an oozing cut on his cheekbone. Swelling on his jaw and split knuckles were testimony that the man in the chair had not gone down easily.

"He took off as soon as he came to," he answered.

"I just passed their friend in the kitchen," Alina told him. She looked at the remaining intruder, slumped in the chair. "What are you going to do with him?"

She studied him curiously. He had brown hair and a brown beard and was built like a pit bull. He was probably still seeing stars, which would account for the vacant look in his face as his head lolled to the side. One eye was already swelling shut and blood was pouring from his nose.

"Charge him," Michael responded shortly.

"He's bleeding onto your carpet."

They both looked down to where blood was dripping onto the carpet and Michael sighed, grabbing the back of the chair. He tilted it onto its back legs and dragged it across the floor and out the door of the dining room. Alina grinned as he continued out the open front door and onto the front porch. Turning the chair so their visitor was facing the road, he moved around it to stare down at him. Alina leaned on the door jam of the front door, her eyes scanning the dark front yard and street beyond. The neighborhood was quiet and still. The neighbors obviously hadn't heard a thing.

"Who are you?" Michael demanded, bringing her attention back to the pit bull in the chair. Her eyes narrowed.

Michael had handcuffed him with his arms behind the chair and Alina found herself staring at a Special Forces tattoo on his right bicep. She glanced at Michael and knew that he had already seen it. This was no ordinary hired thug like the others.

"Who sent you?" Michael asked when there was no answer to the first question. Silence also greeted the second one.

"He won't talk," Alina said, shaking her head.

Michael stepped back and glanced at her.

"He'll talk eventually," he replied grimly. "I'm going to get some ice for his nose." He stepped back into the house, pausing next to her, his face inches from hers. "You're sure you're ok?" he asked softly, his eyes probing hers, and Alina smiled slightly.

"I'm fine," she answered calmly. Michael nodded slowly.

"Ok." He stared at her for a beat, then continued into the hallway. "I'll be right back."

Alina nodded and turned her attention back to the porch and the man in the chair. She missed the sharp, speculative glance from hazel-green eyes as Michael went thoughtfully into the kitchen.

"That tattoo of yours is pretty distinctive. I have a friend who had the same one," Viper remarked softly, staying where she was.

The man twisted his head, trying to see her. She was just out of sight, behind him on the side with the eye swollen shut. He gave up trying to see her and faced forward again silently.

"Now what's a nice American hero like you doing mixed up in a mess like this?" she wondered, her voice as smooth as velvet.

The figure in the chair flinched and Alina studied him thoughtfully.

"Do you even know *why* you were paid to do this?" she asked.

The man stilled and that was all the answer she needed.

"Interesting," she murmured before falling silent.

Alina was still staring at the back of the man's head thoughtfully when a black SUV came rolling down the street. She glanced up, about to alert Michael to the fact that things were going to get awkward, when the vehicle suddenly picked up speed. Alina saw the back window roll down and the barrel of a rifle emerge. She spun inside the door, with her back against the wall, out of sight.

"Michael!" she called. "More company!"

Michael appeared in the entrance to the kitchen just as two cracks echoed outside, followed by the sound of squealing tires as the SUV took off down the street. Alina straightened up quickly and peered around the door jam in time to see the vehicle careen around the corner and disappear.

Michael ran down the hallway, stopping next to her, and they both looked at the chair. The man was slumped forward, unmoving.

"What the hell?!" Michael exclaimed, stepping onto the porch.

Alina followed and they stared at him. Both bullets had entered his chest and blood was starting to spread over his torso. Michael reached out and pressed two fingers on his neck, feeling for a pulse. Alina looked at him and he shook his head.

"Well, this is awkward," Alina murmured, glancing at the street.

Front porch lights were flickering on up and down the street and the neighbors across the road were already outside, looking to see what had happened. Where the sound of breaking glass and Molotov cocktails drew no notice, the unmistakable pop of gunfire got everyone's attention.

Michael glanced up and groaned.

"Time to call the reinforcements," he muttered, pulling his phone out of his pocket and turning toward the front yard.

Alina saw the porch light next door go on and the front door open. She backed into the house slowly.

"Michael, if you don't mind, I'll be inside," she called. He glanced back at her and she did her best to look upset. "The sight of blood and I have never gotten along in large doses," she lied convincingly.

Michael nodded and Alina retreated into the house while he called in the shooting and went out to meet the neighbors. Retrieving her purse from the kitchen, she went into the bathroom, closing and locking the door behind her. She pulled out her phone and hit speed dial quickly. It was picked up on the second ring.

"Tell me you got a plate number," she said.

"I got the plate number," Hawk assured her. "What was that all about?"

"I'm not sure." Alina flipped the toilet lid closed and sank down onto it. "They were here for Michael. The one on the porch was Special Forces."

"That did *not* look like a Special Forces operation," Hawk murmured in her ear.

"He was the only one. The others were just hired thugs." Alina rubbed her forehead and frowned when her hand came away wet. She stood up and looked in the mirror. Blood was oozing from a gash above her eye, next to her temple. "I'm bleeding!" she exclaimed in surprise. "When did that happen?"

"I assume you're not waiting for an answer from me." Hawk sounded amused. "Are you ok?"

Alina turned her head and examined the gash in the mirror briefly, then promptly disregarded it and went back to her seat on the toilet.

"I'm fine," she said. "But I'm in one hell of an awkward position here. This place will be crawling with federal agents in about five minutes."

"I told you not to go," Hawk retorted. Alina's eyes narrowed.

"Not helpful," she snapped, drawing a chuckle from him.

"Well, unless you want them to get an inadvertent DNA sample and make everything worse, you better get whatever's bleeding covered up," he advised. "And do it fast because the first responders are already pulling up."

"Great," Alina said.

"Viper..."

"Yes?"

"Be careful," Hawk said softly.

Alina's heart stopped and then thudded painfully as a rush of warmth coursed through her at the tone in his voice. She couldn't stop the smile that spread across her face as she disconnected the call. She swallowed, sighed, and then opened her purse and pulled out the only thing she had to conceal the gash on her forehead.

Alina stood up and pulled her hair back into a ponytail. She set the red Phillies cap on her head and pulled it down to cover the gash, wincing slightly as it settled over the open wound. Tucking the ponytail through the back of the cap, she looked at herself in the mirror again. The wound was covered. Turning on the water, she splashed it on her face, rinsing away smudges of blood before looking at herself again. She was about as presentable as she was going to get.

"Alina? You ok?" Michael called, tapping on the door.

"Fine," she called back.

She patted her face dry and took a deep breath, turning to open the door. Michael looked at her in concern.

"You sure?" he asked.

Alina looked up at him and brown eyes met hazel. She smiled.

"I'm fine now," she told him.

He nodded and his lips twitched as he tweaked the Phillies cap.

"You know, I have a rule about non-Yankee caps in the house," he murmured, his lips curving into a teasing grin. "But given the circumstances, I'll waive it this once."

"My hair was a disaster," Alina informed him. "If I'd known this was how you do dinner, I would have worn it up."

Michael laughed and pulled her out of the powder room, wrapping his arms around her. He rested his chin on the top of her head.

"You've been wonderful," he said with a heavy sigh. "I'm so glad you're alright."

Alina hugged him back awkwardly. She could see lights flashing in the front yard and people in official jackets and badges were starting to mill around the body on the porch.

"You sure know how to show a girl a good time," Alina told him, pulling away and glancing up into his face. "Too bad I'm still hungry," she added with a wink.

"Well, *you're* the one who threw the lasagna on the fire," Michael pointed out, steering her toward the kitchen and away from the porch as more people arrived.

"It seemed like the best option at the time," she murmured.

They entered the kitchen and he deposited her in a chair in the corner, behind the round kitchen table in front of the bay window.

"You stay here," he told her. "This is going to take a while. I'll make sure they don't bother you too much."

Alina nodded and set her purse on the table. She looked up at him when he didn't move immediately. His expression was gentle and it penetrated her shell suddenly, shaking Alina to her core. She stared into his eyes, caught by the intensity there.

"I'm sorry about dinner," Michael said softly.

"No apologies."

Her voice was just as soft and Michael smiled slowly.

"I'll make it up to you," he promised.

Alina felt like she was caught in a time capsule. There didn't seem to be any movement beyond the two of them.

"I know," she answered.

He grinned suddenly and the intensity in his eyes was replaced with a laugh. The spell shattered and Alina blinked. She was still breathing and Michael was laughing down at her.

"Sit tight," he told her, turning away and disappearing around the corner and up the hallway toward the activity on the front porch.

Alina shook her head slightly and looked around, absurdly dazed. What just happened?

She looked across the table to the fragmented bay window and watched as a multitude of flashlights started to swarm into the backyard. The Feds had arrived.

Her mind registered that fact even as it was grappling with that timeless moment between her and Michael. Alina took a deep breath and frowned. It hadn't been physical. It was something else. She got up impatiently and crossed over to the island. The wine bottle and glasses from earlier were broken, the wine spilled over the counter and floor, but the wine rack on the island had escaped damage. Alina went through the cabinets until she found another a wine glass and, pulling a bottle of red wine from the rack, she carried it back over to the table. Sitting down again, she pulled out her all-purpose utility knife and flipped out the corkscrew.

It was going to be a long night.

Chapter Eleven

Alina stepped into the kitchen and kicked the door closed behind her. Dropping her purse and keys on the table, she looked down the short hall to the living room. Damon was stretched out on the couch facing her, bare feet crossed at the ankles, a laptop open on his lap. His hair fell over his forehead carelessly and he was dressed in old sweats and a t-shirt. Alina thought he had never looked so good as he did in that instant. His blue eyes met hers over the top of the screen and he sat up, swinging his legs off the couch. He stood up and came towards her, frowning slightly as he took in her drawn face and the dark shadows under her eyes.

"You look exhausted," he said, flipping on the over-head light in the kitchen.

Alina sighed as she pulled her gun out of the holster at her back, setting it on the table next to her purse.

"I am," she told him. "I'm starving, tired, and my head is killing me."

"Then it's a good thing I picked up pizza on my way back," Damon murmured, turning toward the oven. Alina watched as he opened the oven and pulled the box out. He set it on top of the stove and turned off the oven. "I kept it warm for you," he said, turning around to face her. "I guessed dinner had been ruined."

He smiled, his deep blue eyes glinting warmly, and Alina was filled with a sudden wave of warmth. She stared at him, unable to think of a single word to say. His smile grew into a grin and Damon walked over to her, looking down into her face. He touched her lips gently with his fingers.

"You can thank me later," he murmured. "Eat. I'm going to have a shower."

Alina watched him go down the hall and disappear up the stairs, still standing rooted to the spot in the kitchen, her lips tingling where he had touched them. The smell of pepperoni suddenly snapped her out of her stupor and she shook her head, going over to flip open the box. She lifted out a piece of pizza, biting into it hungrily as she turned to get a plate from the cabinet next to the sink. Carrying it over to the table, she sat down facing the back door with her back against the wall.

She was exhausted. She hadn't eaten since the morning and between the lack of food and constant rush of adrenaline today, Alina knew that her body was using every last resource it had just to function. She had sat at the table in Michael's kitchen for three hours, sipping wine and watching as federal agents from both the Secret Service and the FBI swarmed around her. True to his word, Michael had ensured that she hadn't been bothered and, to her relief, they seemed to take absolutely no notice of her whatsoever. They approached her only once, and Michael leaned against the wall next to her while they questioned her. He had appeared bored, but the once or twice that she glanced up at him, she got the distinct impression that those hazel-green eyes weren't missing a thing.

Michael was dangerous and, Viper admitted to herself now as she took another bite of pizza, he was paying entirely too much attention to her.

Alina finished her pizza and went back to get another slice. The pipes in the wall banged briefly and the sound of water rushing up to the bathroom upstairs told her that Damon had turned on the shower. She smiled slightly to herself. It was kind of comforting to have someone else in the house for a change. She headed back to the table slowly.

There had been a few times throughout the night when she caught Michael studying her thoughtfully. What he was thinking was anyone's guess, and Alina left uncomfortably aware that Michael saw a lot more than he appeared to see. She frowned, sinking into her seat. The woman in her knew that Michael was attracted to her, and had known it ever since she got out of the taxi and caught him drooling over her legs. That same woman inside her knew that that very attraction, coupled with the investigator in Michael, was garnering much closer scrutiny than she had expected.

And that was an unforeseen problem.

The water upstairs shut off and Alina realized with a start that she had been staring into space for several minutes. She sighed and finished her pizza, putting Michael and all the attached difficulties out of her mind. Getting up, she went to put her plate into the dishwasher. Hawk would have already run the plates on the SUV and she would be able to find out who had wanted the ex-Special Forces man dead rather than have him talk.

Her few moments of rest were over.

Alina was just closing the dishwasher when Damon came into the kitchen. She turned and her breath caught in her throat. He had put the navy sweats back on, but nothing else. His chest and feet were bare and his hair was still wet from the shower. His flat stomach was as hard as a rock,

117

and his broad shoulders tapered into solidly muscled arms that were still glistening with droplets of water. There wasn't an ounce of fat on the man.

"Feel better?" he asked, glancing at her as he opened the fridge to pull out a bottle of water.

"Much," Alina answered.

He held up a bottle of water questioningly and handed it to her when she nodded.

"What's with the Phillies hat?" he asked, closing the fridge and opening his water.

"It was all I had to cover the blood," she said, taking a long drink of water.

Damon's eyes narrowed and he sipped his water.

"Is it still bleeding?" he asked. Alina shrugged.

"I have no idea. I haven't touched it since I put the cap on."

Damon grimaced and stepped forward. He set his water down on the counter behind her and his broad shoulders stopped her from trying to edge around him. Alina was assaulted with the scent of shower gel, shampoo, and Hawk. Her pulse jumped as her heartbeat quickened.

"This isn't going to feel good," Hawk murmured a split second before he swiftly yanked the cap off her head.

Alina gasped as burning pain shot through her left temple and her left eye filled with tears in reaction. Her ponytail came out with the removal of the hat and red waves tumbled down around her shoulders. Damon tossed the hat on the counter and gently tilted her head sideways so he could look at the gash. Dried blood had caked around the edges and fresh blood was oozing out from the wound where it had been ripped open again.

"What did this?" he asked.

"I think it must have been glass, but I'm not sure."

Alina's voice was slightly breathless. The pain receded as quickly as it had come and her eye stopped watering. Hawk was standing so close that his thighs were brushing hers and she could feel the warmth radiating from his skin. Alina's heart started pounding in reaction. She didn't trust herself to look at him, so she kept her head turned and tried to concentrate on the throbbing wound on her head.

"You need to get this cleaned out before it gets infected," Damon told her, seemingly oblivious to her silent struggles. He gently probed around the edges of the gash. "I think you can get by without stitching it." He finally looked down at her averted face. "I seem to remember that you're opposed to stitches."

Alina swallowed and nodded, finally returning her gaze to his face. Their eyes met and silence fell heavily between them as they stared at each other.

"I like you better without the green contacts," Damon finally murmured huskily.

"Michael knows I have brown eyes," Alina whispered. "I have to take them out when I see him."

Damon nodded slowly, his eyes locked with hers. Alina's mind drained of thought as she stared into his deep blue eyes and her mouth went dry. Her heart was thudding in her chest again painfully and she took a deep breath, trying to calm it. She inhaled the warm and comforting smell of woodsy musk that was uniquely his, and her heart simply thudded faster. Damon groaned softly and lowered his lips to hers.

She met him halfway.

Alina slid her hands over his shoulders and felt the smooth skin prickle beneath her fingers. Passion rolled over her, hot and urgent, and she draped her arms around his neck as her eyes slid shut. Damon dropped his hands to her waist and pulled her hard against him as desire took over. Alina heard a moan and dimly realized that it had been her to make the deep, almost haunting, sound of yearning. She couldn't think, couldn't breathe, and couldn't stop touching him. Her feet suddenly left the ground and Alina felt weightless, caught in space for a split second, before she came to rest on the counter. Damon had lifted her up without breaking the kiss and her legs went around his hips on their own. This time the groan didn't come from her, and Damon lifted his head. His eyes were heavy-lidded and filled with desire and Alina felt a shiver streak down her spine as she met his gaze. He was sliding her shirt up and over her head and then his lips were back on hers, hot and demanding.

As soon as her skin touched his, Damon knew it was going to take a miracle to make this stop. The passion between them was simply too strong for him to resist. For the first time since they had been cautiously testing this attraction between them, Damon knew without a doubt that Alina was holding absolutely nothing back. He groaned again. God, she felt so good.

Alina heard a cell phone go off over the blood pounding in her ears. She thought it might be the burn phone that she used for communicating with Michael, but she couldn't seem to make herself care. With every touch and every breath, Damon had swept past every barrier she had tried to erect against *this*. She couldn't seem to get close enough to him. She was surrounded by his strength and his warmth, but it still wasn't enough. She wanted to feel every inch of him. She wanted to love him.

And that sudden thought scared the hell right out of her.

"Stop."

Alina gasped, ripping her mouth away from his, breathing heavily.

The passion coursing through her made her whole body feel like jelly and she rested her chin on his broad shoulder, trying to catch her breath and get herself under control. Damon's heart was pounding against hers, his ragged breathing telling her that he was just as affected by this onslaught of desire. His jaw brushed her cheek as he held her close, taking long, deep breaths.

They both stayed very still, afraid to move until they regained some kind of tenuous control. A laptop alarm beeped from the living room and still they didn't move, wrapped in each other's arms. Damon realized that they were both taking long, deep breaths, trying to calm themselves and he chuckled. The low, rich sound reverberated into Alina's ear and her lips curved in response reluctantly.

"Well, that was unexpected," Hawk murmured finally, his heartbeat slowing at last to a manageable rhythm.

Alina was absently stroking a hand across the back of his shoulders. She was silent, but made no move to pull away. Her pulse was slowly returning to normal and her mind was now racing. What just happened? How had they *both* lost total control? And how were they going to avoid it from happening again? Did she *want* to avoid it from happening again?

"This is going to get complicated, isn't it?" Alina finally spoke, her voice low.

Damon pulled away slightly and looked at her. Her lips were swollen and she looked completely dazed.

"This got complicated five years ago when we both ended up in the same training facility for the Organization," Damon replied quietly. Alina opened her mouth to speak, but Damon swiftly and gently pressed a finger against her lips, his cobalt eyes inches from hers. "And don't pretend that it didn't," he whispered huskily. "You and I have been dancing around this ever since we met and you know it."

Alina stared at him. He was right. This attraction between them had always been there, from the day they met in boot camp ten years ago. They had just pushed it to the side. His finger moved off her lips and Damon leaned his forehead against hers gently, careful to avoid the wound near her temple. Alina inhaled slowly, surrounded by the warmth of his skin. His eyes were sparkling into hers, laughter lurking deep in their depths. Laughter and something else.

"In my defense, we would have killed each other then," Alina whispered a little breathlessly, her lips curving slightly. "And that training course was too damn hard to concentrate on anything else."

"I'll give you that," Damon agreed with a slight laugh.

She moved her head back, breaking contact with his forehead and giving herself some breathing room. Damon let her move back a few inches before his arms, still wrapped around her, stopped her retreat. Alina stared into his eyes, trying to sort out the scrambling thoughts and emotions tumbling through her while Damon watched her, his eyes hooded and the hint of a smile on his lips.

A jumble of memories cascaded through her mind: racing him on the obstacle course in basic training; the bonfire after graduation; seeing him in the training facility and feeling her heart leap; sitting across from him and laughing at a café in Paris; stepping off a commercial flight in Singapore to find him leaning against a railing, smiling at her. Random memories from the past flitted through her mind as she stared into his eyes.

"There just wasn't time," Alina finally whispered.

Damon nodded slowly. He slid his hand slowly up her arm, watching the goosebumps follow his fingers.

"There is now," he said quietly.

His eyes went back to her face in time to see something flash in her eyes before it was effectively hidden.

"Maybe," Alina whispered.

Damon's hand slid over her bare shoulder and across her collarbone before coming to rest gently along the side of her jaw. Alina's mouth went dry again and her heart started thudding.

Damon stared deep into her eyes, seemingly trying to peer straight through to her soul. It was a long moment before he sighed softly. He lifted his other hand to her face, holding her head still, and kissed her softly. It was a long, gentle kiss and when he finally lifted his head, Alina felt like he had stolen some of her soul. He smiled slowly and the twinkle that she knew so well came back into his eyes.

"Well, if we're going to hold off on this for a bit, you'll have to unwrap your legs from around me before I make an executive decision out of pure necessity," he murmured, dropping his hands back to her waist and rubbing his nose teasingly against hers.

Alina felt a blush steal into her cheeks. Damon saw it and grinned, laughter leaping into his eyes. Her eyes narrowed at the grin and Alina released her legs suddenly. As they dropped, it forced her pelvis sharply against his and Damon groaned in reaction, biting his lip. Alina smiled at him and slowly slid her hands off his shoulders, bringing them to rest on his chest.

Hawk lifted his head and looked at her, his eyes dark.

"That was just mean," he growled.

Alina's chuckle was cut short when he pulled her against his chest sharply and dropped his mouth to hers. It was several long moments before either of them could speak again, and when he finally lifted his head, her legs were wrapped around him again. He grinned, his eyes dancing.

"We seem to be right back where we started," he murmured.

121

Alina burst out laughing and disentangled her legs more slowly this time, pushing against his hard chest. Damon winked and stepped back, lifting her back onto the floor. He kept his hands on her waist for a moment and looked down at her. His eyes were suddenly serious.

"We can't avoid this forever," he told her and Alina looked up slowly.

"I know."

Damon nodded and dropped a light kiss on her forehead before letting go of her waist.

"You better go get that gash cleaned out. We have work to do," he said, turning away. "That was your boy's laptop booting up that made that beep earlier. Looks like he's back to work."

After a long shower, Alina descended the stairs again feeling more like herself. Hawk was settled in the center of the couch, with two laptops opened on the coffee table before him. He had put on a shirt and Alina was both grateful and a little disappointed. He glanced up as she came off the stairs.

"We might have a problem," he told her, sitting back.

Alina stopped behind the couch.

"Oh?"

Damon tilted his head back to look up at her.

"Your boy is poking around in things above his pay grade," he told her, then he frowned. "You didn't clean that gash very well."

"The peroxide is down here," Alina retorted. "What's he doing?"

"Go get the peroxide," Damon sat forward again, "then we'll talk."

Alina made a face at the back of his head and continued into the kitchen. She retrieved her first aid box from the pantry and returned with the box and her bottle of water. Damon watched her sink onto the rug, cross legged. She had changed into loose black yoga pants and a tank top. Her feet were bare, her hair was wet, and Damon thought she looked beautiful.

"He texted me earlier," she said, opening the sturdy tool box that was her first aid kit and pulling out a bag of cotton balls and a roll of medical tape. After a second of rummaging, she pulled out a gauze bandage.

"And?" Damon asked, getting up to grab the cotton balls and peroxide. "Come here. I'll do it," he said briskly, sitting back on the couch.

Next Exit, Pay Toll

Alina got up and sat on the couch sideways, one leg pulled up, facing him.

"I'm perfectly capable of doing it myself," she informed him and Hawk winked.

"I know you are," he agreed, holding a cotton ball over the top of the peroxide and flipping the bottle over to drench it. "You can't see what's in there. If there's glass, we need to get it out." He leaned forward and started dabbing gently on the wound. The shower had washed all the dried blood away, but it was oozing slightly and looked angry. "This isn't looking good," he said with a frown.

"It's fine," Alina said impatiently, watching him. "Once it's cleaned out and covered, it'll be fine."

Damon sat back and dropped the cotton ball onto the coffee table, pulling out a fresh one.

"So what did your boy have to say?" he prompted, wetting the new cotton ball with the peroxide.

"He's not my boy," she retorted. "He wanted to make sure I made it home without an issue."

Damon raised an eyebrow.

"Oh really?" he drawled. Alina nodded.

"He wanted to bring me himself, but I told him he was being ridiculous," she said as Damon leaned forward and went to work on her forehead again.

"Tell me what exactly happened," he said.

"Four men were paid cash up front to attack Michael and 'rough him up,'" she told him. "They were supposed to get his laptop as well. At least, that's what the one I questioned said."

"I saw that. Nicely done, by the way," Hawk murmured, concentrating on his task.

"Thank you." Alina winced slightly when he hit a raw spot. "Why did you flip all the power breakers?" she asked suddenly.

"To give you guys an advantage," he answered. Alina smiled.

"It worked," she said.

He nodded and prodded the raw spot again. She sucked in some air and winced again.

"Sorry," he said, getting up.

Alina raised her eyebrow and watched as he dropped the cotton ball onto the table and went over to the first aid box. He returned with tweezers.

"There's glass," he said shortly. Alina scowled.

"And you think *you're* going to dig it out?" she demanded, trying to grab the tweezers. "Thanks, but no. I'll go upstairs and do it myself."

Damon held the tweezers away from her, laughing.

"I can get it," he told her, leaning back as she leaned forward to grab them.

"So can I," she retorted, lunging for his hand.

The resulting struggle ended with him on his back and her sprawled on top of him, without the tweezers.

"Sweetheart, if you want to be on top, just say so," Damon murmured, his eyes dancing with laughter.

Alina grunted and pushed herself up. She stuck her tongue out at him with a glare and Damon burst into laughter, the deep, rich sound filling the room. Alina grinned reluctantly and scrambled off him, settling back down in her corner. Damon sat up, the tweezers reappearing in his hand.

"It won't hurt, I promise," he said with a grin, his eyes dancing. "No need to be scared."

Alina's eyes narrowed into slits and Damon bit back another laugh. She pressed her lips together silently and allowed him to lean forward with the tweezers.

"You know, you really need to let go of these control issues you have," he said conversationally, knowing he was playing a dangerous game but enjoying himself too much to stop. Keeping a wary eye on her right fist, he turned her head slightly so that he could see better. "You don't always have to do it yourself."

"It's what I'm used to," Alina said after a short silence. She grit her teeth as he probed into the heart of the wound with the tweezers.

"Hold out your hand," Damon murmured. Alina held her hand out, palm up. "It's what we're both used to. Maybe we need to learn to let go of some of that and give ourselves a break once in a while."

Alina didn't answer. It was taking every ounce of will power that she had just to sit still and let him dig into an open wound on her head. After what seemed like an eternity, he sat back and dropped a long piece of glass into her palm. It was an inch and a half long, and she stared at it in disbelief.

"THAT was in my head?!" she demanded.

Damon was drenching another cotton ball with peroxide.

"It's just a sliver," he answered, leaning forward again.

Alina started to feel a little light-headed and, glancing at her face, Damon saw it draining of color.

"So, what happened with the guy in the chair on the porch?" he asked, cleaning the wound gently and trying to force her mind onto something else.

"Uh..." Alina swallowed and forced herself to concentrate on what Damon was asking. "Michael detained him because he had a Special Forces tattoo."

"Special Forces tattoo?" Damon paused and looked at her. Alina was watching him steadily.

"The same one you had," she told him quietly.

Damon stared at her for a beat.

"You're sure?" he asked. Alina nodded.

"It's pretty distinctive," she murmured.

Damon finished cleaning out the wound and sat back.

"I'm surprised you remembered it," he said, slowly. "I recognized him. I'm already running checks on him to find out what he was doing there."

"Michael took him onto the porch because he was bleeding on the carpet. He went back to the kitchen to get some ice for his nose." Alina gathered the bloody cotton balls together and stood up. "That's when the SUV rolled down the street and shot him. It was a good shot. Double-tap to the chest from a moving vehicle," she added thoughtfully. "Not your average drive-by."

She turned and went into the kitchen to throw the cotton balls away. When she returned, some of the color had returned to her face.

"Did you talk to my brother in arms?" Damon asked her as she sat back on the couch. He ripped open the gauze bandage and placed it on the gash. Alina held it in place while he tore off the tape.

"Yes. He didn't say anything, but I got what I needed," she answered. "He was hired by someone he believed was in the government and he had no idea why he was attacking an ex-Marine. He also had no idea that there was anything fishy going on until he was handcuffed to a chair. I think then he realized he'd been used. I'm pretty sure he was feeling more than a little guilty." Damon taped the bandage down and sat back. His lips were pressed together grimly. "What was his name?"

"Jason Rogers." Hawk turned away and went to one of the laptops. "Your boy's running a search on the tattoo. It won't take him long to uncover it. My whole team got it after one of the raids in Afghanistan."

Alina looked at Damon's arm where the tattoo used to be. It had been the first thing to go when they were in training for The Organization. All identifying marks were lasered off. Standard operating procedure.

"What are you worried about?" Alina turned on the couch and sat back, sipping her water. "You're hedging around something. Is it the tattoo?"

"The tattoo doesn't worry me. All he'll get from that is who was in that particular team with Jason, and my name won't appear anywhere he can find it." Hawk glanced at her and turned the laptop to face her. "But if he gets access to this, it'll tell him a hell of a lot more."

125

Alina looked at Hawk and then sat forward to look at the screen. On it was a screenshot of the remote view to Michael's computer. It showed a formal request for access to Alina's classified military file.

"If he gets access to that, we're done," Hawk told her grimly.

Chapter Twelve

Alina stood next to the window in the small bedroom and stared out into the night. The room was dark and the house was silent. She had left Hawk stretched out on the couch downstairs to sleep, but Alina couldn't sleep just yet. Her mind was churning. A sudden scratching sound on the roof pulled her attention away from the window and she smiled as Raven appeared at the makeshift swinging window she had rigged up in the corner. He nudged it and the glass swung inward, allowing him to step on the sill and then hop onto his perch in the corner of the room. His black eyes gleamed as they latched onto her, standing across the room.

"Good hunting?" Alina murmured.

Raven stretched his wings and settled down on his perch, his eyes fixed on his mistress as she turned her attention back outside. The sky was starting to lighten to a pale gray in the distance and she knew she needed to rest. She was exhausted, and it was counter-productive to think when she was exhausted. Yet, she didn't move from the window.

Hawk had traced the plates of the SUV. The current registered driver of the vehicle was a man named Billy Conners. It took absolutely no time at all to pull up a rap sheet on Billy going back to his juvenile days. He was bad news all around, his criminal career spanning everything from petty theft all the way through the ranks to rape and murder. He had done hard time in Illinois for the rape and murder, and was released on good behavior two years ago. He was placed under the care of a parole officer that, at the time, was working on the grassroots campaign supporting the candidacy of Alex Ludmere for Vice President.

Alina's eyes narrowed and stared sightlessly out the window. The parole officer was dead now. He died of a heart attack a year ago, but Alina discovered that before his death, he had given a stellar report to the parole commission. As a result, Billy's parole ended three months earlier than originally scheduled. Billy then quit his job at the factory where he was working and promptly disappeared from the paper trail of employment records. The last mention of him Alina was able to find was six months ago when his name popped up on a lease for an apartment on the outskirts of DC. He was listed as occupant, but the apartment was leased to Morganston Security, the parent company listed for the lease on the SUV. A background check on the company had offered up a woman's name as the sole shareholder. Regina Cummings. Alina's gut told her that Regina was the mystery woman in the photos from London two years ago.

Viper had a name. She just needed the face.

Alina turned from the window slowly and moved toward the bed. Raven watched her as she got into bed tiredly, his eyes full of moonlight. She smiled at him and he suddenly lifted off his perch and came to rest on the headboard, next to her head. Alina reached up slowly to stroke his feathers under his beak and Raven made a low cooing noise, tilting his head to the side. She gently stroked his neck for a few moments before taking her hand away and settling against the pillows.

Damon was worried about Michael getting access to her classified file. Alina was worried about Michael himself. He had become a target and Alina was willing to bet that the moment he started asking questions about The Engineer, he became a liability to the very person who was trying to keep Viper quiet.

They were getting desperate now. They had tried to silence her three months ago and failed. They tried to silence Stephanie today and, in the process, pull Viper out of hiding and failed. They tried to take on Michael tonight, and once again failed. Not only were they getting bolder, but they were getting sloppy. The mistakes that she had been patiently waiting for were happening.

Alina's lips curved into a cold, satisfied smile. It was time to beat the grass and see what snakes emerged.

Her eyes slid shut a few moments later with her hawk ever watchful above her.

Michael carried his mug of coffee into the dining room, his bluetooth hooked into his ear, and sipped it while he stared at the map on the wall. The conference call droned in his ear and he turned to sit at the table in front of his laptop grimly. The agency was in an uproar. Anyone would think that it had been the director's house that had been stormed last night. Michael pulled up his email while he listened to two superiors argue over sharing jurisdiction with the FBI.

"Mike, what's the word on that Fed whose car blew up?" one of them asked suddenly, cutting off the other one. Michael set his mug down.

"I haven't spoken to her yet," he said. "I've contacted her department head and they're trying to locate her now. She's on vacation, so they have no itinerary."

"What about her partner?"

"Same," Michael answered shortly. "Neither are answering their cells."

"Fabulous," someone muttered. "Do we know yet who did *that*?"

"Still working on it, sir." Michael took another sip of coffee. "We're trying to get video from the parking garage."

"What about the body from last night? Do we have an ID?" another voice asked.

"Jason Rogers," Michael answered, setting his coffee down and pulling up the email from the lab. "Ex-Special Forces. We're tracing his old team now."

"Ex-Special Forces. Well, isn't that just wonderful," Michael's direct boss, Chris, drawled. "Any idea why an ex-Special Forces hero would want to break into your house, Mike?"

"Not at the moment, sir." Michael went back to his emails. "I'm still working on that one myself. I've never heard of the guy."

"Where are we on finding this missing government agent? This Viper?" Michael recognized the voice of Art Cosgrove, Chris' boss, and he repressed a groan.

"Still working on that too, sir," Michael answered, picking up his mug again.

"I think we need to consider the possibility that Viper is behind this," Art stated soberly.

Michael paused in the act of lifting the mug to his lips.

"Viper is nowhere near DC," Chris objected. "Michael would have found her by now if she was within a hundred miles of here."

"How would he know?" Art demanded. "No one knows what she looks like except her Organization, and they're not giving away diddly-squat. We've got ex-Special Forces involved in an attack on the agent assigned to find her, and we've got the FBI agent who can probably identify her missing after her car gets blown up. What more do you want?"

"What's the tie-in with Special Forces?" Chris asked.

"I don't know. That's your job," Art retorted. "But you can't tell me she doesn't know people in Special Forces. All those people know each other."

Michael felt his blood pressure starting to rise and his eye start twitching.

"Mike? What do you think?" Chris asked him directly.

"With all due respect, I think that's improbable," Michael said, sitting back in his chair and rubbing his neck. "And we don't even know that these two incidents are related."

"Why don't you think it's probable?" Art demanded condescendingly.

"First of all, the assault on my home last night involved multiple people. Everything we have on Viper says she works alone. Second, a government-trained agent doesn't hire street thugs to do their dirty work," Michael replied, unable to keep the impatience out of his voice. "Third, the bomb on the car was apparently a very simple device, not high-tech at all, and that also doesn't line up with someone of Viper's caliber. The CIA doesn't do kitchen-timer bombs. None of these have any of the earmarks of an operative trained by the CIA, and most especially, Viper. She's not sloppy and she's certainly not this visible. No one even knows she's been there until the body shows up."

"Her past methods aren't relevant here," Art snapped and Michael's eyebrows soared into his forehead. "She's up against the whole United States Government. She knows she can't win alone. I say she's hiring people to do the dirty work for her."

"You do understand we're talking about a CIA clandestine agent here, right Art?" Chris interjected. Michael took another deep breath.

"Why, exactly, does the administration think she is a security risk again?" he asked. "I was never really clear on that..."

"That's above your pay grade, gunny," was Arts' short reply. Michael grit his teeth. "I'm sending out an alert to all agencies that we believe Viper is in the DC area," Art decided.

"With all due respect, sir, I think that's a mistake," Michael said, getting out of his chair and circling the table impatiently.

"I'll note your opinion," Art told him. "Chris, you'll proceed as we discussed earlier. I'll get the word out now."

"Sir, if you..." Michael began, but was cut off.

"I said, your opinion was noted," Art snapped.

Michael grabbed the blue-tooth off his ear and disconnected, throwing it onto the table angrily. He swung around and stared at the map on the wall furiously. As soon as they put out an alert that Viper was in DC, she would vanish.

"For God's Sake, Viper, tell me where you are," he muttered, staring at the map.

His personal cell phone rang and Michael turned to glance at the number. When he saw Chris's number, he picked up the phone reluctantly.

"I'm sorry, Chris," he answered.

There was a chuckle on the other end.

"No need to apologize to me," he retorted. "I'm surprised you lasted as long as you did before hanging up on that circus."

"Viper isn't behind any of this," Michael said firmly, picking up his coffee cup again and swallowing a big gulp. "I would bet anything on that. And we have absolutely no proof that the bomb on Ms. Walker's car and the attack on my house are even related. They're basing this whole thing on a hunch!"

"You're preaching to the choir, Mike," Chris answered. "But orders are orders." He paused for a moment and Michael was silent. "Unless you know something you're not telling me?"

Michael finished his coffee, thinking about his encounter with Viper and his conversation with Ms. Walker yesterday.

"No," he lied, setting his empty mug on the table.

"Then we'll have to let Art have his way." Chris sounded disgruntled. "What are you doing about the house?"

"The kitchen window I can have replaced tomorrow," Michael said. "The bay window will have to be boarded up. It's a special order."

"It's a miracle that was all the damage done," Chris said.

Michael remembered Alina's quick thinking with the lasagna.

"Yes," he agreed thoughtfully. "I had a friend with me. She was quick on her feet."

"I heard." Chris chuckled. "Did she really use the lasagna?"

"Yes." Michael's lips twitched. "Yes, she did."

"Obviously, she's never had your lasagna," Chris said with another laugh. "Well, keep me posted on any developments, especially any that can slow down the Art Express before it derails."

"Will do," Michael agreed.

He hung up and dropped the phone onto the table, rubbing his eyes. Lord, he was tired! Grabbing his mug, Michael went back to the kitchen to pour himself another cup of coffee. Alina hadn't answered his text until after he'd fallen into a restless sleep. She told him to stop worrying about her. Michael sipped the coffee and stared out the broken window above the sink.

He didn't know what he was expecting to find if he got access to Alina's military file, but he knew she was more than what she had indicated to him. She had been too comfortable with the events the previous night, too calm, and too damned *quick*. She was diving behind that island before he even grasped what was happening. Then, there was the way she handled the two men who came through the back door. Michael had been prepared to help her if needed, but he wasn't needed. She moved so fast that he hadn't even been sure what had happened until the first man went down.

Oh yes. Alina was much more than what she seemed, and Michael wanted to know just what Dave's little sister had been up to these past couple years. As much as he hated to do it, he had to face the fact that ever since she had shown up on Friday, things had been happening. In fact, ever since she had shown up Friday, he hadn't had a single hour of peace.

Michael turned away from the window and glanced at his watch. He was probably seeing shadows where there were none, but he had to be sure he knew who Alina had become. He couldn't keep his promise to Dave if he didn't know what she was up to.

Hawk looked out the window above the sink as he filled the reservoir to the coffeemaker. The sun was just making it over the trees and he yawned, shutting off the faucet and turning to slide the reservoir back into the side of the machine. Viper didn't mess around with her coffee. She had a state-of-the-art espresso maker that did everything except wash out your mug when you were finished, and Hawk loved it. He placed his mug under the spout and pressed a button. The grinder came to life, grinding espresso beans and breaking the early morning silence in the small cabin. He glanced upwards, wondering if she was awake yet.

They were up most of the night and when she finally went to bed, he stared at the ceiling for a long time before sleep claimed him. This morning, as soon as he opened his eyes, he shot off a secure email to his old friend Paul, in London. He felt disloyal for doing it, but Hawk knew that he had to be prepared in case Viper's file got out. While the agency could protect him to a certain extent, his anonymity would be gone and with it, his job.

He had to be prepared to disappear for good.

A shadow in the trees outside caught his eye and Damon glanced out the window as he pulled his mug from under the spout. Raven swooped once around the yard before coming to land on the banister along the back porch. Damon sipped his coffee, watching the bird absently. A moment later, Alina emerged from the trees, dressed in shorts and a tank top. He watched as she stopped in the middle of the backyard and bent over at the waist, catching her breath. She had been out for a morning run in the forest.

He set his mug down and pulled out another one, setting it under the spout and hitting the button again. Alina straightened up again and jogged over to the porch, picking up a bottle of water that was sitting there.

He watched as she chugged it down, wondering how she got past him without waking him. The coffee finished brewing and Damon grabbed their cups and headed outside.

"Morning," he greeted her, handing her the coffee.

"Morning." She took the mug gratefully. "Thank you!"

Alina sipped from the steaming mug before sinking onto the step, cradling the mug in her hands. She stretched her legs out in front of her and stared across the clearing as Damon leaned against the porch support beam, sipping his coffee. They were both silent, listening to the birds chirping in the trees and absorbing the start of a new day. Raven hunkered down a few feet away on the banister, his eyes ever watchful, surveying his territory. A soft breeze stirred the damp tendrils of hair at Alina's temple and she brushed the curl back absently.

"Are you going to visit Billy Conners today?" Hawk broke the silence after a few minutes. Alina continued to stare out over the expanse of scraggly grass.

"Yes."

Hawk glanced down at her thoughtfully.

"I think I'll go check on the Fearless Feds," he said slowly.

Alina glanced at him and her eyes met his. She hadn't put the green contacts in yet and her dark eyes glinted in the shadow of the porch.

"Really?" she drawled, and Damon's lips twitched.

"Really," he replied. "I have some questions for them."

Alina's eyebrow rose and she continued to study him as she took another sip of coffee.

"You think they know something I missed?" she asked.

"It's always good to get a second set of ears on something," he said with a shrug.

Alina smiled slightly and turned her eyes back to the clearing.

"True," she agreed. She didn't believe for a minute that was why he was going to see them, but Viper knew better than to ask. If Hawk wanted her to know what he was up to, he'd tell her. "I'll be out all day. I've been summoned by Charlie. Anything you want me to tell him?"

Hawk finished his coffee and straightened up.

"Yes." He turned to go back into the house. "Tell him to keep your damn file away from the Secret Service," he said shortly over his shoulder.

Chapter Thirteen

Michael was on a ladder, nail gun in hand, attaching a sheet of plywood to the frame of the shattered bay window when Alina rounded the corner of the house. Her hair was loose around her shoulders and large sunglasses concealed most of her face. She tilted her head back and waited for the steady bangs to stop before trying to get his attention.

"Hey!" she called when the nailing ceased.

Michael glanced down, a smile creasing his tanned face when he saw her.

"Hey yourself," he replied, setting the nail gun down and backing down off the ladder. He stepped onto the grass and looked at her. "I didn't expect to see you today. I thought you were leaving."

"I am," Alina said with a smile. "I wasn't going to leave without saying goodbye." She looked at the second sheet of plywood leaning against the back of the house. "Boarding up?"

"I have to special order the windows for this one." Michael looked at the remains of the bay window. "I have people installing the other one tomorrow, but this one will be at least a week."

"What a mess." Alina turned her gaze back to him. "Do you have any new ideas on who did it?"

Michael shook his head and wiped his forehead.

"Not yet," he answered. "Come on inside. Since you're here, I have something for you."

Michael motioned for her to follow him and Alina went up the back steps and into the kitchen warily.

She didn't intend to stay long. She just wanted to see if he would let slip with any information that would give her a clue as to whether or not he thought Viper was behind the attack. Alina was willing to wager dollars to donuts that her mark had already decided Viper was in town. They were going to err on the side of caution now. Too many mistakes had been made in the past few days. They couldn't afford anymore.

Next Exit, Pay Toll

Alina stepped into the kitchen and removed her sunglasses, setting them on top of her head. Michael tossed his onto the island and flashed her a smile. Something deep inside her stirred and Alina's lips curved on their own.

"What?" she asked, her smile growing at the obvious anticipation in his face. His eyes glinted in the dappled light through the broken window above the sink and looked very green.

"Come and see," he said, turning towards the door leading into the garage.

Alina followed, dropping her keys onto the island next to his sunglasses as she went past. Her eyes dropped briefly to the burnt patch of laminate flooring at the base of the island before she followed him into the garage. She watched as he went over to his workbench.

"I was going to give this to you last night, but things got a little crazy," Michael said over his shoulder. Alina grinned.

"Ya think?" she asked in an exaggerated drawl.

Her eyes scanned the garage quickly out of habit and she noted that nothing had moved since last night. She brought her eyes back to Michael as he turned away from the work bench and came towards her, holding a brown paper-wrapped package.

"I found this a few weeks ago, buried in a box that I threw into storage right after I got back stateside from Iraq," Michael told her, handing her the package. His eyes met hers and he smiled. "I want you to have it."

Alina raised her eyebrow and tore away the brown paper. She found herself looking at a picture of Dave's unit, framed in a handmade wood frame. Her stomach lurched as she stared at the photo. They were dressed in full gear and surrounded by sand. Sun beat down on them and they all wore sunglasses, grins spread across their tanned faces. Dave was front and center, kneeling on one knee with his rifle laid across his other leg.

"My God, he looks so alive!"

The words tumbled past her lips before she could stop them. Michael moved to her side to look at the picture with her.

"That was taken a few days before his last mission," he told her.

Alina shifted her gaze from her brother's face to the man standing behind him.

"Look how young you were!" she exclaimed and Michael laughed.

"We all were," he retorted, moving away from her. "We were just kids."

Alina stared at the picture, wondering if she had ever been that young. She couldn't remember.

All she could remember was Viper.

"Yes." Alina took a deep breath and looked at him. For once, no smile hovered around her lips. "Thank you. I appreciate this more than you know."

"I know," Michael said softly.

They shared a smile and Alina wrapped the picture back up.

"Did you make the frame?" she asked as she folded the paper back around it. Michael nodded.

"Yes." He motioned around his garage. "As you probably guessed, wood-working is a hobby of mine."

Alina smiled, her mask firmly back in place when she lifted her face.

"So I see," she said. She nodded to the table top on the saw horses. "Making a table?"

"For the dining room," Michael replied, looking at the table top. "I want something more rustic, like something in a farmhouse." He grinned. "But I don't want to pay for it."

Alina walked over to the wood and ran a hand across it gently.

"I don't blame you," she murmured, glancing at him. "If you have the skills to make it yourself, you should. I'd be interested to see it when it's done. I might pay you to make one for me!" she added with a wink.

"Just pay for the wood," Michael replied with a grin. "I enjoy doing it."

He watched as she slowly walked around the table, her hand sliding along it gently. She seemed lost in thought and Michael was quiet, watching her. She suddenly stopped, removed her hand from the wood, and turned to him. Her lips were once again curved in that half-smile she used to conceal her thoughts.

"I really need to get on the road," Alina said abruptly.

"Where are you headed?" Michael asked as she walked past him toward the door.

"I have to go up into your old neck of the woods, actually," Alina lied smoothly. "I have a meeting with a client in Manhattan before I can head home."

"You said your place is in North Carolina, right?"

Michael followed her, switching out the garage light and closing the door behind them. Alina lifted her keys from his island and turned to face him.

"Yes, not far from Raleigh," she answered. "I'm thinking of moving back north, but we'll see. I've gotten used to the pace down there."

"It's a different world," Michael agreed. Alina nodded.

"I miss the delis though," she confided. Michael burst out laughing. "Seriously! There is not a decent deli to be had for miles!" Alina exclaimed, pulling her sunglasses off her head and settling them on her face.

"And cheesesteak?" Michael asked teasingly.

Alina held up a hand and shook her head.

"Let's not even discuss," she retorted.

With her hand up and her sunglasses on, Alina looked every inch the Jersey girl that she used to be and Michael felt a rush of affection roll through him. *This* was the Alina he had heard so much about from her brother all those years ago. This was the Alina he had been expecting at the restaurant...was it only two nights ago? But in an instant, the hand was lowered and the Jersey girl was gone.

"I'll definitely keep in touch. You have my email."

"Of course." Michael stepped forward and wrapped his arms around her, pulling her into a loose hug. Alina caught the whiff of a fresh scent that reminded her of the ocean before he pulled away and looked down at her with a lopsided smile. "I promised Dave I would look out for you. I plan to keep that promise," he informed her.

Alina chuckled and pulled away.

"Well, you don't have much to do," she told him, turning away. "I can take care of myself."

"So I saw last night."

The words were out before Michael could stop them and he instantly regretted them. She glanced over her shoulder, her lips smiling faintly.

"Military intelligence isn't just code on a computer screen," Alina murmured. There was a slight pause, and then her lips curved into a smile. Michael didn't have to see behind the dark shades to know that the smile didn't reach her eyes. He'd seen that smile from her before. "But I do hope we can keep in touch. I miss talking to someone who knew my brother."

"You don't talk to your folks?" Michael asked, following her to the back door. Alina shook her head.

"Not for about five years now," she answered. She didn't add that it had been her choice and it was made for their safety.

"I'm sorry." Michael opened the back door and they went down the steps into the hot humid sun.

"It is what it is." Alina turned to face him, that smile firmly in place. "It has definitely been interesting, Michael O'Reilly."

Michael laughed, squinting in the sun.

"That it has, Alina Maschik."

He watched as she flashed a grin and a wave before disappearing around the corner of the house. Michael turned to go back into the kitchen for his sunglasses feeling melancholy and not quite knowing why.

Damon stared at John calmly across the room while Stephanie watched warily from the recliner, her legs crossed and the iPad laying forgotten on her lap. John was standing with legs braced and arms crossed over his chest, facing Damon, who stood behind the couch with his hands resting lightly on the back. Stephanie could cut the testosterone in the air with a knife, and she wondered which one would start peeing on the furniture first.

"What the hell do you want my access codes for?!" John was about one octave away from a yell.

"I just told you," Damon replied patiently, his quiet voice a direct contrast to John's belligerence. "If Alina's government file is going to get released, I need to know who receives copies."

"If you guys work for our government, don't you have your own access codes?" John demanded. Damon's lips twitched.

"I wish it was that simple," he murmured. John snorted.

"*Nothing* with you two is simple," he shot back.

"John, don't be an ass," Stephanie interjected when she saw the glint of amusement leap into Damon's eyes. Laughter right now would start an all-out brawl with John and, while she suspected that was exactly what both men secretly wanted, she had no desire to start mopping blood up off the floor. "Of course he can't use his own. Damon's explained everything clearly. Just give him the access codes so he can do what he needs to do to keep Alina safe."

"If you suddenly trust him so much, give him your access codes," John retorted. Stephanie rolled her eyes.

"Mine have definitely been disabled by now," she answered calmly. "Yours are probably still active." Stephanie glanced at Damon. "Mind you, as soon as you log in, they'll have you tagged...but you knew that already."

Damon smiled faintly and nodded, his blue eyes sparkling.

"Don't you worry about me."

Stephanie grinned despite herself, sucked in by the deep blue eyes and the easy mid-western drawl.

"Oh, I don't," she informed him easily.

"Does Alina know you're doing any of this?" John asked after a long moment of silence. His pale blue eyes met Damon's deep blue ones and he chuckled reluctantly. "Of course not," he murmured. Damon glanced at his watch.

"The access codes?" he prompted, lifting his eyes up from his watch. John sighed.

"I'll type them in," he agreed ungraciously.

Damon nodded once and turned to go into the dining area. He pulled a laptop out of his bag and powered it on, keying in several passcodes to get through the security layers he had built into the unit. Once he was in, he motioned for John to come over.

"I can't believe I'm doing this," John muttered, joining him at the table.

"Don't think of it as betraying your agency's trust," Damon told him. "Think of it as justifying hers...in you."

John glared at him and silently brought up the FBI portal, entering in his codes.

"You're a bastard," he informed Damon, straightening up. Damon's only response was a short laugh before he settled down in front of the laptop. John watched him, trying to keep up with the swift key strokes before finally giving up. "Ok. What the hell are you doing?"

"I'm depositing a worm into the routing table," Damon said briefly. "It will attach to all files outgoing to the CIA and, once it's in their network, it will attach to any file with the tags I tell it to." He glanced up at John. "If Viper's file goes anywhere, this will be attached to it and I'll know exactly where it goes."

"So, essentially, you just hacked your own agency," John said. Damon grinned.

"Essentially," he agreed.

"And you used my access codes to do it," John added. Damon struggled to keep from laughing.

"Yep."

"You SON OF A ----"

"John!" Stephanie yelled from the living room and John's mouth snapped shut.

"What?!"

"Knock it off!" Stephanie appeared behind them. "Do you really think he's going to let it be traced back to your access? Really??" she demanded furiously "What the hell is wrong with you?"

John looked at Damon.

"Can they track it back to me?" he demanded.

Damon chuckled, severed the connection with the government databases, and closed the laptop.

"Spoil sport," he said to Stephanie as he stood up.

"I have to live with him for the foreseeable future," she pointed out and Damon grinned.

"Good point," he agreed. "No. They won't be able to track it anywhere. They won't even know it's there. Stop worrying." Damon slid the laptop into his bag. "You guys need anything? Food? Beer?"

"Entertainment?" Stephanie suggested with a grin. Damon smiled.

"Sorry," he replied. "All out of the entertainment package."

He swung the bag over his shoulder and turned to head out of the apartment.

"What's Alina's plan?" John called after him and Damon paused, turning around.

"I have no idea," he answered truthfully.

"Aren't you her partner in this?" John asked with a frown.

"It's not that..."

"Simple," John finished for him disgustedly.

"She's protecting me," Damon explained. "Plausible deniability. If I don't know what she's doing, I can't be held as an accomplice."

"Don't they already have you pegged as an accomplice?" Stephanie asked.

Damon shook his head slightly.

"Not yet." He grinned. "No one knows I'm here. As far as my handlers know, I'm in Peru."

"Someone must know you're here," Stephanie said with a frown.

Damon turned back to the door.

"The only people who know who and where I am, I trust with my life." He paused. "Which is a good thing, given that it *is* my life at stake here," he added thoughtfully. He glanced back at them. "And then, of course, there's you two. Don't be offended when I say that I don't trust either of you. If anything leaks out about either me or Alina, I'll know exactly who's to blame. And trust me, you won't even know I came for you until you're staring at the light at the end of the tunnel."

Hawk gave the warning as a statement of fact, his voice void of any emotion. The blue eyes, normally twinkling, were suddenly arctic and filled with deadly promise. Stephanie shivered as a chill shot down her spine and she glanced at John involuntarily. His face was unreadable.

"You just take care of Lina," John retorted, his voice even. Damon's eyes glinted briefly.

"Oh, I will," he promised softly.

And then he was gone, the door closing silently behind him. Stephanie stared at the closed door, her heart beating a hard tattoo against her chest.

"I don't *ever* want to get on the wrong side of him," she said fervently, breaking the silence as soon as her heart rate slowed. "Did you see his eyes?" she demanded.

John glanced at her, his own slightly amused. He went over to lock the door.

"He's a trained killer," John said, turning and going toward the kitchen. "What did you expect?"

"I don't know." Stephanie rubbed her arms as if she could ward off the chill that still lingered at the memory of those eyes. They had been so completely foreign from the twinkling blue eyes she was used to. "It was like Jekyll and Hyde."

She turned to follow him into the kitchen and watched as he opened the fridge and pulled out a tray filled with bags of deli meat and cheese.

"That's what you get for falling for a pair of blue eyes," John retorted, waggling his eyebrows at her before he turned from the fridge to the counter. Stephanie wrinkled her nose and pulled a bag of rolls off the top of the fridge, joining him at the counter.

"I suppose Alina must have that lurking inside her, too," she said thoughtfully after a moment. "Do you think *she's* that intense when she's working?"

John glanced at her as he pulled plates out of a cabinet.

"Intense?" he repeated, his lips twitching. "Is that what you call it?"

"I don't know *what* to call it," Stephanie frowned, "besides creepy and scary and dangerous, all at the same time."

"That's how you were supposed to feel," John told her. "It's called intimidation."

Stephanie shook her head and took out a roll, tearing it open and reaching for one of the bags of cheese.

"No. I saw something more than that," she muttered. "Something dark."

John grinned and pulled a roll out of the bag.

"Something dark?" he demanded. "Steph, we gotta get you out of here. You're starting to get weird on me. What kinds of books are you reading on that iPad, anyway?"

Stephanie handed him the cheese and pulled out a bag of ham.

"Oh, shut up," she retorted good-naturedly. "You saw it too. You know what I mean."

"I'll tell you what I saw," John said after a minute. "I saw a trained killer warning us that, whatever our past with Alina may be, we don't have any ties to him. He'll have no qualms about getting rid of us to protect her or himself. In light of that, we'd better hope and pray nothing happens to make him think we're in any way involved in anything."

"Exactly," Stephanie agreed, setting her finished sandwich on a plate and turning away from the counter.

"But nothing is going to happen to make him think that," John added. "How can it? We're locked up here until it's all over. We can't do anything. Lina made sure of that."

Stephanie paused in the act of opening a bag of potato chips. The thought crossed her mind that maybe Alina wasn't just protecting them from a traitor.

Intentionally or not, she was protecting them from Damon as well.

Chapter Fourteen

Billy Conners' apartment was on the fourteenth floor in a building where the thirteenth floor did not exist, giving him the dubious pleasure of living on what, in another building, would have been an unlucky floor. Alina never really understood the superstitious custom of skipping the number thirteen in a high-rise. Didn't the truly superstitious realize that they were still thirteen floors up? If the Boogie-Man was coming for you, she was pretty sure he would know how to count.

The SUV from last night was in the parking garage downstairs, the engine cold. Alina glanced around the empty hallway and set her ear briefly to Billy's door, listening. There was no sound on the other side. Glancing at her watch, Viper shot another look around the deserted hallway. The building didn't have a security system once you got past the front door, so there were no cameras to distract her. She turned her back to the hall, bent over the door handle, and disappeared into the apartment a moment later.

Closing the door silently behind her, Alina glanced around the living room. The seating consisted of a leather couch and a navy recliner that looked as if it had seen better days. A fifty-two-inch flat screen TV took up most of the far wall, and an entertainment center below it was packed with high-end electronics and game systems. Across the room, in front of a bay window, was a desk with a laptop and two twenty-two inch monitors. Alina looked to her left and saw the door to an eat-in kitchen and a short hallway that led to two additional doors. One was open and led to a bathroom. The other was partially closed.

Viper moved away from the door and peeked into the empty kitchen. Dishes were piled in the sink and the small kitchen table was littered with empty beer bottles and take-out containers. She grimaced slightly, imagining roaches lurking in the mess, and moved into the short hallway. She paused for just a moment outside the bedroom door, glanced into the empty bathroom, and then pushed open the bedroom door.

Billy never heard a thing. Viper moved swiftly and silently to the

143

side of the full-sized bed, looking down at her prey with detached curiosity. He was sprawled on his back on top of the covers, snoring loud enough to wake the dead. He was wearing only a pair of boxers, giving her an unimpeded view of the tattoos covering his arms and torso. Viper studied the king cobra etched across his chest thoughtfully. The work was good and she took a moment to admire it before pulling out her gun. Billy had clearly paid top dollar for all the artwork on his body. Viper smiled coldly. Now she knew what was important to him.

Casting an experienced eye over him dispassionately, she estimated that he was about five foot ten and maybe a buck ninety in weight. He was wiry, but he clearly lifted weights and his shoulders and biceps were well-defined. His stomach, however, was turning pudgy and Alina guessed the culprit to be too many beers and not enough cardio. She could see him landing maybe one hit before she could put him down. Bracing herself, Viper reached over with one hand and squeezed his nose closed, putting an abrupt end to the loud and God-awful snoring.

He came awake with a choke and a start, his eyes popped open wildly, and Alina was confronted with bloodshot brown eyes in a lean and scraggy face. An old scar ran alongside his nose, giving his face a mean twist, and his thin lips parted as he sucked in air. When he saw Viper standing over him, Billy started to sit up but never got the chance. Pressing the barrel of her gun to his temple, she pushed him back down, staring at him silently as his lips curled into a snarl. She liked him better snoring, she decided, as he swung his arm to knock the gun away. Blocking the blow easily, she cracked him on the temple with the handle of her pistol. His eyes rolled up into his head and Billy sank back down onto the bed, out cold.

Yep. Definitely prefer him unconscious.

A few minutes later, she had him off the bed and into a chair. A quick look around the room offered up a few belts, which she used to secure him to the chair tightly. Once he was trussed up, Viper sat on the edge of the bed to wait. It wasn't long before he started to moan, and a few seconds later those bloodshot eyes opened again, slowly coming into focus.

"What the..." Billy muttered, trying to move his arms.

His face contorted with anger as he realized he couldn't move, and a stream of profanity poured out of his mouth while he strained against his bonds. Viper ignored him. She took a pair of latex gloves out of her pocket, pulling them on slowly and deliberately, her eyes on her hands.

"What the hell are you doing?!" he roared. "Do you know who I am?!"

Billy had a loud, gravelly voice that echoed around the room, but when Viper lifted her eyes to his, he fell suddenly silent. While her green eyes glittered dangerously, it was the look on her face that stopped him cold. His eyes dropped abruptly to the long, serrated military knife that appeared in her hands.

"You should be more worried about who *I* am," she purred.

Billy visibly flinched at the soft tone and Viper let that sink in for a moment, watching as the wheels slowly started to churn in his head. Realization dawned on his mean face and those bloodshot eyes returned to hers suddenly. They were filled with a mix of anger, defiance and fear. It was a strange mix that Alina had seen many times before.

"You're...you're *her!*" Billy's voice cracked and he coughed. "You're the one they're all looking for."

Alina stood up and stretched languidly before slowly circling around until she was directly behind him. When he turned his head to look at her, she pressed his face forward with the flat of her blade against his cheek. Once he was facing forward again, she slowly slid the knife back until its point was pressing lightly into the soft spot behind his left ear. He kept his head perfectly still after that and, leaning forward until her lips were a scant inch away from his ear, she whispered,

"Say my name."

Viper watched dispassionately as Billy swallowed and beads of sweat started to form on his upper lip. He kept his lips pressed together, silent, and she gently increased the pressure on the knife-tip, watching the pulse beneath his Adam's apple start to beat rapidly. He was fighting to remain calm, but she could almost smell the fear starting to build up. She slid the tip of the knife up behind his ear, the razor sharp blade leaving a path of red in its wake. Billy gasped and swallowed again. Alina continued until her blade was resting on the top of his ear. She didn't say a word when she started to apply pressure. The blade began to slice easily through his ear.

"*Viper!!*" Billy choked out, panic edging his voice.

Alina immediately lessened the pressure of the blade and he gasped in relief. Sweat started trickling down his temple and she straightened up, remaining behind him and removing her knife from his ear.

"Do you know why they call me that?" she asked conversationally, her voice an icicle that slid over him. She watched as he shivered slightly.

"Some kind of codename," Billy muttered.

"Ah, but every codename has an origin," Viper told him softly. "Do you know what a Viper is?"

"It's a car," Billy sneered, regaining his courage now that the knife was no longer touching him.

The words had barely left his mouth when the knife slid skillfully into his right bicep above a tribal tattoo. He cried out in shock and tried to jerk his arm against the restraints again, succeeding only in driving the knife in deeper. Viper angled it slightly and it started to slide down under the tattoo.

"Have you ever seen a tattoo skinned?" she asked almost pleasantly. "I've heard it makes a remarkable decoration...almost like leather."

"It's a snake! It's a snake!" Billy cried out, watching as blood started to pour down his arm.

The knife was removed and she draped her arm around his shoulders, bringing her lips close to his bleeding ear.

"That's right," she said quietly. "It's a snake. It kills its prey so quickly that it doesn't even know it's being attacked. Most people never even see me."

Viper straightened up and patted his right shoulder, just above the deep slice in his arm. Blood gushed out in response and Billy flinched. Sweat was pouring freely down his face now and Alina pursed her lips, staring down at the back of his head.

"So you see, you're really very lucky that I'm taking the time to have a nice little chat with you," she told him, her voice cold and steady. "You should feel honored."

Billy was silent and Viper studied him silently. He was still a little too self-restrained for her liking. She walked around slowly to stand in front of him, taking her time and trailing the flat of her blade around his shoulder and across his collarbone as she went. She rested the tip of the knife above the cobra's head on his chest and stared down at him for a long, silent moment.

"But you know all about snakes, don't you?" she murmured.

Billy was silent, shooting daggers out of his eyes. The anger was still prominent over the fear. Alina crouched before him and slowly began to trace the tattoo on his chest with the knife, outlining it with his blood. The skinned tattoo remark hung heavily in the air as she carefully sliced around the cobra slowly.

"Funny. A big, tough man like you, with a big ol' snake tattooed across your chest, and here you're all trussed up like a Thanksgiving turkey," she said mockingly.

Billy spit at her and it landed on her cheek.

Viper didn't hesitate. She rose up and slammed her forehead into his face before he had time to blink. His nose crunched loudly and he howled in pain as blood started pouring from his broken nose. His howl was cut short when Viper whipped behind him again, her arm around his neck, forcing his head back while her knife pressed against his carotid artery. He stared up at her, his eyes wild, fear edging out the anger. Viper kept his head extended back at an odd angle and moved her knife, inserting the tip into the hollow at the base of his throat.

"If you're having problems breathing now, I can make another hole if you like," she offered, watching as the blood poured freely from his nose. "I've seen them do it on TV."

"No!" Billy gasped out, too afraid to shake his head. Viper smiled slowly, her eyes cold.

"No...what?" she whispered.

"No, *Viper!* Please," his voice was hoarse now with fear, "what do you want?"

Viper stopped the pressure on the knife and blood started seeping around it, trickling down to his chest. She considered him silently for a long moment, watching as he tried to gasp for air through his mouth without pressing against the knife-tip inserted in his throat.

"Who do you work for?" she asked after he was finally able to get some breaths in around the knife.

"Regina Cummings," Billy rasped out.

"And why is she interested in me?" Viper asked softly.

Billy took too long to answer and she pressed gently on the knife, inserting it deeper into his throat. He made a panicked noise and she stopped.

"I don't know!" he gasped, his eyes wide and staring up at her. "For real, I don't know. She never told me. All she ever said was that you knew too much. That's it."

"And the hit last night? Why did she do that?"

"She didn't do the hit," Billy told her quickly. "We arranged for the guys to go in and rough up the Marine and get his laptop, but she didn't know about the hit on the SEAL."

Viper raised an eyebrow slightly.

"Then who ordered that?" she asked.

"Marty." Billy was trying to breathe and talk at the same time, but found that it was pressing the knife in further. He resorted to taking short breaths and inserting words in between, his eyes filled with terror now. "Marty...he said...Frankie...Solitto...ordered...it..."

"Who pulled the trigger?" Viper asked, momentarily diverted by Frankie's name.

"One...of...Solitto's...trigger...men..." Billy was trying hard not to move and add pressure on the knife.

"Why did your boss want to attack the Marine?" Alina went back to her main line of questioning.

"She...said...he...was getting...too...nosy..."

Billy paused, trying to take a couple breaths. Blood from his nose was pouring over his face and getting into his mouth, making breathing even harder. Viper didn't move or relieve the pressure of the knife on his throat.

"Something...about...engineers...she wanted...to know what...was on his...laptop." Billy paused again and Viper watched him struggle coldly. "She...wanted...to teach...him...lesson..."

Billy ran out of air and started to choke on his blood. Viper pulled the knife out and let go of his head, stepping back as it fell forward and he gasped for air. The gasp for air turned into a coughing fit and she stood behind him silently, waiting for him to finish coughing and regain his breath.

"Why did she want to teach him a lesson?" she asked softly once he had finished coughing and spitting out blood. Billy shook his head.

"I don't know, man," he confessed. "She's kind of crazy. With men, you know?"

Viper walked around to stand in front of him and Billy lifted his bloody face to look at her. He looked defeated. Blood covered most of his body, mixing with sweat, and his eyes were still filled with fear. He eyed the bloody knife in her gloved hands warily.

"She gets real jealous. I figured the Marine was seeing someone else and Reggie didn't like it."

Viper stared down at him silently, studying him. The fear had taken over completely now and she knew he was incapable of lying at this point.

"You said she's crazy. What kind of crazy?"

Billy tried to shrug but grimaced with pain and stopped mid-shrug.

"She had some kind of thing for a lawyer once," he told her. "He was married. She had me go take care of the wife." A look of pleasure crossed Billy's face and Viper's eyes narrowed. She knew she wasn't going to like what came next. "Best piece of ass I ever had, aside from the bitch that got me locked up for ten years. She screamed so loud I had to cut her throat before I was done." Billy tried to grin through the blood on his face. "Didn't matter, though. I still finished."

He glanced up at her slyly, hoping for some flicker of emotion in Viper's face. He was disappointed when there was none. This woman wasn't a woman at all. She was just a killer.

"Turned out the husband never even looked twice at Reggie," Billy continued. "She made it all up in her head."

Viper filed the information away and went back to her main interest.

"And what do you know about engineers?" she asked, watching him through cold, emotionless eyes.

Billy stared at her. She saw the moment of indecision in his eyes and watched as his fear of her won the inner battle.

"I know that she arranged entry into the country for one a few months ago." Billy was talking quietly now, almost as if he was afraid to say the words out loud. "She brought him in to take care of clean-up for an issue up in New Jersey. She said he was supposed to have taken care of you then."

"What was he cleaning up?"

"I don't know." Billy shook his head slowly. "I heard rumors there was a terrorist up there planning something, but I don't know details. I just know that she brought in this engineer to clean up a mess."

Viper was silent, watching him. When she flipped the knife skillfully in her hand, Billy gasped.

"Ok! Ok!" he exclaimed hurriedly. "In the back of the closet, there's a panel cut into the wall. I keep an external hard-drive there with files and information."

Viper raised an eyebrow, stilling her knife.

"Do you now?" she drawled. "Information on what?"

"Regina. Insurance...just in case, you know. Everything about the Engineer and the terrorist is on there. Dates, memos, flight information, payments, account numbers...it's all there."

Viper studied him silently for a long moment. The only sound in the room was the sound of his ragged wheezing as he stared at her. She believed him. Billy let out a sigh of relief as she calmly leaned down and wiped her knife clean on his bedspread.

"How do you know Marty?" she asked, tilting her head to look at him curiously.

"We work together from time to time on different things," Billy answered, his head drooping.

He was starting to fade and his face was taking on a grayish pallor. Viper inserted the knife back into her sheath on her ankle and straightened up. Billy watched as she pulled her .45 from her back holster. His eyes widened in alarm again.

"Just one more question before I'm finished." Viper raised the gun and aimed it at his forehead. "How did Regina find out where I was three months ago?"

Billy stared at her hopelessly through all the blood.

"She's the Vice President's cousin," he said tiredly. "She can find out anything."

Damon lowered the binoculars and glanced at his watch. Alex

Ludmere was attending a fund-raising dinner at a hotel, and Damon was waiting for him to leave. It was easy enough to determine which exit the Vice President would use simply by watching the Secret Service detail. The dinner would be wrapping up soon, and then Alex would emerge out the side door into the alleyway. Hawk stifled a yawn and lifted the binoculars again. A black SUV pulled into the alley and he watched as the advance detail came out the side door, securing the alley ahead of the Vice President. A few minutes later, Ludmere emerged. Damon watched as he paused outside the door and turned to look behind him. A tall, dark-haired woman followed and Damon adjusted the binoculars to zoom in on her face.

Her dark hair was pulled up into a chignon at the back of her head and she was dressed in a wine-colored suit. Damon clicked the button on the side of his binoculars to snap a picture. She had just pressed a button on her cell phone and long red nails closed around the phone, holding it tightly. He snapped another picture as Alex tilted his head towards her to listen to what she was saying. Whatever he heard, it clearly did not please him. He frowned ferociously before disappearing into the back of the SUV. The woman followed him, unaware of the series of pictures being snapped and saved onto an SD card.

Damon lowered the binoculars with a frown as the SUV started to move out of the alleyway. Given the height and build of the woman, he had no doubt that she was the woman in the grainy pictures from London two years before. He also suspected that she was the mysterious Regina Cummings, the sole shareholder of the security firm that leased the SUV Billy Conners drove last night. Those facts alone made him dislike her, but there was something else. Damon's frown grew as he dropped the binoculars into his cargo short's pocket and departed from his watching post.

He *knew* her. Everything was different; the name, the clothes, even the hair was wrong. He couldn't place where he knew her from, or how, but Hawk was sure that he knew Regina Cummings.

"You're sure about this?" the man asked, his dark eyes probing Alina's as if he could read her soul.

If there was any one man on this forsaken globe that Alina feared, it very well could be this man. This was a man who knew so many secrets, so many classified missions, so many scandals that he was virtually untouchable. In theory, he reported to the Director of the CIA. In reality, he answered to no one. He knew something about everyone, everything, and everywhere, and that magnitude of knowledge placed him in a class all his own. He was intimidating. He was ruthless. He was her boss.

"Absolutely." Alina nodded once, her gaze firm.

Charlie, as they all called him, watched her quietly for a moment, his face unreadable.

"It's a huge risk," he finally said, "even for you."

Alina smiled slightly and turned her head to look out the window of the hotel room where they were meeting. She looked out over the city thoughtfully. The sun was setting, bathing the city in a beautiful, purple hue and casting pale pink and orange light between the tops of the buildings. It was probably the only time of day that she thought the city looked pretty.

"You told me once that it was my job to take risks," she murmured, her eyes dropping to the city far below. She watched the traffic on the street absently.

"Calculated risks, yes," Charlie retorted.

Alina turned her head and he encountered a flash of amused ruthlessness in her glance.

"Oh, trust me," she assured him. "This is far from uncalculated."

"Of course," Charlie said with a slight smile. "I should have known," he added, walking over to stand beside her at the window. He only stood a few inches taller than her, but she felt dwarfed by him. "You never do anything without evaluating it first. You have a plan for everything. You would be perfect for running ops."

Alina was surprised into a quick laugh.

"Not for me, thanks," she replied, a grimace passing fleetingly across her face. "I'm better suited to field work."

"Perhaps," Charlie answered thoughtfully.

Alina was left to wonder at the meaning of that comment as he turned his attention, with her, out the window. The purple hue over the city was already fading and gray shadows were lengthening between the buildings and into the streets below. In another half hour, the light would be gone completely. Street lights were already on, insignificant now, but holding promise of light for the coming darkness.

"This is my favorite time of day," Charlie told her suddenly. Alina glanced at him under her lashes. His eyes were fixed out over the city and his hands were in his suit pants pockets. He was relaxed. "The light's fading. All the creatures of the day are settling down and this is when the night begins to stir. This is when all the action starts."

Alina stared at the pink, orange and purple streaked sky over the city in the distance. She could almost feel the sun breathing its last sigh over the city. She stood in silence with Charlie, both staring out the window at different things. He stared downward, into the streets, where the shadows grew darker and the night creatures began to stir and spill out into the city. Alina stared up at the fading light in the sky, watching the promise and hope of a new day fade as it came to a close. She didn't need to look at the shadows below. She lived in them.

"You've had the agency's support throughout this whole operation." Charlie finally spoke again, turning away from the window as the last bit of light left the sky and darkness fell to cloak the city.

"I appreciate what you did." Alina turned away from the window and followed him across the sitting area of the hotel suite. "I didn't expect it. When Hawk told me that you told the other agencies to pound sand, I was surprised."

Charlie flashed her a quick grin.

"When I can do so, I *will* protect my agents," he said humorously. "The fact is, this administration has a serious problem on its hands. It has a traitor. Worse, it doesn't even know it. I need you to take care of it. I'll protect you as much as I can so you can do your job."

Alina raised an eyebrow.

"You really think they don't know?" she demanded. Charlie shrugged.

"If they do, we have an even bigger problem," he replied obscurely. "I'll arrange what you requested." Charlie picked up his suit jacket from the back of a chair and put it on. "I don't know that I'm happy about it, but I'll trust you on this. God knows you've never let me down before."

"Never?" Alina prompted, her lips twisting humorlessly despite herself. Charlie looked her right in the eye.

"Never," he reiterated. "Cairo was a success, as far as *my* objective was concerned."

Alina stared back at him steadily as the meaning behind his words sunk in.

"You mean..."

"It was a success," Charlie said firmly and Alina sucked in a deep breath.

"One day, I hope you'll explain that remark," she said grimly and Charlie smiled.

"One day," he agreed, heading toward the door. He paused at the door and glanced back. "You know how to reach me if you need to."

Alina nodded. She would wait half an hour before leaving herself, and then she would be on her own. There would be no more contact between her and the agency until this was over, barring a national security emergency. They stared at each other for a long moment and Charlie smiled again.

"Happy hunting," he murmured.

Alina smiled slowly, her eyes glinting dangerously, and nodded. Charlie returned the nod and then was gone, closing the door softly behind him.

Chapter Fifteen

"This is the second one, tied to a chair and shot. You starting an epidemic, Mike?"

Michael raised an eyebrow and grasped Blake Hanover's hand in a firm greeting. When Blake had shown up at Michael's house last night with the Feds, Michael had been relieved. An old friend from the Corps, and one of Michael's monthly poker buddies, he was the FBI agent working with him on the parking garage debacle yesterday. When his house was raided last night, Blake had appeared again as the Agent in Charge. Working with Blake meant that any information he came across would be shared, and Blake hadn't disappointed. Michael had just finished eating dinner when Blake called and told him to meet him at a high-rise just outside Georgetown.

"Care to explain?" Michael replied, glancing around at the bevy of activity in the apartment living room. Blake shrugged.

"Come and see for yourself," he said, motioning for Michael to follow him through the living room and down a short hall. "A traffic camera on the next block picked up the SUV leaving your neighborhood last night and we ran the plates. The vehicle was registered to our boy in the chair here. We showed up the same time the police did. They were responding to a call from the building manager."

Blake led Michael into the bedroom and he glanced around, taking in the careless disorder of an untidy man. The shades on the window were drawn and there didn't appear to be anything out of place. It wasn't a robbery, then. Blake motioned to the main attraction.

Michael stared down at the body tied to the chair with what appeared to be his own leather belts in disbelief. The man was dressed only in a pair of boxer shorts, and dried blood covered most of his body. He was covered in tattoos, some of which, absurdly, looked as if they had begun to be removed with a blade. Michael glanced at Blake and encountered an unusually solemn look from his old friend. With a frown, Michael crouched down to examine the body. A bullet hole was perfectly centered in his forehead and the back of his head had a hole the size of a grapefruit, leaving no doubt as to the cause of death. Michael stared at the king cobra tattooed across his chest and grimaced. Someone had traced around most of it with something very sharp, leaving an eerie outline of dried blood around the snake.

"Have you found the bullet yet?" Michael asked after staring at the body for a few moments in silence.

"We dug it out of the wall over there." Blake nodded to the wall to the side of the door. "It looks to be either a .40 or a .45. I'm sure you've noticed the back of his head is missing."

Michael nodded and stood up, turning to look at Blake.

"And the ones from my place?" he asked.

Blake met his look steadily.

"They were .45's." he answered. "The lab will tell us if this was fired from the same gun, but my bet is that it's the same shooter. And there's more."

"There always is," Michael retorted. "Tell me."

"The bullets from those cameras your boy pulled down from the parking garage?" Blake said, nodding. "They're .45's."

Michael stared at him.

"So, we've got the same shooter in all three places?" he demanded.

Blake shrugged and shook his head.

"Can't say for sure until we compare them all, but it sure looks like it." He looked at Michael, concern in his eyes. "If we do, you need to watch your back. Someone is trying to send you a very clear message."

Michael ran a hand through his short hair.

"Why?" he muttered.

Blake leaned against the dresser and crossed his arms over his chest.

"Have you been poking around in anything lately that might piss anyone off?" he asked. Michael let out a short laugh.

"Would you like a list?"

Blake grinned, but it was short-lived.

"I got an urgent memo about an hour ago," he said slowly. "It said that the rogue operative that everyone's looking for, from the CIA, is believed to be in DC. You wouldn't happen to be involved in that, would you?"

Michael looked up and his eyes met Blake's.

"I don't know what you're talking about," he said, his gaze steady. "I didn't get the memo yet."

Blake stared at him for a moment, then nodded slowly.

"That's what I thought," he said. "Read it. You'll enjoy the wording. It's about as vague and arbitrary as you can get."

Michael shared a reluctant grin with his old friend and then sighed.

"What a mess." Michael shook his head and glanced down at the body again. "What was his name?"

"Billy." Blake turned to lead Michael out of the room and nodded to the medical examiner. "Billy Conners. He had a rap sheet longer than...well, it's long."

Blake and Michael stepped out of the way as the medical examiner's assistant rolled a gurney down the short hallway. They watched it go by in silence before continuing to the living room.

"Any ideas who he was working for these days?" Michael asked. Blake shrugged.

"Not yet." He motioned to the computer electronics that were being boxed up. "We'll find out. His computer should tell us something."

"Do you think he knew the shooter?"

"There was no obvious signs of forced entry," Blake answered. "It's possible."

Michael nodded and took one last glance around before turning toward the door reluctantly.

"Thank you for calling me," he said, walking with Blake to the door.

"Hey, I told you I'd keep you informed," Blake answered with a grin. "I'm hoping it'll encourage you to go easy on me in the next poker game."

Michael chuckled and held out his hand again.

"Not a chance," he retorted good-naturedly. "Let me know what you find out about the bullet, will you?"

"Sure." Blake shook his hand firmly and held it for a moment. "Be careful, Mike. I don't like the feelings my gut's throwing up. I don't think this is finished yet."

"Solitto?" Hawk repeated, frowning. Alina nodded, not lifting her eyes from the sirloin steak that was laying on a grate over the fire. Damon sipped his beer and watched as she flipped the steak carefully. "Why does that mobster keep popping up? What part does *he* have in all of this?"

"Well, that may be my fault," Alina admitted, glancing at him ruefully. "I went to see him a few days ago."

Damon raised an eyebrow and stared at her.

"I'm sure you had your reasons," he murmured.

Alina smiled slightly and turned her attention back to their dinner. Damon had joined her at the fire in the clearing when he returned, bouncing into the clearing in a new Land Rover. The Jeep was gone, wiped down and abandoned after the explosion in the parking garage. Damon watched her in silence for a moment before giving in to his curiosity.

"Ok. Tell me," he said. "Why did you go see Solitto?"

"Are you sure you want to know?" she asked. Hawk shook his head.

"I'm pretty sure I *don't* want to know," he retorted. "Tell me anyway."

Alina flipped the steak once more and sat back from the fire.

"Remember I told you one of his family is one of Michael's informants?" she asked him, picking up a glass of wine she had set on a flat rock nearby. She sipped it appreciatively and watched as Damon nodded. "Well, I've been keeping an eye on him. He's essentially harmless, but he was getting his information about me from somewhere. I went up to Frankie's to see who was talking."

"And what did you find out?" Damon asked. Alina shrugged.

"Frankie wasn't intentionally feeding the Feds information about me." Alina set her glass down. "In fact, he had already taken care of the person he believed was the leak before I showed up to chat."

"That's inconvenient," Damon murmured. Alina nodded.

"That's what I told Solitto, in not so many words," she agreed.

Damon blinked, his lips starting to twitch.

"Wait." He set his beer down and leaned forward. "Let me make sure I'm understanding this right." The flames from the fire cast shadows over his face, but even in the dancing firelight Alina could see that Hawk's eyes were alight with laughter. "You went into Solitto's house and told him to take care of his leak?"

Alina shrugged and nodded.

"Pretty much," she answered, picking up her glass of wine again and sipping it. Hawk burst into laughter.

"You're something else, Viper," he chortled. "You really are. How did Frankie take it?"

"Quite well, actually," Alina replied. "He already knew he had a leak to the Feds. I was just the catalyst he needed to do something about it. You know, the more I talk to Frankie, the more I like him," she added thoughtfully. "I think I'll keep him on my list of assets."

"That's a dangerous game," Damon warned, his shoulders still shaking with laughter. "God, I wish I could have seen his face."

"He sends you his regards," Alina told him with a wink. "He also reiterated his offer of employment for both of us."

"Great! If we live through this debacle you've pulled me into, I may consider it," Damon said with a laugh. "Working for the mob would be significantly safer!"

"Don't go blaming me for this mess," Alina shot back, leaning forward to check the steak. "*My* debacles are much more sophisticated than this one!"

She picked up a plate from the grass nearby and transferred the steak onto it, standing up with the plate and her glass of wine. Damon followed and they walked back to the cabin slowly.

"So, if Solitto ordered the hit on Jason, it's safe to assume that he found out Jason was the leak." The laughter was gone from Damon's voice now. "How the hell did Jason end up on Solitto's payroll?"

"We can add that to our growing list of hows and whys," Alina answered. "It's getting longer and longer."

"Means we're getting somewhere," Damon murmured. Alina nodded.

"We're definitely hitting some nerves," she agreed.

Damon was silent as they entered the kitchen. He smiled when he saw the table. Two plates were already set out and a bowl of salad was in the center. He watched as Alina set the steak and her wine on the table before turning to the oven. She pulled out two baked potatoes and transferred them onto the plates on the table.

"You've been busy."

Damon sat down gratefully and the smell of potato and steak filled his nostrils. His stomach growled in reaction. Alina smiled slightly and sat opposite him. He was already cutting the large steak in half.

"I think better when my hands are busy," she said. "Besides, I haven't had steak cooked over a fire in years."

Damon glanced up from the steak and his eyes met hers warmly.

"No one I know makes it like you," he told her. Alina smiled slightly and lifted her plate so he could slide her half of the steak onto it. It was perfect, medium-rare on the inside and seared on the outside. "The last time I had this was at that bonfire on the beach after boot camp."

"I'm surprised you remember it," Alina retorted with a grin. "Were any of us sober that night?"

"I was," Damon said after swallowing a piece of meat. "You weren't."

Alina was silent as she cut into her steak. She remembered everything from that last night with Damon. She had stored it all away, thinking she would never see him again.

"I went and saw our suspect earlier," Damon said after a few moments of silence. Alina glanced up sharply.

"And?"

"He was leaving a dinner." Damon missed the searching glance, intent on his steak. "This is amazing," he mumbled. "You need to do this for me regularly. We can set up a yearly date for fire-grilled steak."

"Just name the beach and I'll be there."

Damon looked up, his eyes glinting.

"Oh, I'll hold you to that," he assured her.

"You were saying?" Alina prompted, changing the subject back.

"He had Regina Cummings with him," Damon said, reaching for his beer.

Alina paused in cutting her potato and looked at him.

"Really?" she asked. Damon nodded.

"I got pictures," he added, setting his beer down. "I know her."

Alina raised an eyebrow.

"How is that?"

"I don't know," he answered thoughtfully. "It will come to me. I know I know her."

"Could you just remember seeing her during the election? Or in the background on TV?" Alina asked, setting down her knife and fork and picking up her wine glass. Damon shook his head.

"No. I've spoken to her," he said decisively. "I know her personally."

Alina sipped her wine and looked at him consideringly.

"According to Billy Conners, she's Ludmere's cousin," she said slowly.

Damon looked up quickly.

"Well, that explains a lot," he said. "It explains her constant presence, for one."

Before Alina could answer, her laptop dinged from the living room. She frowned and set her glass down, getting up from the table.

"Excuse me," she said, turning to leave the kitchen. "I have to check that."

She headed down the short hallway to the living room and Damon continued eating, setting Regina out of his mind. He would remember how he knew her when he stopped trying to force the memory. A minute later, he heard Alina speaking in a low voice from the living room and knew that she was on a video chat. As much as he wanted to go in and see who she was talking to, Hawk stayed put and finished his late dinner. Viper had her sources, just as he had his, and they were confidential. She respected his privacy, and so he had to respect hers. All the same, every minute or so his eyes wandered down the hallway. She was on the couch, the laptop on her lap, dinner completely forgotten for the moment.

Damon finished eating and glanced down the hallway yet again. Viper was still speaking in a low voice. He looked at her half-eaten dinner and got up, picking up his empty plate and carrying it over to the dishwasher. After putting it away, he went back to pick up her plate and wine glass and carried it out to the living room. He set the plate beside her with a smile and put the wine glass on the coffee table. He noticed her gun then, in pieces on the table. She had been cleaning it and it was laying on a cloth, waiting to be put back together.

"Thanks." Alina glanced up at him with a smile.

Damon nodded and headed for the stairs to go take a shower. He tried to ignore the sudden feeling of belonging that washed over him. This whole working with a partner thing was getting more and more complicated. Hawk wasn't sure that he liked it.

Damon turned off the old-fashioned knobs to the shower and pulled the shower curtain back. He started at the sight of Alina perched on the edge of the sink.

"Boot camp," she told him, holding out a towel as he stepped out of the old, claw-footed tub. Damon took the towel and wrapped it around his waist quickly.

"Was hell, but at least you weren't there whenever I opened the shower curtain," he answered good-naturedly. Alina grinned, momentarily diverted.

"I bet you wished I was, though," she retorted swiftly. "I'm better looking than some of the guys in that class."

Damon grinned and pushed her legs to the side so that he could stand in front of the sink.

"Infinitely," he agreed, opening the old medicine cabinet hanging on the wall and pulling out his razor. He glanced at her, his blue eyes dancing. "If you showed up in our showers, I wouldn't have made it past the first week," he added with a wink.

Alina's lips curved into a responding smile.

"Me either," she admitted.

Damon smiled slowly and leaned toward her. Alina felt the moist heat coming off his body as the water from the shower evaporated from his skin. She got a big whiff of his shower gel before his lips settled warmly on hers. The action just seemed so natural, so right, and she was lifting her arms to his shoulders when she remembered why she was there. Pulling her lips from his, she pushed him away gently.

"Start that and we won't stop," she told him, slightly breathless.

His dark eyes were unreadable as he smiled slightly and went back to his razor.

"Then you'd better start taking my mind off of *that*," he retorted. He missed Alina's grin.

"Regina Cummings."

"Well, that will do it," he muttered, spreading shaving cream on his jaw. Alina shifted away slightly. "What about her?"

"You know her from boot camp," she told him.

Hawk paused in the act of lifting the razor to his face. His startled gaze met hers.

"Yes!" he exclaimed, staring at her. "You broke her leg!"

"Yes," she agreed with a nod. "Well, I broke Lani Cunningham's leg, to be exact," she qualified.

Damon's chest was gleaming with droplets of water and Alina tucked her hands under her legs on the counter to prevent herself from reaching out to smooth them away.

"Didn't she get discharged after that?" he asked, turning his attention to the shadow growing in on his face.

"Yes." Alina watched him, her mind darting back in time. "She just disappeared from training," she murmured. "I'm almost ashamed to say it, but I never thought of her again."

"I suppose her cousin had something to do with her discharge," Damon commented, turning on the faucet and rinsing his razor under the water before going back to his jaw.

"Yep." Alina turned her attention to the wall opposite, her gaze thoughtful. "Did we know at the time that she had rich relatives in politics?"

"I doubt it," Damon murmured. "I don't think we knew much about anyone. Didn't you break her leg in a training exercise?"

"It was a defense exercise," Alina answered with a nod, the memory coming back. She frowned slightly. "At the time, I just wanted to get through the round so I could move on to a more challenging opponent. She wasn't much of a fighter. She had the basics down, but she wasn't a very *smart* fighter."

Alina paused and her frown deepened. Damon glanced at her. Her eyes were fixed on the wall opposite her, staring at something he couldn't see or remember.

"We got into the ring and she went kind of crazy," Alina said slowly. "I put her down almost immediately, but then she snuck an attack from behind after the instructor called match."

Alina remembered walking to the side of the padded ring, thinking she was finished, when hands suddenly tried to close around her throat. She had reacted on pure instinct, dropping and spinning around, sweeping her leg to take the legs out from under her opponent. Lani, as she was known then, had gone down heavily with a cry and Alina felt the crack when her ankle made contact with Lani's shin. She remembered it now, a long forgotten memory, and grimaced slightly.

"I broke her tibia." Alina's gaze came back into focus and she glanced at Damon to find him watching her, his eyes hooded. "The medic told me later that it was already cracked, probably from the drills."

"I remember now," Hawk said slowly. "You were walking to the side of the ring. You were done." Alina nodded and Damon went back to his face, turning his attention to the other side. "What reminded you of all this?" he asked, focusing his attention on his jaw. "You haven't even seen the pictures yet."

"My contact in Egypt," Alina told him. "That's who I was talking to on the laptop. She dug it up. As soon as she said the name, Lani Cunningham, I remembered."

Damon rinsed his razor, turning off the water, and Alina handed him another towel. He took it with a nod of thanks, wiping his face.

"Why do I feel like there's something more?" he asked her, lowering the towel. His blue eyes met hers and Alina smiled slightly.

"Because you know you haven't asked the one question that you should have asked right away," she retorted.

Hawk grinned and tossed the towel aside, leaning his hip against the vanity and staring at her.

"Why did she change her name?" he asked.

Alina's lips curved into a grin and she couldn't stop herself from leaning forward and pressing a soft kiss on his smooth jaw.

"Because the Cunningham side of the family has a documented history of mental illness, drug addiction, and violence," Viper whispered a moment later.

She leaned back and brown eyes met blue. Damon thought again how much he preferred her deep brown eyes over the strange, green contacts. When she spoke again, those brown eyes glinted slightly.

"The future Vice President of the United States couldn't be associated with that part of the family, now could he?"

Chapter Sixteen

"What do you mean, he's *dead*?!" Regina stalked across the patio angrily, her cell phone pressed against her ear. "What happened?"

She stopped just outside the pool of light cast from the outside spotlights and stared at the blooms of a huge potted Delphinium, listening intently to the voice on the phone. As the voice went on, her grip on the phone tightened.

"Well, where's the body?" she finally demanded, keeping her voice pitched low so that she wouldn't be overheard. The answer didn't please her and she reached out and swatted the tall spike of blue flowers before her ruthlessly. "What the hell are *they* doing with it?!" she exclaimed, swinging around and stalking across the long patio again.

Regina stomped past potted plants and rattan patio furniture without giving them a glance, her eyes narrowed into slits, until she reached the other side of the patio. She came to a stop and glared at her feet while she listened to the report in her ear.

"What about his laptop? Where's that?" she demanded after a few moments. The answer made her let loose with a stream of profanity. "Everything? They took everything?"

"Reggie?"

A tall man stepped outside, glancing around. Regina swung around and waved, pasting a smile on her face. She motioned to the phone apologetically.

"Look, I can't talk now," Regina hissed into the phone. "Find out the cause of death and call me later. And find out why the damn Feds have *everything*!" she added harshly before pressing end on her phone.

"Everything ok?"

Alex moved further onto the patio toward her and Regina smiled brightly, striding forward into the light to meet him.

"Fine," she answered calmly. "Something cropped up at the security firm, that's all. Nothing to be worried about."

Alex looked down at her and nodded.

"Good," he said. "I don't think I can take any more surprises today."

Regina smiled reassuringly at him and tucked her hand into his arm, turning him back toward the house.

"No surprises here," she replied soothingly. "Let's have a cocktail, and then I'm going to head home. I'm just exhausted tonight."

Alex patted her hand.

"It *has* been a long day," he agreed.

Regina nodded and they stepped off the patio and into the house. Neither of them noticed the Secret Service agent that had become a fixture in their vicinity two years before. He faded back into the night silently once they were both safely inside and pulled out his phone.

Michael sipped his scotch and stared at the map on the wall of his dining room broodingly. It was almost two in the morning and he couldn't sleep. He was still trying to wrap his mind around the bizarre events of the past two days. Was it really only two days? It seemed unreal that so much could have happened in one short weekend. It was even more unreal that he couldn't seem to make heads or tails out of any of it. All he knew for certain was that out there, somewhere, was Viper.

And, somehow, everything hinged on her.

A week ago, he would have been convinced that she was somehow responsible for all the events of the past two days. He would have thought, as Blake did, that it was Viper who had shot two men and tried to blow up a Federal Agent. He would have wondered if she was coming after him next.

Now, as he stared at the map with all the red pins dotted over it, Michael was just as sure that she wasn't directly responsible for any of it. Given the massive amount of information he had discovered in the past few days regarding the assassin called The Engineer, coupled with Ms. Walker's remarks, Michael was becoming more and more convinced that Viper was working on the side of justice. The question plaguing him was whose justice she was fighting for: hers or her country's? Or both?

And where was she now? After assaulting him, had she remained in the city? Michael frowned and sipped his scotch again, his eyes drifting to his laptop. He felt that she was still nearby. It was just a gut feeling that he hadn't shared with anyone, but Michael suspected that she hadn't left the area. She was on a manhunt. Viper wouldn't leave until she finished what she was here to do.

Michael was still staring absently at the map when his email alert dinged. He set his glass down and leaned forward, clicking on his email to open the new message. It was another message from a contact in Interpol. It told him the same thing as countless other messages the past few days. Yes, they were aware of an international assassin known as The Engineer. He was a phantom. People said he had a 100% success rate, but they had no information on him other than his existence. They didn't know if he was or had been in the US recently. Michael closed the email with a sigh and deleted it. He sat back in the chair again and reached for the scotch.

Viper seemed to be the only one in the world who thought that the Engineer had been in New Jersey three months ago. Was that because she had seen him? Had she followed him there? Or, as was implied by all her actions since, had something more sinister brought the international assassin there? Had someone in Washington paid him to come to the US? And, if so, why?

Michael frowned ferociously and got up impatiently to refill his glass at the sideboard. He poured two fingers of scotch and turned to stare across the room once more at the map hanging on the wall. He took a slow, deep breath and walked over to the map, staring at the Eastern seaboard of the United States. His mind churned as he gazed at the tiny finger hanging off the coast beneath New York.

Viper wanted him to find out who paid The Engineer to go to Jersey. He had been poking around now for four days and all he had to show for it were more questions, two dead bodies shot while tied to a chair, and two missing windows in his house. Her agency wouldn't release any information to help him, and *his* agency was making his job harder by issuing unfounded alerts saying she was in the area, alerts that they were bound to justify in the morning by pointing to the rash of .45 slugs popping up everywhere.

Michael frowned. It wasn't looking good for the mysterious Viper, he admitted. All they needed now was to find out that her weapon of choice was a .45 and the water-boarding team would be getting the hoses ready. *If* they managed to take her alive, Michael qualified to himself. Somehow, his gut was telling him that whomever hired the Engineer had no intention of doing that.

"Talk to me, Viper," Michael whispered. "Tell me what I need to know so that I can help you."

Hawk was floating on the waves of the ocean, weightless, drifting along the steady rise and fall of the tide. His body felt separated from his mind. If he opened his eyes, Damon was sure he would be looking down at himself, but his eyelids were too heavy to lift. He couldn't see his body being carried along by the waves, he could only feel it.

He had experienced this feeling once before, in the distant past. Hawk reached out his hands, trying to grasp the fleeting memory, but it dissolved like mist as soon his fingers touched it and his hands fell into the water again with a splash.

What happened? Where was Viper? How had he ended up in the ocean?

Questions swirled in and out of his mind, hampered in their progress by his intent concentration on the sensation of floating. The tides were fading now and his body had stopped, no longer being carried forward. He was suspended, bobbing with the under-current. The air above him was silent as the lapping of waves against his ears gently assaulted his senses. The mix of silence and waves confused him. Hawk tried to open his eyes again, but they refused to cooperate.

He frowned, forcing his mind to concentrate. The last thing he remembered was Viper kissing him in the bathroom. He had just finished shaving and she had leaned forward on her own, with no encouragement, and kissed him. She had! Right on his jaw. He remembered it.

A tide pushed up beneath him and Hawk's body rose above it, riding the crest gently before descending into the valley again between waves. It reminded him of surfing when he was younger.

They had gone on vacation out to the beaches of California, where he saw the ocean for the first time. There, he discovered surfing and the rush of catching a perfect wave and riding it in to the shore. His love affair with the water had begun. He decided that summer to join the Navy. At the tender of age of ten, he made up his mind to dedicate his life to his country on the water.

It wasn't until later that Damon learned about the SEALs...

Harry glanced down at his watch and pressed the button to

illuminate the dial. It was just after two in the morning and the silence surrounding the car was deafening. He lifted his eyes from the watch dial and turned his attention back to the darkness of the woods surrounding him. He still got nervous in the trees at night, a throwback from his days in the jungles of Vietnam, when survival depended largely on luck and little on yourself.

Harry sighed and leaned his head back tiredly. He was here only because there was no other choice. He thought back to Vietnam. There hadn't been any choice there, either. They had all gone because they'd been starry-eyed with tales of the Great Second World War from their fathers. They believed that they were there to fight for greatness and freedom. They had believed there was no other choice but to fight for their country as their fathers and grandfathers had done before them. In some ways, they had been right. But in others, they had been terribly wrong.

The jungle had taught him the most valuable survival skills a man could acquire, however, and Harry had the wonderful opportunity of passing them onto his pupils in later years. Hawk and Viper had both excelled in the art of jungle warfare; Hawk through his sheer determination and natural physical abilities, and Viper through her honest love for all things of nature and her grasp of how to use them to her advantage. Viper also had that uncanny ability to understand and communicate with animals, that sixth sense that made her more at home in the wilds then among ordinary civilization. Between them, Hawk and Viper were a true joy to teach. They became Harry's favorite pupils. Once they moved on in their career, they also became his friends. That friendship was about to be tested greatly.

Harry glanced at his watch once more.

It was almost time.

Viper?

Hawk tried in vain to open his eyes as he heard her voice far away. Or was that just his imagination? He couldn't hear her anymore now. His tongue was swollen and when he tried to swallow, his throat wouldn't obey his mind's command either. He was so thirsty! The ocean had made him thirsty.

The ocean...the waves....

They were gone. He wasn't in the water any longer. The rolling of the waves was gone and in its place was a controlled weightlessness. The complete stillness in which it existed was interrupted occasionally by a gentle motion. Hawk tried to determine where his body had landed. He knew what that gentle motion was, but his brain couldn't seem to convey the message to his consciousness.

Where was he?

He tried to lift his hands and found them weightless. He reached into darkness, trying to feel something, anything, to give him a clue as to where he was. His seeking fingers encountered only air. It was like he was in a vacuum. A silent, noiseless vacuum.

Except...there *had* been noise. He had heard Viper's voice...hadn't he?

Damon took a deep breath and tried to relax his mind. His mind knew where he was. His mind knew what had happened. He just had to extract the information he needed in order to know how he could regain control of his motor skills. Hawk exhaled slowly and focused on the sensation of nothingness because that was where the *something* was.

Because he *was* somewhere. He was breathing. He was thinking. He was alive.

He just had to remember....

Michael sat back in his chair, rubbing his eyes and yawning widely. It was past three now and he had been staring at the laptop screen for over an hour, pouring through documents from all the agencies. He had discovered quite a few shocking discrepancies between funding and expenditure within Homeland Security, but nothing to lead him any closer to what he needed to know. Glancing at his watch, Michael sighed and stretched. It was time to call it a night. He would continue tomorrow. God willing, he may get a few hours of sleep in yet.

He was starting to log off when an alert he'd never seen before popped up in the bottom, right-hand corner of the screen. Frowning, he clicked on it. A black DOS box flashed up and rapidly streamed some script, disappearing before he could click it closed. Michael stared at his screen dumbfounded.

What the hell was that?

He was still staring at the screen, waiting for something to happen, when the entire screen suddenly went black. Michael scowled, about to hit the power button to shut the whole thing down, when white text appeared at the top of the screen. He realized with a shock that someone had opened a remote chat screen on his laptop.

Any luck with The Engineer?

Michael stared at the text, his heart thumping almost out of his chest. How the hell had Viper broken into his personal network? He had it secured and locked down so that no one could access it. No one at all.

Except, apparently, Viper.

Cat got your tongue?

Michael grinned despite himself and sat forward.

Not yet, but the night is young.

Michael grimaced to himself at the lame reply before catching himself. He shrugged. He didn't need to impress the woman. He needed answers.

How's the head?

A wave of irritation washed over him at the gloating reminder of their one and only meeting.

Just started hurting again.

Two advil and a shot of vodka always work for me.

I'll be sure to have some on hand for you if we ever meet again.

Michael waited for her response, a grin tugging at his lips. It was slow in coming.

I'll give you a fair shot next time.

And I'll take it, don't worry. Why was The Engineer in Jersey?

Michael sat back and watched the blinking cursor on the screen. Would she answer? She had made contact, which indicated she was willing to talk, but the seconds stretched into minutes and still the cursor blinked mutely on the screen. Michael was just leaning forward to try a different tact when the cursor started moving.

He was paid to kill Johann Topamari after he executed his terrorist attack.

Michael stared at the screen, his breath catching in his throat. Of course! Why hadn't he realized? Viper wasn't just after the person who had brought an assassin into the country. She was after the person who had brought a *terrorist* into the country!

But you killed Johann, didn't you?

My, you have been busy, haven't you?

I had a cozy chat with a nice young woman in the FBI. Stephanie Walker. You know her?

Oh, you can do better than that.

Michael was surprised by the chuckle that bubbled up and out of him. He was grinning freely now and realized, with something of a shock, that he was actually enjoying himself.

Where's The Engineer now?

Do you really think he's anywhere?

Michael stared at the words, surprised despite himself. If she had killed the assassin, then she had to know who brought him into the country already. That meant...she wanted *him* to know. She wanted him to know who she was chasing.

Now who's been busy?

Oh, Gunny, you have no idea.

Enlighten me.

Someday. Would you like some help?

With?

The Engineer

What have you got?

His real name was Dimitrius. Check with the Israeli Secret Service. They can tell you anything you want to know about him.

Michael felt his mouth drop open. The assassin had been Israeli-trained?

Thank you. I have something that might help you too.

Michael typed the words with misgiving. He was about to shoot himself in the foot, but Viper was clearly trying to help him. It was only fair that he reciprocated.

Do tell.

An alert was issued to all the Federal agencies today saying you're in the DC area.

Really? That couldn't be farther from the truth just now...

Michael stared at the screen thoughtfully. A part of him acknowledged relief at the words. Were they true? He suddenly found himself, inexplicably, hoping that they were.

Good, because by tomorrow you'll be the prime suspect in the murder of two men. What kind of gun do you carry?

Thank you for the warning. I'm running short on time. Do you have any more questions?

Aside from the gun? Hundreds.

I'll give you two more, but no comment on the gun.

Michael sat back, his mind spinning. She was giving him two freebies. He quickly sorted through all the questions he had and tried to prioritize them in his head. He was still thinking when the cursor moved again.

Clock's ticking.

Michael sat forward slowly, trying to decide which were the most pressing questions. He may never see or hear from her again.

Why me?

Michael waited, staring at the screen. The answer was a long time coming.

I told you before, I'm partial to gunnies.

Michael smiled slowly. She knew a Marine gunnery sergeant...or had known one. It wasn't much, but it was something. It was a clue to her identity. He had worked with less.

Why kill the assassin? Why not use him as leverage?

Let's just say I took offense to something he tried to do.

Michael was still staring at the screen thoughtfully when the black screen disappeared and his normal desktop returned. He cursed under his breath, quickly going to his system tray. The alert was gone and all trace of the chat had disappeared. He frowned and opened up a system log, cursing more loudly when the log showed no signs of the alert, chat, or script that had run on his laptop.

After a moment of frustrated searching, Michael finally gave up in defeat, logging off and shutting down. He was completely unaware that by doing so, he was initiating a wipe that would remove all traces of the files that Alina had installed on his laptop five days before. Any evidence that she had ever been inside his network was erased as soon as his laptop turned off, severing all connection to Viper.

Damon struggled to pull himself back from the darkness. Had he been sleeping? He must have been, but he had no way of knowing for how long or how much time had passed. The feeling of weightlessness had faded and now every part of his body felt very heavy. He felt like he was being weighted down and was going to sink into...into what? He still couldn't see anything, but he had the impression that he was laying on something soft. A sofa? A bed?

Hawk tried to swallow and discovered that his tongue was no longer swollen but his mouth was still dry. He felt as if he had swallowed a desert. Where was Viper? And how long ago was it that they had eaten steak? It had been so good...just like he remembered from the bonfire at the end of boot camp.

He tried to open his heavy eyelids and they fluttered slightly. Hawk concentrated on the motion, focusing all his limited energy on getting his eyes open. His eyelashes lifted slowly, feeling as if they were glued shut, until a shot of bright light exploded into his head. Damon groaned and hastily let his eyes close again, but it was too late. The light had caused an explosion of pin-pricks and sun-bursts behind his eyelids, and the comfortable darkness that he had been existing in was shattered.

"He's coming around."

A deep voice made it through the fireworks and Hawk stopped trying to sink back into the abyss. He knew that voice. Remembered it well. It had barked orders at him from a loud speaker in the jungle.

"Harry?"

Hawk tried to speak, but his mouth was too dry. He felt his lips moving, but could only hear a croaking noise coming from a distance. Deciding against trying to speak again, Hawk refocused his efforts on trying to get his eyes open. The sunbursts exploding in his head didn't seem as painful as they had before he heard Harry's voice. Harry was there. Harry would know where Viper was. Harry knew everything.

Hawk was still trying to get his eyes opened and focused against the blinding light when something touched his lips. He frowned and tried to turn his head away from the sharp object being pressed against his mouth.

"It's just a straw, Hawk," a voice said soothingly. "Stop fighting me."

Viper!

Hawk turned toward her voice and parted his lips. The sharp object was gently inserted into his mouth and his lips closed around it. Still struggling to get his eyes open again, Damon was grateful for the rush of water that followed a tentative suck on the straw.

"He'll choke."

That was Harry's voice again, deep and even, further away now. Damon could almost hear Viper smiling.

"No, he won't." Her voice was calm and steady, full of assurance. "He knows better than that."

As if on cue, Damon's throat suddenly stopped obeying his commands and closed up abruptly. The straw left his mouth as he started choking. In his heightened state of awareness, he heard a soft sigh above him before his head was forced on its side. The water ran out of his mouth and Damon started coughing, gasping for air as his throat re-opened in protest.

"Well, I thought he did." Viper sounded resigned.

"He doesn't have all his muscle control back yet."

Harry was speaking from directly above him now. How could that be? The rush of air that followed the coughing fit was starting to clear his mind, and Damon realized that he was lying down, his head turned to the side. Was Viper on one side and Harry on the other?

"So I see."

Viper sounded like she was drifting away. Damon shook his head, re-doubling his efforts to get his eyelids unglued.

Wait! No! Don't go anywhere! What happened?

"Leave him to sleep the rest of it off," Harry advised, his voice moving away now.

No! Give me more water. I can fight through this!

Hawk felt the cold fingers of sheer panic grab hold of him for the first time. They couldn't leave! They had to stay until he got his eyes open! He had to see them. He had to touch them. He had to know that he wasn't going insane. Was this all a dream? Damon fought to get his eyes open, focusing all his energy into confronting that painful, blinding light. Shards of white light pierced through the darkness and elation surged through him, holding the panic at bay. The shards became a line and then the line exploded into the blinding whiteness that had caused so much pain and confusion a few moments before.

Hawk forced himself to fight the blinding light, ignoring the pain and pushing it to the back of his head. He blinked once, then forced his eyes back open, confronting the light and trying to see past the white orbs that were blocking her from him. Viper was still there. He could feel her beside him, but it wasn't enough. He needed to *see* her.

And then, suddenly, he did.

The blinding whiteness shifted and broke up, and there she was. Viper was leaning over him, her red hair falling around her face. Her dark eyes were watching him carefully as he struggled to focus. In an instant, Hawk realized he was lying on a narrow couch of some sort, and she was perched on the edge with one hand braced against the wall beside him. He wanted to look around, to see where they were, but the white orbs were blocking his peripheral vision now and Hawk was afraid to move his eyes from her face in case he lost her again. They stared at each other for what seemed to him to be forever, and then she smiled slowly.

"Welcome back," Viper said softly, her brown eyes suddenly warm.

Hawk didn't know if the smile in his heart made it to his lips. He didn't care. He was just happy to see that Viper was alive and well. He reached out his hand to touch her and felt her fingers close around his firmly.

"What...."

Damon tried to speak and his voice croaked out painfully. He frowned and swallowed. Before he could try again, Viper laid her finger against his lips softly.

"Don't speak yet," she told him gently. "Sleep now."

Hawk focused on her dark eyes and was sucked into chocolate lava. They were so warm and dark and, with her words, he was suddenly exhausted. His eyes were growing heavy again.

"You're fine. Rest now."

Viper moved her finger from his lips and he felt her hand smooth his hair back on his forehead. His eyelids started to droop, but he fought to keep them open. He didn't want to rest. He wanted to ask her what had happened! She was smiling slightly, her eyes glinting in that unique way of hers, as if she knew exactly what he was thinking.

"Rest now," she repeated softly.

His mind was racing now, trying to process all the thoughts and impressions of what was around him. Through all the chaos in his head, Viper's dark eyes kept him centered. He stared at them, fighting to keep his own open even as they were sliding closed.

No! Wait!

But the abyss was claiming him again, pulling him under and wrapping him in its darkness.

Viper faded away as Hawk sank back into oblivion, his fingers entwined with hers.

Chapter Seventeen

Stephanie poured herself a mug of coffee and turned to leave the kitchen. Sounds of shooting and random explosions echoed around the living room and she grit her teeth. John was playing Call of Duty on the game system, and had been playing it all morning. When she finished her morning workout and went into the shower, he was shooting people. When she came out of the shower, he was shooting people. When she made breakfast, he was shooting people.

And he was still shooting people.

Stephanie swiped the iPad off the end table as she stalked by and headed down the hall into her bedroom. Slamming the bedroom door behind her, she felt some satisfaction in the resulting bang before immediately feeling a little guilty. She sighed and settled down on the bed with her back against the headboard. It wasn't John's fault she was irritated. His shooter games were distracting him from their forced inactivity, just as her books on the tablet were supposed to be distracting her. It was just that her books didn't make so much noise.

She was swiping the screen to go back to reading one of them when her bedroom door swung open again unceremoniously.

"You ok in here?"

John leaned against the door jam and studied her with lazy eyes. Stephanie sipped her coffee and set it down, not looking up.

"Just swell," she muttered, missing the grin that passed over John's handsome face.

"You sure?" he asked. "Because your door just knocked a picture off the wall out here."

Stephanie did look up then.

"You're lying," she said.

"Come see for yourself."

Stephanie's eyes narrowed and she swung her legs off the bed to stomp over to the door. She looked out into the hallway and saw a picture laying face-down on the floor. John watched as she went into the hallway and picked it up. She hung it back on the wall, straightened it, and turned to go back into her bedroom.

"Oops," she muttered as she passed him.

John forced back a laugh and followed her into the bedroom.

"Now that we've established that I wasn't lying, care to tell me why you're throwing a tantrum?" he asked, following her to the bed and flopping down across the foot of it.

Stephanie glared at him and sat back against the headboard.

"I'm not throwing a tantrum," she retorted. "I'm just irritated. You've been shooting people all morning and it's annoying."

John's eyebrows soared into his forehead.

"I'm sorry," he apologized. "Did you want the TV for something?"

"No!" Stephanie snapped.

John studied her thoughtfully. Stephanie was awkwardly aware that she was acting like a spoiled child, but she couldn't seem to help herself. If they didn't get out of this apartment soon, she felt like she would scream. And it had only been two days!

"You're getting restless," John decided. He stood up and held out his hand to her. "Come on."

Stephanie eyed his outstretched hand.

"Come on where?" she demanded. "Out to the living room? Be still, my heart."

John grinned and reached forward to grab her hand, yanking her up.

"Smart ass." He pulled her across the room and out the door. "You can't go stir-crazy on me after only two days, partner. That will make for a long vacation."

"It's already a long vacation. I should have gone down the shore," Stephanie retorted, following him into the living room. "At least I could be getting a tan right now."

"Quit complaining." John picked up the gun-shaped controller and handed it to her. "Shoot some people instead," he added with a grin.

Stephanie rolled her eyes and turned to walk away, but John grabbed her wrist and pulled her back, laughing.

"I'm serious!" he told her, pulling her over so that she was in front of the couch and in line with the sensor bar. "Try it."

He picked up a second controller and hit a button. The screen came alive and Stephanie found herself moving his character out from behind an army truck, where she was immediately confronted with people in desert camos shooting at her. She shot John a startled look of panic and he grinned. Stepping behind her, he put his arms around her and his hands on the controller.

"Watch."

Stephanie let him take charge of the controller and watched what buttons he was pushing. When he shot all the bad guys, he let her have the controller back and showed her how to move it so that the sensor bar picked up the movements.

"You have to get to that building over there," he pointed to the screen, his cheek next to hers.

Stephanie nodded and John stepped back, moving away to watch from the couch. As he left and the heat of his body disappeared, Stephanie suddenly felt alone. She frowned at the unusual feeling. A second later, someone appeared out of nowhere on the screen before her and she swung the controller up to shoot them. They fell with an unrealistic cry and Stephanie looked at John.

"I got one!" she exclaimed with a big grin. John nodded.

"And you just got shot," he pointed out with a laugh.

Stephanie looked back to the screen and saw her life meter at the bottom of the screen flashing.

"Well, what the hell!?" she cried.

John burst out laughing and pointed.

"Quick! There's another.....too late," he said as the screen flashed and an option came up to save or continue.

Stephanie hit continue and John chuckled as the sequence started over. He settled back on the couch, watching as she began bumbling her way through her first shooter game. He hoped it would help distract her from wondering what Alina was doing the same way it was helping to distract him.

Michael was at his laptop at six-thirty in the morning, coffee in hand. He sent off an email to the only person in Israel that he knew personally, Ori Katchman. Ori just happened to be Mossad. If anyone could dig up information on an ex-Israeli patriot, Michael was confident that person was Ori.

Once the email had gone, Michael started to pull up information on Jason Rogers' SEAL team. He got the names of all the members who received the tattoo and then compared it to a list from the Navy. An hour later, he was still cross-referencing lists and checking names and locations. Two of the team members were still active military and Michael reached out to them to see if they kept in touch with Jason. Someone, somewhere, had to know how he had ended up breaking into Michael's house. He just had to find that someone.

It was a little after eight when he received the email he had been expecting from work. It was the official notification that the bullets found in Jason Rogers and the bullets found in the cameras in the parking garage were the same caliber as the one found in Billy Conners' bedroom. The email instructed him to work on the assumption that it was the same shooter in all instances and proceed accordingly. It had been sent to both agencies involved with the investigation, and Michael knew that the other alphabets would receive a less detailed version alerting them to move Viper up on the Most-Wanted list.

Michael sat back in his chair, rubbing his face with a yawn, and realized that his coffee mug was empty. He stood up with a stretch and picked up the mug, turning to go into the kitchen. So the news was out. The agency thought that Viper was running rampant through DC, breaking into houses, tying people up, shooting them and blowing up cars. He could only imagine the flack that Chris walked into when he got to the office this morning.

Michael's lips tightened as he emptied the used coffee grinds from his coffeemaker and put a clean filter in the basket. Art would be flapping around, laying the blame for just about everything that happened in the city last night at Viper's feet, and Chris would be forced to pull men from other assignments to beef up security. Michael shook his head. He wouldn't be a bit surprised if the White House was evacuated just to bring more pressure to bear on the agency to find Viper.

But she's not in the city, Michael thought absently, filling up the water reservoir to the coffeemaker. *Not just now, anyway.*

Michael's head shot up, his tired eyes widening in understanding. Those had been her words, or something like them. She wasn't here now, but she was coming back.

Michael dropped the water reservoir back into the coffeemaker and hit the button to brew before turning to pace around the kitchen. What made her leave? If he could only find out how The Engineer got into the country! Michael knew that everything hinged on that. But if he was dead, and Michael had no doubt that Viper killed him in Jersey three months ago, what else would drag her away from her manhunt? If someone in Washington brought the terrorist and assassin into the country, what could possibly call Viper away? Had the someone in Washington *left* the city? Was she following them? Was she running? *Had* she shot Jason and Billy?

Michael frowned, sending his mind back to Saturday. He had been in here, filling a bag with ice when Alina called out, saying they had company. He ran to the kitchen door and heard the pops of gunfire. Alina had been crouched low inside the door, her back to the wall, taking cover. The black SUV was just leaving as he came running down the hall to the door. *Could* it have been Viper in the back of the SUV? It was an excellent shot...

The smell of fresh brewing coffee began to fill the kitchen and still Michael paced with a slight frown. Of course it could have been Viper, but he would be willing to bet his next month's salary that it hadn't been. Even if Jason could identify her, which was doubtful since he had yet to find any connection between Jason Rogers and Viper, there would have been no reason to kill him so publicly. That just wasn't her style. She was far from flamboyant. *None* of this was her style.

"Hello?"

Michael was roused from his thoughts by a voice yelling from the backyard. He stopped in front of the sink and looked out the broken window. Blake was standing in the backyard, looking up at the jagged hole in the window. He grinned and waved when he saw Michael.

"Morning! Do I smell coffee?" he called.

Michael grinned, reluctantly letting go of his train of thought and going over to open the back door to his friend.

"You do. Come on in," he answered, leaving the back door open and going back into the kitchen to get a clean mug out of the cabinet. Blake stepped into the house and closed the door.

"You didn't board it up?" he asked, nodding to the broken window. Michael shrugged, closing the cabinet door.

"There wasn't much point. They're coming today to put a new one in."

Blake dropped his keys and sunglasses onto the island and accepted a coffee mug from Michael.

"I guess you weren't worried about security last night," he remarked. Michael snorted.

"I was up half the night working," he retorted. "By the time I went to bed, I was looking for a fight. So no, I wasn't worried about security." Michael pulled the full coffee pot out of the machine and Blake held out his cup. "What brings you around so early?" he asked, pouring coffee into Blake's mug.

"I wanted to see if you got the official word on the bullet casings," Blake answered.

Michael finished filling his cup and Blake sipped it gratefully as Michael turned to refill his own mug.

"Got it a little while ago," Michael murmured, pouring black coffee into his mug. He set the pot back onto the burner, turned around to lean against the counter, and sipped his coffee. "Do you have something unofficial to add?" he asked, eyeing his friend over the rim of his mug. Blake grinned.

"A few things," he said.

Michael raised his eyebrows.

"Well, then you'd better come into my office," he told Blake, walking over and opening the door to the garage. Blake laughed and preceded him down the few steps into the garage. "I sweep this place regularly for bugs," Michael explained, closing the door behind them. He pulled out a stool for his friend to sit on.

"You sweep your garage for bugs?" Blake repeated, staring at him. Michael shrugged and leaned against his work bench.

"What can I say? I'm careful."

"Paranoid is more like it," Blake retorted. Michael grinned.

"Maybe," he agreed. "But at least you know what you say in here won't get out."

Blake chuckled.

"True," he agreed. He drank some more coffee before setting the mug down on the work bench. "Well, here's what I've got. The bullets you know about. All .45's. The lab will be able to confirm that they all came from the same gun and I should know in the next few days. I sweet-talked one of the techs, so I'm hopeful that I'll have confirmation sooner rather than later."

Michael snorted.

"With your idea of sweet-talk, you won't have the results for months."

Blake glared at him, his dancing brown eyes belying the fierce look.

"How's your stalker?" he asked innocently and Michael grinned.

"Point taken," he said, holding up his hand in surrender. Blake chuckled.

"Someday, I want to know who the mysterious stalker is," he said. Michael sipped his coffee and was silent. "Oh! That reminds me!" Michael stifled a groan at the mischievous look stealing into Blake's face. "One of your boys told one of my boys that your date Saturday night was an old buddy's kid sister. Is she legal?"

Michael set his mug down and crossed his arms over his chest.

"Remind me to knock some heads together when this is all over," he muttered.

Blake burst out laughing.

"Who was she? I only got a glimpse of her as she was leaving, but she looked like a knock-out. You might not want to make her your lasagna again, though. She seemed to have an aversion to it," he added.

Michael glared at him and Blake laughed harder.

"Keep it up, buttercup," Michael retorted.

"Anyway, I got the backup tapes from the cameras in the parking garage." Blake calmed down and continued. "They were next to useless. The only thing we were able to pull was a grainy image of someone lurking around Ms. Walker's car on Saturday morning. We tried to clean it up, but it's tentative at best. The person is about the right height and build to be Billy Conners, but there's just no way to tell if it was him or someone else. One of our techs is willing to say positively that she thinks it's a man, based on the size of his hands and the way he moves, but that's far from conclusive."

"Does the film show him approaching the car?" Michael asked, picking up his coffee again. Blake shook his head.

"He, or she, never approached the car in the clips that we have," he said. "But here's where it gets weird. The tapes are all distorted and grainy to begin with, but in that particular portion of the feed, there are other images superimposed over each other. It's almost like someone corrupted the feed somehow."

Michael frowned, remembering the hacked feed the night Viper attacked him.

"This seems to be becoming a trend," he murmured and Blake glanced at him sharply.

"What does?" he asked. Michael shook his head.

"Nothing," he said. "I was just thinking out loud. What about the street cameras?"

"Well, that's where we had some luck." Blake drank some more coffee. "We have solid footage of a black Jeep Wrangler leaving the garage right after the explosion. Good plates and a man driving, although not one camera could pick up any facial features at all. He was wearing a hat and shades. There's also footage of the same Jeep going in, but the angle only catches the rear side of the vehicle, so no help there. We're trying to find the Jeep now."

"Well, that's something at least." Michael set his mug down and crossed his arms again. "Any idea who Billy was working for yet?"

Blake finished his coffee and set the empty mug down.

"We're still going through his PC, but he was being paid by someone. Regular cash deposits into a bank account every week, and the SUV was leased to a security company. Morganston Security, I think it's called," Blake answered.

Michael's eyes narrowed and he frowned.

"Now, why do I know that name?" he wondered and Blake raised his eyebrows.

"You've heard of them?" he asked. Michael nodded.

"Yes." He thought for a moment before shaking his head. "I'll let you know when I remember how I know them." Blake nodded.

"Well, that's what I have so far," he said. "I should have more by tonight. How about you? Are you making any progress?"

"Progress? No," Michael answered with a grimace. "I'm still trying to find out why an ex-SEAL would want to break into my house."

"He was working for someone, that's for sure," Blake murmured, getting to his feet. "I'll keep you posted on any developments." Michael nodded.

"I appreciate that," he said, straightening up and walking with Blake to the kitchen door. "Have you heard anything from your missing agent, Stephanie Walker?"

"Not a peep," Blake replied as they stepped back into the kitchen. "Now her partner is MIA as well." He went to the sink and set his empty mug inside. "Their boss can't reach either of them on their cell phones, and we're not getting any hits on the GPS for either phone. It's like they just disappeared on Saturday."

Michael frowned.

"They can't just disappear," he said. Blake shrugged.

"I know, but that's exactly what they did," he replied. "You met with Ms. Walker on Saturday, didn't you? Did she say anything about where she was headed?"

"No. All she said was that she was on vacation and didn't know how long she'd be staying in the DC area," Michael answered.

Blake glanced at him as he picked up his keys and sunglasses from the island.

"What did you talk about?" he asked.

"I had some questions about something else that I'm working on," Michael replied. "I thought she could help."

"And did she?" Blake settled his sunglasses on his face, but not before Michael caught the piercing glance from brown eyes.

"She did, actually," Michael informed him with a smile.

Blake nodded and turned to the door.

"Good! I hope she checks in soon," he said on his way to the door. "Thanks for the coffee!"

"Anytime," Michael assured him.

Blake disappeared out the back door with a wave and Michael turned to pour himself more coffee. Where had Stephanie Walker disappeared to? Was she with Viper?

Michael turned to go back to the dining room with the unsettling feeling that he was missing something.

Marty wiped his sweaty palms on his khaki pants. He was shown into Frankie's parlor over half an hour ago, and there was still no sign of the boss. He perched on the edge of the leather arm chair and stared at the table in front of him. A vase of sunflowers was in the center, nestled in a bowl of seashells. Marty wondered if Frankie's wife had flowers in all the rooms. He had never seen any room of the shore house, other than this one. This was where business was transacted.

The door opened suddenly and Frankie's large frame filled the doorway. He was dressed in shorts and a polo shirt and looked as if he had just come in from the beach behind the house. Closing the door behind himself, he nodded to Marty.

"Marty! Glad you could make it."

Marty jumped up and held out his hand.

"Anytime, boss, anytime," he said, shaking Frankie's hand energetically. "It's always nice to get to the Jersey shore."

Frankie nodded slightly, pulling his hand away and sitting down in the arm chair opposite him. Marty dropped back into his chair.

"It's a nice break from the city," Frankie agreed, sitting back. "Tell me about DC," he commanded and Marty swallowed.

"Well, like I told you on the phone, I got a call from our contact in the Secret Service," Marty began. "He's part of security at the Admiral's House, assigned to the VP."

Frankie held up a hand, stopping him.

"How long has he been on our payroll?" he asked. Marty thought for a minute.

"About two years now," he answered. Frankie nodded and Marty continued. "So he tells me that the VP's cousin is really upset over Billy Conners. She wants to know how the Feds ended up with the body and what they're doing with all his stuff. Our man thinks she's afraid they'll find something she don't want found."

"Any idea what that might be?" Frankie asked, steepling his fingers under his chin, his elbows on the arms of the chair. Marty shrugged.

"Nah. No one knows. But she's real nervous, or so he says," he answered.

"What about the SEAL?" Frankie asked.

"The ex-Marine whose house they broke into is looking for

answers on him," Marty said, wiping his palms on his khakis again. "He's no joke, boss. He'll find out who he was working for."

Frankie studied him, his gaze steady, until Marty felt like squirming like a schoolboy.

"How can they connect him back to us?" Frankie finally asked softly.

"I don't know, but that guy, Michael O'Reilly, he's smart." Marty swallowed. "He's not an average suit. He'll figure it out."

Frankie released his fingers with a sigh.

"Marty, he'll find out that Jason Rogers was working for Regina Cummings," Frankie informed him patiently. "There won't be any need to look any further than that."

"I hope you're right, boss. I wouldn't want you to have the hassle of that guy breathing down your neck," Marty said. "He's smart. Smarter than the other Feds."

"Yes, you said that already," Frankie murmured. "Did my trigger man get out of the city ok?"

"Without a hitch, boss." Marty nodded. "He's back in the Poconos now." Marty reached down to the messenger bag on the floor next to his chair and picked it up. "Here's the gun, just like you said."

Marty got up and handed the bag to Frankie, who took it and dropped it onto the floor next to his own chair.

"Good." Frankie looked up and Marty swallowed nervously. Even with him standing and the boss sitting, he still felt intimidated. "How's the search going for the woman?"

"They've just about locked DC down looking for her," Marty answered, backing up and perching on the edge of his chair again. "They think she's in the city."

Frankie raised his eyebrows.

"Do they? What do you think?" he asked softly. Marty swallowed again.

"She's crazy if she is," he answered. "I hear they're not so interested in her alive. If they catch her, she's dead."

Frankie was silent for a minute.

"Did you hear that from your contact in the Admiral's House?" he asked.

Marty shook his head.

"Nah. I heard that from the Feds," he said readily. "It's common knowledge down there. I guess she knows too much for her own good. General opinion is that if they *do* take her alive, she'll disappear into Gitmo or worse, but no one thinks she'll live long enough to make it there."

Frankie was studying him again, his dark eyes piercing into him.

"You really are a wealth of information," he commended him and Marty swelled with pride.

"That's what you pay me to do," he said, trying to be modest and not succeeding. "I like talking to people, but I like listening more." Marty tapped his forehead. "It all gets stored up here. You never know if what you hear can be used."

"Indeed." Frankie stood up. "Well, Marty, I want you to do something else for me. I want you to go back and order a Guinness burger with double Guinness in that Irish bar that you go to all the time."

Marty stood up, his startled gaze making Frankie chuckle.

"How...how do you know about Danny's Place?" Marty stammered.

"I know everything, Marty," Frankie retorted. "Even that you are also on the ex-Marine's payroll as an informant," he added softly.

Marty felt the blood drain from his face and he stared at Frankie, speechless. Frankie smiled a Cheshire Cat smile, clapping him on his shoulder.

"Don't worry, Marty," he assured him. "Your usefulness has outweighed my displeasure so far."

"I swear to God, boss, I ain't never given any information about the Family," Marty stuttered. "I swear on my life!"

Frankie led him to the door.

"I know," he said soothingly. "Just go back and order that burger with the extra Guinness."

"When?" Marty asked, stopping at the door. Beads of sweat were breaking out on his forehead and he rubbed his palms on his shirt.

"Every day until I tell you to stop," Frankie answered, holding out his hand.

Marty took it with a shaking hand and then turned to stumble out the door.

Chapter Eighteen

Alina glanced at her watch as she moved swiftly through the airport crowds, heading toward her gate. She would be right on time for the last boarding call, barring any delay on the part of the airline. She hated flying commercial flights, but this time it was necessary. Her eyes were never still as she navigated the crowds, noting every face she passed and storing it away in the back of her mind, just in case. The paranoid habit had saved her life on more than one occasion, and she wasn't about to stop now.

As she passed a group of tourists with hiking gear strapped to their backs, one of the hikers turned and bumped her with his pack. Alina stumbled a step in her stride, throwing the hiker a sharp glare. He shrugged apologetically.

"Sorry, Señorita," he apologized in Spanish, reaching out his hands to steady her. "This pack is bigger than I am. I've been bumping people all morning. My apologies."

"Esta bien," Alina murmured, regaining her balance and nodding.

He nodded and turned back to his group as Alina continued on her way. She weaved through the crowds without further delay and arrived at her gate just as they called last boarding call. She handed over her boarding pass and was striding down the boarding tube a minute later. When she reached the door of the plane, a stewardess looked at her boarding stub and showed her into first class with a smile.

She had the compartment all to herself. Settling into her seat next to the window, Alina requested coffee from the stewardess and pulled her laptop out of its bag. The stewardess moved away and Alina reached into her pocket to extract the flash drive the hiker had slipped into her palm in the airport.

Powering on the computer, she plugged the flash drive into the port and started running the files through her decryption program. The stewardess returned with her coffee while it was still running and Alina accepted the tray with the small coffee pot and cup gratefully. She had been up for over thirty hours now and was running low on both energy and optimism. Sipping her coffee, she checked the progress of the decryption and saw that half the files had been completed. Alina clicked them open and started scrolling through the decrypted documents and memos.

It had begun.

A statement of cooperation had been issued to the Federal Bureau of Investigation this morning by Charlie, after he had been shown "persuasive evidence" that she had been involved in two homicides and an attack on a Secret Service agent in the past forty-two hours. Alina read the official report, her lips curving humorlessly when she read that she had paid an ex-SEAL to assault the Secret Service agent, shooting him afterwards. Alina paused in her reading to sip some more coffee, her eyes wandering to the window to stare sightlessly at the pre-flight bustle below on the tarmac.

Obviously, they hadn't discovered his connection to the Jersey mob or she would have been accused of being on their payroll as well, she was sure. There would be no end to the mud-slinging now. Her target had to convince everyone that she was a dangerous rogue operative, a force that had to be neutralized, a shoot-to-kill threat. She would be blamed for anything and everything that happened within a fifty mile radius of Washington now that her agency had lifted their protection. Viper's eyes narrowed slightly. Ten years of service had come down to this, a game of hard ball between a politician and the agency that trained her.

Had Michael figured out who hired the Engineer? Was he putting it all together yet? Alina hoped she hadn't misjudged her brother's old friend and that he was as smart as he appeared. She needed him to the find the money trail, additional proof that she didn't have access to and that would, hopefully, justify her actions on US soil. If Michael wasn't everything she believed him to be, things were going to get even messier than they already were.

"We're getting ready to taxi." The stewardess was at her side apologetically. "May I take this away?"

Alina looked at her empty coffee cup. She couldn't remember finishing it.

"Yes, thank you."

The stewardess nodded with a smile and took the tray away. Alina returned to the documents. Alerts had been communicated to all the field agents around the world once again, stating that she was believed to be in the DC area but any information should be communicated immediately. Alina skimmed over the rest, pausing only when she got to the copy of her classified file. It had been released to three people in the Secret Service that morning: Michael O'Reilly, Chris Harper, and Art Cosgrove. Alina didn't open the attached copy of her military career. She didn't need to read it. She knew what was in it.

It was done. By now, Michael would know the truth.

Alina closed the documents and pulled the flash drive out, dropping it into her laptop bag. She shut the laptop down and put it in the bag as the plane started backing out of its bay. Turning her attention out the window, Alina watched as the terminal slid by slowly. All at once, she felt suddenly alone, and the hollow feeling in the pit of her stomach that had been missing the past few days settled in heavily. Alina hadn't even noticed that her constant companion had been missing until now, when it fell into her with a thud.

She was alone again. She had only herself to rely on now.

All the pieces were in place. The worst had happened, with her file being released to the very people who wanted her dead, and now it was up to her to make the traitors pay the price for their actions. It was up to her to right a wrong that only a few people knew had even been committed. If she failed, Damon's career would be over. He would be forced into hiding because of his association with her, Michael would more than likely be killed, and her life would be over. Viper held no illusions as to what they would do to her. They didn't want her alive to talk.

The plane rolled to a stop at the beginning of the runway. Alina stared at the terminal, now in the distance, and wondered briefly what would have happened if she hadn't boarded the plane taking her back to Washington. What if she had run, as both Damon and Harry had urged her to do repeatedly? This whole mission was built on her fury that a member of government, who had sworn to uphold the law for the safety of the nation, had disregarded that very oath and tried to impart a heinous act of terror on innocent American lives.

Only a few people knew. The nation was ignorant of just how close they had come to another 9/11. What if she left it at that and walked away? It wasn't her responsibility to enforce justice, after all. Viper rested her head back on her seat as the engines on the plane started to ramp up in preparation for take-off. She could have not taken this flight. She could have disappeared.

The plane started to move forward, quickly picking up speed and hurtling down the runway. Viper watched as the airport terminals flashed by in the distance and knew that she was exactly where she was supposed to be. No one else could do it. No one else was crazy enough to try.

Viper was pressed back into her seat as the plane approached lift off, and she smiled slightly when the wheels abruptly left the tarmac and the plane lifted into the air. Her stomach dropped briefly as solid ground was left behind and she took a deep breath. There were no more what-if's or maybe's. There was no more time for thinking or regrets. Viper made her choice three months ago in a clearing in Pennsylvania.

This was where she was supposed to be.

The airport fell away below her as the plane lifted effortlessly into the sky, carrying her back to finish this, once and for all.

Michael stared at the screen, his half-eaten sandwich forgotten on the plate beside the laptop. The sounds of the workers cleaning up in the kitchen after installing the new window faded into the background as he read through the email from Ori. The amount of information he had sent regarding the Engineer was staggering. The man had been a psychopath, and a very skilled one at that. Michael read through one incident after another of his exploits while still in Mossad, and once he went rogue and became for hire, the stories and rumors got worse. His notoriety knew no bounds, apparently, and Ori had documented every blessed story he had heard. Michael didn't question why Ori had such good records on the assassin, but he trusted them implicitly. He couldn't help but be relieved that the Engineer was no longer with the living. If even half of the information he was reading was correct, Viper had done the world *two* favors that night three months ago.

Michael let out a low whistle when he got to the last known rate that was paid for the Engineer's services. A one hundred percent success rate made people willing to pay fortunes for his services. Michael lifted his eyes thoughtfully for a moment before going back to some of the government files he had been pouring through last night. After a few calculations, Michael sat back, stunned. The financial discrepancies he had discovered the night before added up to the same amount The Engineer was known to charge.

The money had come from Washington.

His work blackberry started ringing, jarring Michael from his thoughts. He glanced at the number and sighed, reaching for his phone.

"Hi Chris," he answered, clicking Ori's file closed on his laptop and going to his email.

"Did you get my email?" his boss asked.

Michael opened the email that had come into his inbox over half an hour ago.

"Just reading it now," Michael told him, scanning the email. His eyebrows soared into his forehead and he went back to the beginning, reading more slowly. "Wait...we have Viper's file?!"

"Yep," Chris answered with a laugh. "I wondered why you weren't banging on my office door yet."

"I was busy with something." Michael felt his heart rate increasing. "They released it this morning?"

"Given the circumstances, they weren't left with much of a choice," Chris replied. "I understand the pressure brought against them to release it was pretty intense. You've been authorized to view it, but it doesn't leave this building."

Michael closed his laptop.

"I'll be there in twenty minutes," he said, getting up and picking up his forgotten sandwich with his free hand.

He disconnected the call and bit into the sandwich as he headed out of the dining room and upstairs to change.

Damon opened his eyes and yawned, blinking in the dim light. He was on a bed in what appeared to be a hotel room, the heavy curtains pulled tight across the windows. Damon stretched and turned his head. The clock beside the bed read 3:47 in big red numbers. He sat up with a frown, rubbing his face and looking around. It was an expensive hotel. The carpet was thick and plush and the furniture was heavy, polished wood. The door to the bedroom was open and, from where he sat, it appeared to lead to another room. It was a suite then.

Where *was* he?

The last thing he remembered was shaving in the tiny bathroom at the cabin, with Alina sitting on the vanity telling him about Regina Cummings. Damon frowned, trying to concentrate. That couldn't be right. Something had happened since then, something bizarre. Memory rushed upon him, and he leaned back against the headboard of the large bed and stared at the opposite wall, stunned.

He had been drugged!

He remembered it all now: the disorientation, the lack of control over his body, the strange dreams, the dry mouth, the sensitivity to light...all symptoms of being heavily drugged. He had only experienced these only once before, in training, when Harry had drugged them all so that they would know how to respond in the event that it happened in the field. Hawk scowled. He hadn't been capable of responding at all this time.

"Oh good! You're finally awake."

Harry appeared in the doorway, as if summoned by Hawk's

thoughts, dressed in linen shorts and a floral, short-sleeved button-down shirt. His bald head gleamed in the filtered light and Damon shifted his bemused gaze to him. He watched silently as Harry went over to the curtains and pulled them back. Bright sunlight filled the room and Harry turned to face the bed, watching as Damon squinted and raised a hand against the afternoon sun.

"What the hell happened??" Hawk demanded.

"You were drugged," Harry answered calmly, walking over to the dresser and pouring a glass of water from the bottle on the tray there. He carried it over to Damon and handed it to him. Damon took it thankfully and drank it down. "A stronger solution than the one I used in your training, I think. You were completely powerless."

"I know," Damon said, setting the empty glass down on the nightstand. "I remember. I knew I had felt the effects before, but my brain wouldn't focus long enough for me to remember what it was."

"We'll have to work on that." Harry took the empty glass back to the water bottle and filled it again. He brought it back with a slight grin. "We can't have you rendered useless like that again. It was downright depressing." Damon shook his head when Harry tried to hand him the glass, but Harry frowned. "If you don't drink, you'll stand up and crash into the floor instead," he said sternly. "After nursing you for the past twelve hours, I have no desire to stitch up a split face as well."

Damon grinned and took the glass, responding to the drill-sergeant tone in Harry's voice.

"So, I was drugged," he repeated, drinking the water. "By who? And where are we?"

Harry turned to head out of the bedroom.

"Why don't you finish that and get up and showered?" he suggested over his shoulder, ignoring the questions. "I'll order room service. You're probably hungry."

"Where's Viper?"

Hawk's sharp question stopped Harry at the door and he turned his head reluctantly.

"On her way back to Washington," he answered.

His eyes met Damon's and he hesitated before adding,

"We're in Peru. Viper was the one who drugged you."

191

Chapter Nineteen

Regina's heels tapped out a rapid rhythm down the hallway as she made her way to her office, late for her one o'clock appointment. He would be waiting for her and Regina moved quickly, replying to an email from her phone as she walked. The Feds had been in possession of Billy's computer now for almost twenty-four hours. Regina could only assume that the lack of outcry meant that nothing had been found on it to incriminate her. She had been worried ever since she learned that they had taken all his electronics and, while she didn't think he was smart enough to keep anything to use against her, you never really knew for sure with men like Billy. They could sometimes surprise you.

Regina hit send on the email and raised her head, relaxing slightly as she continued toward her office. Once Viper and Michael O'Reilly were taken care of, there would be nothing left to worry about.

She and Alex would be safe.

Regina threw open the door to her office and swept inside. Sure enough, there was her one o'clock, seated in a chair at the small conference table, working away on his laptop while he waited for her. He glanced up as she entered, nodding slightly as his fingers moved over the keys rapidly.

"Good afternoon!" Regina greeted him, closing the door behind her. "Sorry to have kept you waiting."

"That's fine." Art Cosgrove finished what he was working on and saved it before standing up and holding out his hand to Regina. "I was just finishing up some emails. I have news for you."

"That's what I like to hear," Regina said, grasping his hand loosely before seating herself at the conference table. "Tell me."

"We got a copy of Viper's file this morning," Art told her, seating himself.

Regina's eyebrows soared into her forehead and her thin lips curved into a feline smile.

"Fantastic!" she exclaimed. "Where is it?"

"I'm risking my career giving this to you," Art said, sliding a thumb drive across the table. Regina's glossy red-tipped fingers snatched it up.

"Are you kidding me?" she demanded, her lips still smiling. "I'll make sure you get a promotion."

"There's more," he said, going back to his laptop. After a moment, he turned it to face her and clicked play on the media player. "I also have the camera footage from the parking garage where that FBI agent's car was blown up."

Regina looked at him sharply. Art got up and came around to stand behind her, missing the quick look.

"The footage of Ms. Walker's car is pretty bad," he explained as they watched the grainy image of a figure loitering near the car. "You can't even tell if it's a woman, although I think the stature is slight enough that it could be." Art leaned forward and fast-forwarded through the file. "In this footage, the figure never actually approaches the car and there are other images flickering through the frames, like old footage was taped over it. It makes it virtually impossible to tell if that person is the one who planted the bomb."

"Who else could it have been?" Regina asked, the thumb drive grasped so tightly in one hand that her knuckles were white. The long nails of her other hand tapped nervously on the table. "It had to have been Viper."

"I'm sure it was," Art agreed, "but based on this, we don't have visible proof."

"Then why are you showing this to me?" Regina demanded impatiently.

"I'm getting to it." Art stopped fast-forwarding. "Here it is. Watch."

Regina glanced at him behind her, then sighed and turned her attention back to the laptop. A black Jeep was driving down a ramp toward the camera.

"What's this?" she asked.

"This is from the camera across the street from the parking garage. It was recorded about three minutes after the car exploded," Art explained.

Regina stared at the laptop screen, her attention arrested. Her eyes narrowed and she watched as the Jeep stopped at the entrance briefly before turning out of the garage. The driver was the only person in the vehicle. He was wearing a baseball cap and sunglasses and his face was partially averted from the camera.

"Who is it?" Regina demanded sharply. Art shrugged.

"We don't know yet," he answered, "but we have a clear shot of the plates and they're looking for the Jeep. We'll find him." He reached over to close the laptop and Regina turned in her chair to look up at him. "He may have seen something. The bomb techs said it was a basic ignition charge, set to explode as soon as the engine started. Someone had to have triggered it. If Viper was there, that guy may have seen her," Art said, straightening up and looking down at Regina. She gazed up at him, her eyes suddenly limpid.

"He could be the witness we need," she murmured. "Do you think you'll find him?" Regina asked. Art nodded.

"I have my best man on it," he told her confidently.

Regina smiled that feline smile again, her lips curving slowly. Her free hand reached out and slid intimately up the inside of his thigh.

"Oh, I doubt that," she murmured seductively, her voice dropping an octave. "At least, not in my opinion."

Art sucked in his breath.

"Reggie, here?" he gasped as her questing fingers slid higher.

"Why not?" she purred. "After all, this calls for a celebration."

Michael stared at the pages in front of him. The coffee he picked up on his way into the office sat cold and forgotten on the desk. The only sound in the room was the very faint ticking of a clock on one of the bookshelves as Michael turned another page of Viper's file.

It started with basic training and followed her short military career until her discharge from the Navy. Most of the file had been blacked out for security reasons, including all instances of her real name, but what was left was impressive enough to make him realize that Viper was certainly a very special agent. She had started off with a bang, breaking every record in boot camp except two, all set by men. After basic training, she was guided into naval intelligence by a superior and it was here that whole pages of thick black lines began. The agent known as Viper had descended into the murky underworld of military intelligence, where she apparently settled in comfortably and excelled. The sections not blacked out were laced with commendations and praise from her superiors. Words like "tenacious," "exemplary," and "dedicated" were sprinkled liberally throughout the file, along with three recommendations for promotion. She had been on a fast track to heights unknown in the Navy when she opted to not re-enlist.

Viper was discharged with honors and snapped up immediately by the CIA, who sent her to a top secret training facility. Most of that section was also blacked out, but Michael was able to deduce enough to realize that it was there that she trained to be the government assassin she had become. After the training facility, she went out into the field. Once again, the parts not concealed had nothing but praise from her handlers. The adjectives "focused" and "aggressive" joined the others, along with notations regarding her commitment to her assignments. She never failed. Her handlers had nothing but utter confidence in her.

Viper was one of the golden children of the Organization.

Michael flipped through the file, scanning page after page, looking for something that would indicate a propensity to turn and go rogue. He could find nothing. By the time he got to the end of the active file, Michael was even more impressed with the woman who had blown into his life and knocked him out cold next to his truck. Her entire career was a non-stop shot straight to the top of everything that she attempted. She had obviously found her niche in the Navy, no easy feat for an enlisted sailor, and excelled beyond the expectations of her superiors. She was on her way to being fully established in military intelligence when she allowed herself to be recruited into one of the most clandestine agencies in the world. Once there, she had repeated her extraordinary success, once again rising above and beyond what was expected of her. She became everything they asked her to be, and then took it even further by becoming a hero several times over. Viper had become a legacy within the elite Organization.

Michael sat back, feeling somewhat stunned. And *this* was the woman they wanted to hang from the nearest tree? This was the woman they said was attacking federal agents and was a threat to national security? This was the agent they said was a threat to the White House?

She had joined her nation's Navy, served with distinction, and then moved on to continue to serve with distinction in the CIA. This was not a rogue agent. Michael was convinced, more than ever, that this was simply a woman who knew too much about a terrorist and an assassin.

He drummed his fingers on his desk, his eyes fixed sightlessly on the closed door to his office. The file had an address of residence in North Carolina, just south of Raleigh. Michael was sure that Art would have him send men to search it, but whether or not they would find anything was anyone's guess. Viper wasn't stupid. If she had been anywhere near her residence, which Michael highly doubted, she would have had plenty of time to get out after his warning to her last night.

He frowned slightly. Why was North Carolina jumping out at him? Michael's fingers stilled and he stiffened, his eyes still fixed on nothing. He stayed like that for a few moments, his mind churning, before he slowly lowered his eyes back to the file as an insidious and dreadful suspicion crept into his mind.

No. No, it's not possible, Michael thought, flipping to the front of the file again.

He looked at the date Viper enlisted into the Navy, staring at the year, his heart rate increasing. Slowly, he flipped forward and looked at the date she had discharged from the Navy.

Michael's frown grew darker as he started flipping through the file again, this time taking note of the dates of the missions and the countries they involved. Viper had been all over the Middle East, Europe, South America and Asia. The last mission was three months ago and, glaringly, did not include a country.

It can't be, Michael thought, sitting back in his chair, staring at the pages as if they had grown horns and a tail. *It's just not possible.*

Viper joining the Navy the same year as Alina didn't mean anything. It was just a coincidence.

"...I ended up in military intelligence."

Michael heard Alina's voice in the back of his head and he shook his head slightly, his mind rebelling at the thought. There were hundreds of people who worked in military intelligence.

"...It also turns out that the whole marksmanship thing runs in the family. I turned out to be a pretty good shot myself..."

Michael's thoughts were spinning now and he was having trouble catching his breath. The shot that killed Johann Topamari was sniper's shot. Michael had known that all along. Only a very experienced marksman could have made that shot in one try.

"...I'm partial to gunnies..."

Realization crashed down upon him mercilessly and Michael's face alternated between hot and cold as color flooded it, only to drain away again as anger warred with denial. The denial eventually gave way to stunned shock as the truth finally sank in. His eyes went to the photo of his Marine unit on the shelf across the office. Viper was partial to gunnies because her brother had been one!

Close upon the heels of that thought came anger, white hot and instant.

"Of course!" Michael whispered, his throat hoarse from the effort not to shout. "How could I be so blind?"

Everything made sudden and perfect sense! Why Alina had contacted him so suddenly after over ten years, why she had reacted so swiftly that night in his kitchen, why she was so comfortable with the gun that she carried in a specially designed holster in the back of her pants...

Michael's head snapped up, his eyes widening suddenly. Through his growing anger, he saw her again in his mind's eye. She was standing with her back to the counter in his kitchen, her gun pointed downwards in her hands...her Ruger SR45, .45 semi-automatic pistol!

Oh Lina, what the hell have you gotten yourself into? And what have you gotten ME into?!

Regina yawned and stretched. The sun was setting outside and her office was getting darker by the minute. She had been too preoccupied to turn on the light, but she got up now to walk over to the light switch. Viper's file was open on her laptop and she had already read through it twice. Regina flipped the switch and the shadows in her office disappeared as fluorescent light flooded the room. Turning, she went back to her desk.

The file had been heavily blacked out, but the important things were visible, things like the residence in North Carolina and the locations of all the safe houses Viper had used in the past. The majority of them were in other countries, but three were on the east coast of the United States: one in Manhattan, one in Baltimore, and one in Miami. There were also references to a few other agents that she had worked with, all code-named, but one name jumped out at her.

Hawk.

Regina sank into her seat again thoughtfully. She knew all about Damon Miles, aka Damon Peterson, aka Hawk. She remembered him very clearly from basic training all those years ago, and she had recognized him instantly in the surveillance photos that Dimitrius had sent down from New Jersey three months ago. She knew that Damon had been working with Viper in New Jersey, and Art's video of the Jeep confirmed her suspicion that Damon was *still* working with her.

Billy had set that bomb to go off when Stephanie Walker turned her ignition, but Stephanie had mysteriously disappeared and the bomb detonated on its own. She didn't know how she had done it, but Regina knew that Viper managed to find out about the bomb. As soon as she saw the Jeep, she knew that Damon had been right there with her.

Regina's lips tightened and her eyes narrowed angrily. Damon always *had* preferred Viper's company, even in basic training. He completely ignored Regina, even though she had indicated repeatedly that she was available. Instead, he had eyes only for Alina Maschik, the Wonder Bitch.

She had been a thorn in Regina's side then, and she was still a thorn in her side. Regina turned back to her laptop and smiled to herself smugly. Four possible locations on the east coast were easily narrowed down to two.

Regina knew Viper was around Washington DC, so that only left the residence outside Raleigh or the apartment in Baltimore as likely places for Alina to be hiding. She would send someone to both places to investigate. When she found out which one Viper was using, she would finally put an end to it all.

Viper's reign was about to end. And, if she was very careful and cunning, perhaps Regina could ensure that Hawk went down with her.

Regina reached for the phone on her desk.

Michael pulled into his driveway and cut the engine to the truck. Grabbing his laptop bag, he climbed out and slammed the door. A Dodge Challenger was parked at the curb in front of his house, and he watched as Blake got out of the driver's side.

"How long have you been sitting there?" Michael called.

Blake shrugged and walked up the driveway to join him, carrying a large brown paper bag.

"Only about twenty minutes," he answered. "I got us Chinese." Blake raised the bag and Michael raised his eyebrows, leading the way to the front door.

"You're bringing food? The news must be bad," he said, unlocking the door and stepping inside. Blake followed him.

"Not bad. Frustrating," he muttered.

Michael turned on the hall light and disappeared into the dining room to drop his laptop on the table before coming back to lead the way to the kitchen.

"Welcome to my day," he said, flipping on the light to kitchen and heading for the refrigerator. "We can take turns."

Blake set the bag of food on the island and opened it as Michael pulled two bottles of beer out of the fridge. He started pulling the cardboard containers out of the bag, setting them on the island.

"I've got shrimp or beef lo mein and pork fried rice," Blake said, taking the beer with a nod of thanks.

Michael grabbed one of the lo mein cartons and a set of chop sticks and headed toward the garage with the food and his beer. Blake grinned at his single-mindedness, turning to follow with the other lo mein carton.

"We can use the half-finished table," Michael said over his

shoulder.

Blake followed him down the steps and headed to the table-top resting on the saw horses in the middle of the garage.

"Hold on," Michael told him, turning to the shelving unit inside the door and grabbing a tarp from the top shelf.

"A tablecloth?" Blake watched as Michael tossed it over the table. "If you pull out candles, we're done here," he warned.

Michael let out a short laugh and set his food and beer down on the tarp while Blake pulled a stool over to the table.

"You know I like to keep it classy for you," he retorted, settling down on another stool and opening his lo mein.

"Much appreciated," Blake mumbled before shoveling in a mouth full of shrimp lo mein.

They ate in silence for a few moments, the food taking precedence over conversation. While he ate, Michael debated how much he wanted to share with his old friend. He desperately needed an unbiased view on Viper. He knew his own anger was preventing him from thinking clearly. He hesitated, however, to bring Blake into his problem. Everyone connected with Viper seemed to have a very short life-expectancy these days. However, that being the case, Michael knew that he might need Blake's assistance. He was the only person in Washington that Michael knew he could trust.

"I got the report back on the slugs." Blake finally broke the silence, looking up from his lo mein.

"Ok." Michael sipped his beer, waiting expectantly to hear that they all matched.

"They don't match," Blake informed him, setting the carton down on the tarp and picking up his beer. Michael stared at him blankly.

"Come again?"

"They don't match," Blake repeated morosely. "A little embarrassing for both our agencies, given the high alert that was issued this morning, don't you think?"

Michael slowly set down his half-empty food carton.

"What, exactly, didn't match?" he asked slowly.

Blake watched as his friend picked up his beer absently and his eyes narrowed slightly. Michael seemed almost dazed.

"The bullets from the parking garage all match," he explained, sipping his beer. "They all came from the same gun. The slugs that killed your SEAL and Billy Conners all match too, but they came from a *different* gun. The gun that shot out the cameras in the parking garage isn't the same gun that killed those two men."

"They're sure?" Michael demanded sharply. The look he got from

Blake made him smile a little sheepishly. "Ok, ok. I'm sorry," he said apologetically.

"They're sure," Blake assured him, slightly mollified. "The tech working on it double-checked before sending the results to me. Given the high-profile of the case, she bumped it to the top for me. I think she was a little afraid to tell me what she found out," Blake added thoughtfully.

"I warned Art that we didn't know the two incidents were related!" Michael exclaimed, his mind spinning with all the ramifications. "Good Lord, what a disaster!"

"Yup," Blake agreed glumly. "Billy was a nasty character. Anyone could have popped him. We can't work on the assumption that it was this Viper everyone's looking for, which leads me to my next bit of news."

Michael looked up sharply.

"What else?" he asked.

"There was something missing from Billy's apartment after all," Blake told him, sipping his beer. "My people found references on his laptop to an external hard-drive, but there was no external hard-drive anywhere in that apartment."

"Maybe he kept it somewhere else," Michael suggested. Blake grinned.

"I would think that too, except we *did* find a hidden compartment in the wall at the back of his closet," he said. "And it was open and empty."

"So you think whoever shot Billy has whatever was in that compartment?" Michael asked. Blake nodded.

"I think it's a safe bet," he answered. "You saw the evidence on his body. Someone was trying to get information out of him before they killed him. He could have told them about the hard-drive before they killed him."

"What's on the hard-drive?" Michael asked. Blake shrugged.

"My best guess? Insurance," he replied. "The references on the laptop are for file numbers, and all indications are that the files contain emails and deposit information. Obviously, we won't know until we get the hard-drive, but it looks like Billy was either blackmailing someone or keeping track of information so that he *could* blackmail someone in the future."

Michael was silent for a moment.

"He worked for Morganston Securities, right?" he asked suddenly. Blake nodded.

"Yep. You said you knew them," he said. Michael frowned slightly.

"I do, but I still don't remember how," he answered, shaking his head.

He fell silent again and Blake watched as Michael stared unseeingly at the floor. After a moment, he looked up.

200

"What do you think?" he asked Blake. "What's your gut reaction to all of this? Do you think the shootings are related? The parking garage, the SEAL on my porch, and Billy?"

"I don't know," Blake answered slowly, picking up his lo mein again. He picked at it absently, popping a shrimp into his mouth. "My knee-jerk reaction is that they're all related, but I can't give you one good reason why I think that. Do I think this Viper is involved with any of it? Again, my gut thinks so, but I can't give you one logical reason why."

Michael was silent for a moment, sipping his beer. Blake watched him from under his lashes, picking up at the food with his chopsticks.

"What do you think?" he finally asked when Michael showed no signs of breaking the silence. Michael glanced up.

"Well, I have a little more information than you do," he answered slowly. Blake nodded.

"I guessed as much," he said before lifting lo mein into his mouth. Michael shrugged and set down his beer.

"I know," he said simply.

Blake chewed patiently while Michael was silent for another long moment, struggling with himself before finally making up his mind.

"I'm willing to read you into my own private hell of an investigation, but I have to warn you that if I do, your life-expectancy is likely to decrease significantly," Michael finally told him. Blake raised his eyebrows, a laugh leaping into his eyes.

"You and I both know *that* particular danger has never stopped me in the past," Blake retorted, swallowing and setting down the food container. He picked up his beer and settled back on his stool comfortably.

"Tell me what I need to know."

Chapter Twenty

Alina settled down on the couch in the living room, two laptops open on the coffee table before her. She tried to ignore the silence of the cabin as she plugged Billy Conners' external hard-drive into one of the laptops. Ever since she stepped foot back inside the cabin, the feeling of guilt and loneliness had been almost overwhelming. Alina had tried to ignore it then, as she was trying to ignore it now, but it seemed to be screaming accusingly from every corner of the small cabin. Raven had met her in the yard and she could hear him now, opening the window upstairs to come inside. Even *his* comforting presence wasn't soothing her unrest.

Hawk was in Peru.

She had betrayed his trust in her, ruthlessly drugging him and relocating him to the one country where she knew he had contacts who could conceal him. It was where his handler already thought he was, and it was where she knew he would be safe until this was all over.

Alina sat back on the couch, staring blindly at the empty fireplace. When her source in Egypt contacted her last night, Alina came into the living room expecting to find out information about the mystery woman in the photo with Alex Ludmere. She *hadn't* expected to learn that Hawk had joined her on the Most Wanted list.

Viper's eyes narrowed and her lips tightened into a grim line. As Damon had showered obliviously upstairs, her contact told Alina of the bounty that went out, not through the normal government channels, but through the underground. Mercenaries, assassins, and agents alike were informed of the price on Hawk's head, winner takes all.

Alina got up restlessly and went into the kitchen to get one of the beers Damon had brought into the house. Popping the cap off, she headed back into the living room, filled with an intense longing to see him lounging on the couch with a beer of his own. She pushed the feeling aside impatiently and strode around the living room aimlessly, filled with restless energy.

Next Exit, Pay Toll

When Regina couldn't draw Viper out with Stephanie, she turned to the only other person she knew Viper would give her life to protect. Alina sipped the beer, pausing next to the empty fireplace and staring down at the cold stone. She was willing to bet anything that Regina had gone after Hawk out of pure spite. Alina remembered how Regina had followed Damon around in training camp. After learning from Billy just what kind of woman she was, Alina realized that Damon was probably the reason that Regina had attacked her in training that day so long ago.

She turned to continue her restless loop around the living room. When her contact had finished telling her about the exorbitant price on Hawk's head, Viper had been furious; furious enough to do whatever it took to get Hawk out of harm's way and finish Lani Cunningham, aka Regina Cummings, once and for all.

Unfortunately, it took drugging Damon to get him out of the country.

Viper knew without a doubt that Hawk would never leave voluntarily. She had called Harry while Damon was still in the shower, quickly telling him everything she had learned. Between the two of them, they came up with the only plan they could think of to get Hawk to safety immediately.

Alina sighed heavily and went back to the couch, suddenly exhausted. Damon would be absolutely furious when he found out what she'd done. Harry seemed to think that he would get over the anger, but Alina wasn't so sure. She knew how *she* would feel if the situation were reversed. If Hawk ever drugged her, she would bloody well kill him.

Sinking back down onto the couch, Alina took another sip of beer and set the bottle down. Pushing aside her thoughts, she turned her attention to the laptop and Billy's hard-drive. It didn't take her any time at all to get through the standard security password that Billy had on the drive and within minutes, Viper was staring at a number of folders, all labeled by month and year, starting with the beginning of Billy's employment with Morganston Security.

Alina started at the beginning, clicking open the folders and examining the files inside. Billy had been thorough in his documentation. There were text files, media files consisting of both video and audio clips, scanned documents, photos, and even GPS tracking in some files. With each file, Billy had included the times and dates of each job, and the bank deposit slip with each cash payment paid by Morganston Security. While Viper appreciated his attention to every detail, she had only gone through three months' worth of files before she was feeling sick.

Nothing was off-limits to the woman. Man, woman or child, Regina had no compunction about torturing, mutilating and murdering anyone who she perceived as being in her way. In Billy, she had found the perfect accomplice. Regina told him what she wanted to happen, Billy enjoyed doing it, and then got paid for the pleasure.

As the shadows outside deepened, Alina read through the files, looking at the pictures and listening to the media files. Viper was a killer, and she had seen and done things that would haunt her until the day she died, but her disgust grew with each file she clicked open. Where she had been trained to kill for a purpose, these two monsters had killed for the sheer enjoyment of it. While she had been hunting down terrorists and insurgents all over the globe, these two had been hunting down and torturing innocent people stateside under the protection of the office of the Vice President of the United States.

When Alina reached the file with the wife Billy had bragged to her about, she picked up her forgotten beer and drained it. The photos sickened her. The woman had been a gorgeous blonde, young and fresh-faced, and visibly pregnant at the time of Billy's attack. Billy's cash deposit the following day was a mere five hundred dollars. Two lives for the bargain price of five hundred dollars.

Alina felt bile starting to rise in her throat. She got up to take the empty bottle into the kitchen and took some deep, cleansing breaths. She wished now that she had slit Billy's throat when she had it in her hands.

She got a cold bottle of water out of the fridge and took a long drink before turning to head back into the living room. Whether she liked it or not, she had to finish going through all the files. She had to find the proof that Regina had brought a terrorist into the country.

Without it, Viper couldn't kill the monster.

Blake stared at Michael, the Chinese food forgotten, while Michael sipped his beer and patiently waited for his friend to process it all. Michael had told him everything, from his search for the notorious Viper to his investigation into The Engineer. He told Blake about the funding discrepancies he had found last night, and the information Ori had sent him. Michael held nothing back, pausing every so often to make sure Blake wanted him to continue. He started with his introduction to Viper in the parking garage at work, and had finished up with his realization this afternoon that Viper and his dinner guest on Saturday were one and the same.

"Let me get this straight." Blake finally broke his stunned silence. "Let me just make sure I'm understanding you correctly."

Michael's lips twitched as Blake picked up his beer, draining what was left in one swallow. He set the empty bottle down and took a deep breath.

"Someone in Washington, someone on Capitol Hill, diverted substantial anti-terrorist funding in order to bring Johann Topamari, leader of Mossavid, into the country three months ago. He was paid to commit what would have been the biggest terrorist attack on US soil since 9/11, instantly guaranteeing Congressional approval for additional funding. That same person, at the same time, also paid an international assassin to come into the country and kill Johann after he had done his job."

Blake paused, looking at Michael. Michael nodded and Blake shook his head slightly in disbelief.

"So, now we have a terrorist and an assassin, just hanging out in New Jersey, when Viper, our own government assassin, shows up to save the day," Blake continued.

Michael grinned and nodded again when Blake glanced at him. Shaking his head again, Blake got up to prowl around the garage while he talked.

"After saving the day, Viper disappears. Now the person in Washington who started all this is spooked. They don't know if Viper knows they're responsible for everything or not. So, they need to find her to see what she knows," Blake went on.

Michael held up his hand and Blake stopped, looking at him.

"That part is conjecture on my part," Michael said. "I'm just assuming that's where the manhunt for Viper started. For all I know, Viper could have known all along who the person responsible was, why they were doing it, and how they were doing it. That person could have known that she knew. Maybe Viper wasn't supposed to succeed three months ago. Maybe they expected her to get killed by either Johann or the Engineer."

"The odds were certainly not in her favor," Blake agreed thoughtfully.

He and Michael were silent for a moment, both thinking.

"Let's say, just for the sake of argument, that Viper was sent after Johann by the same person who brought him into the country," Michael suggested. Blake scoffed.

"Why would they risk her finding him and stopping him?" he demanded.

Michael was staring at the far wall of the garage thoughtfully.

"Because they brought in the best assassin money could buy," he said slowly. Blake's eyebrows soared into his forehead as he followed

Michael's train of thought. "They brought in someone with a one hundred percent success rate."

"I follow you," Blake said. "Bring in the assassin to take care of both the terrorist *and* the agent who might be able to blow the lid off the whole thing."

Michael nodded. He thought for a moment, then shook his head.

"Viper had to have known something about who was doing this before going into Jersey," he said. "That's the only way that makes sense. They wouldn't bring her in without already having a reason to want her dead."

"She knew something all right," Blake agreed with a nod.

He and Michael stared at each other.

"Well, damn it! Viper's not the bad guy here. She's the victim!" Blake finally exclaimed. Michael nodded.

"Yep," he agreed.

Blake sighed loudly and ran his hand through his hair.

"Ok. Let's leave that for a minute and go back to this past weekend," he said, resuming his trek around the garage.

Michael turned on his stool to watch him, glad to have someone else doing the pacing for a change.

"So the whole world and his dog is looking for Viper, including you. Meanwhile, she's right here the whole time, waiting. She finally approaches you and tips you off to the Engineer." Blake paused thoughtfully. "We can only assume she did that so that you would start investigating and find out who brought him into the country. She needed another person to know what she knew, someone who could find the money trail without drawing questions."

"At least now I know why she picked me." Michael felt his temper starting to simmer again. "Who better to help her than her brother's old Marine buddy, who already swore that he would watch out for her?"

Blake glanced at him.

"Yes, well, we'll get to that later," he said hastily. "Calm your britches, gunny, and save the fire for the enemy."

Michael grinned reluctantly and nodded. Blake continued on.

"After getting you to focus on what was really going on, what did she do next? I don't see her trying to blow up Stephanie Walker's car. Where does Stephanie Walker fit into this? What am I missing?"

"Viper saved Stephanie Walker's life on Three Mile Island," Michael told him. Blake swung around to stare at him and Michael shrugged. "That's what Ms. Walker told me on Saturday morning in my office."

"You could have told me that," Blake muttered with a frown and

Michael shrugged.

"Sorry. I forgot," he retorted.

"Well, that just makes everything more confused," Blake complained. "If Viper saved Stephanie's life three months ago, she's hardly going to plant a bomb in her car now, is she?"

"That's why I don't think Viper had anything to do with the car bomb," Michael said.

Blake glanced at him.

"But you think she was there," he stated rather than asked. Michael nodded.

"Here's what I think happened," he said, taking over the commentary. "I think somehow Ms. Walker managed to get herself involved with this whole mess. I think she got some time off, came down here to try to find some answers herself, and became a target. Viper found out Ms. Walker had become a target because she was with me when *I* found out."

Michael paused for a moment, finishing his beer.

"That's why Stephanie disappeared!" Blake interjected before Michael could continue. "Viper probably has her squirreled away somewhere safe."

"I think Ms. Walker was probably bait to bring Viper out into the open," Michael said, setting his empty bottle on the tarp. Blake nodded thoughtfully.

"Once Stephanie showed up, they probably thought they could kill two birds with one stone," he said slowly. "Viper gets Stephanie out of the way, but in the meantime, the people try again by planting a car bomb in Stephanie's car." He stopped and looked at Michael helplessly. "I'm still not seeing where Viper plays into that."

"I don't know," Michael admitted, shaking his head. "Maybe she was there to get the car?"

As soon as the words left his mouth, Michael knew he was right. He looked at Blake and saw the same glint of comprehension in his eyes.

"If she went to get the car, she wouldn't want the cameras to pick her up," Blake said slowly and Michael nodded.

"Everything happened so fast, she wouldn't have had time to hack the camera's, so she just shot them out," he added.

"She shoots out the cameras, hits the remote starter, and boom," Blake finished.

Michael ran a hand through his hair and they were both silent for several minutes, thinking.

"That's thin," he finally admitted.

"It's very thin," Blake agreed, a grin starting to spread across his face. Michael shared his grin.

"I think that's exactly what happened," he told him and Blake nodded in agreement.

"Yep." Blake continued pacing. "You're her alibi for the SEAL," he said, his mind moving on. "You saw her in the hallway when the shots came from the road. There's no disputing that. And, the bullet that killed Billy is a match to the ones that killed the SEAL, so by default, she's in the clear on that as well."

"Which brings us back to the person responsible for everything," Michael said.

Blake looked at him.

"Do you have any ideas?" he asked. Michael shook his head.

"I know it's someone on the Hill," he answered. "That's all I know."

"Well, we're going to need more than that to clear your buddy's kid sister," Blake muttered and Michael got up impatiently.

"I know," he agreed. "I'm getting another beer."

"Grab me one too," Blake said, stretching. "If I'd known this was going to turn into a brainstorming session, I would have brought vodka."

Michael grinned as he headed out of the garage.

"Look on the bright side! If we can sort this all out, we can make ourselves look good in the wake of what's going to be the biggest embarrassment either of our agencies have seen in a long time," he said over his shoulder. Blake snorted.

"I'll settle for just catching the bastard responsible for all this," he retorted.

Regina set the phone down and tapped her long red nails on her desk absently, a frown creasing her lips as she stared at the desk, lost in thought.

Harry, that meddlesome old fart from Homeland Security, had gone to Peru suddenly last night. Her spy had just confirmed it. Now why on earth would Harry take off to Peru in the middle of the night unexpectedly?

Harry had been a thorn in her side for the past two years. His dark eyes saw much more than they were supposed to, and he had connections out the whazoo all over this town. He was one of the old-school relics, left over from the cold war, and one of the more dangerous men in Washington. Alex had warned her repeatedly to steer clear of Harry, Homeland Security, and the CIA. Those were his areas of expertise and he would handle them. Regina had done as he asked, watching helplessly as Harry became more and more suspicious of them. Alex didn't seem to be capable of handling Harry, but she knew better than to suggest anything of the kind to the Vice President. Regina planted her own spy in DHS six months ago, and now was glad she had.

What made Harry go tearing off to Peru?

Regina opened her desk drawer and pulled out a big bottle of antacids. If Harry was suddenly mobilizing, there had to be a damn good reason. He didn't just take off anymore, and he certainly didn't do it on a private jet with no flight plan logged until it was taking off.

She popped a handful of antacids in her mouth and reached for the phone again. *Someone* had to know.

Alina sat back on the couch and rubbed her eyes. As much as she now loathed the man, Billy had certainly delivered as promised. Copies of emails between Regina and The Engineer, arranging payment and arrival, were included in the March folder of this year. Also in the March folder were visa forms for Johann, emails including classified information on Three Mile Island and flight arrangements for both Johann and his brother-in-law. Billy had also included proof of money paid to TSA agents and customs officials, with names and amounts, on both days that Johann and The Engineer had entered the country. Alina shook her head, almost impressed at the level of careful planning that had ensured seamless entry into the country for both men.

The April folder had offered up even more documentation, including wire transfers into the Engineer's offshore account. Alina read the details of the accident that had killed Stephanie's friend, Shannon Gleason, with interest. She was forced off the road and over the edge a ravine by a truck. Billy made over a grand on that job and a notation on the deposit slip indicated he had been paid cash by A.L. Alina smiled coldly. Even if Alex Ludmere tried to claim ignorance on everything else, he couldn't talk his way out of his initials on a deposit slip. Regardless of what he tried to say, even the press couldn't believe he was blameless when faced with that.

But it was the last folder on the drive that riveted her attention.

Viper scrolled through detailed descriptions, emailed instructions, and deposit slips for payment for both the hit and run attempt on Stephanie and the car bomb planted on her car. Billy also had detailed documentation on the attack on Michael, with notations of how much he had been instructed to pay the four participants and corresponding money transfers into his account. Alina read with interest the email from Regina to both Billy and Jason, telling them to make sure to get Michael's laptop and make it look like a robbery. Billy had also somehow landed copies of emails between Regina and Art Cosgrove, of the Secret Service. Alina was sure Michael would be interested to know that Regina was really the one guiding his investigation, not Art.

The laptop dinged, breaking the silence in the living room and alerting Alina to the fact that her copy of the files from the external harddrive was complete. She leaned forward, glancing at her watch with a yawn. It was about time for breakfast in Egypt.

Alina smiled slightly as she encrypted the copy of the files and zipped them into another encrypted file. Her contact in Egypt was about to get a surprise with her morning coffee. If anything happened and Viper failed, her contact would make sure Charlie got the encrypted file. She sent the file through the secure server and sat back, stretching her arms high above her head. Standing up with another wide yawn, she picked up her empty water bottle and wandered into the kitchen, setting it on the counter before opening the back door and stepping out into the night.

Leaning against the worn wooden banister, she stared out into the pitch darkness, the night alive with music around her. Owls were hooting in the trees, crickets were singing loudly everywhere, and a soft breeze carried the scent of the forest as it brushed against her face. Alina breathed deeply and felt her muscles relax on her exhale. The night was perfect and peaceful, soothing away her stress and surrounding her with its comfort. Tomorrow she would start stalking Regina. Her connection to the White House and the resulting protection made things tricky, but Viper was confident that she would find a way to get the woman out of her comfort zone. If she could do it with foreign national leaders, she could do it with Regina Cummings. Alina smiled slowly in the darkness.

After all, this was *exactly* what she had been trained to do.

Raven appeared out of the darkness and landed on the banister next to her hand. Alina smiled at her bird and lifted her hand to stroke his head. Raven bobbed his head, blinking his shiny eyes and staring at her intently. She let her hand fall away from his head and he bobbed it once more before launching off the banister again. Alina heard him land a few seconds later on the overhang above her head. He was going into the bedroom to settle down for what was left of the night.

She turned to go back into the cabin, closing the door and locking out the night. She flipped the light off in the kitchen and headed down the short hall to the living room. Alina was just passing the couch, on her way upstairs to bed, when her laptop made a familiar noise.

Viper smiled slightly as she went up the stairs. Her contact in Egypt had received the file. Her insurance was in place.

Blake watched as Michael pressed end on his cell phone and dropped it onto the bed next to the open carry-on bag.

"Who's Damon Peterson again?" he demanded from where he was leaning against the door jam.

"The missing DHS agent who was helping Ms. Walker and her partner three months ago," Michael answered, turning toward the dresser.

"And why do we care about him?" Blake asked, sipping his beer and watching as Michael grabbed a change of clothes from the dresser and stuffed them into the bag.

"*I* don't," Michael retorted, "but Art wants me to go Peru and bring him back. Now."

"Do you think he knows something?" Blake asked after a moment.

Michael glanced at him before he disappeared into the master bathroom.

"Art thinks he does," he called from within the bathroom. He reappeared a moment later with a black shaving kit in his hand.

"No offense, but so far Art hasn't impressed me with his intelligence," Blake muttered as Michael dropped the shaving kit into the carry-on and zipped up the bag.

"None taken." Michael picked up the bag and his phone and turned toward the door. "I think it's a wild goose-chase. Damon Peterson is no more a DHS agent than I'm Peter Pan."

He brushed past Blake and headed down the hall, Blake trailing after him down the stairs.

"So we think he's working with Viper?" he asked.

Michael glanced over his shoulder.

"I'm sure of it," he said.

He dropped his bag next to the front door, glanced at his watch, and went down the hall toward the kitchen. Blake followed with his beer.

"Then why is he in Peru?" he asked logically. "Viper's here. Isn't she?"

"Only God Himself knows where Viper is," Michael muttered, grabbing his half-empty beer off the island in the kitchen and lifting it to his mouth. Blake perched on one of the bar stools and frowned thoughtfully.

"How did Art find out Damon was in Peru?" he asked. Michael shrugged.

"He wouldn't say," he answered. "If he's still there when I get there, I'll be shocked."

"You think he's running?" Blake asked.

Michael shook his head.

"I don't know," he muttered, finishing his beer and turning to set the empty bottle into the sink. "I just don't know."

"Did Art say what reason to give to detain him?" Blake asked. Michael's lips twisted.

"National security," he answered grimly.

Blake stared at him and shook his head.

"This isn't a wild goose-chase. It's a witch hunt," he said.

Michael's eyes were troubled when they met his.

"I know."

"Well, I'll take care of my part here." Blake finished his beer and got up to put his bottle with Michael's in the sink. "I'll contact you as soon as I have something."

"I appreciate that," Michael said as they walked back toward the front door. "I'm sorry to drop all of this on you and then fly away."

Blake laughed.

"No worries," he answered, stopping at the door and turning to face Michael. His eyes were alight with a new sparkle. "You were always good for keeping it interesting," he added, holding out his hand. Michael grinned and grasped his hand.

"You be careful," he said, growing serious. "Everyone involved in this mess ends up with a bulls-eye on their back."

Blake's eyes met his and he nodded briefly, his jaw hardening.

"It won't be the first time we've had targets on our backs," he replied. "It's never ended well for the people who put them there. This time won't be any different."

Chapter Twenty-One

Damon sat at the table in the back corner of the hotel bar and stared at the handwritten note in his hands. After a long silence, he slowly lifted his eyes to the young local man sitting across from him. The man shivered at the look of icy fury in his eyes.

"This comes from your brother?" Hawk asked softly in Spanish.

The man nodded nervously.

"He sent me to you as soon as he heard you were here," he answered.

Hawk stared at him for a moment with those glacial eyes before folding up the note and slipping it into his pocket. He lifted the pint of beer in front of him and sipped it, watching the man across from him fidget.

"Your brother is a good friend, Marcus," he finally said, setting his glass down.

The young man visibly relaxed and managed a smile, revealing a missing tooth.

"He says the same of you," Marcus replied.

Hawk nodded and reached out to pull a small notepad toward him. He ripped the top page off the pad and placed it on the table before scrawling a quick note on the paper.

"Take this back to your brother, with my thanks," he said, folding it and handing it to Marcus. "Tell him I won't stay in the city. I'll be gone by morning."

"Si, Señor."

The young man stood up and turned to leave the bar without a backward glance. Damon watched him go, his eyes narrowed. Santiago was his closest contact in Lima, and his younger brother was as loyal as they came. When Marcus came to the hotel looking for him, Damon knew that something was wrong. Santiago never sent Marcus unless the situation was serious. Hawk sat back and sipped his beer again. The anger that had been simmering since yesterday, waiting to boil over, was now even closer to the surface.

They wanted him dead.

That was the message tucked into his pocket from Santiago. There was a price on his head high enough to attract most of the mercenaries and assassins worldwide. They were coming after *him* now.

Damon stared across the dimly lit restaurant, his eyes on the door. The bounty had been issued two nights ago, but the word had gone out this morning that he was in Lima. Santiago wrote that two mercenaries from Brazil were already in the city looking for him. He could delay them by sending them into the country, but there would be more.

Damon sipped his beer, his eyes remaining fixed absently on the door to the bar. He would leave the city today and go into the mountains until he decided on the best course of action. He wasn't staying in Peru. Viper may have got him here, but she couldn't make him stay.

Viper.

Hawk frowned ferociously. Obviously her contact in Egypt had alerted her to the bounty on his head when she spoke with her that last night. Harry told him that he and Viper were trying to protect him, and now Hawk knew just *what* they were trying to protect him from. When Regina couldn't get to Viper through Stephanie, she had come after him.

Damon set his beer down and crossed his arms over his chest, sitting back in his chair and glaring at the door. He set aside his anger with Viper for the moment and focused it on Regina Cummings instead. She was ruthless in her pursuit of Viper and, while he understood that Viper had witnessed a very inconvenient meeting between the Vice President of the United States and a terrorist leader, Regina's viciousness indicated that there was something more. For the life of him, Damon couldn't think what it could possibly be. The broken leg wouldn't warrant such spite...would it?

Hawk was still pondering the question when a large shadow filled the door of the bar. He noted the height and military bearing even as he raised his eyes to the newcomers face. His blue eyes met hazel-green ones across the near empty bar, and Damon recognized the Secret Service agent instantly. The two men stared at each other for a moment, weighing each other silently, one suddenly amused and the other cautiously curious.

Michael studied what he could see of the man seated in the shadows at the back of the bar. He had his back to the wall, his arms crossed over his chest, and he was staring right back at Michael intently. He looked perfectly at ease in the wooden bar chair, his legs stretched out comfortably beneath the dark, scarred table. In fact, Michael got the absurd impression that he was suddenly amused.

He turned to the bar with a frown and ordered a beer in Spanish, aware that the man in the corner never took his eyes off him. Once he was handed his beer, he turned toward the table in the back corner, noting the big shoulders and thick biceps as he moved closer. He sighed inwardly. If it came down to a fight, Damon Peterson would clearly be able to hold his own. Michael suddenly hoped his diplomacy wasn't as tired as his body was right now. The last thing he wanted was a fight with this brute on less than three hours of sleep in the past thirty-one hours.

"Mind if I join you?" Michael asked in English, stopping at the other side of the table.

"Not at all," Damon replied.

Michael pulled out the chair and set his pint down on the table. Hawk watched him, his blue eyes glinting in the dim light. Viper's gunny was larger and more solid up close and in person. He moved with precision that told Hawk he would make a worthy opponent in a fight, and he suddenly hoped the gunny would pick one. He needed a good fight to blow out some of this anger and frustration.

"You're a hard man to find," Michael told him, seating himself.

Hawk silent as Michael studied him, sitting back in his chair. The man before him exuded powerful confidence. This was a man who was capable of handling himself in any situation, and right now he was perfectly comfortable facing a federal agent across the table in a little hotel bar in Peru. Michael smiled.

"Is your name really Peterson?" he asked softly.

"No."

"I didn't think so," Michael murmured, sipping his beer. He grimaced slightly and set it down.

"Who do *you* think I am?" Hawk asked, his voice soft and dangerous.

"Does it matter?" Michael asked.

Damon studied the agent before him and saw the look of sharp intelligence in his eyes. *He knows exactly who I am,* Hawk thought in surprise. *He's already put it all together.*

"How did you find out?" he asked, dropping any pretense and uncrossing his arms.

Michael watched as Damon sipped his beer, his demeanor calm and disinterested. Yet, Michael had the impression that he was being tested.

"Do you want the long version or the short version?" he asked dryly.

Damon raised an eyebrow slightly and his lips twitched.

"Short," he answered. "Long versions bore me."

"A Navy SEAL was shot to death on my front porch and something had to link him to Viper," Michael told him, sipping his beer again. "I was halfway here before the light bulb went on. The connection wasn't a some*thing*, it was a some*one*. Someone whose name only showed up once in connection with Jason's unit."

"I'll have to look into that," Hawk murmured. "It shouldn't have shown up at all."

"Don't worry." Michael smiled slightly. "It won't show up again." Hawk glanced at him sharply and Michael shrugged. "It was the least I could do for you."

"Why are you here?" Damon asked after a moment of silence. "Did she send you away too?"

"Is that why you're here?" Michael asked in surprise. Hawk stared at him silently and he sighed. "No. She didn't send me. She's disappeared again. I was sent to bring you to Washington for questioning."

Hawk sat back, his face impassive.

"How did you find out where I was?" he asked softly.

"My boss's boss sent me," Michael answered, watching as Damon's eyes narrowed and his lips pressed together into a hard line.

"So, that's her game," Hawk murmured grimly, the anger surging toward the surface again. Send the Secret Service after him as well and, if the mercenaries didn't get him, she would.

"Who's game?" Michael repeated.

Hawk looked at him and Michael was confronted with icy fury in the cold blue eyes.

"Regina Cummings," Damon replied coldly.

Michael's eyebrows soared into his forehead.

"Regina?" he repeated in surprise. Damon noted the genuine surprise in Michael's eyes before it was almost instantly replaced with understanding. "Of course!" Michael exclaimed. "That explains almost everything!"

"Well, you've clearly figured most of this mess out," Damon observed in grudging respect.

"I knew someone close to the White House was responsible for everything," Michael said quietly, leaning forward. "Regina is the VP's right hand. What does Viper have on *her*?"

"Not her," Hawk told him softly. "Her boss."

He watched as Michael sat back, stunned. Hawk finished his beer and set the empty glass on the scarred table, waiting for Michael to work through what he had just heard. Michael lifted his beer and drained it two swallows.

"This is not good," he muttered, running his hand over his short hair. "Do you realize what you're saying?" Michael leaned forward and lowered his voice even lower. "You're saying the Vice President of the United States committed *treason*, not only aiding and abetting a terrorist on

US soil, but actually *bringing him here!*" he hissed.

Damon returned Michael's stare impassively, his arms crossed again, for all the world looking like he was bored out of his mind. Michael sat back in his chair, hitting the chair back with a thud, and stared at him while his mind raced. He had realized it had to be someone pretty far up in the pecking order in Washington, but Michael had never once considered the possibility that the guilty party was the Vice President himself.

"Well, no wonder they want Viper silenced at all costs," Michael finally said, breaking the silence.

"Nothing is ever easy with Viper," Damon murmured, his lips twitching.

"Does she have proof?" Michael asked sharply.

Hawk met his gaze squarely, all traces of humor gone.

"*We* have proof," he replied. Michael nodded shortly.

"I'll need to see it," he said.

"Oh, you will," Hawk promised, his voice still soft and laced with danger. "Don't worry."

"You don't understand." Michael leaned forward. "If you have proof, I need to see it *now*. My orders are to take you in for questioning. If what you say is true, then you're in just as much danger as she is and I need to protect you."

"Do you really think I need *your* protection?" Hawk demanded, his eyes lighting up with laughter. Michael grinned in spite of himself.

"Ok. Poor choice of words," he admitted. "Let me put it this way, I can't help you, or Viper, if I don't know the full facts."

"You already know the important facts," Damon pointed out, "but, in the interest of clarity, I'll fill in the holes." Damon uncrossed his arms and leaned on the table, waiting for Michael to lean forward to listen. "Two years ago, Viper was assigned to eliminate Johann Topamari. She followed him to Cairo, where she saw him walk out of a private meeting with Senator Ludmere. Ludmere *saw* her. She disappeared after that, went on hiatus, and wasn't heard from again until three months ago, when Johann appeared on US soil."

"She actually witnessed him walk out of a private room with Johann?" Michael asked. Damon nodded.

"But don't take her word for it," he said. "I went to Cairo myself three months ago and got sworn affidavits from both the hotel manager and one of the hotel workers who were there that morning. They observed both men going into the meeting together."

"What about what happened on Three Mile Island?" Michael demanded. "Do we have proof that Ludmere brought Johann into the country three months ago?"

"Viper was working on it," Damon sat back. "What she got, I don't know. She was onto something the last time I saw her. She didn't tell me, but she'd found something."

"How do you know?" Michael asked.

Damon's eyes met his and he smiled.

"She made steak."

Regina glanced at her phone, vibrating across her coffee table. She paused the press conference she was watching and picked up the phone.

"Tell me good news," she said, sitting back on her couch.

"Someone's in the apartment in Baltimore," the voice on the other end told her. Regina's lips curved into a smile.

"That *is* good news," she purred. "Tell me."

"I haven't seen them yet, but someone's definitely there. Food gets delivered through a local grocery store and there's electric and cable running to the apartment."

"Have the neighbors seen anyone?"

Regina got up and started walking around her couch slowly.

"No."

"Well, I suppose that doesn't mean anything," she said thoughtfully. "She was trained to be a ghost. No one ever sees her. Can you get in?"

"I think so."

"Then do it." Regina stopped at the back of the couch, a long red nail tracing circles on the microfiber. "And kill her."

She hung up and stared across the room at the huge arrangement of blood red roses on her sideboard. It had to be Viper. No one else would be in her safe house. The house outside Raleigh was empty. The apartment in Baltimore was the only other logical place, and someone was living there.

Regina smiled, her lips curling cruelly. She finally found the bitch. All their worries were about to end.

The doorbell rang and Regina swiveled around to go down the stairs to the marble-floored foyer at the bottom. She peeked through the peep-hole before throwing back the deadbolt and unlocking the door.

"Art!" Regina exclaimed, opening the door wide. "What a surprise! Thank you for the lovely roses. They're exquisite."

"I'm glad you like them." Art stepped into the foyer and Regina closed the door. "Are you busy?" he asked, peering up the stairs.

"Just watching this morning's press conference," she told him. "Come up."

"I won't stay long," Art said, following her up the stairs to the living room. "I have to make a three o'clock meeting, but I came to give you an update. We're getting closer."

"Really?" Regina dropped gracefully onto the couch and patted the seat next to her with her long nails. "Do tell!"

"I sent O'Reilly to Peru to bring back Damon Peterson." Art sat down and Regina turned to face him, bringing one knee up on the couch and laying her arm along the back.

"Oh good!" she exclaimed. "Did he find him?"

"He landed and called Chris about an hour and a half ago," Art told her. "He was going to check into the hotel you gave me, the one you said Damon had gone to."

"Have you heard from him since?" Regina asked, her nails tracing circles on the back of the couch again.

"No." Art shrugged. "But if Damon's there, O'Reilly will bring him back. The man's a boy scout. He doesn't know how to disobey orders. It's not in his DNA."

"Hmm." Regina looked at him, her dark eyes narrowing. "I always rather liked boy scouts," she murmured. "They follow instructions so well."

"Yes," Art agreed, his eyes glinting. "We should have the missing Peterson by tomorrow. How did you find out he was in Peru?"

"Luck." Regina waved her hand vaguely. "Someone from DHS took off unexpectedly to Peru the other night. Upon investigation, it turned out that he checked into the hotel with someone matching Peterson's description."

"Your information never ceases to amaze me," Art told her with a smile. "You missed your calling when you went into politics."

Regina chuckled and leaned forward to kiss him.

"You always know what to say," she murmured. "*You* should have gone into politics."

She wrapped her arms around his neck and pulled him to her. A long while later, Art pulled away firmly.

"I told you, I have to make it to a meeting," he said breathlessly.

Regina looked up at him limpidly.

"I'm not stopping you," she said with a wicked grin, her hand sliding off his thigh. Art grinned and glanced at his watch, cursing when he saw the time.

"I have to leave," he said, getting up and adjusting his shirt and pants hastily.

"Was that all you stopped by to tell me?" Regina asked, standing up and following him to the stairs. Art turned at the top of the stairs.

"Oh! There *was* something else I thought you might like to know," he said. "I heard from the Fed in charge of Billy's investigation and, since he was an employee of your security firm, I thought you'd be interested in what he told me."

"Yes?" Regina asked, her smile suddenly tense. "Are they any closer to finding out who did such a horrible thing?"

"Possibly." Art smiled. "The Feds found references on his laptop to an external hard-drive."

"Oh?" Regina's smile was frozen on her face.

"Yes." Art didn't notice her sudden stiffness or the arrested look in her eyes. "They think he may have been blackmailing someone. If they can find the hard-drive, they think it will lead them to his killer."

"It wasn't in the apartment?" Regina choked out, her mind spinning. Art shook his head.

"No," he answered, leaning forward to kiss her quickly before turning and jogging down the stairs. "They're looking for it now. I'll call you tonight!" Art called from the bottom of the stairs and a minute later, the front door slammed closed behind him.

Regina went blindly down the stairs after him, locking the door absently. There was another hard-drive? And the Feds thought Billy was blackmailing someone? She turned to go back up the stairs, her unease growing with each step she took. The sneaky son of a bitch! He kept a back-up drive with insurance, and there was no doubt who it was insurance against. In death, Billy had released his final act of mischief, directed at the woman who had enabled it all.

This was what she had been afraid of ever since the FBI took all his electronics. When there had been no outcry immediately forthcoming, she began to relax. After all, Billy had just as much to lose as she did in everything they had done. If he kept a record of everything and it had been exposed while he was still alive, he would have gone back to prison for life. Regina had convinced herself that she was safe.

She reached the top of the stairs, her blood running cold and her stomach dropping inside her. Grabbing the corner of the wall at the top of the stairs, she leaned against it for support. Billy had been a mean, conniving and evil man. It made him perfect for her purposes, but now she realized she should have kept a shorter leash on him. Knowing him as well as she did, she knew he would have taken perverse pleasure in documenting everything. There would be pictures, and documents, and videos. There would be audio. Billy had loved audio. He would tape his victims so that he could play back the sound of their screams later. He told her he got off on it. He would have saved *everything*.

And now it was all *missing!*

Regina released the wall and reached out blindly to snatch a glass bowl off the sideboard. Hurling it across the room, she screamed in fury, watching it shatter against the far wall.

She was ruined!

Ruined!

Viper leaned against the wall, arms crossed, and absorbed the noise around her. People milled around as the bells and mechanical music of slot machines flowed over them, drawn by the flashing lights and promising clink of coins. Time was suspended here, the lights at a constant brightness and the cascading sound of money never ending. Even in the high-roller rooms, the soft tapping of chips and murmured conversation never ceased, lending credibility to the impression of timelessness. There were no clocks and no windows, no way to gauge the passing of time. The casinos were self-contained worlds, adhering to their own schedule, and shunning the natural order of night and day. Whether it was six in the morning, noon, or midnight, the casino floors were always the same. You went there to have fun, and stayed there when you got lost in the excitement.

Frankie Solitto was at a poker table behind the door a few feet away. Alina stifled a yawn and watched as one of his black-suited henchmen disappeared through the door, carrying a message from her. He wasn't happy to be doing it, but Viper had convinced him with a few softly spoken, well-chosen words. A moment later, the man was back.

"He says he'll meet you at the bar in the lounge," he told her grudgingly.

He motioned to the martini lounge not far away, nestled in the corner behind the roulette tables. Viper glanced at him and nodded once, turning to make her way to the lounge. When she had gone to Danny's Place for her weekday check-in, she hadn't been there ten minutes before Marty sauntered in, sat down in the booth, and ordered the Guinness burger, with extra Guinness. She had cut her scotch short and headed north, responding to Frankie's message. She debated waiting for him at his house, but followed him to Atlantic City instead. She was short on time. She had to get back to Washington to check on her target. Regina received a visit from Art at her home in Georgetown earlier, and she went straight to her office shortly afterwards. Viper knew the news from Art hadn't been good, and she was uneasy not being on hand to watch her target. Not for the first time today, she wished she had Hawk as a second set of eyes on Regina.

Alina stepped into the martini lounge and looked around. The lights were dim, mood lighting in full effect even though it wasn't even six o'clock yet. A blue LED light snaked its way along the floor in the center of the lounge, outlining a huge martini glass on the dark carpet. Two bars ran the length of the room on both sides and a stage stretched across the back wall. Tables spaced intimately throughout the lounge had votives burning in the center, and the candlelight cast an ambiance of subdued elegance.

Viper turned toward the bar on the left, which had only one customer seated midway down. She moved to the far end of the bar, away from the door, and settled herself with her back to the empty stage and a clear view of the door and the lounge.

"Ketel martini with a twist," she said to the bartender.

The bartender nodded and turned away to make the drink as Viper watched the door patiently. She didn't have long to wait. The bartender was just setting her martini down in front of her when Frankie strode through the doors. He glanced around, spotted her at the far end and came toward her, his suited henchman following at a discreet distance.

"Scotch," Frankie told the bartender as he seated himself next to Viper. "The usual." The bartender nodded with a smile and Frankie turned his attention to Alina. "You got my message."

"You have news for me?" Alina asked, sipping her martini. Frankie nodded.

"News, and a present," he told her. Viper raised an eyebrow.

"A present?" she repeated, her lips curving. "Will I like it?"

"I hope so," Frankie smiled at her. "Do you enjoy the casinos?" he asked as the bartender returned with his scotch. Alina smiled slightly.

"I don't usually have much time to play," she murmured, sipping her martini again. Frankie chuckled and took a sip of scotch.

"Then I'll keep this brief," he said after the bartender had moved away to the other end of the bar again. "You were right about the leak. It's been taken care of."

"I know," Viper told him, setting her glass down. "I was there."

Frankie stared at her, speechless, and Viper smiled. The smile didn't reach her eyes, he noticed, and he swallowed.

"Where, exactly, were you?" Frankie demanded finally.

"About three feet away."

Frankie blinked and reached for his scotch.

"Tell me," he commanded.

Viper raised an eyebrow slightly and looked at him. The head of the Jersey Family flushed at the look in her eyes.

"If you want to..." he added awkwardly.

"Why don't *you* tell *me* how an ex-Navy SEAL came to be on your payroll?" Viper suggested softly. Frankie shrugged.

"He was at a loose end when he got out and came back home," he told her. "He suffered from that post-trauma syndrome that most of the boys are coming back with and he needed work. I put him to work in good faith."

"Who was he really working for?" Alina asked.

Frankie looked at her and his lips twitched.

"You already know the answer to that if you were there when he was popped," he replied.

Alina grinned suddenly.

"I like you, Frankie," she announced, her eyes dancing. "Yes, I know who he was working for. How did he get into your ranks?"

"That idiot Marty," Frankie said. "He sent him here with a recommendation."

"Ah, of course. Marty." Alina sipped her martini. "And he was convinced of Jason's legitimacy by one of his associates outside of the Family?"

"Marty has a lot of associates outside the Family," Frankie said carefully. "He trades in information and, as such, he comes into contact with a lot of different types down there. One of them introduced Jason to Marty, and the rest is history."

"Billy Conners?" Alina asked. Frankie nodded, his lips curving in another grin.

"You really don't miss anything, do you?" he asked. Alina smiled slightly.

"I can't afford to," she murmured. "What's the present you have for me?" she asked, glancing at her watch.

"I took care of something for you," Frankie told her with a smile.

Viper raised an eyebrow.

"Oh, do tell."

"I heard there was some trouble down in Washington with a hit and run and a car bomb," Frankie said, sipping his scotch and watching her over the rim of the glass. She didn't flinch, but continued to look back at him with a faint smile.

"Marty said Billy was running his mouth pretty freely about it," Frankie continued. "He said the target was a Fed who was down there from Jersey, on vacation, poking around in something Billy said didn't concern her. Well, I thought to myself, I know a young Fed from Jersey. She was involved in that incident three months ago, when you did my Family a favor. Then I think to myself, what's Billy got against her? So I had Marty poke around for me. Guess what he found out?"

Frankie smiled. Viper was staring at him, arrested.

"He found out Billy was being paid to get rid of the Fed, once and for all," Frankie said softly. "He was told to get rid of the Fed and watch for you. He was told you would come out of hiding for that."

Frankie nodded, sipping his scotch and watching Viper. She lifted her martini, her hand perfectly steady, and sipped it, her eyes never leaving his face.

"Marty certainly *is* good at information," Alina murmured. Frankie nodded again.

"That he is," he admitted.

"So what did you do when he told you all this?" Alina asked.

"I had it taken care of," Frankie told her. "You *and* your Fed are safe from Billy now."

Alina slowly set the martini glass down, her eyes never leaving Frankie's face. She stared at him, her heart pounding while her mind clamored to grasp what he was telling her. Frankie took care of Billy Conners? Frankie had Billy *killed?* Michael's warning popped into her head, *'Good, because by tomorrow you're going to be the prime suspect in the murder of two men.'*

Good God, she'd left Billy tied to a chair, bleeding and unconscious, but alive!

"In his apartment?" Viper asked, somehow managing to keep her voice steady.

"Yes. Nice and clean." Frankie set down his glass and motioned to his henchman lurking near the door. The man disappeared.

"Nice and clean for whom?" Viper muttered. It was bad enough that they were trying to pin Jason's death on her, but now she was suspected of shooting Billy Conners?

"I thought you would be grateful." Frankie frowned. "You don't look very grateful," he told her accusingly.

Alina stifled the sudden desire to laugh hysterically.

"I'm just overwhelmed," she replied honestly. Frankie glanced at her suspiciously.

"The way I see it, we're almost even now," he said.

Viper raised an eyebrow and looked at him.

"Almost even?" she repeated.

"I don't like owing anyone any favors," Frankie explained quietly. "In my mind, this takes care of one."

"As I recall, you don't owe me anything," Viper said, finishing her martini as Frankie's henchman appeared again in the door to the lounge. He was carrying a shopping bag from one of the boutique shops that Alina had passed on her way through the casino.

"We all owe you something," Frankie retorted obscurely. He turned to take the bag from his employee and the man returned to the door. "This is your present. Don't open it here. Wait until you're alone."

"It's not a horse's head, is it?" Alina asked, taking the bag.

Frankie laughed, the booming sound making the bartender glance over in surprise.

"Take it with peace," Frankie told her, standing. Alina stood with him and he held out his hand to her. "Think of it as a token of my appreciation."

"Thank you." Alina grasped his hand and Frankie held it for a long moment, his eyes meeting hers. He stared at her, his lips curving into a soft smile.

"Vai con Dio," he murmured.

Alina smiled, her fingers tightening briefly on his.

"Grazie amico mio," she replied softly, her Italian impeccable.

Frankie nodded in approval before releasing her hand and turning to leave the lounge. When he got to the door, he glanced behind him for one last look at the mysterious woman who had risked so much three months ago, and continued to risk so much now.

Frankie stopped abruptly, turned around, and scanned the lounge with a frown.

She had already disappeared.

Chapter Twenty-Two

Michael hung up with Blake and turned back to Damon. They had moved from the hotel bar to the luxury suite at the top of the hotel and Damon was typing away on his laptop.

"Do you think that was wise?" Damon asked without looking up.

Michael raised an eyebrow.

"Blake is helping in DC while I'm here," he said. "He needs to know who our prime suspects are."

"Well, you just made him a target." Damon lifted his eyes to him. "Everyone who touches this mess becomes a liability to them. They're going after anyone they think can expose them."

"He's already aware of that," Michael retorted, setting his phone down on the table next Damon. "We were both already aware of that much last night before I left."

"Do you trust him?" Hawk asked, glancing up at him.

"With my life."

"That's exactly what's hanging in the balance," he told him, turning his attention back to his laptop.

"I know." Michael watched him for a minute. "What are you doing?"

"Making arrangements," Damon answered shortly.

Michael frowned and turned to wander aimlessly around the sitting room.

"Viper's going after them, isn't she?" he asked, glancing back at Damon. "So far she hasn't done anything wrong," Michael continued when it became apparent that his companion wasn't going to offer a comment. "As of right now, I have nothing to charge her with, except maybe destroying private property when she shot out the cameras in the parking garage, and I can't even prove *that* without her gun. Right now, she's free and clear. But, if she goes after the VP, she'll cross over to where I can't help her."

"She won't go after the VP."

Damon finally spoke. Michael glanced at him from across the room.

"How can you be so sure?" he demanded. Damon looked up.

"Because she doesn't need to," he said simply.

"You think she'll just go after Regina?" Michael asked, his forehead creasing in a frown. Damon sat back in his chair.

"Regina is the only one who counts now," he explained. "We have enough evidence between us all to hang Ludmere without having to make him a target. I think Viper realized that when they decided to go after you. You were a threat because you could track down the money trail that would lead back to Ludmere. Regina was the one Viper needed to pin down."

"Morganston Securities," Michael muttered, shaking his head.

"Excuse me?"

"I've been trying to remember how I knew Morganston Securities," Michael explained. "I know it from Regina. She mentioned it the one and only time we ever had dinner."

"It's her shell company," Damon said. "She's the sole shareholder."

"Billy's hard-drive!" Michael exclaimed suddenly, cutting Damon short and banging his hands together. He swung around to face Damon. "Of course!"

"Billy's what?" Michael had Damon's full attention now.

"Billy had an external hard-drive," Michael explained, his eyes alight. "Blake told me last night they found references to it on his laptop when they took it from his apartment."

"Wait. What were the Feds doing in Billy's apartment?" Hawk demanded.

Michael strode over to the table and turned a chair so that he could straddle it, facing Damon.

"Billy Conners was shot in the head Sunday," he told him and Damon's eyebrows soared into his forehead in surprise. "Blake called me over to Billy's apartment because he'd been tied to a chair in his bedroom and shot, just like Jason was on my porch."

"This was Sunday?" Hawk's mind was working backwards quickly.

"Yes. Same caliber as the shots that killed Jason," Michael said. Damon stared at him, his face impassive. "Blake thought Viper had done them both."

Damon remained silent, listening. Michael watched him in grudging admiration. The man wasn't betraying a single thought, even though it was clear this was all news to him.

"Forensics on both sets of bullets showed that they were fired from the same gun," Michael continued, "but two factors eliminated Viper.

227

One, the bullets in the parking garage did *not* match the others, and we're pretty damn sure it was Viper who shot out the cameras in the parking garage. Two, *I* am Viper's alibi for Jason."

"Ah." Damon's lips twitched. "You know, then."

"Yes," Michael said shortly, anger swelling inside him again.

Damon watched Michael's eyes turn a stormy, glittering green and suddenly had some sympathy for him. He understood completely what Michael was feeling. They were both furious at the same woman.

"Well, I know who shot Jason," Hawk told him, deciding to give him something to take his mind off of how Alina had lied to him. It was Michael's turn to be surprised.

"Who?" he demanded.

"Frankie Solitto had him popped," Damon informed him with a grin.

Michael stared at him.

"Frankie...as in Jersey mob Frankie Solitto?" he demanded. Damon nodded. "What the hell does the *Jersey Mob* have to with any of this??" Michael roared and Damon couldn't contain his laugh.

"I told you, nothing is ever simple with Viper."

Michael got up and took a turn around the room again, muttering under his breath while Damon watched, his shoulders still shaking with inward laughter.

"I'm sure that once you explain it to me, it'll make perfect sense." Michael finally returned to his seat. "So tell me."

"Viper told Solitto that he had a leak to the Feds, and she advised him to find it," Damon explained, his eyes dancing.

Michael blinked.

"She told...she advised...a mob boss...to *clean house??*" he sputtered.

"Once you get to know Viper, you'll learn it's all part of her charm," Damon advised him.

Michael ran his hand over his hair, staring at Damon in disbelief.

"You're serious, aren't you?"

"Yes."

Michael continued to stare at Damon for a long moment in silence. Hawk glanced back at his laptop as a message flashed up and, while Michael was mulling over the random and unwelcome entrance of the Jersey mob into his life, Damon answered the message quickly before closing the laptop.

"So what you're saying is, Jason was Frankie's leak," Michael said.

"Yes."

"What was he doing in my house?" Michael demanded.

The laughter faded from Damon's blue eyes.

228

"He was paid, along with the others, to break in and beat the daylights out of you," he said. "Viper believes Regina ordered it to get your laptop. She thinks Regina was getting worried about your research on The Engineer."

"Of course." Michael nodded shortly. "That makes sense, but are you saying it was just coincidence that Jason was there?"

"Absolutely not." Damon shook his head. "I fought with Jason. He was as good a man as you could ever want to meet," he said quietly. "He wouldn't have worked for Solitto unless he thought he was doing something else."

"He wasn't working for Solitto." Michael suddenly understood. "He was working for Regina. Regina put him in Solitto's employment as a spy."

"And a leak back to the government," Damon finished. "My guess is that she inserted Jason up there around the same time that Johann came into the States. She would have wanted to have an extra set of ears and eyes up there. Johann was using a member of the Solitto family in his network, so that's where she put him."

"So Frankie found out about Jason. How did he know he was going to be at my house that night?"

Michael got up and went over to the sideboard and the coffeemaker there. He poured himself a cup of coffee, stifling a yawn. His long flight was catching up with him and he couldn't seem to wrap his mind around all this.

"Billy," Damon answered.

Michael drank some coffee and came back to the table.

"Ok, but then why did Solitto kill Billy?"

"You have me there," Damon replied. "I didn't know Billy was dead until you told me. Where's this external hard-drive?"

"No one knows," Michael answered, sipping the coffee. "There was no hard-drive in the apartment. Blake found a compartment at the back of the closet where he thinks it was kept, but the compartment was empty and no one's been able to find it."

"Of course not," Damon murmured, his lips curving into a soft smile. Michael saw it and nodded reluctantly.

"Billy must have kept a record of all his dealings with Regina," he said. "If Viper somehow got that hard-drive, she probably has all the evidence she's looking for against Regina Cummings."

"And everything she needs to justify making her a target," Damon murmured. "That's my girl."

Michael looked at him sharply but Damon's face was already impassive again. If Michael thought he had glimpsed a soft look of

229

admiration in Damon's cold eyes, he must have been mistaken. Damon was as cold and distant as he had been for most of their short acquaintance.

"Regina must have seen the file," Michael said suddenly. "Viper's file was released yesterday. Against my advice, my agency jumped to the conclusion that the bullets that killed both Jason and Billy were all fired by Viper. Given the pressure, your agency finally released her file. They released it to me, my boss, and my boss's boss."

"The same boss's boss that sent you here?" Damon pointed out softly.

Michael nodded, his eyes meeting Damon's.

"Art must have shown Regina the file. It's the only way she could have known to look for you," Michael said thoughtfully.

"Oh, she was looking for me before that file got released," Damon muttered, "but I know Regina has seen the file."

"Your codename was in the file, and your picture was in the evidence from Three Mile Island three months ago," Michael continued. "Even if she put two and two together before now, the file would have confirmed it."

Damon was silent, waiting for the full ramifications of that thought to hit Michael. He didn't have long to wait.

"Dammit! That means Art was feeding her information all along!" Michael exploded, his eyes flashing green again. "I've been taking orders from *them!*"

"Yep." Damon stood up and stretched, his own eyes narrowing slightly. "What else was in that file?"

"They blacked most of it out," Michael answered. "A couple of code-names, yours included, and the locations of her safe houses were in there. Dates and locations of missions, but no details. Nothing really that useful, actually," he added thoughtfully.

"Safe houses?" Damon glanced at him sharply. "What safe houses?"

Michael looked at him, frowning slightly at the sharp tone in Damon's voice.

"All of them," he answered simply.

Damon swore softly and Michael was filled with a sense of foreboding.

"Tell me Viper isn't in one of them," he said.

"No," Damon told him, turning back to his laptop and flipping it open, "but Stephanie Walker and her partner *are!*"

Alina sipped her coffee and raised her military binoculars to her eyes. She was ensconced on a rooftop diagonal from Regina's townhouse. The sun had set about an hour ago, and a warm evening breeze blew gently against her face. Regina had returned from her office carrying a cardboard file box and hadn't left the house since. Alina watched her now through the living room window. She was on the phone, pacing around the couch. Lowering the binoculars, Alina frowned and sipped her coffee again.

Cardboard boxes never boded well.

This morning, her target had gone to a press conference and stood in the back, watching as Ludmere fielded questions from the press. She left the press conference and accompanied the Vice President back to his house, where she had brunch before heading back to her townhouse. Regina was, at that point, what appeared to be her normal, hurried self. When she arrived home, she showered, changed into slacks, and settled in front of the TV to watch the press conference again, making notes as she watched. She received a phone call in the middle of it and whatever was said had made Regina very happy. She was all smiles when she hung up the phone.

And then Art arrived.

Viper recognized Michael's superior from his statement to the agencies, addressing the very serious issue of the 'rogue agent running amok' in DC. Her Egyptian contact sent her the clip, including an audio snippet of *Werewolves of London* with the link, and Viper had watched it early that morning. She had been humming the song ever since, her sense of humor tickled. When Art arrived on Regina's doorstep, Viper saw in person the man who was causing her so much discomfort with his witch hunt. She had studied him, and was unimpressed. Art had the seal of the town in which he worked stamped all over him, and Viper had never been in awe of the power in Washington.

But something Art said upset Regina terribly. Viper had watched as as Regina threw a fit in the living room after he left. She broke two glass bowls and a vase of roses before she was finished. Reggie had a temper, and Viper had a pretty good idea what had brought it to the surface.

Alina lifted the binoculars again and slowly scanned the street in front of the townhouse, stopping when she picked out the black Dodge Challenger parked half a block away. She zoomed in and watched as the man settled behind the wheel unwrapped a burger and bit into it.

Blake Hanover.

She saw him for the first time this morning. He had been at the press conference, not far from Regina. Regina smiled at him as she was entering and Blake nodded briefly in acknowledgement. He caught Viper's attention again when the press conference was ending and he answered his phone as he turned to leave. He was turning towards Alina and his voice rose slightly before he remembered where he was and lowered it quickly. She watched curiously as he hung up and pushed through the media throng, disappearing into the crowds. When she spotted him again a few hours later, parked outside Regina's office, Viper knew she had another player. On her way to New Jersey, she ran his picture through the databases on her laptop. By the time she pulled into the parking garage for the casino in Atlantic City, she knew all about Blake Hanover.

Viper watched him for a moment thoughtfully. Michael had disappeared, and now here was Blake. The two were former Marine buddies, and Blake was heading the FBI portion of the investigation into Stephanie's car and Michael's dead Navy SEAL. He was also the Agent in Charge of Billy Conners' murder. But what had led Blake to Regina? Who had tipped him off?

For Blake had clearly been tipped off. He had been stuck to Regina like glue all afternoon and evening. When Viper left to go to Danny's Place at four, Blake was parked down the street from Regina's office in the black Challenger. When she came back from her meeting with Frankie, the Challenger was still parked in the same spot. Now, here he was again. Blake was watching Regina as intently as she was herself. Now why was that? If he was investigating Billy Conners' death, then he had to have discovered that there was a missing hard-drive. Had there been something else on his laptop? Something to lead Blake to Regina?

Alina hadn't bothered wiping Billy's laptop or trying to hide the compartment in the bedroom. She left Billy alive and had all expectations that he would tell Regina what was in Viper's hands. She *wanted* Regina to know. Viper wanted her to know that she was coming for her, but Billy had apparently been shot before he could pass on the message.

Now, however, Viper was confident that she had been warned by Art. He was too involved with the mess to not be getting daily updates from both his own people and the Feds. He would have heard about the hard-drive by now, if Blake did indeed know about its existence. If he didn't, the empty compartment in the closet would have alerted any Federal agent worth his salt that *something* was missing. Even if they didn't know what it was, they would know something had been taken. Regina wouldn't be able to take the chance that whatever was missing would not incriminate her.

The very fact that Blake was seated in a car now, watching Regina, told Viper that he knew she was guilty of something. But *HOW?* Had Michael figured it out? Had he found the money trail? Had the phone call Blake took at the press conference been from Michael?

Alina shook her head with a slight frown. The only thing she knew for sure was that Blake was a Federal agent and he was watching Regina. That could only mean one thing: he was watching her with a view to apprehend her.

Viper moved her binoculars back to the living room window where Regina was still pacing around the room, her phone still stuck to her ear. Her eyes narrowed slightly and she lowered the binoculars, lifting her coffee to her lips again.

She had no intention of allowing Blake, or anyone else, to apprehend her.

Regina Cummings was hers.

Michael glanced at Damon as they left the city of Lima behind them and bounced over a pothole in the middle of the barely-paved road, the mountains looming above them in the distance. They were headed into the country and the buildings fell away behind them as the road snaked around rugged hills. The air was fresh out here, and the sky was transitioning from blinding blue to a stunning mauve as the sun began to set. Michael took a deep breath, looking out over the craggy landscape and enjoying his first view of the Peruvian countryside.

Damon hadn't been very talkative since they left the hotel. The speed with which he arranged for them to leave Peru and get back to the States should have surprised Michael, but he was beyond surprise at this point. He had offered his government contacts, but Damon laughed briefly and otherwise ignored him. When pressed with the reminder that Michael was a federal agent and Damon was his temporary charge, Hawk informed him bluntly that he would get them back to the States his way, or Michael would go alone. Michael had no doubt that he meant it and, still torn between his job and his personal opinions, he caved. Until this was sorted out one way or another, he had to stay with Damon.

Damon had their departure arranged within twenty minutes of turning to his laptop. Michael hadn't asked what those arrangements were, sensing that it would be a fruitless exercise. After closing his laptop, Damon produced an extra duffel bag and tossed it to him, saying that his carry-on made him look like a tourist. He hadn't said much since.

Michael grabbed the roll-bar of the old Jeep as Damon veered off the road and onto little more than a goat track that snaked up the side of a very steep, vertical incline. Damon glanced at him and, for the first time since leaving the hotel, a grin creased his face.

"Getting worried yet?" he asked, shifting gears and pressing the gas. Michael grinned back.

"Should I be?" he retorted.

Damon guided the topless, door-less Jeep up the side of the mountain incline. He was surprised at how much he liked Viper's gunny. Michael O'Reilly had turned out to be an intelligent and rugged military man, earning Hawk's grudging respect in the few short hours that he'd been with him. Not only was he willing to compromise to get what he wanted, evident in the fact that Damon was driving them to his private exit point in Peru instead of the international airport, but Michael was genuinely concerned about the many ramifications of this whole mess. He wasn't just another ex-military suit who had landed in Washington and was working his way through agency life. He was still a Marine. He still thought like a Marine, he still acted like a Marine, and he still believed in what had *made* him a Marine. Damon couldn't help but respect that.

Hawk followed the track as fast as he knew the old Jeep could take it while Michael hung on next to him. With every mile that separated them from the city, he wondered again why he was doing this. The Fearless Feds could take care of themselves. They were federal agents. If they couldn't take care of themselves, that was certainly not *his* responsibility. Viper had taken that upon herself.

Viper.

Damon clenched his jaw. He was doing this for her. He knew she was focused on Regina and wouldn't, *couldn't*, know that she had put the Fearless Feds in danger. They were sitting ducks. Regina would send her minions to the safe house's closest to DC, hoping to find Viper. When she found them instead, it would be nice and tidy clean-up. He couldn't let that happen, not if he had the ability to protect them. Hawk had promised to help Viper any way he could, no questions asked, and if that meant protecting her friends, then so be it. He couldn't just walk away from her, even if she had walked away from him first.

Anger washed over him anew.

Alina drugged him, kidnapped him, and dumped him in Lima, leaving him there while she went back to Washington to fight a losing battle. It didn't make any difference to him that she did it for his safety. He didn't care. She walked away from him purposefully, leaving him on a different continent while she faced the biggest enemy she had ever faced yet. Alone.

How dare she?

Hawk punched the Jeep over the rise and they bounced onto flat land again. After everything they had been through, she just up and left. Worse, she drugged him, dumped him in a different country, and *then* up and left. How could she do it?

Damon's eyes narrowed slightly. He knew with a sinking sense of doom inside him that he would never be able to walk away from Viper like that.

Dammit. He loved her.

With that admission to himself, Hawk felt as if he'd been sucker-punched right in the gut. He stared through the windshield across the craggy plateau, stunned. Alina was complicated, independent and intimidating on her best day, and on *all* days, she was controlling. What she couldn't control, she shot. She was so completely her own person that Damon couldn't even begin to imagine her as a partner, even though he had been actively pursuing just that for three months now. She was a rock, and an enigma. She was just beyond reach.

Yet, three months ago, he caught glimpses of the Jersey girl. Alina was still a woman, fused deep within Viper's armor, and he was in love with that woman. When had *that* happened? *How* had it happened? And what on earth was he going to do about it?

"Should I be getting worried now?" Michael interrupted Damon's thoughts.

He glanced at him, brought back to earth suddenly. Michael nodded ahead of them and Damon slowed the Jeep, his eyes taking in the three local men standing in the middle of the goat track. Their hair was long and unkempt and they were dressed in work clothes, military-style boots on their feet. They had rifles slung over their shoulders and were blocking their progress. Hawk smiled slightly.

"Are you rethinking traveling with me now?" he asked, glancing at Michael again.

Michael's eyes met his and Damon saw the glint of amusement in them.

"I give us two to one odds," Michael retorted.

Damon let out a short bark of laughter and slowed to a stop before the armed locals. He left the engine running and studied them for a moment before standing up in the Jeep.

"You picked a bad time to block the road," he called out in Spanish. "I'm in a hurry."

The men looked at each other and back to him. One of them

stepped forward and a wide grin split his face, exposing several gaps in his teeth. He fingered his rifle suggestively.

"In a hurry to leave our beautiful country?" he called back before spitting on the ground. "You just got here, Señor Peterson."

"Friends of yours?" Michael asked.

Hawk glanced down at him, his eyes glinting.

"Two to one, huh?" he replied. "What do we win?"

"I like beer," Michael suggested with a shrug. "I prefer to keep it simple with new acquaintances. I haven't seen you in action yet."

"Don't want to commit to a steak dinner just yet?" Damon asked, his lips twitching. Michael grinned.

"No offense."

"Hey! Señores!" Toothless yelled, growing impatient. "Get out of the car. We have guns! See?"

He waved his rifle in the air and Damon sighed.

"We don't really have time for this," he muttered, leaving the engine running and jumping out.

Michael climbed out of the Jeep grinning and met Damon in front of the hood as the three locals advanced on them, rifles in hand.

"Care to explain this at all?" he asked him. Hawk shrugged.

"I have a price on my head."

"You could have told me that sooner," Michael muttered. Hawk grinned.

"Where's the fun in that?" he demanded.

"Hey! We still have guns," Toothless snapped in Spanish. "Stop talking."

"He keeps mentioning the guns," Michael said in Spanish, raising his voice slightly. "Is that some kind of cultural thing?"

The men had moved close enough now for Hawk to reach out and grab the barrel of Toothless's rifle and wrench it upwards, hitting him sharply in the face with his own gun. It happened so fast that no one saw it coming. Toothless let out a howl of instant rage and pain as his nose cracked and blood started pouring down his face. Within seconds, both Michael and Damon were armed with rifles, which they used as weapons without ever having to fire a shot. Michael got one of the men around the neck with his rifle, using him as a shield to prevent the third from firing. While that local was yelling threats in Spanish, Damon hit Toothless with a debilitating jab to his kidneys, followed by a blow to his temple that knocked him out. Once he fell to the ground, Hawk turned and kicked the back of the legs of the third man, bringing him to his knees with a cry. A second later, he was also unconscious on the ground. Michael released his prisoner, spinning him around and cracking him on the side of the head with the rifle.

Less than a minute after the fight had begun, the last man was sinking to the ground silently.

"Bring the guns," Hawk said, grabbing the extra rounds of ammunition off Toothless. "We might need them."

"Will there be more of them?" Michael asked, grabbing the third man's rifle and turning back to the Jeep. Hawk followed.

"You never know," he answered, tossing his rifle and the ammunition into the back of the Jeep before climbing in. Michael tossed the other two rifles in and got back into the passenger's seat.

"Ok then." Michael grabbed the roll bar again as Damon put the Jeep in gear and drove around the pile of men left in the middle of the goat track. "Are you always this boring?"

"Only when I'm forced to deal with Marines," Hawk retorted with a quick grin, drawing a laugh from Michael.

Damon maneuvered the Jeep up another incline, this one even steeper than the last. The fight hadn't even *been* a fight according to Hawk's standards, but he felt a hundred times better nonetheless. Some of his simmering frustration and anger had disappeared with the satisfying crack of the unknown assailant's nose. One or two more scuffles like that before he laid eyes on Viper again and he might not be tempted to wring her bloody neck.

"Do you think we'll make it back in time?" Michael asked, breaking the silence a few moments later, his mind on Stephanie Walker and her partner.

"I don't know," Damon answered after a short silence.

"Blake is watching Regina," Michael told him, glancing at him, "but she might send someone else to Baltimore."

"Oh, she won't go herself," Hawk said derisively. "She won't face Viper. She prefers to hide behind her cousin."

"I still can't wrap my mind around it all," Michael muttered, more to himself than to his companion. "What was Ludmere meeting with Johann about in Cairo?" Damon glanced at Michael, and Michael caught the considering look. "You know!" he exclaimed. "You *know* what the meeting was about!"

"That's Viper's story to tell," Hawk said after a short silence. "You'll know when she wants you to know."

"What if she doesn't get the chance?" Michael demanded.

Damon ignored the lurch in his gut at the agent's words.

"Then I'll re-evaluate," he said shortly, indicating that the conversation was over.

Michael lapsed into silence as they rounded a bend in the goat track, turning past a copse of trees at the base of another incline. As they rounded the trees, a huge flat clearing came into view, and settled in the center was a black helicopter. Damon stopped the Jeep and switched off the engine, hopping out as a tall man separated himself from the chopper.

"I was getting worried!" he called in Spanish. Damon waved as he grabbed one of the rifles and his duffel bag from the back. "I heard there is a price for your head."

"When has that ever stopped me, Pietro?" Hawk demanded, striding up to him and holding his hand out with a grin. Pietro gripped it, his face creasing in an answering smile.

"That is because you are half-insane!" he exclaimed. He turned his head as Michael strode up, carrying his bag and a second rifle. "This is the American? He's big. He looks like a Marine."

"He also speaks Spanish," Michael said dryly.

Damon chuckled and Pietro continued to grin unabashedly.

"Then there's hope for you yet!" he retorted. "But enough talk. You have to leave now to get to Columbia on time." Pietro turned back to Damon. "Everything you need is in the chopper. I will take the car back to Santiago."

Damon nodded and handed him the keys.

"Thank you, my friend," he said, holding out his hand again. "Give Santiago my thanks, for both the message he sent and the use of the Jeep."

"Of course. You are always welcome, Hawk. You know that," Pietro told him with a nod.

Damon smiled and clapped him on the shoulder before turning and heading towards the chopper.

"There's a rifle in the back, should you need it," he called over his shoulder.

Pietro waved and jogged toward the Jeep while Michael followed Damon up to the helicopter. He climbed in after him, wondering what on earth he had gotten himself into.

Chapter Twenty-Three

Blake rubbed his eyes and yawned widely. He lifted up an almost empty, forty-two-ounce cup of watery soda and sucked the rest of it down, glancing up at the windows of Regina's townhouse. She was moving between rooms and every light was on. Blake dropped the empty cup into his cup holder and raised his binoculars, zooming in on the living room. He could just make out her moving in front of the windows again, her phone on ear. She had been on the phone since she returned from her office over three hours ago. Blake dropped the binoculars as his own cell phone started ringing. Glancing at the name, he reached over and picked it up.

"How's Peru?" he answered.

"Don't know. Not there," Michael retorted. Blake frowned.

"Sight-seeing already?" he asked.

"You could say that." Michael sounded amused. Wind was buffeting the cellphone on Michael's end and Blake turned up the volume on his phone in an effort to hear more clearly. "How's our rat?"

"At home in her barrel," Blake told him. "If you're not in Peru, where are you?"

"Bogotá."

Blake's eyebrows soared into his forehead. What on earth was Michael doing in Columbia?

"Pick me up some coffee," he said, stifling another yawn. "What are you doing there?"

"We're on our way back," Michael said.

"So you found him?"

"Yes." The rushing sound of wind ended abruptly and Blake listened for the sound of a door closing, but there was none. "We should be back soon. What's going on there?" Michael asked, his voice suddenly loud in the absence of howling wind.

"Not much." Blake glanced back up to the townhouse. "She brought back a box from her office, and there's a lot of light and a lot of movement going on up there. I think our rat is getting ready to run."

"Don't let her out of your sight," Michael said. Blake frowned.

"I have no reason to detain her," he pointed out. "Do we have proof yet?"

"In a way," Michael said obscurely. "Don't detain her, but don't lose her."

"I'll do my best," Blake said. He scratched at the stubble growing on his jaw. "I might have one of my guys take over when she goes to bed so I can go home and shower. Not being prepared for a stake-out, I didn't leave the house with the appropriate supplies," he added accusingly.

"You should always be prepared," Michael retorted. "I'll let you know when we land."

"Are you flying into Dulles?" Blake asked, lifting his binoculars again with one hand and watching as Regina disappeared from the living room and reappeared in the kitchen.

"Philly," Michael answered and Blake's eyebrows soared once more into his forehead.

"You really *are* sight-seeing, aren't you?" he exclaimed. Michael laughed shortly.

"You have no idea."

Michael disconnected after that cryptic remark and Blake dropped the phone back onto the seat next to him, shaking his head. Michael always did have a way of complicating things. He watched as the kitchen light went out and glanced at his watch. Quarter past eleven. Lowering the binoculars, he leaned his head back on the seat. It was going to be a long night.

Alina slid behind the wheel of the Land Rover and sat for a moment thoughtfully. The windows of the townhouse were finally dark, her target in bed. Regina was getting ready to run, that much was clear. She had just spent four hours on the phone while systematically shredding the entire contents of the file box from her office, one page at a time. In between shredding evidence, she worked on her laptop and Viper had watched as she connected an external hard-drive to the laptop, moving files.

Oh yes. She was getting ready to run. Alina smiled slowly.

Instead of her finding a way to Regina, Regina would come to her.

Alina started the engine and was about to pull out of her spot in the alleyway when the bag Frankie handed her in the casino caught her eye.

Next Exit, Pay Toll

She put the Land Rover back into park and reached over to pull the bag up onto the seat next to her. Inside was a wooden box wrapped in brown paper and Alina pulled it out, tossing the shopping bag aside and resting the box on her lap. She stared at it for a moment, wondering if she really wanted to open it. Wooden boxes given as gifts from mob bosses never turned out well in the movies.

Frankie, if this is a dead anything, I'll find you and scar you for the rest of your life, she thought, reaching into her pocket for her leather gloves.

Alina pulled them on and opened the box. Blinking, she stared down at the semi-automatic, .45 Beretta that lay inside. It was a few years old and was most definitely a used gun. Slowly, her lips started to curve upwards. Frankie said it was a present, and it most definitely was that.

Closing the box again, Alina set it on the seat next to her, staring out the windshield. Jason and Billy had both been shot with a .45. She didn't need to run ballistics to know that Frankie had given her the smoking gun.

Oh Frankie, you don't miss much yourself, Viper thought with a smile.

He must have realized what he had done shortly after he had Billy killed. He must have realized that he had created yet another complication for her. Frankie was going through a lot of trouble to stay on her good side, Viper realized, and this present was more than just a token of appreciation.

This was her ticket to total exoneration, and she knew exactly what to do with it.

Michael hung up and dropped into the leather recliner opposite Damon. The stewardess moved past them to take her seat in the front of the private jet as the engines geared up for take-off.

"Blake says Regina is getting ready to bolt," he said as he fastened his seatbelt. Damon turned his eyes from where he was staring out the window broodingly.

"She won't get far," he replied.

"You think Viper is watching her now?"

"Undoubtedly." Damon stretched and glanced out the window again as the small jet turned on the isolated runway on the outskirts of Aeropuerto el Dorado International. "She's probably been watching her all day."

"Blake didn't say anything about seeing anyone else," Michael said.

The look he received made him feel like a schoolboy who just announced that Santa Claus was real.

"He won't see her," Damon said simply.

Michael watched as his companion turned his attention back out the window. The engines kicked up more as the jet began moving down the runway, picking up speed rapidly. Michael rested his head on the headrest as he was pressed back into the seat, his eyes resting on Damon's face. He wondered who this man was, that he could arrange chopper transport from Peru to Columbia and a private jet from Bogotá to Philly in less than half an hour. Was this who Alina had become? Did *she* have private pilots on speed dial as well? Michael's lips twitched. And, would *she* fly the helicopter herself?

Just as quickly as the flash of amusement came, it was replaced with irritation. Viper was a government assassin with a life that he didn't want to know about, and Alina was Dave's kid sister whom he had promised to look after and was sexy as hell. Michael still couldn't reconcile the two in his head. He watched Damon lean his head back on his seat, his eyes still fixed out the window, as the wheels left the tarmac and the jet lifted effortlessly into the air. Michael's stomach dropped as they left solid ground behind and arched up into the clouds. Damon was more a part of Viper's life than he could ever be. He knew more about the way she worked and the way she thought, and Michael suspected that Damon was closer to Alina than anyone. He frowned slightly at the thought.

"You should get some sleep," Damon spoke suddenly, his blue eyes catching Michael mid-stare.

"Are you going to sleep?" Michael asked.

"I have some work to do first," Damon said, reaching down under the seat and pulling his laptop from his bag. "But you need to rest. You look half-dead and no amount of coffee will fix it. Sleep is the best weapon we have."

Michael got the impression that Damon was repeating an axiom that he lived by religiously. He watched as he opened his laptop and powered it on before those deep blue eyes flicked to his face again. They glinted briefly with something resembling amusement.

"You're no good to me if you're too tired to fight."

"You know more fighting means more beer," Michael said and Damon grinned.

"Agreed."

Michael reclined his seat back tiredly. Damon was right. He was flat exhausted, not having slept now for almost two days. He needed to sleep. He settled back, staring at the ceiling of the cabin.

Why *had* Ludmere met with a terrorist two years ago? It would have been before the election, while they were still campaigning as

Presidential candidates. Why would he have taken time from the all-important campaign trail to go halfway around the world and meet with a known terrorist? Why would he have risked it?

Michael's eyes shifted to Hawk, typing away on his laptop. Hawk knew why, and so did Viper. They both knew secrets far above even *his* security level, but they weren't telling anyone. Michael realized with a start that he may *never* know why Alex had met with Johann two years ago. Hawk and Viper were bound by oaths of silence as strong as his own, and Michael had no doubt that they would stick to them if they didn't deem the information need-to-know.

As Michael's eyes slid shut out of pure exhaustion, his last waking thought was that it really didn't matter why. What mattered was that his Vice President and Regina Cummings were guilty of treason, and he had no idea how he was going to convince anyone of their guilt.

Blake unlocked the door to his condo and opened it, flipping on the light as he stepped into the small entryway. He yawned widely and kicked the door closed behind him before tossing his keys onto the hall stand inside the door. A large, brown and white speckled pit bull charged out of the living room, rearing himself up and planting his front paws on Blake's sternum. He barked once and Blake grinned, leaning his face down to be licked mercilessly.

"Hey Buddy," he murmured, rubbing the dog's ears.

Buddy dropped down to all fours and stretched before turning to trot back into the living room. Blake locked the door and followed, switching on the lamp next to his favorite arm chair.

"I hope Martha came and took you out because I'm too tired," he informed his pet. Buddy's answer was to jump onto the couch, circle once and plop down heavily with a big yawn. Blake grinned. "Exactly. I have time to shower, shave, and grab half an hour of sleep before I have to get back to relieve Anthony."

Buddy responded to that statement by crossing his front paws and resting his head on them, his eyes gazing up at his master adoringly. Blake rubbed a hand through his hair and turned to go down the hallway, past the dining room and galley-style kitchen, to the master bedroom at the far end of the hallway. He was half-way down the hall before he stopped abruptly with a frown. Spinning around, he strode back to the dining room and flipped on the light.

Sitting on his dining table, right in the middle where he couldn't fail to miss it, was a wooden box.

Blake glanced around the dining room and back-tracked to the living room again. Buddy lifted his head as he entered the living room, watching as Blake looked around carefully. The windows were closed and locked, the shades and curtains drawn. Nothing was out of place and everything was quiet. He turned and went slowly through his home, checking the windows and finding them all locked securely. He went through the kitchen, guest room, guest bath, master bedroom and master bath. They were all empty of intruders and nothing was out of place.

Blake was scowling by the time he went back into the dining room to stare at the wooden box. A piece of white paper, torn off his memo pad in the living room, was in front of the box. He walked up to the table and glanced down at the note.

> *You looked a little sleepy tonight. Try alternating water with the coffee. It helps. Here's a little something that should perk you up. I think you'll find it helpful.*

> *V*

A swift, cold chill streaked down Blake's spine and he spun around, scanning the space behind him. No one was there. The chill was from the note, and the scrawled drawing of a snake next to the V.

Viper.

She had been here. In his house. *With his dog!*

Blake frowned and backed up to glance accusingly into the living room where Buddy was going back to sleep on the couch. Buddy never let anyone into the house without Blake there. Martha was the only exception. She had been coming to clean the house and take Buddy out since he was a wee puppy and he knew her well. Other than her, no one got through the door.

Except Viper.

Blake returned to the table with a frown. He reached into his pocket for the pair of latex gloves that he always carried with him. Pulling them on, he lifted the note and examined it with a frown. It was written on his own memo paper with his own pen. He recognized the tell-tale blots of ink. Dropping the note back onto the table, Blake turned his attention to the box. He lifted it carefully, testing the weight and moving it closer to him. He debated whether or not to open it, wondering if it was booby-trapped, but then shook his head impatiently. If Viper was going to try to kill him, she would have shot him earlier when she had obviously been watching him outside Regina's.

He opened the lid to the box. His mind registered the fact that it was a .45 Beretta as soon as he opened the lid and he stared at it, stunned. What did this mean? Was this her gun? Was this the gun that shot out the cameras in the parking garage?

Blake tilted his head, studying the pistol. It was an older model, two years old at least, and maybe more. He didn't picture Viper using an older gun like this. Perhaps as a backup, but not as her primary weapon. If everything Michael had told him was true, Blake imagined she would carry something newer as her primary weapon.

Was this the gun that shot Billy and Jason?

Blake flipped the lid to the box closed and went out into the living room to get some evidence bags from his work bag. Whichever gun it was, it was now evidence.

And Viper had handed it to him.

Alina finished transferring the final encrypted file and sat back on the couch. She stared at the big, empty fireplace and leaned her head back tiredly. Like many others in her profession, she had set up fail-safes and avenues of escape for herself. Unlike Hawk's friend Paul, she didn't have servers full of information on every job she had ever done, but she *did* have what she liked to call her "insurance agent." It was a single, secure server that she had set up five years ago. It was untraceable, unhackable, and she was the only one who knew of its existence. She set it up in case she would ever have need of insurance to protect herself, in case anything like *this* ever happened.

She closed her eyes and breathed deeply, listening to the silence around her. She wondered what Hawk was doing. Had he moved on to his next assignment? Or was he taking a break, hiking in the Andes? Was he still in the city where she had left him? Alina doubted it. He would have heard by now of the price on his head. The mountains were his friend, just as they were hers, and he would have disappeared into them, waiting to hear what happened in Washington.

Once she took care of Regina, he would be safe again. He would go back to his life and she would be free to return to hers. She could get back to the life she had been living before any of the events in the past three months had happened. She could get back to normal.

Alina opened her eyes as a wave of crushing depression washed over her. Her mountain retreat that had proved to be such a healing haven for her was now part of the past. She couldn't go back there, and she had known that when she left. They knew about that place now. The people who lived there, trained there, and prayed there would be in danger if she ever went back. The sensei who had guided her through her healing process, teaching her how to keep her body and mind strong while her soul healed, would be put at risk. Alina would never allow that to happen.

She could return to her adopted city in Europe, buy a new apartment in a new section, and go back to her old life of work and constant travel. However, that life suddenly seemed cold and lonely to her. Alina remembered the nights spent alone and, while they hadn't bothered her then, now they filled her with an unfamiliar kind of dread.

She didn't want to be alone anymore.

She didn't want to go back to her isolated existence, surrounded by people yet knowing no one. Returning to Jersey three months ago had reminded her of what her life should be and used to be, filled with a few close and trusted friends, and moments of laughter and belonging. And emotion. Between her old friends and Hawk, Viper had learned to feel again. She didn't *want* to go back to the emotionless existence she led before.

Alina sat quietly, wondering if there was a possibility that she could change her life. She had purchased the house in Medford, buried in the pine barrens of New Jersey. Only five other people knew of it, four of whom she trusted and one of whom was dead. Would it be possible to shift her living arrangements and base herself out of New Jersey? To continue her work and still have some semblance of a normal life outside of it?

Viper frowned thoughtfully. Logistically it could be done. She would be further away from the location of most of her targets, but travel was nothing new to her and she would still have her apartments dotted throughout the world. The change wouldn't impact her effectiveness, and she would have a true retreat to come back to in between assignments. She would have a home, and for the first time in years, that thought didn't scare her. She would have a home and a few friends that she could trust. Alina stared into the fireplace, her mind shifting to a pair of dark blue eyes.

Hawk would always know where to find her.

Alina closed her laptop and stood up, turning to switch out the lights and go upstairs to bed. She firmly pushed all thoughts of Damon and his blue eyes out of her mind. She didn't have time to dwell on him and the strange mess of emotions that he evoked. *If* she decided to return to New Jersey permanently, then she would allow herself to explore the "maybes" and "what-ifs" of a possible relationship with Damon Miles. Right now, she had to focus on Regina Cummings.

And getting them all out of this god-awful mess Regina had started three months ago.

Chapter Twenty-Four

Stephanie came awake with a start. The room was pitch black and the apartment was silent, but something had awoken her. She sat up and listened intently to the silence, staring at the closed bedroom door. When there was no sound after a few seconds, she glanced at the phone, plugged into the charger on her bedside table next to her holstered 9mm Glock. Stephanie reached out and swiftly pulled her gun from the holster, swinging her legs out of bed and standing in the darkness. She heard John's bedroom door open and crossed to her door swiftly, opening it and looking out into the hallway. John was disappearing into the living room, his phone pressed to his ear. Stephanie followed him silently.

"Are you serious?" John was demanding as she stepped into the living room.

He turned and saw her, his eyes dropping to her gun. He smiled briefly in the darkness at the sight of it. Stephanie watched him curiously. Only two people had the number to the clean phones that Alina had given them.

"How reliable is the information?" John asked, standing in the middle of the living room, listening intently. After a moment, he sighed. "You don't need to come here. I think we can handle it," he muttered.

Whatever the response was to that, it didn't make John happy. He scowled ferociously and the muscle in his jaw pulsed as he clamped his jaw shut. Stephanie had her answer as to which of the two people had called the secure phone. Only one of them had the knack of irritating John so swiftly.

"Fine."

John hung up and tossed the phone onto the coffee table before turning to face Stephanie. His lips curved into a grin and he looked at her gun again.

"You expecting company?" he asked humorously.

"I didn't know what woke me up," Stephanie retorted, setting the gun down on the end table. "Now I know it was your phone. What did

Damon say?"

"We'll be having company," John answered, sinking down onto the couch with a yawn and propping his bare feet onto the coffee table. Stephanie frowned and sat next to him. "You might want to keep that gun handy. Apparently, you had the right idea."

"What happened?" Stephanie asked.

"He didn't say much." John yawned again and rubbed his face. "The gist of it was that Alina's government file was released yesterday, and in it was a list of all her safe houses, this one included."

Stephanie sat back on the couch, a chill running through her.

"So, the person who tried to kill me now knows where we are."

John nodded and glanced at her.

"That's about it," he answered. He watched as she stared straight-ahead, her lips pressed together slightly. "Are you worried?" he asked softly.

Stephanie glanced at him.

"I'd be a fool not to be," she retorted. "They tried twice and failed. Alina was right. They won't stop until I'm dead."

"Or until they are."

"Did Damon say how much time we have?" Stephanie asked. John shook his head.

"No. He just landed in Philly and is coming straight here," he told her. "He wants us to be on our guard."

"Why isn't he with Alina?" Stephanie demanded.

John leaned his head back on the couch.

"I don't know. I didn't get the chance to ask," he muttered.

Stephanie was silent as they both stared at the numbers illuminated on the cable box. 3:32am.

"I have two guns," Stephanie finally broke the silence. "This one and Alina's back-up. How about you?"

"Two."

They fell silent again, both listening to the silence around them. Going back to sleep was out of the question now.

"Damon sounded pretty sure of the threat?" Stephanie asked after a moment.

"He's coming here," John retorted and Stephanie nodded. They both knew Damon wouldn't make the trip unless he was sure.

"I guess I'd better get dressed then."

Stephanie stood up and John glanced at her t-shirt and boxer shorts with a grin.

"I kind of like the pj's," he told her, standing with her.

Stephanie rolled her eyes and picked up her gun, starting down the hallway to her bedroom. She turned her head when she realized that John was right behind her.

"What are you doing?" she demanded, stopping and facing him in the dark hallway.

John looked down at her, his face inches from hers.

"Coming with you," he said, all traces of humor gone from his face. "Until this is over, I'm not leaving your side."

"I think I can get dressed without you," Stephanie retorted.

John shook his head slowly and that familiar twinkle came back into his eyes.

"But where would the fun be in that?" he murmured.

Stephanie huffed and turned to go into her bedroom, John close behind her.

"Sometimes I really do think you're still stuck in grade school," she muttered.

Viper glanced at her watch and then lifted the binoculars to her eyes. She scanned the quiet street in front of Regina's house, pausing for a moment on the black Challenger parked halfway down. The sun was just starting to lighten the sky to a pale gray and the birds were starting to wake up, interrupting the silence occasionally with their song. Regina's house was still and quiet, but Alina knew that she was awake. Her cellphone had just received an incoming call.

Viper lowered her binoculars and turned to the small laptop next to her. She had hacked into Regina's cell carrier and set a patch on Regina's line before she left the cabin. Now, she ran a trace on the number that had just called Regina's cell phone. It was another cell phone and the GPS link placed it in Miami. Alina watched as the call time reached just over three minutes before it ended. She raised the binoculars again and waited, watching Regina's house. After a few minutes, a light flicked on in the hallway and then the light in the kitchen turned on. Viper glanced at her watch again. Just after five in the morning. Regina was getting an early start today.

Alina lowered the binoculars and turned back to her laptop. Within seconds, she had the name of the person who owned the phone in Miami. She ran it through one of her programs and, a few minutes later, knew that they were a private charter pilot. Viper raised her head and lifted her travel mug of coffee to her lips thoughtfully.

Regina was definitely running. From Miami, she could easily reach any of the islands, Latin America, or South America. Or she could could cross the ocean and disappear into Europe. Alina narrowed her eyes, staring at the townhouse from her rooftop. She couldn't see Regina going to Europe right away. She would need funds, and the islands were notorious for offshore accounts. If she was arranging to fly by private charter out of Miami, Alina liked the odds of the islands as the destination. But when? When was she flying out?

Lifting the binoculars again, Viper watched as Regina made herself coffee before going into the dining room where her laptop was sitting on the dining room table. She settled herself before it with her coffee and Alina shifted her binoculars to the black Challenger.

It was in the same spot as it had been last night and Alina wondered if Blake had been home yet to see the present she left him. She studied the car thoughtfully and zoomed in on him. He was sipping bottled water, binoculars to his eyes, watching Regina's living room window. Alina smiled slowly, noting the freshly-shaved face and different shirt. He had been home. He had the gun.

She moved the binoculars back to Regina's window and watched for another moment before lowering them again. She drank some more coffee, stifling a yawn, and turned to her bag. Alina pulled out an earbud and a hand-held, digital scanner. Plugging the earbud into the scanner, she adjusted the frequency before picking up the binoculars again. She watched as Regina typed away on her laptop, her cell phone next to her on the table. Alina lowered the binoculars again. She would be able to listen to the next call that was made on Regina's phone. She settled down to wait patiently.

Viper was in the middle of sipping her coffee a few minutes later when the scanner in her hand picked up a signal coming from Regina's cell. Setting her coffee down, she glanced at the laptop and saw that the call was outgoing. Viper hooked the earbud into her ear and lifted the binoculars, watching as Regina drummed her long nails on the table, her phone on her ear.

"Hello?" a voice sounded groggy in Viper's ear.

"Leon?" Regina asked, getting up from her chair and starting to pace around her dining room.

"Yeah. Who's this?"

"This is Regina Cummings." Regina wandered out of the dining room and into the living room. "I need a ride to Miami and I don't want anyone to know I'm going. Are you available to fly me down there?"

"That depends on when you want to go," Leon answered with a loud yawn. "I have a run to Boston this morning, and I have a client booked to Cali tomorrow afternoon."

"Tonight?" Regina asked.

"Where do you want to leave from?" Leon asked after a moment of silence.

"Somewhere quiet. Remote," Regina answered, pausing at the couch and running her finger along the back. "Not one of the usual airports."

"Hm." There was a short silence as Leon thought for a moment. "There's Shannon, outside Fredericksburg. I can arrange to fly you out from there later tonight."

"Wonderful!" Regina exclaimed, spinning around and heading back to the laptop on the table. "What time?"

"Any time after nine tonight." Leon was yawning again. "Why don't we say nine-thirty to be safe. Is that too late for you?"

"No, that's perfect," Regina said, sinking down into her chair at the table.

"Ok. Send me the details," Leon said. "I'll be ready to take-off at nine-thirty tonight."

"Thanks, Leon." Regina disconnected and set the phone down on the table.

Across the street on her rooftop, Viper smiled coldly in the dim light of the rising sun and pulled the earbud out of her ear, reaching for her coffee again.

Regina would never see that flight.

"I know you."

Stephanie made that accusation as she opened the door to the apartment, standing aside so that Michael could step inside out of the hall. Michael smiled and she glanced out into the hallway before closing the door behind him.

"Nice to see you alive and well," Michael replied, holding out his hand. Stephanie took it, smiling at him warmly.

"I do my best," she answered, her eyes meeting his. "Where's Damon?"

"He's coming. He wanted to do a sweep of the neighborhood first," Michael told her, setting his duffel bag down.

He looked at the tall blond man coming towards him from the hallway. He had a badge clipped to his belt and his standard issue in a holster beside it.

"John Smithe?" he asked him and the blond nodded.

"And you are?" John asked.

"Michael O'Reilly." Michael held out his hand. "I'm with the Secret Service."

"Oh, you're..." John started to say something as he gripped Michael's hand, but Stephanie cut him off quickly.

"You look half-dead," she told Michael. "I have coffee in the kitchen. Come on in."

"Thanks." Michael glanced at John and turned to follow Stephanie into the kitchen. "Have you guys seen anything? Heard anything?" he asked as she poured coffee into a mug for him.

"Not a thing," Stephanie answered, handing him the mug. "It's been quiet as a..."

"Don't say it!" John exclaimed from the doorway.

Michael grinned and sipped the black coffee thankfully. They landed in Philly at three and cleared customs by three-thirty. Damon picked up a black SUV at the airport and drove straight to Baltimore, not taking time to stop for breakfast or even coffee. They pulled into the underground parking garage a little after five in the morning and, after satisfying himself that the building was secure, he told Michael which apartment to go to before disappearing to sweep the neighborhood for any obvious signs of surveillance.

"Well, I'm glad about that, at any rate," Michael told Stephanie. "I don't want to have to explain to your boss that you came down to Washington and got yourself killed."

"How did you end up coming here with Damon?" John asked, his pale eyes studying Michael.

"It's a very long story," Michael told him.

"At least you didn't say it was complicated," John muttered, turning to go back into the living room.

"Don't mind John," Stephanie said, rolling her eyes. "He's not known for his social graces."

"Don't make excuses for me," John called from the living room and Stephanie grinned.

"There *is* no excuse for you," she retorted.

Michael carried his coffee into the living room and looked around, taking note of the position of the rooms to the windows and the hallway down to the bedrooms.

"Is this the only door in?" he asked, motioning to the front door.

Stephanie glanced at him and nodded, passing him on her way to the living room.

"Yes," she said. "No balcony and no trash chute," she added, sitting next to John on the couch.

Michael nodded and turned to go over to the window in the living room, lifting one of the slats in the shade and peering out. There was a beautiful view out over the harbor, but a sheer drop down to the water. No entry possible there.

"Well, that makes security fairly easy," he murmured, turning away from the window. "Did Viper arrange for food?"

"Yes." Stephanie watched as Michael settled himself on the recliner. "The same person brings it each time. Are you still trying to track her down?" she asked.

Michael's hazel green eyes met hers over the rim of his coffee mug.

"*She* tracked *me* down," he replied.

"Is *that* how you ended up with Damon?" John asked, glancing at him.

Michael sighed. John was like a terrier with a bone.

"No. I was sent to bring him to Washington for questioning," he answered.

"How did you know where to find him?" Stephanie demanded. "No one's been able to track him or Ali...Viper down in three months," she corrected herself quickly and Michael's eyes narrowed slightly.

"I think I'll let Damon explain that part," he said, watching as the front door opened silently behind Stephanie and John. "He seems to have his own ideas as to what should be known and by whom."

"Of course he does," John said, sitting back on the couch. "He'll just say that it's complicated."

"It is."

Damon spoke directly behind them and Stephanie and John both jumped, turning on the couch to stare up at him. He smiled at them faintly.

"It's very complicated, but I'll tell you if you're sure you want to know."

"How bad is it?" Stephanie demanded, standing up and facing him.

"No worse than I'm sure you've already guessed," he answered with a shrug. He glanced at Michael. "What have you told them?"

"Nothing." Michael grinned. "I was waiting for you. There's coffee in the kitchen," he added.

Damon nodded and turned to go into the kitchen, but Stephanie beat him there. She got another mug out of the cabinet and turned to pour him coffee.

"You don't have to serve me," he murmured.

"I know," she retorted. "How's Alina?"

"She was fine the last time I saw her," Damon answered shortly.

Stephanie caught the edge to his voice and looked at him sharply.

"Why aren't you with her?" she asked him, lowering her voice.

Damon looked down at her consideringly and Stephanie saw the shadows under his eyes and the grimness about his mouth.

"She decided she didn't need me."

Hawk heard himself say it before he could think twice. Stephanie studied him for a long moment before smiling slightly.

"Alina needs you more than you know," she said softly, handing him the mug of coffee. "And more than she knows."

Damon took the coffee and watched as Stephanie went back into the living room after imparting that little gem of wisdom. He frowned and sipped his coffee thoughtfully before turning and following her.

"Let's start with Viper's file," John said as Damon carried his coffee over to the window. Like Michael, he lifted one of the slats of the shade and glanced out, looking down to the lapping harbor far below. "You said when you called that her file had been released and that's how they know about this place. Let's start there."

"It was released Monday morning," Michael told him.

"Why? How in God's name did it get released?" John demanded with a frown. "I thought it was classified."

Damon turned from the window and sipped his coffee, his eyes resting on John in amusement.

"It's a long story," Damon said before Michael could answer.

"That's not an answer," John retorted.

Michael glanced at Damon and his lips twitched as he saw the glint of pure devilry in his eyes.

"Nevertheless, it's the truth," Damon replied calmly.

"Dammit Damon, stop baiting him!" Stephanie exclaimed. "Just tell us!" she added when Damon glanced at her, his lips twitching.

"I take it you've been down this road before?" Michael asked Stephanie and she shook her head, rolling her eyes.

"You have no idea," she muttered.

Michael glanced at Damon with a grin.

"Oh, I think I do," he murmured.

Damon looked at him and laughed reluctantly. Michael didn't miss much.

"What do you want to know?" Damon asked, leaning his back against the wall next to the window.

"Viper's file," John said through gritted teeth.

"My agency pressured her agency to release it," Michael told him.

"How?"

"That's the long story," Damon murmured, sipping his coffee.

John started to stand up to face Damon and Stephanie grabbed his arm to stop him.

"For God's sake, John!" she exclaimed in exasperation. She looked at Michael beseechingly only to find him fighting back a laugh.

"Will you two just explain what the hell is going on?" she demanded. "We've been locked up here since Saturday, with no idea what's happening, and we're a little cranky. We get a call in the middle of the night telling us that we're no longer in a 'safe' place, and we still have no idea why that is. I don't know where my friend is, whether she's dead or alive, and right now I really don't care about being diplomatic. Forget John. If you guys don't tell me what's going on, *I'm* going to lose it!"

Michael looked at her, all traces of laughter gone from his face.

"It really *is* a long, complicated story," he told her.

Stephanie met his look squarely.

"Then start talking."

Harry glanced at his watch before walking up to the coffee cart at the side of the path. It was a little before nine and he was early, a habit he still carried over from his days in the field. He ordered a large coffee, looking around while he waited for the vendor to pour it into the travel cup. The sun was shining and the day was clear. A hot breeze blew over his bald head and Harry sighed. He would be glad when fall arrived. The summer heat was wearing on him.

He paid for his coffee and turned away from the cart, securing the lid on the cup before lifting it to his lips. His eyes scanned the people moving through the park. Some were businessmen and women, but most were mothers with jogging strollers. He moved to the side of the path and walked toward a bench a few feet away. Charlie would be right on time, as always. In fact, Harry knew Charlie was probably watching him right now. He settled on the bench and set the coffee next to him, pulling his paper from under his arm and flicking it open with a practiced movement.

"Do you ever actually read the paper?"

Harry glanced up at the man who seemed to have materialized next to him. He grinned and folded the paper closed again.

"Never," he answered, standing and shaking Charlie's hand.

Charlie grinned back, his brown eyes dancing.

"Neither do I," he said. "Let's walk."

Harry nodded and picked up his coffee, falling into step beside the man who had trained next to him years ago. They followed similar paths throughout their careers and when Charlie had advanced to the upper echelons of the agency, Harry had been glad to see him get there. Charlie had the impersonal and dispassionate nature needed to run his section with the kind of success that he had achieved. Harry eventually moved over to the Department of Homeland Security, not because he wanted to, but because Charlie had asked him to. Charlie needed someone he could trust in that agency, and Harry had gone as a personal favor to him.

"How was Peru?" Charlie asked after a few moments of silence.

Harry glanced at him with a grin.

"When did you find out?" he asked.

Charlie tossed him a tolerant smile.

"When your plane left Dulles," he replied. "I wasn't surprised. As soon as I heard about the price on Hawk's head, I knew she'd do something. I must admit, I didn't expect that she would physically force him to leave. How did she manage it?"

"She drugged him," Harry answered and Charlie let out a bark of laughter.

"That's my girl," he chortled. "How did he take it?"

"How do you think?" Harry muttered. "I've never seen Hawk that angry, and I pray to God I never do again."

Charlie fell silent again and Harry sipped his coffee patiently.

"He's not there anymore," Charlie finally told him.

"I never expected that he would stay," Harry admitted. "Where is he?"

"Back in the states." Charlie moved out of the way of a couple of runners before continuing. "I lost track of them after they landed in Philadelphia, but I would imagine they're either in Baltimore or headed back into Washington."

"They?"

"Michael O'Reilly went to Peru after him." Charlie glanced at Harry in time to catch his surprise. He nodded. "Viper was right. The file worked like a charm. They fell right into the trap."

"Tell me," Harry said.

"I released a heavily edited, fake file to the Secret Service," Charlie told him, his voice low. "It's not Viper's real file. She wanted it to be total fiction, but I had to include a few details that could be verified to make it authentic. I added some of her safe houses and a few unimportant mission details. I released it, eyes-only, to three people."

"Which one passed it on?" Harry demanded.

"Art Cosgrove," Charlie said. "I've been watching him for a few months now. I had a feeling it would be him. He's been seeing a lot of

Regina Cummings lately and, of course, that's where the file ended up."

"I'm not surprised," Harry murmured. "We knew it was Ludmere that met with Johann. It makes sense that it would be his assistant that was managing it all."

"Yes." Charlie clasped his hands together behind his back as they walked. "Viper knew that the file would lead us to who was responsible."

"This is a good thing," Harry said, glancing at Charlie. "So why are you worried?"

"Viper is off radar until this thing is finished," Charlie said slowly. "I have no way of knowing whether or not there was any additional fall-out from releasing the file. I wasn't happy about doing it, but she seemed sure that it was the only way to prove the leak."

"She was right," Harry said, finishing his coffee and dropping it into a trash can. "Now we know their whole network."

"Regina had you followed, you know. She has a spy in DHS," Charlie told him. "That's how she knew to send O'Reilly to Peru after Hawk. She's trying to tie up all her loose ends."

"I've known about her spy for three months now," Harry replied. "I've been monitoring him. So far, he's been harmless. Are you worried about O'Reilly?"

"I don't know," Charlie admitted. "I don't think he was in on it, but there's no way to know for sure until Viper wraps it up."

Harry stopped walking and faced his old friend. Charlie stopped and looked at him.

"Charlie, what has you so worried?" Harry demanded. "We both know Viper and Hawk can handle this. We wouldn't have done this, otherwise. Everything is working out just as we planned. You're worried about something, and it's not them."

Charlie smiled slightly, his eyes concealed behind his sunglasses.

"You know me too well, my friend," he murmured. "I'm worried about Ludmere and how we'll handle him. When Viper takes care of the head, we can roll up the body. But Ludmere is rather more than just part of the network. The President will have to be read in on the whole operation."

"Ah." Harry turned and started to walk again. "You're worried about what he'll do when he finds out just *why* Ludmere met with Johann two years ago."

"Exactly." Charlie looked up at the blue sky and the green trees arching over the path. "This is a scandal the likes of which the White House has never seen before, and we're going to need to contain it without the country knowing anything. The President will agree with that whole-heartedly."

"He'll do what needs to be done," Harry assured Charlie. "And he'll empower you to do what needs to be done on your end. He won't have a choice."

"I know." Charlie nodded and looked at Harry. "But how will he react when I tell him the truth? And how the hell am I supposed to tell the President that, on top of everything else, his Vice-President was going to have him assassinated two years ago?"

Chapter Twenty-Five

Blake hit the hands-free button in his car as he turned the corner, keeping the black SUV ahead of him within sight. It looked like Regina was headed to the Admiral's House to visit her cousin and he allowed the distance between them to grow slightly. He didn't need the Secret Service noticing him tailing her.

"Talk to me gorgeous," he answered the phone.

There was a short laugh on his cell phone.

"I bet you say that to all the techs," the female voice told him. Blake grinned.

"Yep," he agreed. "What've you got for me?"

"Where did you get this from?" the tech demanded, the small talk over. "This gun is the smorgasbord of cold cases."

"How so?" Blake demanded, slowing down and stopping at a red light.

He watched as the black SUV turned a corner far ahead. Regina was definitely going to the Admiral's House. He glanced at his watch. Almost noon. She must be joining him for lunch. Blake glanced in his rear-view mirror and flipped on his turn signal, pulling out as the light turned green and cutting in front of the lane next to him to turn right. The car he cut off laid on the horn, but he ignored it, continuing down the side street.

"Well, so far, I've connected the slugs from this gun to no less than seven cold cases in the past three years," the tech informed him. Blake's eyebrows rose in surprise. "It's also a match to the bullets in the SEAL *and* to the bullet from Billy's apartment."

"So, you're telling me this gun has a history?" Blake demanded.

"And a long one," the tech agreed.

"Give me some dates." Blake pulled over to the side of the road and reached for his tablet.

"I emailed all the information to you," the tech answered, "but the first date was March, 2010. The second was July of 2010, and the third was

October of the same year."

"Got it." Blake finished typing them onto a notepad on his tablet. "That's good work."

"I'm not finished yet," the tech replied smugly. Blake grinned.

"Amaze me," he invited.

"The slugs from the parking garage came from a Ruger SR45," she said triumphantly.

"You're a doll," Blake told her.

"I know."

Blake disconnected the call and glanced at his phone. Michael had called just after three in the morning to say that he had landed in Philly and would be in touch, but he hadn't heard from him yet. Blake debated for a moment, then shrugged and hit speed dial.

"Hello?" Michael picked up on the second ring.

"Still sight-seeing?" Blake asked.

"Yep," Michael answered. "What's up?"

"How good is your memory?" Blake asked.

There was a short silence.

"If this is going to turn into another discussion about my age, I'm hanging up now," Michael informed him. Blake chuckled.

"Not this time," he assured him. "Your girlfriend left me a present last night."

"I didn't realize you two were close," Michael said after another short silence.

"Neither did I, and I want to know how the hell she got by Buddy," Blake muttered. "Next time you see her, you might ask her for me."

"She left it in your *house?*" Michael exclaimed.

Blake caught the note of amusement in his voice and sighed.

"Yes," he said. "She's very unnerving, isn't she?"

"Very. What was it?"

"The smoking gun," Blake answered bluntly.

There was another long silence.

"Tell me," Michael finally said.

"I just heard from my tech in ballistics," Blake said, satisfied that he had Michael's full attention now. "The gun that killed Jason and Billy can be linked to seven cold cases, all in the past three years. She emailed me all the information and I'll forward it to you, but she gave me the dates of the first three cold cases."

"Hold on." Michael sounded muffled for a minute, like he was holding something in his mouth and Blake pictured him pulling the lid off a pen. "What are they?"

"March, July and October of 2010," Blake told him. "Do you remember where your girlfriend was those months?"

"Hold on." Michael set the phone down and Blake was able to catch murmured voices in the background. He strained to listen, but couldn't make out any words. "I'm just pulling up my notes."

Michael was back and Blake heard him typing on a laptop.

"Not sure about March, but according to her file, she was in Sudan in July," Michael said after a minute. "Where was the cold case?"

"I'll send you the email, but I'm pretty sure it wasn't in Sudan," Blake retorted. "Looks like Viper is officially in the clear on the murders of Jason and Billy."

"That's good news," Michael replied. "Send me the email and I'll get back to you on all the dates."

"Will do."

"Where's the rat?" Michael asked.

Blake swiped the screen on his tablet and pulled up the email from the tech.

"Headed to lunch at the Admiral's House," he answered, forwarding the email to Michael. "I just forwarded the email to your personal address."

"Got it," Michael said after a minute. "I'll let you know on these dates as soon as I can. Stick with her until you hear from me. Your surveillance duty may be almost over."

"I'll keep my phone on," Blake answered, putting the car in gear and easing out into traffic again.

Alina watched through her binoculars as Regina and Ludmere engaged in an energetic discussion in the back study of the Admiral's House. The French doors to the patio were closed, but the curtains hadn't been pulled and Alina had a clear view of the two inside. The conversation had started off calm enough, with Alex sitting in a chair and Regina pacing restlessly around the room. Now, it had escalated to both of them pacing around the room.

Viper lowered her binoculars and brushed an errant leaf out of her hair. She had navigated around the Secret Service details easily enough and was settled high in the branches of a massive tree behind the Vice President's house. Leaning her head against the wide trunk at her back, Viper watched two squirrels chase each other across the ground and up a tree not far away. She smiled slightly as they chattered to each other loudly before disappearing into the branches and out of view. A rustling noise above her head drew her attention upward, and Viper looked up to find herself confronting the hooked beak and dark eyes of a red-tailed hawk. He stared at her, unblinking, and Alina smiled slowly. He was perched on the branch right above her head, less than a foot away. They stared at each other for a moment before the hawk blinked and settled down comfortably above her. He shifted his gaze from her to something in the distance and Alina dropped her eyes back to the French doors in the distance.

Raising her binoculars again, she put the hawk out of her mind and turned her attention back to the couple inside the house. Regina had stopped pacing now and was gesturing with her hands while Alex gripped the back of an armchair. Alina zoomed in on his face and pursed her lips at his ferocious scowl. The Vice President looked downright mean and ugly. She zoomed out again and watched thoughtfully as the two continued to go back and forth.

There was little doubt in her mind what the argument was about. Regina was getting ready to run. Even if she wasn't telling Alex her immediate intentions, she had to be telling him that everything was about to blow up in their faces. The Vice President would have to be warned. Viper's lips curved slowly into a cold smile.

All sins are punished one day, she thought as Alex threw his hands up in the air and started pacing again. *Even yours.*

The argument in the room continued and, after a few minutes, Regina grabbed Alex's arm and said something that stopped him in his tracks. Alina watched as he dropped into a chair, staring at Regina. Regina was still talking animatedly as she picked up her purse from a chair and slung it over her shoulder. She faced Alex, her hands moving almost as fast as her mouth appeared to be, and he stared up at her, nodding every so often. Then, she bent down and kissed him on the cheek before turning to leave the room.

Alina was starting to lower the binoculars, glancing at her watch, when Alex stood up abruptly and gained her attention. She frowned as he took two steps toward the door, and then stopped. She zoomed quickly in as Alex suddenly collapsed, falling to the floor. As he fell, his hand reached out and made contact with a three-legged side table. The table came crashing down with him and a moment later, the door to the room flew open and two men rushed in, kneeling beside the fallen Vice President.

Viper quickly lowered the binoculars and dropped out of the tree silently, disappearing into the woods as chaos erupted in the Admiral's House behind her.

Damon pulled the shower curtain back and caught himself scanning the bathroom quickly for Alina. He frowned as he stepped out of the shower. Of course she wasn't there.

She had left him in Lima, Peru.

He toweled off, tamping down the rising anger at the thought. She had done it with the best of intentions and, while he was starting to understand that, the wound was still raw enough to smart. If he didn't get some kind of physical release soon, he was still going to be a simmering pot of rage when he saw her again, and that was the last thing Hawk wanted. Emotion spooked his Viper in a way that no assassin, traitor or terrorist could. If he showed her how upset he really was, Damon knew he would risk widening that emotional moat that she kept around herself, and he wasn't sure he would be able to cross it at all if that happened.

Damon toyed with the idea of baiting John beyond what Stephanie could control, his lips twitching. It was just so easy! Michael would help. He had caught on right away to the pleasure Damon took in baiting Alina's ex.

By the time Damon entered the living room, dressed and refreshed, his lips were curving and he was almost in a good mood. He walked through to the dining room and dropped his bag on the floor before turning and raising an eyebrow slightly.

Stephanie and Michael were seated on the couch facing the TV, controllers in hand, playing what looked like one of the Call of Duty games. John lounged in the recliner watching, calling out pointers to Stephanie every few minutes. Damon watched for a moment, his lips curving into a grin. He supposed there wasn't much else to do when you were cooped up in a safe house indefinitely, but he was still amused that Stephanie was playing Call of Duty.

"Don't go--too late," John exclaimed as Stephanie got blown apart and her life meter expired.

Michael laughed and continued playing as Stephanie threw her controller down and stood up with a huff.

"That's ridiculous!" she exclaimed. "I should be able to cross behind that truck. Look!!! There was no one there!"

"Yes there was!!" John retorted. "He was around the corner!"

"I would have *heard* him!" Stephanie shot back, drawing laughter from both Michael and John. She swung around and faced Damon beseechingly. "You get what I'm saying, right?" she demanded. Damon grinned.

"Yep," he answered.

"Bullshit!" John exclaimed. "Are you telling me that you would have gone behind the truck?" he demanded. Damon shook his head.

"Nope."

"But you just said..." Stephanie began before getting cut off by a loud knock at the door.

Michael instantly paused the game and got to his feet swiftly, pulling out his real gun and motioning for Stephanie to stay back. He missed her narrowed eyes and seemed surprised when she pushed past him, her own Glock in her hands.

"We ordered food earlier," she announced. "It's probably the grocery boy."

Damon beat them all to the door, moving so swiftly and silently that he seemed to materialize to the right of it before Stephanie or Michael had taken more than a few steps. He motioned for silence and gestured for them to stay back. Michael reached out and grabbed Stephanie's arm when she would have ignored Damon and moved forward anyway. She glared at him impatiently, but Michael shook his head slightly and nodded to the floor.

Stephanie followed his gaze and watched as a red beam snaked across the wooden floor, coming from the other side of the door. She froze, watching as the beam slowly swept left to right. Stephanie felt John move up silently behind her and place his hand on the small of her back. Glancing back, she met his pale blue eyes. For once, they were serious and his mouth was drawn in a grim line. He, too, was watching the red beam that was searching for movement.

Damon motioned to Michael and pointed to the peephole. Michael nodded and reached behind him to grab a small cushion off the couch, tossing it to Damon. Hawk caught it with one hand, and the silence in the apartment was deafening as they all watched him pull out his gun. He flipped off the safety, motioning them back. Stephanie felt John pull her back and around the couch until they were standing outside the dining room while Michael moved to the other side of the living room, near the hallway leading to the bedrooms. She looked at Damon and felt a shiver run down her spine.

The dark stranger was back, and his eyes were like chips of sapphire ice.

Hawk reached out and moved the cushion in front of the peephole. A second later, there was a sound like a pop from a cork gun and the cushion blew apart in his hand. Stephanie jumped, tightening her grip on her Glock.

"I don't think that's the grocery boy," Michael said, just before all hell broke loose.

Damon tossed the pillow away and turned his attention to the door. A second later, there was a loud crack and the door flew open as the lock ripped away from the door jam, sending splintered wood skidding across the floor. The chain snapped easily with the force of the impact and Damon waited for the door to hit his outstretched hand before slamming it back. It flew closed again, driven by the full force of Hawk's arm, hitting someone solidly as they were moving in.

Hawk wasted no time, moving with a speed that made Stephanie blink. He rounded the door and grabbed the dazed intruder by his neck before the assailant realized what was happening. Yanking the would-be assassin into the apartment, he kicked the door closed with his foot while he pinned the intruder to the wall next to the door, his strong hand holding him by his throat.

There was a brief second of shocked silence before the intruder hit Damon against the side of his head with the handle of a gun. Damon snarled as his head snapped to the side, but his grip on the man's neck never lessened. He turned and threw him to the floor easily, kicking the gun out of his hand and following him down in one smooth motion, planting his knee on the man's chest heavily.

Hawk found himself staring into the cold, dark eyes of a killer, and he smiled.

His fist slammed into the killer's face, snapping his head back against the floor with a satisfying crack. Damon hoped that wouldn't be the end of it, and he wasn't disappointed. The killer tried to get the gun out of Hawk's hand, grabbing his wrist and wrenching it sideways. He succeeded in angling the gun away from himself and throwing Damon off balance. As soon as he felt himself start to slip, Hawk countered with a sharp jab to his opponent's throat that made Michael, watching from behind, wince in reaction. The killer released his grip on his wrist as he choked and started gagging from the impact against his esophagus. Taking advantage of the momentary lack of defense, Hawk grabbed the killer by his hair and lifted his head, slamming it into the floor sharply before removing his knee and getting to his feet.

Stephanie got a good look at Damon's face then, and she gasped silently, backing up instinctively until she hit John's unmovable chest. He didn't even look like Damon anymore. His eyes were hollow chips of ice and the man was *smiling!* It was a terrifying, twisted look of wrath that made Stephanie shiver. She realized with a shock that went straight through her that she was staring at the face of an assassin, trained to kill without compunction and without emotion. The Damon she met three months ago, and who had been teasing John a few hours ago, was gone. In his place was a cold and methodical machine, waiting for their intruder to come to his senses and get up to fight. Reaching behind her, Stephanie found and gripped John's hand, unable to tear her gaze away from the chilling blue eyes staring down at the man sent to kill them.

Hawk waited for Viper's would-be killer to regain his senses, his whole body taut and ready to strike out. Tucking his gun into the holster at his back, he watched him with narrowed eyes, studying every twitch and every breath as if he were a specimen under a microscope. When the killer finally focused his eyes on Hawk's face, Hawk motioned him up with a quick, inviting movement of his hand. The killer's eyes narrowed and he sprang to his feet, advancing.

Hawk blocked a blow aimed at his head easily and countered with one to his opponent's midsection, doubling him over with a grunt. Grabbing him by his neck, Hawk forced him upright and was about to land another blow to his face when the killer blocked his fist and landed a hit of his own to his abdomen. Damon grunted and blocked a follow-up hit before grabbing one of the man's wrists and twisting his arm around and up behind his back at an odd angle. Using the twisted arm as a steering bar, Hawk swung him around slammed him into the wall face first, wrenching the arm up higher and watching as the killer flinched in pain. Stepping close, Hawk leaned his face down close to his ear.

"You picked the wrong day to come calling," he hissed.

"All I'm saying is that I don't know how I feel about the ethical position we now find ourselves in," Stephanie muttered, watching as Michael finished hammering a piece of wood to the front door jam.

After examining the dead bolt and finding it still intact, Michael had disappeared into John's bedroom, returning with a slat of wood he took from one of the shelves in the closet. John produced a toolbox and, between the two of them, they managed to get the replacement wood pared down to fit along the edge of the door jam, temporarily fixing the door so that it would lock securely until repairmen could be sent for.

"I'm not sure that we're actually *in* an ethical position," John retorted from the kitchen. He emerged with three beers, handing her one as he passed. "We don't actually know what he's doing to him in there," he added over his shoulder, handing a beer to Michael.

Michael accepted it with thanks and stepped back from the door. He unscrewed the lid to the bottle and took a sip before setting it down and going back to the door. He closed it, locked it, and pulled hard. The wood held.

"I think that'll work until someone can get out here to fix it," Michael announced, leaving the door locked and picking up his beer again.

"Well, we know that Damon forced him into the bathroom forty minutes ago and we haven't heard anything since, except vomiting at regular intervals," Stephanie snapped, ignoring Michael. "What do *you* think is going on in there?"

"Maybe Damon is being a good Samaritan and holding his head," John answered with a grin.

Stephanie rolled her eyes and sipped the cold beer. Clearly, she was the only one in the room who felt uncomfortable with what was undoubtedly transpiring down the hall and behind the locked bathroom door. Even Michael seemed content to turn a blind eye.

"Don't worry," Michael smiled at her as he stepped past her on his way to the recliner. "He might still be alive when they come out."

"It doesn't bother you at all?" Stephanie demanded, turning on the arm of the couch to face them. "Don't you want to know what's going on in there?"

"I think I'd rather not," Michael answered, settling into the recliner. "If I don't see it, I can't testify to it. That's something you should know all about," he added pointedly and Stephanie had the grace to flush red.

"I was protecting a friend," she muttered defensively.

"I know you were," Michael said gently. "While we're on the subject, you both can stop being so careful about not using her real name. I know the truth." Stephanie and John looked at him, startled, and he nodded briefly. "I promised Dave I'd take care of her. Her identity is safe."

"I wanted to tell you in your office that morning," Stephanie told him. "But I had to protect her."

"I understand."

"My guess is that's Damon's goal as well, right now," John remarked, sinking onto the couch next to her. "He's trying to protect her as well. That man was sent to kill Alina."

"I know." Stephanie drank some more and pursed her lips. "He would have killed us too."

"He certainly would have tried," John agreed, sipping his beer. They were silent for a moment, considering that.

"Why did we all just stand back and let Damon handle it?" Stephanie asked suddenly, looking at the other two.

"It all happened too fast to do much else," Michael answered with a shrug. "Besides, I think he needed the exercise. He's been like a caged animal ever since I met him in Peru," he added thoughtfully.

"What *was* he doing in Peru?" John demanded.

"Don't know," Michael answered with a shrug. "He never said."

"It doesn't make any sense," Stephanie said with a frown. "He was supposed to be helping Alina, and he clearly still is or you wouldn't be here now."

Michael was opening his mouth to respond when they all heard the bathroom door open and a single pair of footsteps come out. Conversation came to an abrupt halt as three pairs of eyes turned to the hallway, waiting. When Hawk stepped into the living room a second later, he found all three of them staring at him. His lips twitched as he returned their stare.

"Where is he?" Stephanie was the first one to break the silence, standing up and looking past him to the empty hallway.

"In the bathtub," Hawk answered calmly.

"Is he *alive?*" Stephanie demanded, her eyes meeting his. She noticed that those eyes had returned to their normal dark blue, and a glint of amusement leapt into them as she stared at him.

"Of course he is," Damon replied. *Barely.*

"Unconscious?" John asked.

"For now." Damon went into the kitchen. He emerged a moment later with a bottle of water to find all three of them staring at him again. "What?"

"What did you find out?" Michael asked, grinning at the speechlessness of the other two.

"Regina's leaving on a plane tonight at nine-thirty. She's flying out of Shannon Airfield to Miami and, from there, to the Virgin Islands," Damon answered, sipping the water.

"Once she gets to the Islands, she'll be out of reach," John said. "She'll disappear."

"I don't think we have to worry about her getting to Miami, let alone the Islands," Stephanie said slowly, watching Damon's face. He met her gaze and smiled slightly.

"Regina thinks Viper was here," he told her. "She thinks she's won."

"Won't she wait for confirmation of that?" Michael asked from his recliner.

"She'll get confirmation," Damon held up a smartphone, "courtesy of our unconscious killer."

"Nice." Michael grinned. "Well played."

"I'll give Viper every advantage I can," Hawk answered softly.

"How do we know Alina knows about the flight plans?" John asked.

"She knows," Michael murmured. "Blake knew Regina was getting ready to run. Viper would have been a few steps ahead of him."

"Have you heard from Blake recently?" Damon asked, perching on

269

the other arm of the couch.

"No." Michael pulled out his phone. "That reminds me, I have to call Chris and have him check Viper's file. I need to know where she was on these dates Blake sent me."

"Don't bother." Damon stopped him. "She wasn't in the country for any of them."

"How do you know?" Michael asked, pausing and glancing at him with sharp eyes.

"The first time Viper set foot stateside was three months ago," Damon answered, sipping his water. "Before that, she was in South America for two years."

"You can prove it?" Michael demanded. Damon smiled slightly.

"Our agency can," he murmured. "In the meantime, I think it's a safe bet that the smoking gun belongs to one of Frankie Solitto's triggermen."

"Solitto!" Both John and Stephanie exclaimed together.

Damon glanced at them, his eyes dancing.

"Didn't I mention that before?" he asked innocently.

"No!" Stephanie retorted. "What the hell does Frankie have to do with all of this?"

"I think we might not want to know," John murmured tiredly. "He seems to be popping up a lot lately. Last time he did, we didn't make out so well."

"That was my thought too, when Blake said he had the gun," Michael told Damon, nodding in agreement. "But how did Viper get it?"

"One guess," Damon answered with a grin.

"Why would Frankie hand Alina the gun that would incriminate one of his own?" Stephanie demanded. "That makes no sense."

"It does if he's afraid of her," Damon said softly.

"You think that's what happened?" Stephanie asked as John whistled softly.

"I think Frankie's keeping himself on Viper's good side," Damon said. "Let's just leave it at that."

"I'll call Blake now and tell him she's in the clear on the cold cases," Michael said. "You're sure about this?"

"I'm sure," Damon replied. Michael nodded and hit speed dial on his phone. "While you're at it, tell him to stop watching Regina," Damon added. Michael looked at him sharply.

"Why?" he demanded.

"Viper will have her well-covered. No need to risk Blake running into Viper's nest and startling the target," Damon answered, capping his water and standing up. "And, no offense, but too many of you Feds know what she looks like now. Her anonymity is already in shreds. Let's not make it any worse than it has to be."

Chapter Twenty-Six

Blake squinted against the afternoon sun and watched as another press truck rolled into the hospital parking lot. He had been waiting within view of the gates when Regina's vehicle had pulled out earlier, only to turn right around and go back in. A few moments later, an ambulance came flying by and through the gates. Tuning to the scanner, he heard that the Vice President had collapsed a few minutes before the ambulance re-emerged with lights flashing, surrounded by the secret service. Now, he was sitting outside the hospital, sweltering in the afternoon heat, watching as the press gathered outside to hypothesize on what had happened to the Vice President. It was all over the news, and Blake knew that the White House press team was already inside the hospital.

Glancing at his watch, Blake was surprised to see that it was already after four o'clock. His stomach rumbled, reminding him that he hadn't eaten since early morning, and Blake frowned tiredly. He was hot, tired and hungry. The last thing he wanted to do was sit outside a hospital and watch the circus of the press feed the machine that paid them. When his phone rang, he reached for it eagerly.

"Tell me good news," he answered, leaning his head back on his headrest.

"Viper was out of the country on the dates you sent me. I'm told her agency will be able to verify it," Michael told him. Blake smiled.

"Wonderful," he murmured. "She's in the clear then. Any ideas on the origin of the smoking gun?"

"You're not going to like it," Michael warned.

"I don't like any of this. What's your point?" Blake retorted.

"Frankie Solitto."

"You're right. I don't like it," Blake muttered, then after a moment, he roared, "What the hell does the Jersey Mob have to do with this?!"

"I'll explain later," Michael laughed. "Trust me. It's worth the wait."

"It better be!" Blake exclaimed. "I'll bring the vodka."

"Deal," Michael answered promptly. "Oh, and you can knock off the rat detail," Michael told him. Blake lifted his head, his spirits lifting.

"Really?" he asked. "What happened?"

"We know where she's headed," Michael answered. "I don't want to run the risk of you being seen and tipping her off. She's leaving tonight on a plane to Miami."

"I knew it!" Blake exclaimed in satisfaction. "I told you she was getting ready to run. How did you find out?"

"She sent a hit man after Stephanie Walker. We were able to intercept him."

"Is he still breathing?" Blake demanded.

There was a slight chuckle on the end of the phone.

"Barely," Michael replied. "Where are you now?"

"Outside the hospital," Blake's smile faded. "Alex Ludmere collapsed at his house a few hours ago."

"*What!?*" Michael bellowed.

"Regina went to see him around him lunchtime. As soon as she left, he collapsed," Blake told him. "They haven't released an official statement yet, but they will soon. Apparently, he was sitting up and talking when they hustled him into the ambulance, so it can't be too serious."

"Regina is there with him?" Michael asked after a moment.

"For now." Blake yawned. "You really want me to just leave?"

"Yes," Michael said. "I'll keep you updated."

"Are you headed back from your sight-seeing tour yet?" Blake asked, starting the engine. He hit the button to roll up his windows and cranked up the air conditioner.

"In a little bit."

"I'm assuming Regina will not make her flight to Miami?" Blake prompted when there was a long silence and no more information forthcoming. Michael chuckled.

"I'd say that's a safe bet," he murmured. "I'll call you when I have news."

"I'll be waiting."

Blake hung up and dropped the phone onto the seat next to him, sitting for a moment with the air blowing full-blast on his face. *Frankie Solitto???* How had the head of the Jersey mob become involved in this mess? And, more to the point, how had *Viper* ended up with the gun?

Shaking his head, Blake put the car in gear and eased out of his parking spot. He turned toward the exit of the hospital, unaware of the pair of sparkling green eyes watching his exit with interest.

Viper watched him pull out into traffic before turning and making her way through the throng of press and into the hospital.

"You're letting him go?" Hawk demanded, staring at Michael incredulously.

"I have no reason to detain him," Michael retorted with a shrug. "I can't even get him on assaulting a federal officer, thanks to you."

"If I'd known that's all you wanted, I would have thrown him your way," Damon shot back. Michael grinned at him.

"No, you wouldn't," he said. "You were enjoying yourself too much."

Damon paused in the act of slipping his laptop back into his bag and grinned reluctantly. He glanced at Michael, leaning against the wall in the dining room.

"I won't deny that," he admitted. "You're leaving him free to continue killing people for money. You know that."

"That's ironic coming from you," Michael murmured.

"Ah, but I get paid by my government to kill very bad people who go bump in the night and scare all the good little boys and girls," Damon retorted, his lips twisting briefly.

Michael watched him thoughtfully, wondering if the trace of self-derision in Damon's voice was aimed at himself or his government. He thought it might be a little bit of both, but Damon's face was giving nothing away.

"Either I let him go now or a judge lets him go in a few days," Michael said. "I don't deny it kills me to do it, but it's better than wasting time and raising questions as to what happened to him. It's times like these, I hope that Karma does exist, and what he does comes back on him."

"I'm still trying to figure out why you get to make that decision," Stephanie said, coming into the dining room carrying a gun in a holster.

"I'm the ranking federal agent here. You and John are technically on vacation, and you're MIA to boot," Michael informed her with a wink. "That's why I get to make that decision."

"That rationalization is seriously flawed," Stephanie retorted. "When I figure out how, I'll let you know."

She turned to Damon and handed him the holster, her eyes meeting his.

"Give this back to Viper for me," she told him.

Damon straightened up and reached out to take the holster, pulling out the modified Glock that Alina gave Stephanie three months ago to use as a back-up. It was a gun he knew well. Alina had modified it herself, with the assistance of the armorer, while they were still at the training facility together. Smiling slightly at the memory, he slid it back into the holster and handed it back to Stephanie.

"You can give it to her yourself," he told her, his blue eyes glinting as they met hers. "You'll see her again."

Stephanie took the gun back and smiled. She was strangely comforted by the assurance in Damon's voice. The chilling killer was gone and the man she had gotten to know was back, making her wonder if he ever really disappeared.

"Do we know or care that our visitor is creeping out the front door?" John called from the living room.

Michael leaned back so that he could see the front door. He was just in time to see the back of a man disappearing out the door silently. Michael glanced back at Damon.

"You took his weapon, right?" he asked.

"Of course." Hawk zipped up his bag and picked it up, carrying it out of the dining room and dropping it behind the couch. "Captain America over there made the executive decision to let our visitor go," he told John.

John looked up from the iPad in his hands.

"Typical," he muttered. "I was all for locking him in the bathroom and leaving him there."

Damon glanced at him and blue eyes met blue in a sudden moment of understanding. Hawk nodded slightly. John had been every bit as enraged as he was himself when that pillow blew apart in his hand. Damon saw him start forward toward the door before stopping himself, and Hawk had seen the look of satisfaction in John's face when he stood over the hit man, waiting for him to get up and fight. Now, he realized that John was just as emotionally invested in Alina as he was himself. But, while John still cared for the Jersey girl from long ago, Damon was in love with the complex woman she had become.

"I would have supported that," Hawk murmured, his lips twitching.

"Is the bathroom clean, at least?" John asked, lowering his voice and glancing at Stephanie. "She has a thing about the ethics of it all. It would probably be best for her not to see any blood."

"I didn't have to draw blood," Damon told him simply. "There are other ways."

"Good." John went back to his iPad. "Did you see this yet?"

Damon glanced over his shoulder and stared at the headline.

BREAKING NEWS: VICE PRESIDENT ALEX LUDMERE COLLAPSES AT HOME

"Hey, O'Reilly!" he swung around. "Did you know about this?"

Michael came across the room and glanced at the headline.

"Blake told me when I talked to him," he replied. "Regina was at the hospital. It's not serious. If it was, I would have been recalled by now."

"We have to get going." Hawk glanced at his watch. It was five-thirty. "With Ludmere in the hospital, Regina will be even more careful about leaving. She'll have to avoid the press now, which means she'll have to leave even earlier, and she'll have lost time at the hospital."

"You said Viper would have her covered," Michael reminded him, glancing at his own watch.

"She will." Damon turned to go into the kitchen. "But that doesn't mean I'm going to let her go into that fight alone," he added over his shoulder.

"I'm coming with you," Stephanie suddenly announced.

John and Michael turned to stare at her and she lifted her chin stubbornly, her eyes narrowing and daring them to disagree with her.

"That's not a good idea."

Damon emerged from the kitchen with two bottles of water. He tossed one to Michael and Stephanie moved swiftly, catching the bottle instead. Damon's lips twitched.

"I'm coming with you," Stephanie repeated firmly, staring at him.

Damon met her glare for a long moment, considering her, and suddenly grinned.

"Far be it from me to argue with you," he murmured. "You're a big girl. But you're taking your safety on yourself the second you step out that door."

"Agreed," Stephanie said with a nod and Damon winked at her.

"I knew I liked you for a reason," he said.

"Wait a minute." John was standing up now, scowling. "If you go, I go."

"What is this, *Backdraft?*" Michael exclaimed. "Neither of you are going! I'm not making myself responsible for two federal agents *and* a...a...whatever *you* are." He motioned to Damon, drawing a laugh from him.

"You're cute." Stephanie swung around and patted Michael on his cheek before turning and heading down the hall toward the bedrooms, John right behind her. "Give me five minutes," she called over her shoulder.

"Did she just call me cute?" Michael asked Hawk, stunned.

"Yep." Damon grinned and tucked his water into the outside pocket of his duffel bag. He glanced at his watch. "You've got three minutes!" he called out to the other two.

"You're not seriously bringing them with us," Michael exclaimed. "We'll look like a damn circus!"

"Do you have a better idea?" Damon demanded. "If we leave them here, she'll just follow us. She knows the name of the airfield. She knows what time the plane leaves. You don't think she won't just show up there? At least this way we can control her."

"What if we all walk into a firestorm?" Michael demanded.

"They're Federal agents," Hawk said with a shrug. "They'll have to hold their own...just like you."

"Hmpf." Michael acknowledged the insult with a grin. "You still owe me beer."

"Bullshit," Damon retorted. "You owe *me* beer."

Alina glanced at her watch, pressing the button to illuminate the face. There was still plenty of time. She was on a motorcycle, hidden in the woods about a mile from the small airfield located in Fredericksburg, Virginia. The sun had disappeared half an hour ago, after Viper settled on her point of ambush. There were more possibilities around the airfield than she was expecting, and she was pleased with her final decision. The trees were thick here and a slight rise above the road gave her an unexpectedly good view of the traffic coming toward her. While there were any number of routes Regina could take from DC to Fredericksburg, the road below her was the main road leading to the airport and the most likely one her target would take. If Regina *did* take a little-known back way into the airport, the tracking dot Viper had placed on Regina's SUV would alert her in enough time to improvise.

After making sure Regina hadn't changed plans after Ludmere's collapse this afternoon, Viper came down to Fredericksburg ahead of time, leaving straight from the hospital where Regina had received two text messages to her phone. One was from Leon, confirming the flight for that evening in light of Ludmere's health situation. The other was from an unnamed number, informing her that the target had been eliminated. The first made her frown before she assured him that they were still on for the flight to Miami, and the second had wreathed her in such smiles as to leave Alina in little doubt as to who the intended 'target' was. She had wondered at the time, and wondered again now, who was the woman Regina's assassin had mistaken for her? As soon as the question entered her mind, Alina put it out of her head. The identity of the unknown victim didn't matter. All that mattered was that Regina now thought Viper was dead.

And that gave Viper the biggest advantage of all.

Alina got off her bike and walked it over to rest against the trunk of a tree in the midst of some underbrush. Breaking off some low-hanging branches, she draped them over the motorcycle, concealing it as much as possible. She checked her watch again, flipping the screen on the digital display and checking her co-ordinates before flipping it back. She tightened the straps on her backpack, lifting her head to breathe in the smells of the forest around her, then turned and set off for the rise above the road.

It was going to end tonight.

Three months ago, Regina and Alex opened up Pandora's box by inviting Viper back into their world, convinced that they could control and destroy not only her, but every last shred of evidence that the Vice President had knowingly, and willfully, engaged in treason against the government and people of the country which he served. They had both grossly under-estimated their opponent.

Alina would probably have been content to remain silent about what she saw two years ago in Cairo, never looking any further than the unfortunate fact that the Vice President had been in the wrong place, with the wrong person, at the wrong time. In the course of her career, she had seen a lot of things that she would never mention and never expose due to national security risks, personal ethics, and just plain old-fashioned morals. Some things were never meant to be made public, and the word public to Alina encompassed anyone other than the direct people involved. She would have kept silent on what she had seen in Cairo.

If they hadn't imported a terrorist to kill thousands of Americans.

Alina was very prosaic about her job. She was a government-paid assassin, and her job was to kill people. Many people would consider her job no different from that of a terrorist, but they didn't know the truth. She was sent after the worst of the bad people. The people Viper dispatched to their terminal end were *not* innocent. They were *not* misunderstood. They were *not* victims of random profiling. They were the people no one else could touch.

They were people who believed they were above not only man-made laws, but the higher ethical and moral laws that governed every human being on the planet. The second Alex Ludmere and Regina Cummings decided to pay Johann to kill thousands of innocent Americans, they had joined those ranks. They had gone beyond what was acceptable even by the current intrusive and entitled policies sweeping their nation. They had joined the ranks of the doomed, and Viper was coming for them.

Next Exit, Pay Toll

Alina paused at a break in the trees, looking down the slight rise and along the road. She crouched down, casting an experienced eye along the road and shook her head slightly. Straightening, she moved a few feet over to the left and crouched again, looking between two tree trunks that were close enough together that a man would be unable to squeeze between them. Satisfied with the angle, she swung her backpack off her back and unzipped it.

The darkness was thickening as night started to set in, and Viper listened as crickets grew louder and the night creatures of the woods stirred around her. She pulled a smaller bag out of her backpack and opened it, setting it on the ground. Her hands moved swiftly, assembling her rifle with sure and silent movements. She attached her night-vision scope and silencer last, then slung the rifle over her head so that it hung diagonally across her body. Picking up a stick from nearby, Alina used it to break-up a thick spider web that was strung between the two tree trunks before she settled on her stomach and positioned the rifle between the trees. She lowered her eye to the scope and adjusted the focus until she was satisfied before raising her head and settling in to wait.

Who had Regina's thug killed in mistake for her?

The question popped back into her head persistently. And why were they convinced it was her? Alina knew from long experience that the most bizarre coincidences could conspire to make even the clearest fact appear distorted, but something had to have happened to convince Regina that she had found Viper at last. It must have been that phone call right before Art arrived yesterday, when Regina had been visibly ecstatic.

Viper pursed her lips in displeasure. She should have had her listening gear with her yesterday. There was no excuse for not having it. It had been a miscalculation on her part to think it was unnecessary on the first day of surveillance.

Headlights blinked in the distance, drawing her attention from her thoughts. Setting the few unanswered questions she had aside, Viper lowered her head to the night-vision scope on her rifle and adjusted it slightly, focusing in on the black SUV traveling along the dark and deserted road at high speed. A sense of anticipation washed over her.

Regina was right on time.

Chapter Twenty-Seven

Viper slid her finger over the trigger and watched through the scope as the SUV sped closer. Adjusting the angle ever so slightly, she centered the cross-hairs and exhaled slowly as she squeezed the trigger. The SUV swerved violently as the driver was thrown back, killed instantly by the round that went through the windshield and into his forehead. The armed guard, seated in the passenger's seat, reached over to grab the wheel as Viper fired again. The SUV skidded out of control as the second round entered the guards heart.

Raising her head, Viper watched as the SUV veered toward the edge of the road and careened into the slight incline. The speed with which the vehicle was traveling caused the SUV to hit the rise and travel halfway up before gravity rolled it over. It rolled twice before coming to rest on its side, all four wheels spinning, about fifty yards from where Viper was concealed.

She sat up quickly and grabbed her backpack, swinging it onto her back with a smooth motion as she rose to her feet. Backing away from the two trees, she turned and ran swiftly along the rise toward the incapacitated vehicle in the distance. She knew from her surveillance that the only security Regina traveled with was in the front seat, dead. She would be alone in the back of the truck.

Adrenaline coursed through Alina as she ran, her legs covering the ground quickly. She darted through trees and leaped over underbrush, reaching the incline above the vehicle a bare minute or two after the crash. Even so, the back door to the SUV was open and Alina knew the backseat would be empty. Viper whipped out her night-vision binoculars, scanning the area quickly. She smiled slowly a few seconds later.

Regina was stumbling through the woods a few yards away, heading away from her.

Viper tucked the binoculars away and turned to follow her target, moving silently and allowing the sounds of cracking underbrush to guide her. Once she was behind her, Alina looked down in the darkness and followed the trampled underbrush as a trail. Regina was moving quickly, but Alina didn't pick up her pace. She didn't have to see clearly in the darkness to follow her prey, she just had to listen. Keeping her target several yards ahead, she stalked her silently, listening to the sound of her stumbling through the woods. Viper reached out and moved a low-hanging branch out of her way, stepping past it and releasing it without a sound. Her attention was focused entirely on the woman in front of her, heading through the woods in the direction of the airfield. When the sound of movement suddenly stopped, Viper paused, frowning slightly. She moved forward quickly until she came to a break in the trees.

Alina found herself at the edge of a clearing of sorts. The ground was flat and grassy here, with a stream running along the far side. Regina was bent over in the middle of the clearing, gasping, and Viper watched her dispassionately for a moment. Dressed in slacks and platform sandals, Regina looked sharply out of place in the woods. Viper set her bag on the ground and removed her rifle, leaning it against a tree before advancing into the clearing silently, her eyes narrowed and focused on the woman struggling to catch her breath.

Intense anger flowed through her as she moved toward the woman who had caused such chaos in so many lives. Memories of the files on Billy's hard-drive flitted through her mind, fueling the anger. This woman had willfully and intentionally ruined hundreds of lives through her selfishness and disregard for basic human principles. She had arranged for Billy to torture and kill innocent men, women and children. She had arranged for Johann to come into the United States and kill thousands of Americans. Because of her, an innocent DHS agent from Washington was dead, run off the road for asking too many questions. Because of her, three of Alina's old friends from long ago had been dragged into an international mess that got one shot and had two others in hiding in Baltimore. It was because of this woman that Hawk was God-knew where, evading international killers of every type, instead of here to witness the end of their joint mission. Regina had gone after everything and everyone that Alina held dear.

And then she had gone after Viper.

Regina was just straightening up when Viper grabbed her shoulder and swung her around. Her fist smashed into Regina's jaw, catching her by surprise. Regina's head snapped back sharply as she stumbled backwards, lost her balance and fell to the ground on her back.

"Remember me?"

Regina stared up at her with wide eyes, stunned.

"You're supposed to be dead!" she exclaimed, fingering her jaw.

"Clearly, I'm not," Viper retorted coldly. "*Get up!*"

Regina's mouth twisted into a snarl as she leapt to her feet, facing Viper with all the hatred of years blazing across her face. Alina met the burning onslaught of loathing head on, her eyes narrowing slightly. In an instant, she set her own anger aside, her gaze becoming cold and clinical. Regina was going to attack, her reflexes impeded by emotion, giving Alina the opportunity to toy with her. She had some questions she wanted answered, and if Regina could be encouraged to expend all her energy on rash moves and bragging talk, Alina would get all the answers she needed.

Viper smiled coldly in the darkness as Regina came at her.

Damon pulled to a stop a few feet away from the over-turned SUV on the side of the road. His lips twitched slightly as he switched off the engine and got out, moving toward the vehicle quickly. He was aware of the others following him, but Damon had eyes only for the undoubted handiwork of Viper's rifle. He felt an unfamiliar sense of pride wash through him. The professional in him noted the two identical bullet holes in the windshield as he shone his flashlight through the glass, the beam of light catching and illuminating the dead driver and guard. Switching off the light, Hawk glanced around briefly.

"Back's empty," John announced from the other side of the vehicle.

"Which way did she go?" Stephanie asked, looking around.

"She would have headed into the trees," Hawk answered, nodding toward the woods at the top of the rise. "The airfield is that way."

"Viper must have been waiting for her," Michael said, turning to head up the slight incline at the side of road. "How did Regina get past her?"

"Let me look into my crystal ball and I'll tell you," Damon retorted, bounding past him and into the trees.

Michael grinned and topped the incline. Stephanie and John joined him and they followed Hawk into the woods. A few yards into the trees, Michael stopped them and they watched as Damon stood silently, listening. After a moment, he pulled out the small powerful flashlight again and flicked it around the area, pausing for a brief moment before switching it off and motioning to them.

"They went this way," he murmured. "Keep quiet. We're not very far behind them."

"How can you tell?" John whispered.

"Because this is what I do," Hawk replied shortly.

They followed him deeper into the woods, falling into single file on the trail behind him. Stephanie moved a branch out of her way, being careful not to make too much noise, and glanced back at John. His face was unreadable in the darkness and she turned her attention forward again. Michael was ahead of her, moving through the trees silently, and Stephanie followed his footsteps, careful to avoid any underbrush that would make noise. The trees loomed over them, thick and silent, and she felt oppressed by the heavy darkness. She didn't know what to expect when they found Alina and Regina, but the over-turned SUV spoke volumes for Viper's intentions. Stephanie hadn't missed the two bullet holes in the windshield, and she knew from experience just how good Alina was at that particular shot.

Viper had been waiting for Regina, and she had no intention of letting her stand trial for her crimes.

Damon halted a few moments later and held his hand up, motioning for silence. Muffled noises came from ahead of them, but it was difficult to make out just what they were hearing. Stephanie tried to peer past Michael's wide shoulders but could only see a tree. Standing on tip-toe, she was trying to look over Michael's shoulder when he moved suddenly, trying to push past Damon. Damon grabbed his arm and pulled him back firmly, but in the few seconds that Michael was out of the way, Stephanie saw what was ahead. Two women were fighting in a kind of clearing ahead of them, and one of them was taking repeated hits to her body.

Stephanie picked her way carefully to the right and stopped behind a tree on the edge of the clearing. Shock rolled through her as she stared at the scene in front of her. Alina was fighting with another woman, who was landing hit after hit on Alina's face and abdomen. In the darkness, it was hard to tell if Regina had any wounds herself, but she had certainly gained the upper-hand with Alina. Stephanie felt John move up silently behind her, watching over her head, and she heard his sharp intake of breath when Regina landed a solid kick to Alina that lifted her off her feet and sent her to the ground on her back.

"She's getting her ass kicked," Michael muttered, trying to start forward again. Once again, Hawk stopped him.

Michael looked at him and saw a smile on Damon's face in the darkness.

"No," Hawk disagreed softly. "She's making Regina feel superior. She wants information."

Michael looked back at the woman on the ground with a frown, but he stood still beside Hawk, watching.

"I heard you were a hell of an assassin," Regina's taunting voice carried across the night. "Is that all you've got?"

Alina's answer was muffled and unintelligible, but she rolled out of Regina's way when she would have landed another kick. With one motion, Alina was back on her feet and she blocked a blow from Regina, landing one of her own on Regina's neck, bringing the woman to her knees.

"You remember what happened last time you tried to fight me, don't you?" Viper's voice wasn't loud by any means, yet all four people watching from the trees heard her clearly.

"I've learned a lot since then," Regina retorted, twisting and tackling Alina at her knees.

Viper allowed herself to be wrestled to the ground and blocked two blows to her head before rolling out of the way and jumping to her feet again. Regina followed and they circled each other warily. Viper noted the tear in Regina's shirt and gash on her forehead, both a result of the crash. Blood was oozing from a split in her bottom lip, courtesy of Viper's fist, and Alina smiled faintly. She could feel blood dripping down her own face from a cut under her eye and her abdomen was starting to throb from the several hits she had allowed Regina to land, but the look on Regina's face made it all worth it. She looked smug, and Alina knew she was feeling confident.

"Why did Ludmere meet with Johann in Cairo?" Alina asked, ducking as Regina tried to land a punch to her face. She grunted when Regina's elbow slammed into her shoulder instead.

"You mean the all-knowing Viper, Mistress of All Intelligence, hasn't figured that one out yet?" Regina mocked, striking out and landing another solid hit to Alina's midsection. "Really, I'm disappointed."

"I didn't get that far," Alina retorted, blocking another hit and landing a blow to Regina's shoulder that pushed her back a few feet.

"Alex was arranging for Johann to hire the Engineer on our behalf," Regina informed her. "The plan was for The Engineer to kill the President-elect after the Electoral College voted him in in December, but before the Inauguration."

"That would have made Ludmere President!" Viper exclaimed.

Regina smiled a feline smile and nodded, pausing to catch her breath and brush her hair out of her eyes.

"Yes," she agreed, "and Johann would have had an ally in the White House. It would have been perfect for everyone, except you showed up and ruined everything. Johann didn't trust Alex after you appeared and botched up your attempt to assassinate him, so no more Engineer and we had to settle for the Vice Presidency."

"But Johann trusted him enough to come back three months ago," Viper pointed out, wincing as Regina caught her jaw with her elbow and snapped her head back. Pain shot through Alina's temple, but she ignored it, blocking a follow-up blow.

"Johann didn't know who was paying him," Regina answered. "I made sure of that. Johann thought he was doing it to pave the way for a homegrown jihadist group."

Alina digested that nugget of information while she swept her leg up and landed a solid blow with her heel on Regina's gut. Regina stumbled backwards but remained standing.

"The funding was drying up on Ludmere's pet terrorist project, wasn't it?" Alina asked, following up with a punch to Regina's jaw. "He made Mossavid his personal vendetta when Johann refused to hire the Engineer after Cairo. When the funding started to dry up, he decided to kick-start it again by running a fear-mongering fundraiser."

"Again, it would have worked if the Engineer had been able to handle you," Regina snarled, coming back at Viper with a sharp kick to her abdomen that made Alina lose her breath and double over. Stars appeared in her peripheral vision and she sucked in air, trying to force them back. "Instead, Johann is killed, months of planning goes down the drain, and then you cause added complications by disappearing!"

Regina kicked out again and her foot caught Alina under her chin. The stars exploded in her eyes and Alina felt herself falling backward again, nothing but emptiness behind her until she hit the ground with a thud. The wind knocked out of her chest with a rush and Alina fought to stay conscious as she tried to get enough air into her lungs to stop herself from choking.

Pain shot through her body and Viper knew she had to end this soon. She couldn't take another hit to her head.

"And the DHS agent who went over the ravine?" Viper choked out, rolling out of the way of Regina's foot, aimed for her middle.

"That was all Alex." Regina sounded disgusted. "I was stupid enough to tell him that I recognized Damon when we got the surveillance photos from the Engineer, and he panicked when she started asking questions about him. In retrospect, I should have kept that observation to myself. Alex took matters into his own hands and ordered Billy to take care of her. That was a huge mess I had to clean up."

"And then Stephanie Walker came down here anyway." Alina struggled to her feet, drawing strength from somewhere deep inside her. "Guess you didn't clean it up as well as you thought you did."

"It was clean!" Regina screamed. "You people just don't know when to let it go!"

"So you had Billy try to run Stephanie down. When that didn't work, you had him plant a bomb in her car," Alina continued, ignoring the outburst.

"She had to be silenced," Regina replied with a shrug. "If she had stayed in New Jersey and minded her own business, I wouldn't have touched her. But she didn't. She came down here and tried to get involved again, playing avenging angel after some worthless DHS agent."

"And Michael O'Reilly?" Alina asked. "Was he asking too many questions too? Getting too close to the truth about the Engineer?"

"Mike should have stayed away from you!" Regina screamed and Viper raised an eyebrow slightly. "It's all *your* fault! You told him about the Engineer! It had to be you. You're the only other person who knew about him. If you hadn't told him, I wouldn't have had to send those men to his house to get his laptop."

"Just to get his laptop?" Alina sneered, watching as Regina came toward her again. She side-stepped swiftly as Regina tried to lunge toward her. "I heard you wanted to teach him a lesson."

"He was mine! *MINE!*" Regina yelled, swinging around and confronting Alina furiously. "Then you came along and he started sniffing after you like a junkyard dog, just like Damon did in boot camp!"

"Is that why you put out the hit on Hawk?" Viper demanded incredulously, her eyes narrowed. "Payback for an *imagined* slight ten years ago?"

"It *wasn't* imagined! He would have wanted *me* if it wasn't for you!"

Regina was screeching now, her face pale in the moonlight. She rushed at her and Alina side-stepped again, reaching out and clamping her hand on Regina's shoulder at the base of her neck. Spinning her around, Viper tossed Regina to the ground as effortlessly as if she were a rag doll. Regina landed on her stomach, stunned at the speed with which she hit the ground. Viper shook her head to clear the remaining fog in her vision and watched as Regina struggled to her knees.

"You really are insane, aren't you?" she asked her conversationally. "Tell me, why did you think I was dead?"

"Your file." Regina turned her head to look Viper malevolently, hatred dripping from her lips. "It listed all your safe houses. You weren't in Raleigh, so that only left Baltimore. When my employee told me someone was living there, I assumed it was you."

Alina stared at Regina, watching as she got slowly to her feet, her back to her. Shock washed over her and Alina felt as if Regina just landed another physical blow to her gut, followed immediately by the bubbling eruption of white hot anger.

Stephanie!

Next Exit, Pay Toll

"That idiot obviously didn't bother to confirm that it was you before he told me you were dead," Regina continued, oblivious to the pressure valve of fury she had just released behind her. "That's not a mistake I'll make."

Regina swung around, a knife in her hand. Viper saw the blade a second before it left Regina's hand, hurled with the full force of her arm. She moved swiftly to the right and the blade embedded itself to the hilt into the front of her shoulder, rather than the center of her chest where it had been aimed. Regina's smug smile of satisfaction froze on her face as Viper smiled slowly.

It was the most frightening thing she had ever seen.

Regina started to back up instinctively as Viper moved toward her, a look of cold, deadly intent on her face. In an instant, the woman Regina had been fighting for the past ten minutes had disappeared. In her place was a chilling killer.

Reaching up with her right hand, Viper pulled the six-inch blade out of her shoulder without breaking stride and threw it away into the trees. Any pain that she might have felt at the wound was blocked by her own anger, and Alina was blind to anything other than Regina's smug and evil face.

Sensing that something had tipped the scales out of her favor, and suddenly terrified of the stranger advancing upon her, Regina turned to run. She hadn't gone two steps before Alina's hand clamped down on her wrist, jerking her backwards sharply. Viper twisted her wrist, forcing Regina to turn and face those blazing dark eyes or risk a broken wrist. As she turned, Viper's right hook drove into her jaw and Regina's head snapped back. The force of the blow would have thrown her off her feet if Viper's hand wasn't still clamped to her wrist. Through the stars and ringing in her head, Regina realized that none of Viper's punches had been full-force.

Until now.

Viper released her wrist and followed up with two jabs, one to her abdomen that doubled her over and another to her chin, throwing her upright again. Regina swayed on her feet, dazed by both the swiftness and the strength behind the hits. Without pausing, Viper landed a strong kick to Regina's chest, throwing her backward with such force that her feet left the ground and she traveled a good four or five feet before landing flat on her back. Regina was just opening her stunned eyes when Viper came down on top of her, her knees pinning her arms to the ground and preventing any movement at all. She gazed up at Alina with loathing.

"No jury will ever convict the Vice President's cousin," Regina gasped out.

Viper's lips curved coldly as she met Regina's defiant glare.

"Oh, I know they won't," she answered softly.

Stephanie flinched when Alina reached down and gripped Regina's head, twisting it swiftly. They all heard her neck crack sickeningly, and her body went limp. Stephanie stared in stunned silence as Alina slowly rose to her feet, staring down at the dead body of Regina Cummings.

They heard every word that had been said between the two women and Stephanie realized, even as she watched the terrible transformation from her friend to a killer, that Alina had been confirming Regina's guilt. She hadn't known she had an audience of witnesses. Viper had been getting the answers she needed, absorbing blow after blow in the process, in order to justify killing a traitor. Stephanie was rooted to the spot, shocked and stunned, still reeling from the confession...and the sound of that horrible crack.

Viper rose to her feet and stepped away from Regina's lifeless body, feeling suddenly hollow and drained. Coldness embraced her as she realized that it was over.

She raised her eyes at movement in the trees and felt her heart surge into her throat as Hawk materialized from the shadows, moving with that jungle cat stealth she knew so well. She blinked, staring at him blankly as he moved towards her, and Alina wondered briefly if she was hallucinating.

"*Viper.*"

The word whispered on the breeze and Alina knew that she wasn't seeing things. Hawk was coming towards her, solid and real, with a grim look on his face. He reached her and, instead of looking at her face, focused on her shoulder. Without saying a word, he pulled his shirt over his head and starting ripping it into strips. It was only then that Alina realized the entire front of her tank top was saturated with something wet and sticky.

"You just can't help getting yourself hurt when I'm not around, can you?" Hawk demanded gently, folding one of the strips of t-shirt into a square and pressing it against her shoulder.

He took her right hand, pressing it firmly against the fabric to hold it there, and Alina's lips curved on their own. Burning pain suddenly seared through her as her mind finally acknowledged the fact that she had been stabbed with a six-inch long blade through her shoulder. She gasped softly as Hawk took a longer strip of t-shirt and wrapped it over her shoulder and under her arm, pulling it firmly into a knot over the makeshift bandage.

"You're supposed to be in Peru," Alina finally murmured, trying to focus on Damon's face and not the pain coursing through her body.

"Funny how that worked out," Hawk retorted, finally bringing his blue eyes to hers. "I brought your gunny back with me."

"She sent him after you?" Alina asked, her lips curving.

Damon nodded slowly before turning his attention back to her shoulder. He wrapped another strip of fabric around it tightly, tying it off. Alina lifted her eyes at more movement in the shadows and raised an eyebrow as Michael, John and Stephanie all emerged from the trees.

"Did you guys get a group rate?" she murmured, drawing a laugh from Hawk. He turned to glance at the others.

"As you can see, Stephanie is fine," he told her, bringing his eyes back to hers. He smiled slightly. "I'm the one that sent the text to Regina. I intercepted her hit man and...had a little chat with him."

"Is he still alive?" Alina asked.

"Everyone keeps asking that," he murmured, his eyes glinting. Alina grinned.

"Please tell me that you have proof of everything she just confessed to," Michael called before she could answer.

Alina reached around to her back with her right hand and slid her hand up under her tank top. Her fingers closed around the wire that was taped there and she pulled it off, holding it up to show Michael.

"Every word," she answered. "I also have pictures, documents, emails, videos, audio clips, bank statements, you name it."

"Thank God!" Michael exclaimed, his face breaking into a grin. "Well done, you!"

Alina smiled, and then laughed as Stephanie unceremoniously pushed Damon out of the way. Throwing her arms around Alina, she hugged her tightly. Alina grit her teeth in pain, but raised her arms to hug Stephanie back.

"I thought you were dead," she murmured in her ear.

"He didn't have a chance," Stephanie whispered back. "I was surrounded by the three gorillas here."

Alina started laughing again, and then laughed harder as John wrapped his arms around both her and Stephanie.

"If you *ever* put us through anything like this again, I'll kill you myself," he informed her gruffly.

"Awww, how cute!" Michael exclaimed. "Group hug!"

"It won't be cute when she collapses," Damon snapped and Stephanie and John both fell away, looking at Alina's roughly bandaged shoulder guiltily.

"Oh my God, I'm sorry!" Stephanie exclaimed, her hand flying to her mouth. "Are you ok?"

"I'm fine," Alina replied.

Nevertheless, she was grateful when Hawk moved back to her side and slid a supporting arm around her waist.

"That needs to be stitched," he informed her briskly. "You've lost a

289

fair amount of blood already. Where's your transport?"

"In the woods," Alina answered.

Damon nodded and tossed his keys to Michael.

"I'll take her," he told him. "You take them."

Michael caught the keys with one hand and nodded. He turned to head into the trees, then stopped and looked back at Alina.

"Where's the receiver for the wire?" he asked.

Alina smiled slowly.

"Somewhere safe," she answered.

"Fair enough," Michael said with a grin and turned to head back into the woods with Stephanie and John. Alina glanced up at Hawk's profile.

"Are you mad at me?" she asked. Damon glanced down at her and she read the answer in his eyes. Oh, he was mad alright. "It was the best thing I could think of at the time. In retrospect, maybe it wasn't the most tactful response to the threat against you."

"You think?" Damon muttered, guiding her into the woods. "We'll discuss it later. Where's your transport?"

"This way," Alina motioned with her right arm and he steered her in that direction. "There's still just one question I want answered, and I'll probably never get it answered," she said tiredly.

Hawk glanced down at her in the darkness.

"What's that?"

"How the hell did Jason Rogers know who I was?" Alina demanded, stopping and looking up at him. Her eyes narrowed at the guilty look on Damon's face. "What?" she asked with misgiving.

"That was my fault," Hawk told her grimly. She stared at him. "*Your* fault??"

"Yes." Damon looked uncomfortable and Alina raised an eyebrow, waiting. "When we were in Afghanistan, I carried a picture of you," Hawk admitted. "Jason saw it more than once."

Alina stared at him, dumbfounded, and he stared back, his eyes glinting in amusement.

"You don't have to look so shocked," he muttered, getting them moving again. "I didn't know we'd end up as two government assassins, relying on our invisibility."

"Why?" Alina finally got out.

Hawk debated telling her the truth, then decided against it. Something told him she wasn't quite ready for that yet.

"I wanted to remind myself that if I could beat you in boot camp, I could beat anything they threw at me in Afghanistan," he told her.

Alina gasped indignantly and tried to pull away from him. His arm tightened around her shoulders, hauling her closer.

"Oh no you don't," he murmured. "I don't trust you not to fall over. You look like hell."

"Thanks," Alina muttered. "I just let that bitch beat the crap out of me so I could get her confession documented. I'm entitled to look like hell."

Damon chuckled.

"Like your gunny said, 'well done, you,'" he said, squeezing her gently.

Alina felt a rush of warmth at the tone in his voice and she smiled in the darkness.

"He's *not* my gunny," she retorted, resting her head tiredly on Damon's strong shoulder, suddenly exhausted.

"Good."

Hawk murmured the word so softly that Alina wondered if she had really heard it.

Neither of them gave another thought to the lifeless body of the traitor left behind.

Epilogue

Alina drifted in a pleasant state between dozing and wakefulness, the hot sun warming her skin as she laid back in a reclining chair. The sound of waves lapping gently against the sand a few feet away had lulled her into a relaxed state of mindlessness as a soft breeze blew in off the water. She breathed in the scent of sun-baked sand, enjoying the state of just being.

A shadow fell over her and she opened her eyes reluctantly behind her sunglasses, watching as Hawk set down a drink on the table beside her. It was in a hollowed out pineapple and had a straw and an umbrella sticking out of it.

"That's a pineapple," she said, sitting up.

Damon settled in the recliner on the other side of the little square table and glanced at her with a grin. He set a bottle of beer next to the pineapple and shrugged.

"You told me to get you a drink with an umbrella," he retorted. "As you can see, it has an umbrella."

"That it does," Alina agreed with a laugh, picking it up and stirring it with the straw. "What is it?"

"I don't know," Damon answered with a yawn, laying back on his chair. "The bartender said it's their best-selling drink."

"Well, who am I to argue with the masses," Alina murmured, sipping the drink. It was pineapple and coconut and tasted like a sugary piece of heaven. "Mmmm. It's good."

Alina sipped her pineapple and stared out over the startlingly blue water lapping at the island beach before them. It was Saturday. Raven was back at the house in Medford, where Alina would join him as soon as she and Hawk got the all clear. Harry and Charlie had hustled them out of the country as soon as Alina handed over her evidence. Charlie wanted them both out of the way while he cleaned up the loose-ends in Washington, and Alina was glad to be away from the chaos. She had intended to go to

Europe and begin the tedious task of selling her safe houses and locating new ones, ones that would *not* go into any file, fake or otherwise, but Damon suggested the Islands instead. Viper felt guilty enough about Peru to agree, and now she was very glad that she had.

"I'm glad I let you talk me into this," Alina said, setting her pineapple down at last and settling back on her chair. Damon glanced at her with a faint smile.

"You've earned it," he murmured. "But I can't take all the credit. Harry was the one who suggested it."

"Harry! Of course he did." Alina closed her eyes behind her sunglasses.

"Here is the paper, Señor." A resort employee appeared next to Damon, handing him a thick newspaper. "Just came."

"Thank you." Damon took the paper and the man headed back to the beach-front bar behind them.

Alina opened her eyes and glanced over, watching as Damon opened the New York Times and scanned the headlines. After a moment, he folded it again and passed it over to her without a word. Alina grabbed it and unfolded it, her eyes falling on the block letters:

ALEX LUDMERE DIES UNEXPECTEDLY TWO DAYS AFTER RESIGNING THE VICE PRESIDENCY

Raising an eyebrow, Alina scanned the article quickly. Ludmere had died the night before at his southern estate, the cause of death unknown.

She folded the paper again and dropped it onto the sand between the two chairs. Glancing over, she found Hawk watching her.

"Charlie?" he asked.

"It wouldn't surprise me," she answered.

Damon nodded and settled back again on his seat, keeping his head turned toward her. Alina followed suit and they looked at each other for a moment in silence, absorbing the news. It really was over.

He reached out his hand and Alina's fingers touched his, entwining with them over the sand. She smiled slowly as their hands hung, joined, between their seats.

"Viper?"

"Yes?"

"If you ever drug me again, I'll kill you."

"Understood."

Damon nodded and turned his head back to the sun, closing his eyes and tightening his fingers on hers. Alina smiled and closed her eyes.

The sun was hot and the breeze was cool, and there was nowhere else she could imagine being at that moment.

It was over, and they were free.

The resort employee who had taken the paper over to the couple on the sand watched them from behind the bar. After a moment, he turned away and made his way to the phone at the back. Dialing, he kept an eye on the couple and waited while the phone rang. It was picked up on the second ring.

"It's definitely him. The Hawk."

"You're sure?" the voice on the other end demanded.

"I'm sure. I have the picture the woman in Washington sent."

"Good. I will let the new head of the Cartel know," the voice paused. "Keep an eye on him."

"Of course."

The man hung up and went back to the front of the bar, smiling at the customers and leaning forward to greet them, all the while keeping an eye on the couple holding hands between chairs on the white sands of the island beach.

About the Author

CW Browning was writing before she could spell. Making up stories with her childhood best friend in the backyard in Olathe, Kansas, imagination ran wild from the very beginning. At the age of eight, she printed out her first full-length novel on a dot-matrix printer. All eighteen chapters of it. Through the years, the writing took a backseat to the mechanics of life as she pursued other avenues of interest. Those mechanics, however, have a great way of underlining what truly lifts a spirt and makes the soul sing. After attending Rutgers University and studying History, her love for writing was rekindled. It became apparent where her heart lay. Picking up an old manuscript, she dusted it off and went back to what made her whole. CW still makes up stories in her backyard, but now she crafts them for her readers to enjoy. She makes her home in Southern New Jersey, where she loves to grill steak and sip red wine on the patio.

Visit her at: www.cwbrowning.com

Also find her on Facebook, Instagram and Twitter!

Made in the USA
Las Vegas, NV
22 July 2023

75084098R00164